KING OF ITHACA

Glyn Iliffe studied English and Classics at Reading University, where he developed a passion for the ancient stories of Greek history and mythology. Well travelled, Glyn has visited nearly forty countries, trekked in the Himalayas, spent six weeks hitchhiking across North America and had his collarbone broken by a bull in Pamplona. He is married with two daughters and lives in Leicestershire. *King of Ithaca* is his first novel, and it is followed by *The Gates of Troy*.

KING OF ITHACA

GLYN ILIFFE

PAN BOOKS

First published 2008 by Macmillan

First published in paperback 2009 by Pan Books
an imprint of Pan Macmillan, a division of Macmillan Publishers Limited
Pan Macmillan, 20 New Wharf Road, London N1 9RR
Basingstoke and Oxford
Associated companies throughout the world
www.panmacmillan.com

ISBN 978-0-330-45249-6

A CIP catalogue record for this book is available from
the British Library.

Printed and bound in the UK by
CPI Group (UK), Croydon, CR0 4YY

Visit *www.panmacmillan.com* to read more about all our books
and to buy them. You will also find features, author interviews and
news of any author events, and you can sign up for e-newsletters
so that you're always first to hear about our new releases.

FOR JANE

Acknowledgements

My thanks go to my editor, Julie Crisp, for her persistence and faith in *King of Ithaca*, as well as her hard work in making this book what it is. I would also like to thank Professor Helen King of Reading University for providing notes and comments on the original manuscripts.

GLOSSARY

A

Achilles	— Myrmidon prince; later the principal hero of the Trojan War
Actoris	— Penelope's body slave
Aegisthus	— son of Thyestes; he murdered his uncle and foster-parent, Atreus, the father of Agamemnon and Menelaus
Agamemnon	— king of Mycenae, and most powerful of the Greeks
Ajax (greater)	— king of Salamis
Ajax (lesser)	— prince of Locris
Alybas	— home city of Eperitus, in northern Greece
Anticleia	— queen of Ithaca; mother of Odysseus
Antiphus	— Ithacan guardsman
Aphrodite	— goddess of love
Apollo	— archer god, associated with music, song and healing
Arcadia	— region in the central Peloponnese
Arceisius	— shepherd boy named after a former king of Ithaca
Ares	— god of war
Argos	— powerful city in the north-eastern Peloponnese
Artemis	— hunter goddess, noted for her virginity and her vengefulness

GLOSSARY

Athena	— goddess of wisdom and warfare
Athens	— city on Aegean seaboard
Atreides	— the sons of Atreus: Agamemnon and Menelaus
Atreus	— former king of Mycenae
Attica	— region of which Athens was the capital

C

Castor	— Cretan prince
Cedalion	— former apprentice of Hephaistos, taken by the blind Orion to act as his guide
chelonion	— flower native to Ithaca
Clytaemnestra	— daughter of Tyndareus and wife of Agamemnon
Crete	— island to the south of Greece
Ctymene	— sister of Odysseus

D

Damastor	— Ithacan guardsman
Demeter	— goddess of agriculture
Diocles	— Spartan warrior
Diomedes	— king of Argos and ally of Agamemnon
Dulichium	— Ionian island forming northernmost part of Laertes's kingdom

E

Echidna	— monster with the upper torso of a beautiful woman and the body of a serpent
Elatos	— chief priest of the oracle at Pythia
Eperitus	— warrior from Alybas, exiled for refusing to support his father after he had murdered King Pandion
Epigoni	— collective name for the sons of seven Argive heroes who led a doomed expedition against

Thebes; the Epigoni, amongst them
Diomedes, later avenged their fathers by
laying waste to the city

Eumaeus	– faithful slave to Laertes
Eupeithes	– ambitious and treacherous Ithacan noble
Eurotas	– Spartan river, named after the king who drowned himself in its waters
Eurycleia	– slave to Laertes, formerly Odysseus's nurse
Eurytus	– father of Iphitus

G

Gaea	– earth goddess
Gyrtias	– warrior from Rhodes

H

Hades	– god of the Underworld
Halitherses	– captain of Ithacan royal guard
Helen	– foster-daughter of Tyndareus (actually fathered by Zeus); renowned for her beauty
Hephaistos	– god of fire; blacksmith to the gods of Olympus
Hera	– goddess married to Zeus
Heracles	– greatest of all Greek heroes (otherwise known as Hercules)
Hermes	– messenger of the gods; his duties also include shepherding the souls of the dead to the Underworld
Hestia	– goddess of the hearth and protectress of the household

I

Icarius	– co-king of Sparta, with his brother Tyndareus; father of Penelope
Idomeneus	– king of Crete
Ilium	– the region of which Troy was the capital
Ionian Sea	– sea to the west of the Greek mainland
Iphitus	– Oechalian prince who befriends Odysseus
Ithaca	– island in the Ionian Sea

K

Kerosia	– Ithacan council meeting
Koronos	– wealthy Ithacan noble

L

Lacedaemon	– Sparta
Laertes	– king of Ithaca
Leda	– unfaithful wife of Tyndareus
Locris	– region in north-eastern Greece

M

Menelaus	– brother of Agamemnon
Menestheus	– king of Athens
Mentes	– Taphian warrior
Mentor	– close friend of Odysseus
Messene	– city in south-western Peloponnese
Mycenae	– most powerful city in Greece, situated in north-eastern Peloponnese
Myrmidons	– the followers of Achilles

N

Neaera	– Helen's body slave

O

Odysseus	— prince of Ithaca, son of Laertes
Oechalia	— city in Thessaly, northern Greece
Olympus	— mountain home of the gods
Orion	— legendary hunter

P

Palamedes	— suitor to Helen
Pandion	— murdered king of Alybas
Parnassus (Mount)	— mountain in central Greece and home of the Pythian oracle
Patroclus	— friend of Achilles and captain of the Myrmidons
Peisandros	— Myrmidon spearman
Peloponnese	— southernmost landmass of Greek mainland
Penelope	— Spartan princess, daughter of Icarius
Philoctetes	— shepherd who lit the pyre of Heracles, for which he was awarded the hero's bow and arrows
Phronius	— Ithacan elder
Polybus	— henchman of Eupeithes
Polytherses	— twin brother of Polybus
Poseidon	— god of the sea
Priam	— king of Troy
Pythia	— home of the chief oracle in Greece
Python	— giant serpent, guardian of the Pythian oracle
Pythoness	— high priestess of the Pythian oracle

R

Rhodes	— island in the south-eastern Aegean

GLOSSARY

S

Salamis — island in the Saronic Gulf, west of Athens

Samos — neighbouring island to Ithaca, also under the rule of Laertes

Sparta — city in the south-eastern Peloponnese

T

Taphians — pirate race from Taphos

Taygetus Mountains — mountain range to the west of Sparta

Teucer — half-brother and companion to the greater Ajax

Thebes — city in central Greece

Theseus — Athenian hero who slew the Minotaur

Thrasios — priest of the Pythian oracle

Tiryns — city in north-eastern Peloponnese

Tlepolemos — prince of Rhodes

Troy — chief city of Ilium, on the eastern seaboard of the Aegean

Tyndareus — co-king of Sparta and father of Helen and Clytaemnestra

X

xenia — the custom of friendship towards strangers

Z

Zacynthos — southernmost of the Ionian islands under Laertes's rule

Zeus — the king of the gods

KING OF ITHACA

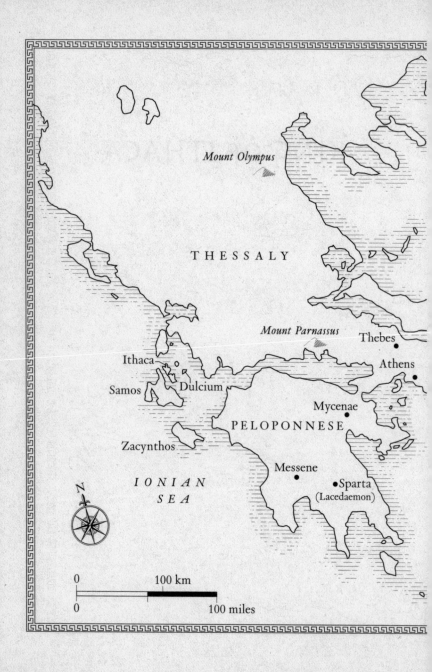

Mount Olympus

THESSALY

Mount Parnassus

Thebes

Athens

Ithaca

Samos

Dulcium

Mycenae

PELOPONNESE

Zacynthos

Messene

Sparta
(Lacedaemon)

N

*IONIAN
SEA*

0   100 km

0   100 miles

book

ONE

Chapter One

MOUNT PARNASSUS

It was a chill dawn on the foothills of Mount Parnassus. The sun rose slowly in the east, infusing the dark, empty skies with a pale radiance. A collar of mist clung to the upper reaches of the purple mountainsides, shifting restlessly with the morning breeze. Eperitus shook the stiffness from his limbs and sniffed the air, which was sharp with the savoury prick of smoke. Pilgrims, he guessed, warming themselves by freshly made fires before the trek up to the oracle.

He decided against the luxury of heat. After a frugal breakfast of cold porridge he gathered his few possessions and followed the bank of a stream that fed down from the hills. The sloping route was crooked and stony, but it gave an even footing and its steep banks were topped with twisted olive trees that hid his progress from unwelcome eyes. In his right hand he carried two ash spears, their shafts smooth and black. He also kept a sword slung in a scabbard under his left arm, its blade sharpened to a keen edge. Hanging from his shoulder was his grandfather's ox-hide shield, given to him by the old man before his death, whilst for added protection he wore a shaped leather corselet and greaves. A bronze helmet hid his long, black hair, its cheekguards tied loosely beneath his clean-shaven chin. His only other possessions were a thick cloak of brown wool, a bag of oats and stale bread, a skin of water and a pouch of copper pieces.

For a while as he walked the only sounds were the clear water washing over the stones of the riverbed and the sighing of the wind in the trees. Birdsong greeted the winter sun as it edged above the green hilltops, and he felt a lightness in his mood that he had not sensed since leaving his home in the north. The journey to Mount Parnassus had taken several days, during which he had walked alone with sombre thoughts, pondering the fateful events that had forced him from his home. But now, with his goal only a few hours' march away, his spirits were reviving with every step.

His peace was suddenly disturbed when harsh shouts erupted from the other side of the river, followed by the angry clash of weapons. Men cried out in fear and confusion before, as suddenly as it had occurred, the din of combat ceased and left a ringing silence in its wake.

Like most young Greek nobles, Eperitus had been taught to fight from an early age and this training came to the fore as he crouched low and glanced about himself, his spears clutched tightly in his sweating palm. Taking up his shield by its handgrip, he strained his ears for further sounds of battle. Although he had yearned to see combat for as long as he could remember, as battle lurked unseen amidst the troughs and swells of the landscape opposite he felt his mouth grow dry and the blood pump thicker through his veins.

He took a moment to calm his nerves, then splashed across the riverbed and threw himself down against the bank, his heart rampaging against the hard earth. Crawling cautiously up the slope, he eased into a position where he could spy on whatever waited beyond.

Before him lay a broad bowl scooped out of the rocky landscape, filled with scrubby grass and circumvented by a low ridge. In the centre were the remains of a disturbed camp: the ashes of an extinguished fire, some wooden dishes and a few trampled cloaks. Two bands of warriors faced each other across the debris, waiting in taut readiness for a movement from the others.

The smaller group, whose camp had been attacked, had formed a line of perhaps a dozen shields. They were half dressed and had obviously armed in a hurry, but were organized and ready to defend themselves. At their centre, casually wiping blood from the point of his spear, stood a short and powerful warrior with a chest as broad as his shield and muscular arms that looked strong enough to break a man's spine. He was clearly of noble blood and stared at the opposing force with disdain, his eyes calm and untouched by fear.

Facing him were fully twenty men, standing in a line with the sun glinting on their raised spear points. They were too well armed to be bandits, so could only be deserters from the war in Thebes, where a siege was raging only a short march away. They had lost their discipline and looked haggard and weary. Their armour was scarred and covered in dust; some men bore the wounds of recent battles, and all looked as if they had not slept for days. Already one of them lay face-down in the dirt.

Standing head and shoulders above them all was their champion. A colossus with a booming voice, he strode about shouting crude challenges to the nobleman. 'Your father's ghost rots nameless in Hades and your mother whores to feed her starving belly. Your children suckle at the breasts of slaves while your wife ruts with swineherds. And as for you!' He snapped his fingers in derision. 'I'll be stripping that armour from your dead body before breakfast.'

The giant's insults received no response from his stocky opponent, who remained indifferent to the tirade. Eperitus, however, had heard enough. Driven by his hatred of deserters – and of all men who had surrendered their honour – he leapt to his feet on top of the ridge and thrust one of his spears into the dirt by his sandals. Kissing the shaft of the other, he drew back his arm and launched it with all the momentum his body could command. A moment later it thumped into the spine of the foul-mouthed braggart, sending his vast bulk crashing forward into the dead fire. His thick fingers clawed furrows through the ashes as, with a final curse on his lips, his open mouth gushed blood over the blackened stumps of wood.

Eperitus did not stop to exult over a lucky throw. Plucking his remaining spear from the ground he ran at the twisting backs of the deserters, yelling at the top of his voice. Leaderless and taken by surprise, they dissolved into confusion before him. A spear was hurriedly thrown from one flank, but the aim was poor and the missile skimmed the ground before his feet. Then three men in the centre of the group hurled their own weapons in another hasty attack. One split the air over Eperitus's head; the second clattered off the thick hide of his shield; the point of the third glanced off his left greave, crushing the leather against his shinbone.

The pain coursed up his leg and almost caused him to fall, but the momentum of his attack carried him on towards his assailants. Seeing the nearest fumbling to bring up his shield from his shoulder, he quickly sank the bronze head of his spear into his groin. The man fell backwards with a scream, doubling into himself and wrenching the spear from Eperitus's grip.

At once his two comrades drew their swords and rushed to attack, yelling with fear and anger as their weapons crashed against Eperitus's shield. He fell back before the onslaught, somehow keeping a grip on the heavy ox-hide as he held it out against their repeated blows. Meanwhile, with his free hand he tried desperately to pull his sword from its scabbard, knowing that his death was surely but a heartbeat away.

At that moment, the rank of men he had rushed to help cast their own spears into the disarrayed ranks of their opponents, laying several out in the dead grass. Then they raised their swords and charged across the gap that separated the two sides. Eperitus's attackers threw fearful glances over their shoulders, uncertain whether to rush to the help of their friends or to finish the newcomer first.

Their indecision was an opportunity Eperitus did not waste. Tugging his sword free, he swung the obsessively sharpened blade in a wide arc around the side of his shield, shearing the leg off one of his enemies from above the knee. Blood spurted in great gouts over the dust and, with a look of disbelief in his red-rimmed eyes, the man toppled over into the mess of his own gore, there to thrash out the last moments of his life.

KING OF ITHACA

Eperitus leapt back from a thrust of the other man's sword. The attack was not forced, though, and for a moment they eyed each other from behind their shields. The surviving warrior was much older than Eperitus, a greybeard with the marks of previous battles on his face and body. It was also obvious that he had come to the limit of his endurance: his bloodshot eyes were fearful and desperate, pleading for mercy. But Eperitus knew that if he lowered his guard for one moment, this same enemy would happily strike him down and send his ghost to the ignominious death the young soldier feared above all.

Breathing heavily, he gripped the leather-bound handle of his sword more firmly, turning his knuckles white. The ringing of bronze against bronze came from nearby, punctuated by shouting and the screams of the wounded. His opponent looked nervously over his shoulder, and in that instant Eperitus sprang forward, knocked the man's shield aside, and hacked his sword down through his ear and into the skull. He tugged the blade free and with a second, heavier swing, cut off his head.

By this time a new leader had gathered what remained of the deserters into a knot on one side of the hollow, where they struggled to hold off the attacks of their more disciplined opponents. Almost immediately another of their number fell writhing in the dust, struck down by a strong and stern-faced man, worn by age, battle and the elements. His grey hair and beard were long like a priest's, his armour old-fashioned but full. He used his shield to force a gap in the enemy line where his victim had fallen, but by then the battle was collapsing into a brawl, with men struggling against each other and seeking security in the closeness of their comrades. There was little room now to use the point of a spear or the edge of a sword. Each side was pushing its weight behind their shields, trying by brute force alone to break the wall of their foes. Men swapped curses instead of blows, so closely locked were they, and neither side gave ground.

Suddenly from the top of the ridge came the shouts of newcomers. A group of nine soldiers stood there with the plumes on their helmets fanning in the wind and the dawn sun flashing a savage red from their armour. Eperitus grew hopeful at the sight, thinking them reinforcements, but as the remaining deserters pulled back from the melee and ran up the slope to join them he realized that the battle was far from over. Pulling a spear from its lifeless victim he ran across to where the stocky noble was shouting orders at his men to re-form in the base of the hollow.

The grey-haired warrior slapped Eperitus on the back. 'Well done, lad,' he welcomed him, without taking his eyes off the enemy line forming on the brow of the ridge. 'It's a while since I've seen that much courage in battle. Or that much luck.'

Grinning, Eperitus looked over to where their opponents were advancing down the slope towards them, pulling back their spears and choosing their targets. At that moment, the short nobleman stepped forward and held the palm of his hand out towards the enemy spearmen.

'Lower your weapons!' he ordered, his great voice stopping them in their tracks. 'Too many men have died today already, and for what purpose? For the few copper pieces we carry? Don't be fools – return to your homes and preserve your lives and your honour.'

In reply, one of the newcomers stepped forward and spat into the dust. His face was scarred and mocking and he spoke with a thick accent.

'Thebes was our home, and now it's nothing more than a smoking ruin. But if you want to preserve your own miserable lives, give us the coppers you do have and we'll let you go on your way. We'll have your weapons and cloaks, too, and whatever else you might be carrying.'

'There are easier pickings than us in these hills, friend,' the nobleman responded, his voice calm and assuring. 'Why waste more of your men's blood when you can find yourselves some rich, defenceless pilgrims?'

There was a murmur of agreement from the line of spearmen, which stopped as the scar-faced man raised his hand for silence.

'We've had our fill of pilgrims,' he said. 'Besides, our dead comrades are calling out for vengeance – you didn't think we would just leave their deaths unpunished, did you?'

The nobleman sighed and then with surprising speed launched himself up the slope, hurling his heavy spear at the line of warriors and sending one toppling backwards under the weight of its impact. Eperitus felt the excitement rush through his veins as he charged with the others towards their foe, screaming and casting their spears before them. A few found their targets, causing the new arrivals to fall back as their confidence wavered. The scar-faced man hurried to rejoin his comrades, who threw their own spears a moment later. Their aim was hasty and sporadic, but a lucky cast found the eye of a young soldier running beside Eperitus, splitting his head like a watermelon and spraying the contents over his arm.

The next moment Eperitus's sword was raised and he was driving into the enemy line with his shield. One man fell backwards before him, catching his heel on a stone. There was no time to plunge his sword into his prostrate body, however, as a much larger and stronger man leapt forward and thrust a blade straight through his shield. The point stopped a finger's breadth from Eperitus's stomach, before jamming tight in the layered ox-hide.

Eperitus snatched the shield to one side, tugging the sword from his opponent's hand and opening his guard. Without hesitation, he sank the point of his blade into the man's throat, killing him instantly.

As he fell another man lunged at his ribs with a spear, but before the point could spill his lifeblood onto the rocky ground, the grey-haired warrior appeared from nowhere and kicked the shaft to one side. With a sharp and instinctive movement that belied his age, he hacked off its owner's arm below the elbow and pushed his gored blade into the man's gut.

Covered in sweat and blood, they turned to face the next assault, but their remaining foes were fleeing over the ridge, leaving their dead behind them.

Chapter Two

CASTOR

Eperitus looked around at the carnage of his first battle. The surrounding rocks were splashed with blood and littered with corpses; the cries of the enemy wounded were silenced one by one as the victors slit their throats. He knew he should feel triumphant that he had killed five men. Instead, his limbs were heavy, his mouth was parched and his shin throbbed painfully where the spear had hit his greave. All he wanted was to cast off his armour and wash the blood and dirt from his body in the nearby stream, but that would have to wait. The stocky leader of the men he had helped was sheathing his sword and walking towards him, accompanied by the old warrior who had saved Eperitus's life.

'My name is Castor, son of Hylax,' he announced, holding out his hand in a formal token of friendship. A glimmer of mischief burned in his quick, green eyes, like sunlight caught in a stream. 'This is Halitherses, captain of my guard. We're pilgrims from Crete, here to consult the oracle.'

Eperitus grasped his hand. 'My name is Eperitus, from the city of Alybas in the north. My grandfather was captain of the palace guard, before his death five years ago.'

Castor released his fierce grip on the young warrior's hand and removed his helmet, his nail-bitten fingers thick and dirty against the burnished bronze. A mess of auburn hair, which he flicked aside with a toss of his head, fell down almost to his eyes. Though not a handsome man, he had an amicable smile that broke through his deep tan.

'And your father?'

Eperitus felt anger flush his cheeks. 'I have no father.'

Castor looked at him piercingly but pressed no further. 'Well, we're indebted to you, Eperitus,' he continued. 'Things would have gone badly if you hadn't come along.'

'You could have handled them without my help,' Eperitus replied, dismissing the compliment with a shrug of his shoulders. 'Just a band of deserters, by the look of them.'

'You're doing yourself a disservice,' Halitherses assured him. 'And perhaps you overestimate our abilities. We're just pilgrims, after all.'

'Perhaps,' Eperitus replied. 'But not many pilgrims go about armed to the teeth, or can fight like a trained unit.'

'These are dangerous times,' Castor answered, blinking in the early morning sun. 'Are you here to speak to the Pythoness, too? It's no business of mine, of course, but you're a long way from home if not.'

Eperitus again felt his cheeks flush with the sting of the unspoken shame that had driven him from Alybas.

'Our crops failed this year and we haven't enough in store to see us through the winter,' Castor continued, realizing the young warrior was in no mood to talk. 'We want to fit out a fleet with oil and pottery to trade abroad for food, but won't lift a finger until we've consulted the gods on the matter first. If the seas are calm and pirate-free, then we can sail in confidence. If not,' he shrugged his massive shoulders, 'then our people will starve.'

There was a mournful cry behind them and they turned to see a man kneeling beside the torso of the young soldier who had died during the charge up the slope. His hands hovered over the corpse, wanting to touch it but repelled by the scraps of hanging flesh where his friend's head had once been. Finally, he collapsed across the bloody chest and began to sob.

Eperitus watched as his new comrades, joined by Castor and

Halitherses, quickly began the process of digging a grave with the sword blades of their enemies. Once this was done they laid the body inside and threw the swords at its feet, followed by the dead man's own weapons and shield. Then they piled rocks over the grave, carefully placing the stones so that no scavenging animal could find an easy passage into the flesh beneath.

Eperitus stood silently as they saluted the young soldier three times, their shouts carrying a long way through the cool mid-morning air. Afterwards he helped bury the sixteen enemy dead, digging a shallow pit for the bodies and casting stones on top. The men did not exult over these corpses, nor did they bury them out of respect. They merely put them in the ground so that their souls would go to Hades and not stay on the earth to haunt the living.

By midday the burials were finished. Castor ordered his men to make a fire and fetch water from the nearby stream for porridge, and invited Eperitus to share their rations. A bag of fresh olives had been found on one of the bodies, and as they spat the stones into the fire and drank draughts of cold water Eperitus eyed his eleven new companions in silence.

On the opposite side of the fire was a handsome warrior with a short beard and an athletic build. He held clear authority within the group – seemingly subordinate only to Castor and Halitherses – but his eyes were cold and hard as they focused on the newcomer. Sensing his hostility, Eperitus turned his gaze to the man's neighbour, a dark-skinned soldier with a head of thick, black curls, a full beard that reached into the hollows of his cheeks, and a chest and arms that were matted like a woollen tunic. He was regarding Eperitus with an icy curiosity, but as their eyes met he offered a quick smile and rose to his feet.

'We owe you our gratitude, friend,' he said with a low bow, but as he raised his head and stared at Eperitus the questioning look had returned. 'Perhaps you will tell us what brings you to Mount Parnassus?'

Eperitus looked thoughtfully into the dying flames. He was an exile, banished from Alybas for resisting the man who had killed its king. Now his only hope – indeed, his only desire – was to become a warrior like his grandfather before him, and so he had come to seek guidance from the oracle. But the agony of his shame was still too raw, and he was not prepared to share this with a stranger. Besides, something in the questioner's manner told him to keep the details of his past a secret – at least for the time being.

'I'm here to seek the will of Zeus,' he said, raising his head. 'Beyond that, I don't know.'

Castor raised his eyebrows. 'That's a bigger question than you might think. The answer could be difficult to accept.'

'What do you mean?'

'Zeus doesn't give his favour lightly, and once he makes his plan clear you have to follow it with a true heart. Do that and honour and glory will be heaped on you, and the bards will sing your name for eternity. But if you fail . . .' Castor tossed a piece of bread into the flames. 'Your name will be blasted from the world for ever, forgotten even in Hades.'

Eperitus's heart kicked with excitement, heedless of Castor's warning. The thought of his name being put into song, to be revered long after his death, was everything a fighting man wanted to hear. This was the only immortality a man could win, and every warrior sought it. An unlooked-for shaft of light had illuminated the shadowy path to Eperitus's destiny and in his excitement he decided to depart at once.

'Castor, your words are god-given. You'll forgive my haste, but I want to be on my way to the oracle. Farewell, and I pray the gods will protect you all and bring you good fortune.'

He picked up the shield his grandfather had given him, with its fourfold hide and the new wounds that decorated it, and slung it across his back. But before he could pluck his spears from the ground, Castor stepped forward to bar his way.

'Slow down, friend. We're all going to the same place; I say let's go together. We could do with your protection.'

Eperitus laughed. 'And I could do with your rations! But I can't wait here any longer – Mount Parnassus is still a three- or four-hour march and the afternoon won't last for ever.'

'Let him go his own way,' said the handsome soldier, stepping into the circle of his countrymen. His eyes were dark and full of suspicion as he fixed his stare on the newcomer. 'We didn't need your help or ask for it, stranger. If you think that running into a fight which we were winning, killing a couple of Theban deserters while their backs are turned and then claiming all the glory for yourself has put us in your debt, then I'll be happy to show you your error. We don't need scavengers.'

Eperitus placed a hand on the hilt of his sword. Quickly glancing around the circle of Cretans he could see that every eye was on him, waiting for his reaction to the insult. If he drew his blade, surely they would aid their countryman and all his hopes of glory would perish in a short, frenzied death. But his soldier's pride would not permit him to back down from such a slur on his name. He felt suddenly alone.

'I agree, Mentor: we don't need scavengers,' Castor said, taking the man's arm and gently steering him to one side. 'Or parasites or hangers-on of any kind. But we do want fighting men.' He lowered his voice, though the slight wind carried his words to Eperitus's keen ears. 'You know there's trouble brewing at home. He could be useful, and his spirit impresses me.'

Mentor muttered something inaudible. Castor nodded then turned back to the others, announcing that matters were settled and – if Eperitus was willing – they would journey to the oracle together. The young warrior released his grip on his sword and exhaled.

'And what's more, Eperitus, after we've heard the Pythoness we can give you safe escort to the harbour where our ship is moored. It's a busy place, and if you're looking for adventure you could do worse than start in a port. What do you say?'

Eperitus nodded. 'A stranger in a foreign land has to accept offers of friendship whenever they're made.'

14

At this Castor took a dagger from within the folds of his tunic and offered the hilt towards him.

'Then you should be a stranger no more. Take the dagger. Go on, take it. As Zeus, protector of strangers, is my witness, I swear to you my lasting friendship and loyalty. By this token I promise to honour and protect you whenever you're in my home or on my lands; never to oppose you in arms; and always to help you in your need. This oath will be true for myself and my children, to you and yours until seven generations have passed, as our customs require.'

Nervously Eperitus took the dagger and held it in his sweating palm. It was rich in gold and the handle was inlaid with a scene from a boar hunt – a work of great craftsmanship. Closing his fingers about it, hiding its enthralling wonder, he looked gratefully at Castor. The prince's eyes were expectant.

Eperitus was familiar with the noble custom of *xenia*, offering friendship to guests, which he had seen his grandfather carry out many times. It was not merely good manners, but a promise of unbreakable friendship. An alliance for life. It lay at the heart of the code by which warriors brought themselves renown, the code that made their names both feared and celebrated throughout Greece.

After a moment's pause he unslung the scabbard from his shoulder and removed the sword. Sliding the blade into his belt, he offered the leather sheath to Castor.

'I've nothing more to give you than this,' he said solemnly. 'It was given to my grandfather by the father of our king, after he saved his life in battle. It belonged to a great man and I offer it to you freely, happy it's given to a warrior of noble blood. With it I offer you my own oath of allegiance. I swear to honour you whenever we meet. I will never take up arms against you, but will defend you from your enemies. As Zeus is my witness, for myself and my children to you and yours until seven generations have passed.'

Castor took the scabbard and winked at the young warrior, while behind him Mentor glowered with displeasure.

They marched silently in single file, tracing the mountain path-ways that had been worn smooth by thousands of pilgrims over hundreds of years. A shower of rain in the late afternoon had made the stones slippery, so they picked their way carefully and used their spears as staffs. Upon reaching the upper slopes they could see a large plain spread below them. A wide body of water lay beyond it, which Eperitus fancied led to the sea. Above them the sky was grey with the passing rain clouds; evening was closing and soon the moon would rise above the crest of the hills.

Castor and Halitherses were striding ahead of the rest of the group, who, after the exertion of the battle, were beginning to lag as the relentless march continued, their strained breathing fill-ing the air. Eperitus, who was tiring of Mentor's watchful presence only two or three paces behind, left his place in the file and stretched his pace out to join the two leaders.

'Evening's nearly upon us, Castor,' he said as he caught them. 'Are we to make camp or march into the night?'

'Is the walk taking its toll on you?' the Cretan grinned.

'I can match you step for step, friend, unlike the rest of your men. Their arms weigh them down and the air back there is heavy with their constant sighing.'

Halitherses looked back and grunted. 'Too much peace has made them soft. They're good lads – plenty of spirit – but may the gods help them if they ever find themselves shield to shield in a real scrap.'

By now the chariot of the sun had slipped below the horizon and the detail was draining out of the world, making it difficult to be sure of their footing on the wet and smooth-trodden path. Despite this and the state of his men, Castor did not slacken the pace for one moment. It was clear he would reach the oracle at Pythia tonight, even if they did not.

'It's dark now,' he said, 'but the full moon will be up before long. The temple's only a short march away and I want to be there before the Pythoness drinks one too many of her potions.'

'You speak like you've been there before,' Eperitus said,

intrigued. For days on his solitary journey he had turned over the stories he knew about the oracle. Mount Parnassus was a magical and sacred place, full of mystery and terror. Returning pilgrims in Alybas had told of a fire-breathing hole at the heart of a mountain, guarded by a monstrous serpent, where men descended after offering a sacrifice to Gaea, the earth mother. Inside was the Pythoness herself, upon whom the goddess had bestowed the power to know all things past and present, and all the secrets of the future. Wreathed in smoke, she would speak in mysterious riddles that only her priests could interpret, whilst all around her the cloud of stinking fumes would shift to depict ghosts of ages past, or spectres of things to come.

'Not into the oracle itself,' Castor answered, 'though I've waited outside while my uncles went in. They live here on the slopes of Mount Parnassus and consult the oracle two or three times a year. I came here in my youth to claim an inheritance promised by my grandfather, so I remember the place well.' He looked about himself. 'We hunted boar a number of times in these hills.'

Halitherses, who had taken the lead from Castor, called back over his shoulder. 'Show him the scar.'

Castor paused to pull aside his cloak, revealing a long white scar that ran up half the length of his thigh from the knee. It was still visible in the fast-failing light beneath the thin canopy of trees, though Eperitus had not noticed it before then.

'A boar?' he asked.

'Not just any boar,' Castor replied. 'It was a monster, a gigantic beast of untold years. His hide was thicker than a four-fold shield and you could see the scars of old spear thrusts through his coarse hair. Two great tusks jutted from his mouth,' he held up his forefingers before his chin and glared boar-like at the young warrior, 'as long and as sharp as daggers, though twice as deadly with his bulk behind them. But most terrifying of all were his eyes: as black as obsidian, burning with hate for all mankind. They were filled with the experience of a beast that'd outwitted more than one huntsman, and I knew I wasn't his first victim. Though I was his last.'

'Your uncles killed him?'

'I killed him!' Castor told him proudly. 'I was the first of our party to see him charging out of a thicket with his breath clouding the morning air. Though only a boy, I threw my spear between his shoulders as his head was lowered at my belly. My grandfather and uncles tell me he was dead before he hit me and only the momentum of his great bulk carried his tusk into my thigh. As for me, he knocked my legs away and I hit my head on a rock. I woke up a day later with my wounds bound and every bone in my body aching.'

'You were fortunate.'

'Fortune has nothing to do with it,' Castor snorted, turning to walk back up the path as his men finally caught up with them. He held open the inside of his shield, revealing a painted image of a maiden in full armour. 'Athena protects me. I honour her above all other gods, excepting Zeus of course, and in return she keeps me from harm. She saved me from the boar, not fortune.'

Castor's choice of deity intrigued Eperitus. Most men had their favourite Olympian, whom they prayed to more than any other and in whose honour they would make an extra offering at every meal. For sailors it was Poseidon, god of the sea; for farmers Demeter, goddess of the harvest; for craftsmen it was Hephaistos, the smith-god. Merchants would make offerings to Hermes to bring them good trade; young women would pray to Aphrodite to make them into wives; and wives would pray to Hestia, protectress of the home. The hunter would worship Artemis and the poet would dedicate his songs to Apollo. And Castor, like all soldiers, should have paid homage to Ares, whose realm was the battlefield. The ferocious god of war gave his followers a strong arm in the fight and, if it was their day to die, an honourable death surrounded by their fallen foes. Instead he chose Athena, the goddess of wisdom. She was the symbol not of brutality in battle – which all fighting men valued – but of skill with weaponry and warcraft.

She gave her favourites cunning, resourcefulness and the ability to outwit their enemies, not the blood-thirsty joy of killing with which Ares endowed his followers. It seemed a strange choice for a man.

The moon showed her pockmarked face above the line of the hills, like a gigantic gorgon transforming the landscape to stone. The plain below their right flank remained dark, though the shard of water that pierced it sparkled like ice. Deep shadows stalked the silvered hillsides about the file of warriors, who were made conspicuous by their movement and glinting armour.

During their whole march they had barely seen more than half a dozen other pilgrims. Winter had just begun, of course, and it was not the season for travelling to and fro across Greece. Nevertheless, there would always be people who needed to consult the gods. Maybe fear of deserters from the siege of Thebes kept them away, Eperitus speculated, or perhaps the need for the gods was less urgent, now that the civil wars of Greece had all but ceased. Peace had brought prosperity and a brittle sense of security to the people.

Suddenly Castor brought his men to a halt, pointing up at the hillside ahead where trails of smoke drifted up through the treetops into the clear night air.

'See?' he said. 'The oracle is up there.'

'Thank the gods,' groaned a voice from the back of the file. 'My feet are dying beneath me and my stomach needs food.'

Castor was unmoved by the self-pitying complaints of his men.

'We can make camp later. First I must see the Pythoness. Those of you who can wait until morning had better set up camp here, where you won't gag on the smell from the fumes. And make sure Damastor doesn't stand guard again, in case his snoring attracts another band of roaming deserters.'

The soldier who had spoken to Eperitus by the fire lowered his head as his comrades jeered him, their good humour surprising considering the danger he must have left them in by sleeping on guard duty that morning. Then they started to shed their armour

GLYN ILIFFE

and baggage, clearly having no intention of taking another step that night.

Castor threw a heavily muscled arm about Eperitus's shoulders. 'Meanwhile, you and I can go and question the hag about what the gods have planned for us.'

Eperitus watched the skeins of smoke trailing into the night air and quickly forgot his fatigue from the day's trials. At last, he was nearing the oracle itself.

'We'll come with you as well,' said Halitherses.

He was joined by a lean, grubby-looking man with hollow cheeks and a big nose. He introduced himself as Antiphus, and as Eperitus took his hand he realized he was missing his two bow-string fingers. This was the harshest and most effective punishment for hunting without leave on a noble's land, and was usually meted out only to the low-born: by hacking off the index and forefingers the man was made ineffective as an archer. It was this that caused Eperitus to note with curiosity that Antiphus still carried a bow on his shoulder.

'There's a sacred spring ahead,' Castor informed them as they walked up the slope towards the trees. 'We should bathe there before we enter the temple.'

They walked into a circle of trees that stood about a wide, dark pool. Water broke from a rock on the far side, gurgling softly in the still night air. As Eperitus watched, the moon emerged from behind a veiling cloud and transformed the clearing with her ghostly light. He found himself in a dreamscape, a place of unmatchable beauty where the simple glade had shed its earthly guise to reveal a heart of magic. The moon's disc moved in the water, wavering, slowing towards stillness but never quite achieving solid form. The boles of the trees became pillars of silver, as if the men had stepped inside an enchanted hall where the glistening pool took the place of the hearth and the whispering branches formed a roof over their heads. Not without reason was the spring considered sacred: Eperitus almost expected to see a deer leap into the clearing, pursued by Artemis herself, bow in hand.

20

Then Castor removed his cloak, armour and tunic and quickly lowered himself into the water. He was soon out again, replacing his garments. The others followed, each one flinching from the icy bite of the water, their complaints echoing about the ring of trees.

Slowly Eperitus scooped up handfuls of water and tipped them over his arms, shoulders and chest. The cold was sharp, initially, but as he became used to it he started to feel a new sensation tingling across his skin, like the breath of a god.

'Don't stay too long,' Castor warned. 'The gods tolerate bathers in the daylight, but the darkness is a time for water nymphs and other supernatural beings. Be quick.'

The water poured off Eperitus as he stepped out. He put his tunic back on and hugged his thick cloak about his body to keep off the chill night air. Yet at the same time he could feel a transformation: the tiredness had lifted and the bruising on his shin where the spear had hit the greave no longer pained him. He felt alive, alert and awake.

As they emerged from the trees they could smell wood smoke and roasting meat. They saw the glow of flames from a plateau further up the hill and scrambled their way up the slope to reach the blaze of several camp fires surrounded by clouds of moths, where groups of pilgrims had laid down their blankets for the night. They avoided looking at the warriors as they walked between their lighted circles, reluctant to attract the attention of the heavily armed men. Eperitus paid the pilgrims no mind either: he was engrossed by the large, pillared edifice ahead of him, built against a sheer face of rock where the mountain rose again from the plateau. A faint red glow came from inside, like a bloody wound cut into the dark of the night, and swirling out of the entrance was a trail of white smoke. They had found the oracle.

'They won't let you in now. They never lets you in after dark.'

They turned to see a young man dressed in a coarse black tunic with a fleece draped over his shoulders against the cold. He sat by his own small fire next to a pen full of goats. The animals were subdued by the night and lay pressed against each other for warmth. Occasionally a kid would bleat or the tangled mass of bodies would kick and shift as one of its members repositioned itself. The herdsman pointed up at the temple.

'Just got a new Pythoness from the village. The ol' one died, see, and this un's only been at it a few weeks. Makes the priests a bit protective, it does, an' they want 'er to get plenty of rest at night.'

'She'll speak for me,' Castor responded. 'I've got business that won't wait.'

The herdsman smiled sympathetically. 'You'll be lucky to get by those priests, m'lord. I've seen rich folk, nobles like you lot, offer 'em a gold piece to see her after dark, but the priests just laugh at 'em. Say she's special, is this'n, and they don't want to tire her any more'n what they have to. Breathing them fumes all day takes years out of a Pythoness, so it does. The one what died looked old enough to be my grandmother's mother, though in truth she were only a few years older than what I am. Those fumes rot the flesh as well as the brain, y'know.'

Castor turned and carried on up the slope. It was all the persuasion the others needed to leave the herdsman to his advice.

''Ang on,' the herdsman shouted, springing up from his fire and running after them. 'If you're goin' anyway, you ought to buy one of my goats. You can torture the priests and hold the Pythoness upside down by her ankles, but the goddess won't speak unless you take her a sacrifice. Ain't your lordships respecters of the gods?'

Castor grabbed the man by his tunic and pulled him close. 'Don't ever question my loyalty to the gods. Now, go and fetch me a one-year-old goat, pure black with no markings.'

'Get me one, too,' Eperitus ordered. If Castor could not wait until morning, neither would he.

The herdsman returned with an animal under each arm. The beast he gave to Castor was as black as night and wriggled like a hydra. Eperitus's was brown and white and had hardly managed to rouse itself from sleep. They threw them over their shoulders and held them by their cloven hoofs.

'Tha's one silver piece for blackie, and six coppers for the other, sirs.'

'We'll give you five copper pieces for them both,' Eperitus corrected, disgusted at the man's audacity.

The herdsman turned to him with a broad smile on his dirty face. 'That black un's my best animal. If your lord wants . . .'

'Here,' said Castor, impatient to get on. He handed the goat herder two silver pieces and started towards the temple.

'You should learn the good grace of yer master,' the trader told Eperitus, before turning to walk back down the slope. Eperitus gave him a swift kick to the buttocks to speed him on his way, which provoked a stream of insults hurled towards his departing back.

As they rejoined Castor and the others a great belch of smoke swirled out of the temple door and coiled into the night air. For the first time Eperitus consciously recognized the faint stench that had been growing since they left the pool. He turned to Antiphus, who wrinkled his large nose in response. It smelled of rotten eggs, the nauseating, throat-drying stink that poets associate with Hades itself. Suddenly Eperitus wished he had waited until morning.

'Perhaps she's asleep like the herdsman said,' Antiphus suggested, uncertainly. 'Wouldn't those other pilgrims be here otherwise? Let's come back tomorrow.'

'Go back if you want,' Castor replied, holding the struggling goat tighter about his shoulders and looking up at the steps to the temple. 'You can all wait until morning if you're afraid. But I'm going in now.'

After a brief pause, the others followed him up to the mouth of the oracle.

Chapter Three

PYTHON

They approached the dark portico that led to the most famous oracle in all Greece. Its rough grey pillars glowed red with the light of whatever burned within and the stench of sulphur was nauseating. A man appeared at the entrance and walked quickly down to bar the way. He was dressed all in black and carried a long staff.

'The Pythoness sleeps. Now leave before I put a curse on you all.'

'Don't be so hasty,' Castor said, stepping up to the holy man and fixing him with narrowed eyes. 'How much will it cost to wake her up?'

'Your money won't make any difference here,' the priest answered, his gaze shifting uncertainly under the scrutiny of the fierce-looking warrior. 'Whole cities send tribute to the oracle, so your pitiful . . .'

'Then you leave me no choice but to wake her myself! Stand aside.'

It shocked Eperitus that his new friend dared talk in such a way to a member of the most powerful priesthood in Greece. It surprised the cleric too, who for a moment looked as if he would merely slip away into the shadows. But his arrogant manner soon got the better of him, used as he was to bullying pilgrims from every station in Greek life. In an instant he jerked his rakish arms into the air and in a quivering moan began to invoke the goddess Gaea.

Eperitus squirmed nervously as his chants filled the air about them. He feared the goddess would take her supernatural revenge on them at any moment, angry they had offended one of her earthly representatives. But Castor was not so easily intimidated and simply walked around the man.

The others followed, only for the priest to bound up the steps and throw himself in front of them again, his arms extended and his voice raised to Gaea. His outstretched palms halted the intruders in their tracks and Eperitus, for one, was filled with terror by his wailing. Though he would happily fight any number of armed men, who was he to stand up to a goddess?

'We'll have to turn back, Castor,' he said. 'Unless you want to bring the wrath of the gods down on us.'

'Athena will protect me, even from Gaea,' he answered, calmly stroking the nose of the goat about his shoulders and looking up at the priest. 'Antiphus! Take this animal, will you.'

The priest's chants were growing louder and more urgent as he saw the armed pilgrims were not retreating. Already he had called down fire from the heavens, cursed them with sudden blindness and invoked several diseases. He was condemning their future wives to barrenness when Castor held up a hand and began to talk through the cacophony.

'Your incantations don't work, so save your breath and let me speak. King Menestheus of Athens has sent me to consult the oracle. And in return for an answer to his question he promises three bronze tripods and cauldrons to match, as well as twenty talents of silver.'

The wailing stopped and the priest came down a few cautious steps. 'What's the question?'

'A great sea monster – a kraken – has been smashing our ships into kindling and devouring the crews and cargoes whole. Our merchants are afraid to leave port and we Athenians are starting to feel the pinch. The king's desperate for the wisdom of Gaea to help rid his city of the beast, and so I must speak to the Pythoness. Every wasted day puts more of our ships in peril and starves Athens of much-needed trade.'

As Eperitus listened to Castor's story he began to wonder further about his friend's identity. Did he really come from Crete – as he had told him – or was he in truth an envoy from King Menestheus? Surely he could not cheat his way into an audience with the Pythoness on the pretence of being an Athenian, then ask about a voyage from Crete? He glanced at Halitherses and Antiphus, but they avoided his eyes.

'There were Athenian merchants here only the day before yesterday,' the priest responded suspiciously. 'Why didn't they mention this kraken?'

'Because they buy goods from the ships of other cities,' Castor replied. 'If they came here and put it about that a sea monster was attacking vessels just off the harbour at Piraeus, the rumour would spread and no foreign merchant would dare come to Athens – they'd be out of business within weeks. Didn't they appear a little nervous?'

At that moment, a husky female voice called out faintly from deep within the temple. 'Lies within lies!' it echoed. 'Don't let him in! A maze he is, that man, unto others and unto himself. Though not to us. Not to me.'

The voice laughed, a horrible, retching chuckle.

'Through the fumes we see him clearly,' it continued. 'We know him, then, now and tomorrow. Send him away, quickly. Sleep matters more than poor island princes.'

The priest looked angrily at Castor, who stared back even more determined than ever.

'I'm not some dog who'll sleep by the footstool of its master, waiting to be woken with a kick,' he said, gripping the hilt of his sword. 'In the name of Athena, you will let me in!'

'Indeed,' said a voice from behind the warriors. They turned to see another priest, an older man this time with white robes, a purple cloak draped over one arm and carrying a staff the length of a spear. There was something ethereal about him; his long hair and beard appeared to be filled with strands of bright silver and he had big, round eyes like an owl and a nose that ran straight and did not dip at the bridge.

'Let them in, let them in,' the old man said authoritatively, striding towards the pilgrims and waving them up the steps.

'But Elatos,' the other priest protested, 'the Pythoness said to send them away.'

'We may be priests, Thrasios, but it sometimes makes us arrogant and heedless of our duties as human beings.' The head priest reached the entrance to the temple and Eperitus suddenly noticed how tall he was – a full head and shoulders above everybody else, even Halitherses. He placed a hand on the younger priest's arm. 'Now then, you can see these men are nobles; warriors, no less. Take their animals and sacrifice them, as is required, and call on the presence of the gods this sombre night. Unless I'm greatly mistaken, the prince here will not be kept waiting.'

'That's right, my lord. I'm Castor, son of Hylax, come from the island of Crete to consult the oracle.'

'Are you and have you?' said the priest sceptically. He placed his fists on his hips and spat irreverently on the step. 'My name is Elatos, and if you wish to speak with the Pythoness you will first give me three copper pieces. As you've brought two animals I assume one of your friends also wishes to receive her wisdom? That will be another three copper pieces.'

Eperitus pulled three of the dwindling number of coins from his pouch and handed them cautiously to the man. 'I seek the will of the gods.'

'A wise thing to do,' the head priest replied, taking his payment along with Castor's and hiding the pieces in a fold of his robe. 'Once the sacrifice has been made, follow Thrasios through the crack in the rock at the back of the temple. He will lead you to the Pythoness, but stay close to him! A serpent – Gaea's own son – protects the priestess, and he's been known to pick off the odd stray pilgrim.

'Thrasios will also interpret the Pythoness's ramblings for you. I find his devotion to the gods helps him understand the precise meaning of the priestess's gibberish. She's quite unconscious of it herself, of course. Spouts the stuff all day long yet can't remember a word of it, let alone interpret it.'

At that point Thrasios appeared on the broad top step. He held Castor's goat under one arm and a sacrificial knife in his free hand.

'Come through,' he ordered, impatiently.

Antiphus led the way. Only Elatos remained, wishing the men goodbye before turning to retreat down the steps. As he placed his foot on the first step, though, he caught Castor's eye and said in a hushed voice, 'Meet me by the sacred pool when this is over. I have something to discuss with you.' Eperitus was not given time to ponder Elatos's words, as Castor pushed him in through the high, pillared doorway.

Viewed from the outside the temple looked small, but inside it had been delved into the rock-face and was as big as the great hall of the king's palace in Alybas. The ceiling was high and dark, punctured by a hole through which the blue evening sky was visible. A large, well-stocked fire in the centre of the temple sent trails of smoke through the room, most of which eventually escaped out of the vent in the roof. In the side walls were alcoves that housed rough terracotta images of various gods, each of them lit by a flaming torch that left great black scars on the limestone plaster above. The plaster itself was decorated with what had once been colourful images of animals and men moving through a landscape of rivers and trees, but now these pictures were fading and in places had peeled away. The smoke of the fire and the torches had dulled some beyond recognition.

Only the far wall remained untouched. This was the sheer face of the mountain: rugged, grey and cold. Eating a line straight through its centre was a dark crack, just wide enough for two men to enter side by side. Eperitus strained his eyes to see into its blackness, but the firelight that filled the temple revealed nothing of whatever lay beyond. Then, as he watched, he heard a faint hissing that made his flesh creep. Suddenly he was reminded of what Elatos had said about the serpent that guarded the oracle. His hand instinctively sought the hilt of his sword and with a shudder he turned away.

To his left Thrasios was kneeling and holding the two goats by their stumpy horns. A second priest appeared from a side door and placed shallow bowls of water on the floor. A moment later the animals bowed their heads to drink, unconsciously giving their consent to be sacrificed. Hardly allowing the black animal to take a second lap of the water, Thrasios lifted it to the altar and, picking up his knife, cut off a wisp of its wiry hair. This he threw into the blazing fire whilst uttering prayers to Gaea, conducting the ritual with practised ease and with the relish of a man who enjoyed his work. Eperitus watched in admiration as he controlled the struggling beast with one hand then stunned it with a blow from the handle of his knife. A moment later, still calling on the goddess, he placed a large bowl beneath the goat's limp head and slit its throat. Thrasios waited for the gush of blood to stop then handed the carcass to the other priest, who finished the work of cutting it up. The second animal met the same efficient death and its various parts were shared between the fire, as a burnt offering to the gods, and the priests, for their evening meal.

Once the act of sacrifice was complete, Thrasios took a torch from the wall and led them into the narrow crack at the back of the temple. It led into an unlit chamber where they waited as the priest cast the light of his torch this way and that, searching keenly for something in the blackness.

As the only light came from this single flame, it took their eyes a moment to adjust to the dimness. Eperitus could sense by the feel of the air and the echo of the small sounds they made that they were in a large cave, a pocket within the solid stone of the mountain. As Thrasios moved his torch through the gloom Eperitus glimpsed a natural archway leading into even deeper darkness beyond. Nothing else was visible, making him feel unnervingly exposed and vulnerable. Then he saw the light catch on something to his left, something shining that moved at incredible speed. Suddenly the torch was whipped out of the priest's hand and they were plunged into darkness.

'Don't move!' Thrasios hissed, his voice strangely distant, as if he stood on the far side of the cave. 'If you draw your weapons you'll be killed. It's Python. He's watching you.' He sounded frightened. 'You shouldn't have insisted on coming so late. He's confused.'

'Don't you have any power over the creature?' Halitherses whispered urgently.

'I can calm him, but you must remain silent. Don't move.'

The great beast shifted across the stone floor not two strides away from them. Eperitus realized this was no mere snake but an animal of supernatural proportions. Fighting the urge to take out his sword, he dared to turn his head and behold the full horror of the monster.

Snakes, to Eperitus, were loathsome creatures. Their hideous limbless torsos, their cold skins and lipless mouths froze his flesh with disgust. As he beheld Python, with its vast coils contracting and stretching, it circled them once and then, to Eperitus's horror, paused opposite him.

Slowly it raised its heavy triangular head and extended it towards his face. Even in the dull light each individual scale was now clear to the terrified warrior as Python's slender nostrils fanned his face with its cold breath, the ageless eyes regarding him with a malice that dwarfed the hatred of any man. As Eperitus watched, transfixed by mind-numbing horror, its mouth parted with a long hiss to release a glistening, forked tongue, which flickered out and touched his lips.

At that moment a number of things happened. Eperitus reached for his sword but his hand was seized, preventing him from drawing the weapon. The creature pulled its head back as if to strike, and then a female voice called to it from the archway. It was the same husky voice that had denounced Castor's lies when they had stood outside in the night air. Quickly the serpent turned its head in response to the voice, just as the other priest appeared with another torch from the entrance behind them.

The stuttering flame threw back the void and to Eperitus's relief he saw that the guardian of the oracle had slid back into a corner of the cave, its scales glittering like a thousand eyes amongst the shadows. Thrasios hurried the pilgrims across the open floor and through the archway at the far end. Eperitus was the last through and collided with Antiphus's back in his eagerness to reach safety.

With his torch held before him Thrasios now took them into a low-ceilinged passageway. They followed its short course as it descended sharply to below the level of the temple. It was warm, stuffy and claustrophobic and the sickening stench of sulphur was much stronger now. Then a new light appeared, and within moments they had turned a bend in the passageway and stood at the threshold of a second, smaller cavern, its floor split by a great crack from which foul-smelling fumes hissed upward to the high ceiling to be lost in the darkness above their heads. A few torches struggled against the stifling vapours, but served only to lend the place a sombre, strangulated life.

The vent in the rock opened up lengthways before them. At the far end a large black tripod had been set up directly over the abyss with a young woman seated on it. She wore a long white robe of a thin and revealing material, and her hair hung loose over her shoulders. There were dark rings about her eyes as if she had not slept for many nights, and her yellow skin was deeply lined, like that of a much older woman.

As Eperitus looked at her he inhaled a lungful of the pungent smoke rising from the vent. It made his eyes water and his vision cloud; shadows crawled about the walls like wraiths. Then the Pythoness looked up wearily at the newcomers.

'Sit down,' she said. Her voice was weak and quiet, but the

men obeyed. Only Thrasios remained standing, in attendance on his mistress, whose eyes and cheeks appeared deeply sunken in the shifting half-light.

He handed her a wooden bowl and, with a fragile and almost helpless movement, she took something from it and put it into her mouth. Eperitus watched her lower her head and chew. After a while her chin fell on her chest and her body went limp, remaining still for some time. He looked at Castor, but the prince was watching the priestess with a hawklike stare.

Suddenly her body jerked upwards as she sucked in a lungful of the vapour through her nostrils, held it, and then exhaled with a long sigh. Thrasios took a step towards her, excited, twitching restlessly in his eagerness to help his mistress. The Pythoness began to inhale deeply now, lifting her head to take in the fumes that coiled about her. Her eyes remained closed as her breathing grew quicker, heavier, her shoulders thrown back and her small breasts thrust outwards with each breath. Thrasios snatched the bowl from her lap, threw the long, dark leaves that filled it onto the floor, and used it to waft more of the vapours into the face of the priestess.

Gradually her breathing slowed and the Pythoness relaxed. Then she turned to face her visitors. But it was not the same tired woman the men had seen earlier. Now she was self-assured, even arrogant as she surveyed them. And there was something else about her: her eyes had changed.

With horror Eperitus saw that the irises were now yellow and the pupils were vertical slits. She opened her mouth and hissed, a forked tongue lolling out of her lipless mouth.

'Who seeks the future?'

'I do,' Castor answered, showing no fear. He stood and kicked Eperitus's sandalled foot. Struggling against the fear within him, he rose to his feet to face the Pythoness.

'And I,' he whispered.

They were the only ones standing. The others knelt before

her, touching their hands and foreheads to the cave floor. The Pythoness pointed at Castor.

'What is it you seek, Odysseus of Ithaca?'

Eperitus stared at his companion and then at the Pythoness. Castor looked equally shocked, but a moment later was kneeling before her with his head bowed.

'Yes, I know you,' she continued. 'Long have I waited for you: the hero who will make a name so large it will take an ocean to swallow. Ask.'

'My father's kingdom is threatened, goddess. I must know if I will rise to become king in his place, or whether the throne will be seized by his enemies. Will I reign, or will I be exiled by usurpers?'

The Pythoness gave her answer without hesitation.

'Find a daughter of Lacedaemon and she will keep the thieves from your house. As father of your people you will count the harvests on your fingers. But if ever you seek Priam's city, the wide waters will swallow you. For the time it takes a baby to become a man, you will know no home. Then, when friends and fortune have departed from you, you will rise again from the dead.'

'Thank you, goddess,' he said, and sat down beside Antiphus. He placed his head in his hands and was silent.

'Do you understand the prophecy?' Thrasios asked.

'Aren't you the interpreter?' Halitherses retorted.

'I've had more difficult riddles to decipher. You must fetch a princess from Sparta, Odysseus, and she will defend your palace from usurpers. You will become king and reign over a prosperous kingdom for ten years. From then you have a choice: to stay at home, or go to the city of Troy far away in the east. But be warned, if you choose Troy you will not see your homeland for twenty years; and when you return you will be alone and destitute.'

Eperitus glanced inquisitively at Castor, or Odysseus if that was his true name, but the prince did not look up as Thrasios interpreted his fate. Instead he fixed his eyes on the chasm and said nothing.

'And you, Eperitus of Alybas?' the Pythoness asked, pointing at the tall young warrior. 'What is your question?'

Chapter Four

HELEN OF SPARTA

The great hall of the palace at Sparta was dark but for the glow of a fire at its centre. Colossal shadows stalked each other about the high walls, whilst the sputtering of the flames echoed in the emptiness of the vast space. Around the large circular hearth four pillars stood sentinel, as thick as tree trunks, their heads lost in the gloom of the high ceiling.

On ornate chairs between two of the columns sat three richly clad men. Before them stood an old priest with a long, white beard and beside him knelt a scribe, taking notes as one of the seated men spoke.

'A bad summer usually means a bad winter, in my experience,' he said in a deep voice, looking down at the scribe.

The slave glanced up from his clay tablet and nodded. 'Yes, my lord.'

His master was Tyndareus, co-king of Sparta, a fierce-looking man with wild hair and a thick beard, not yet touched by grey despite his respectable age. His large bulk seemed to embody the power he held, though disuse was turning his muscles to fat and excessive feasting had swollen the proportions of his stomach.

'We'll need to demand more grain from the farmers for the winter provision,' Tyndareus continued. 'They won't be happy about it, of course, but I'll not risk the people starving. It also means the potters will have to make more storage jars, and quickly.'

'At least the extra work will make them happy, brother,' commented the man to his right.

'But with this year's poor harvest, my lord, we could hardly take any more grain from the farmers without starving them to death.' The scribe held up one of the baked tablets at his side as if the dashed figures were all the proof he required.

Tyndareus passed his golden cup behind his head, where it was hurriedly refilled by one of the attending wine stewards. He took a swallow and nodded at the priest, who was fidgeting for attention.

'Speak, priest. What do the gods say I should do?'

'The signs are that the winter will be mild, my lord.'

Tyndareus's brother spoke up again. 'So does that mean we won't have to store extra grain?'

'Not quite, Lord Icarius,' the priest said. 'There will be more than the winter to provision against.'

'And what does that mean?' Tyndareus growled.

'The gods have sent me a dream that, as joint rulers of the city, you should both be wary of.' Tyndareus scowled; he did not like to be reminded that he and his younger brother were officially co-kings, when in reality Icarius had little say in state affairs. The priest continued undeterred, waving his hands about in a fussy manner. 'Seven nights ago I was asleep in the temple when I dreamed the palace was filled with great men. There were warriors from all over Greece, men of wonderful renown accompanied by their squires and soldiers. I saw this very hall filled with banqueting: men emptying your best golden wine cups as quickly as the slaves could refill them; the women hardly able to do their work for the attentions of so many men; voices calling for more meat, and yet the courtyard outside already swimming with the blood of sacrificed oxen.'

'Perhaps the dream refers to King Agamemnon's visit?' Icarius suggested, nodding towards the other seated man.

Agamemnon, king of Mycenae and son-in-law to Tyndareus,

had arrived in Sparta the day before. He was a full score of years younger than his hosts, and yet had a more authoritative bearing than either of them. Tall, athletically built and handsome, his hair was long and brown with a hint of red and his beard was cropped neatly to his jawline. He wore a tunic of purest white beneath a blood-red cloak which was clasped together at his left shoulder by a golden brooch. This depicted a lion tearing apart a fallen deer, and captured with great skill the majesty, power and ruthlessness of the man. Yet his cold expression revealed nothing of his emotions. He ignored Icarius and focused his icy blue eyes on the priest.

'Well, damn it?' thundered Tyndareus. 'What does the dream mean? Are we going to be invaded? Will our halls be filled with enemies?'

'No,' declared Agamemnon, quietly. 'The Greeks are at peace with each other for the first time in years, and I'll see that maintained. Even if the old man's dream was sent by the gods, it won't mean that.'

'Then what does it mean?' Tyndareus demanded.

'This isn't the only time I've had the dream, my lord,' said the priest, stroking his long beard thoughtfully. 'For six consecutive nights I suffered the same images, until the gods released me from them last night. I interpret this to mean the men will be guests at the palace. What's more, they will be here one month for each night I had the dreams.'

'Six months!' Icarius exclaimed. 'How in Zeus's name are we to feed an army of Greece's finest warriors until next summer? We can barely even feed our own people.'

Tyndareus waved over his chief steward and ordered more fruit to be brought. 'I assume, priest, you've sent an envoy to consult one of the oracles.'

'Oh yes, my lord. Naturally.'

'Then we shall wait on the advice of the gods. Not that I can see any reason for inviting a horde of kings here for winter residence. Can you imagine the fights? No, I think you've made a mistake this time; your dreams mean something else, or nothing at all.'

Tyndareus turned from the priest to focus on the Mycenaean king.

'I'm intrigued by these fantasies of yours, though, Agamemnon. Do you really expect to preserve peace between the Greek nations?'

The fruit arrived and Agamemnon selected a slice of melon. He took a bite without spilling a drop of juice.

'Yes, I do. Greece is tired of civil war. I used to go to the marketplaces and hear the women bemoan the loss of sons and husbands in distant battles, whilst the merchants grumbled about the trade they'd lost because of one war or another. But I've seen how happy the people have become during this lull. They're hungry for peace, and I intend to give them what they want.'

Tyndareus scoffed. 'How? The merchants and women can pine for peace, Agamemnon, but there are too many fighting men in Greece now. The wars have bred a new class of professional soldier. Each state has a standing army, just waiting for the next call to war – and they're getting restless. For every shepherd, farmer, potter and bronze-smith in Sparta there's a warrior. Do you think they'll be willing – or able – to trade their swords for pottery and ivory trinkets? Maybe you think they can sail to Crete in their upturned shields and sell unwanted helmets to farmers and fishermen? And already your so-called "peace" is falling apart again: what about Diomedes and the Epigoni, laying siege to Thebes?'

Agamemnon gave a pained smile. 'Diomedes desires peace more than anything else. I've spoken about this with him and he's given me his word that he only makes war to avenge the death of his father. That's all. He doesn't fight the Thebans for slaves or plunder.'

'He may not,' said Icarius. 'But his men do. Why else would they fight?'

'I said peace will continue in Greece, and it will,' Agamemnon insisted. 'When the nations realize the benefits of commerce over war, attitudes will change. The people want peace with their neighbours and their rulers are prospering already from the free flow of goods. That's where peace starts. But commerce alone won't unite us, nor will even the most solemn oaths. And there's your question about our restless armies, Tyndareus, always itching to be heroes.'

Tyndareus slurped down the last of his wine and the squire refilled his cup. 'So what do you propose to do?'

'If we're to grow rich through commerce, we need to trade freely outside of Greece.'

'And we do,' said Icarius.

'Not any more,' Agamemnon corrected. He chose another piece of melon from the platter and took a bite, spitting the seeds one by one into the flames. 'Have you heard of King Priam?'

'Yes, of course,' Tyndareus said. 'Ruler of Troy, and a powerful man by all accounts.'

'Too powerful.' Agamemnon frowned. 'He's started imposing a tax on trade passing over the Aegean. He claims the sea for Troy and says all ships must pay him tribute. Something I won't tolerate.'

Tyndareus finished another cup of wine and belched loudly. 'You may have to, son. You can't dictate terms to Priam on his own territory.'

'I don't regard the Aegean as Trojan territory!' Agamemnon told him coldly. 'Besides, Mycenaean ships are not the only target, Tyndareus. Your own merchants will soon feel the pinch, as will the rest of the Greek states. Which is why I'm here – to offer a solution that will ensure free trade throughout the Mediterranean, keep the peace here and give our armies their wish for glory. I propose to call the Greek kings to a council of war. We'll raid Ilium and teach Priam to respect us!'

Agamemnon gripped the arms of his chair and stared at the Spartan kings, the flames reflecting vividly in his eyes. With his son-in-law's words ringing in his ears, Tyndareus stood and began pacing up and down by the fire, shaking his head.

GLYN ILIFFE

'Don't be a fool. It's impossible.'

'Is it?' asked Icarius, leaning back and tugging thoughtfully at an earlobe.

'Yes it is,' Tyndareus snapped. He held out his cup to a slave, who rushed to refill it. 'Take it away, you idiot! I need a clear head if I'm to avoid being talked into one of my son's wars. Now listen to me, Agamemnon, you come here talking peace and propose a war. That's fine by me, but can you really see the Greek kings joining forces for anything – even to sack foreign cities? Can you imagine all those generations of petty hatreds and family feuds simply being pushed aside so that Mycenaean merchants don't have to pay tribute to Troy? Can you hear all those proud men swearing oaths of fealty to each other?'

Icarius stood. 'Listen to him, Tyndareus. Of course we could bring them together, even with all their hatred for each other. Most of them only hold grudges because of what their fathers and grand-fathers did to one another. The feuds can't continue for ever. We need an objective that'll unite the Greek-speaking cities and make us into a people.'

'A great people,' Agamemnon added fiercely. 'Can you even imagine the power of a united Greece?'

'United under your leadership, Agamemnon?' Tyndareus said, looking at him suspiciously. 'Even with your political skills you couldn't lead the Greeks. If you could ever get them under one roof, they'd only kill each other. Or is that what you want?'

'Of course not. But ask yourself this: would you rather take a Spartan army to fight Greek-speaking Argives, or Corinthians, or Athenians; or would you rather kill Trojans with their unintelli-gible bar-bar-barring, their strange dress and the way they insult the gods with their outlandish worship?'

'You know my answer to that . . .'

'And wouldn't you like to see peace at home and all our wars fought abroad? Don't you want a unified Greece where a man can go about his business in safety, whether it be a journey to Pythia or a visit to a neighbouring city?'

40

Agamemnon stared hard at his father-in-law, demanding an answer.

'Son, you have great vision and I don't doubt Greece has the potential of which you speak,' Tyndareus sighed. 'But if you couldn't convince Diomedes, your closest friend, to forget his family's feud with Thebes, what chance will you have of making the kings of Greece swear allegiance to each other? We can't be reined in like a team of horses, you know, and we're too damned paranoid about each other to join forces against Troy.'

Agamemnon sighed and looked into the flames as a slave placed an armful of fresh logs in the fire. He had come to Sparta to seek the support of the second most powerful king in Greece, after himself, and instead had found wisdom greater than his own. If Tyndareus had supported him, or if Icarius had been king, he would have convened a council of war. But the older man had spoken with authority and truth: decades and even centuries of feuds would not be cast aside lightly. Even the gods themselves could not command the Greek kings to come together under one roof.

He shook his head in resignation.

'I'm glad you see sense now, Agamemnon,' Tyndareus said, smiling broadly. 'Shall I call the bard for a song? Something light, preferably – perhaps a poem in Aphrodite's honour?'

Agamemnon sat up and snapped his fingers. 'That could be the answer.'

'What? A poem?'

'No – the goddess of love! What man can refuse her?'

The Spartan brothers exchanged puzzled looks. Agamemnon stood and began pacing the floor. 'Your daughter, Helen, she's about fifteen or sixteen years, yes?'

'Thereabouts.'

'So she's old enough to marry.'

'What of it?'

'She's the most desired woman in all Greece!' Agamemnon enthused. 'You see her with the eyes of a father, Tyndareus, but other men . . . they would kill to marry her.'

Moments of silence slipped by as Agamemnon continued to pace the floor, his leather sandals soft on the flagstones. 'Have you considered Menelaus as a son-in-law?' he said after a while.

'I haven't given Helen's marriage any thought at all, if that's what you mean,' Tyndareus replied defensively. 'But your brother's a good man. I've liked him ever since you two were boys, when I threw your uncle – that scoundrel Thyestes – out of Mycenae. Yes, Menelaus would probably be my first consideration.'

'Good. I wanted to know that before I asked you about inviting suitors for Helen.'

Tyndareus shook his head. 'Oh, I wish I hadn't drunk so much wine; a man needs a clear brain whenever you're around. Why should I want to invite suitors to my palace?'

'You asked how I would gather the best of the Greeks under one roof,' said Agamemnon. 'Well, that's my answer. What prince or king would ignore an invitation to pay court to the most beautiful woman of our time? And there's another lure: I would have become heir to your throne when I married Clytaemnestra, had I not already ruled my own kingdom; that means the right to your kingship will now be passed to the man who marries Helen. With her beauty, power and wealth, the suitors will come flocking to Sparta. Don't you see, Tyndareus? It's the priest's dream.'

Icarius lifted his cup in a toast to Agamemnon. 'And when you have them here you'll convene your council of war. You're a clever man, Agamemnon. One day you'll be leader of all the Greeks, and then you can take us to glory.'

'Or death,' Tyndareus added.

❧

A figure watched them from a shadowy alcove above. Her raven-black hair was covered by the hood of her white robe and her face was hidden behind a thin veil. Only the gleam of her dark eyes was visible in the shadows as she listened to the plans of the men below.

Helen's heart sank. Tyndareus was not even her real father –

Zeus had that honour, though Tyndareus did not know it — and yet he had the audacity to put her up for auction like a slave. As for Agamemnon, he was nothing but a butchering megalomaniac. His mind was a maze of political stratagems and his black heart beat only for the glory of the Greeks. If she were a man she would take a sword down to the courtyard and kill all three of them.

But she was not a man. If she was to stop the king of Mycenae weaving his web about her, she would need subtler weapons than swords or spears. But Helen had learned that the weapons she possessed were more powerful than bronze. She smiled bitterly. From an early age she had been forced to veil her beauty because of the effect it had on the men around her. But as she grew older she had learned how to use that effect to her advantage. Power belonged to men, of course, but men could be manipulated.

Helen looked down at the three kings. Why should she give herself meekly to Menelaus, or any other man they could force on her? She was no brood mare to be traded on the whim of kings. She was a daughter of Zeus and had a right to choose her own lover, one who would take her as far away from the confining walls of Sparta as she could get.

Chapter Five

THE SACRED POOL

'I've come to ask the will of the gods,' Eperitus said. 'What is their plan for me, and how do I seek out my destiny?'

The Pythoness ran her tongue along her lips and hissed.

'Ares's sword has forged a bond that will lead to Olympus. But the hero should beware love, for if she clouds his desires he will fall into the Abyss.'

Those were her last words to them, as with a final hissing laugh she pulled the hood of her robe over her face and lowered her head.

'The audience is over,' Thrasios declared. 'You must leave now.'

'And the prophecy?'

The priest gave an arrogant sneer.

'The gods are already moving in your life. A friendship forged in battle may steer you to glory and a name that survives death. But instead love will lead you astray and you will become nothing.'

He announced the last part with satisfaction, as if this was a fitting end for a soldier.

'That's a lie!' Eperitus responded angrily. 'I'll never sacrifice glory for love.'

'Eperitus!' Odysseus cautioned him, putting his arm about his shoulders and leading him out in the wake of the priest. 'The oracle only warned you to beware love. That part of your destiny is still in your own hands. I've never heard of a man who wasn't given a choice by the gods. And besides, did you listen to the first part? Glory and a name that will survive death! What more could a warrior ask for?'

The prince was right, Eperitus thought: his destiny was still his own, and what woman could make him surrender his honour? He looked at Odysseus, who was smiling reassuringly at him; surely their new-found friendship was the one spoken of by the Pythoness. If he was permitted to join the small band of warriors, then his promised destiny would hopefully follow, leading inexorably to fame and glory.

Python was nowhere to be seen in the first cave and they were soon outside again, standing beneath a night sky stuck full of stars. It was good to be away from self-important priests, stinking fumes, the snake-priestess and her vile protector. Eperitus breathed the night air deeply and grinned. Life was just beginning.

As they approached the camp, Odysseus took Eperitus to one side.

'Eperitus, you heard what the Pythoness called me?'

Eperitus frowned, 'Odysseus of Ithaca, yes.'

Odysseus let the others go on ahead. When they were out of sight he folded his arms and gave the young soldier a searching look.

'So what are you thinking?' he asked.

'That depends on whether you are Castor of Crete, or Odysseus of Ithaca.'

'My name is Odysseus,' he answered. 'Perhaps you've heard of me?'

Eperitus shrugged and shook his head apologetically.

'No matter. Like you, my name is yet to become famous in Greece. I apologize that I was forced to deceive you, though.' He pointed at the dagger tucked into Eperitus's belt. 'That's a fine weapon. It belonged to my father's grandfather and I can assure you I didn't give it lightly, nor as part of a trick. I gave it because I meant what I said, and I want you to keep it as a sign of our continuing friendship.'

'So why were you forced to deceive me? And how do I know you truly are Odysseus of Ithaca? I don't even know where Ithaca is.'

Odysseus smiled and for the first time since Eperitus had met him his expression was not guarded. A happy light filled his eyes as for a few moments he forgot the trials of his day.

'Ithaca is a rocky island off the west coast of Acarnania,' he began. 'It isn't particularly beautiful, but we're happy there and it's our home. Its people are the most pigheaded, stupid, idle, yet doughty and lovable folk in the whole of Greece; they live at peace amongst themselves and I would freely give up my life to keep them that way. When I'm away from my island I think of it every moment, and when I'm there I think of nowhere else.' He shrugged his shoulders and shook his head, as if to acknowledge he had failed to do his home justice. 'One day you will come and see for yourself. Then we can sit around a blazing fire with plenty of wine to hand, and I'll ask you about Alybas and your own people, eh?'

Eperitus smiled lamely, hoping he would never have to reveal the shame that had led to his exile.

'As for who I really am,' Odysseus continued, 'the Pythoness doesn't lie. You can be assured of that.'

'And Castor, son of Hylax, prince of Crete?' Eperitus asked. 'Who's he?'

'Castor is a disguise, made up when I left the shores of my home. You see, friend, for all its outward appearance of peace and simplicity, Ithaca is torn. Some of its nobles don't agree with my father's rule. They're plotting to rebel, but lack the strength until they can persuade more of the people to choose them over their rightful ruler. As Laertes's son and heir, they want me out of the way even more: if my father gave me the throne the island would have a young king again, and the nobles are afraid the people of Ithaca would then give their support to me. So when we first met I had to be sure you weren't another assassin, sent by my father's enemies to kill me.'

'But would an enemy have helped save your life?'

'Maybe not, if he could identify me. But Eupeithes, my father's chief opponent, employs Taphian mercenaries to do his dirty work. These men aren't from Ithaca and wouldn't know me on sight, hence any assassin would have had to find out my name before he could kill me. That's why I travel under the name of Castor.'

'It's difficult to think of you as anybody else now,' Eperitus said. 'But I believe you, Odysseus. Perhaps you'll do me a service in return?'

'Of course I will. It's the very least I can do.'

Eperitus pointed back over his shoulder with his thumb, indicating the temple at the top of the slope. 'The Pythoness said a friendship forged in battle would lead to glory.'

'I heard her clearly. Then you also think ours is that friendship?'

'Yes, I do. And I want the glory she spoke of, and a name that will outlive death. Indeed, the name of Eperitus is all I have left. So I want to join your men and sail back with you to Ithaca.'

'You're not likely to find much glory there.' Odysseus laughed.

'I trust in the priestess.'

'Then can I rely on you to defend my father's throne?'

'I've sworn to fight for you and your causes,' Eperitus reminded him. 'And I'm no lover of usurpers.'

'That's settled then,' Odysseus said, taking his hand to seal the agreement. 'We'll leave at dawn and you can join the palace guard. Return to camp and inform Halitherses – he'll tell you your duties. I'll join you later.'

'Later? Where are you going at this time of night?'

'To the camp, to see if anybody has any meat to sell. I haven't eaten properly in a week.' With that Odysseus turned about and retreated up the hill towards the dying glow of the fires.

Eperitus was about to go back and rejoin the others when he suddenly remembered the tall priest, Elatos. Had he not told Odysseus to meet him by the spring? So was the prince off to find the old priest, and had his story about buying food been just another deception? Eperitus realized then that honesty was not something that came easily to his perfidious new friend. But he was also interested in finding out what secrets the priest was keeping for Odysseus's ears only, and planned to find out for himself.

In order to maintain his deception Odysseus had to go back up to the plateau and then work his way around to the grove that surrounded the sacred pool, so Eperitus was at the meeting place long before him and was able to conceal himself behind a screen of bushes on the edge of the clearing. Odysseus appeared some time later, alone, and sat down at the edge of the pool to await Elatos. He did not have long to wait.

The priest emerged from the trees like a ghost in his flowing white robes, dominating the space with his great height and presence. He planted the unusually long staff in the dust and spat into the sacred pool.

'Well, Odysseus, do you know me yet?'

Odysseus stood and looked about the clearing to be certain they were alone. Eperitus remained still, hidden by the bushes and yet able to observe their meeting through a gap between the leaves.

'Yes,' the prince replied formally, crossing his arms and staring hard at the old man. 'You are Elatos, high priest of Gaea.'

Elatos laughed and walked towards the Ithacan prince. He reached out a hand to touch Odysseus's ear, but Odysseus stepped back out of his long reach, a warning look furrowing his brow.

'Don't be afraid,' the priest told him. 'You aren't the only one who can put on a convincing disguise. The real Elatos is asleep with his mistress. He is lying in a hut in the village, where he has been since sunset.'

'Then who are you? And what do you want with me?'

Eperitus placed a hand on the hilt of his sword, wary that the man might be an agent of Eupeithes. But if he was, he appeared to be in no hurry to make an attempt on Odysseus's life. Instead, he eyed the shorter man in motionless silence, allowing his question to hang unanswered in the air between them.

As Eperitus looked on he noticed that the clearing had taken on a strange luminescence. It was not moonlight, for the moon had long since disappeared behind the hills, and it was not starlight, as the stars were hidden by a thin screen of cloud which was creeping across the night sky. Whatever the source, it appeared to be captured within the folds of Elatos's robe, from where it was filtered out to the whole clearing.

'Do you remember when you were a boy, Odysseus,' the man suddenly asked, 'pretending to be asleep when your nurse, Eurycleia, came to check on you? And when she was gone The Lady would come and visit you. Do you remember The Lady, how tall and beautiful she seemed to you? The way she would come out of the darkest corner of your room and sit at the end of your bed, her weight drawing the blankets tight across your legs?'

Odysseus looked astounded.

'How can you know these things?' he demanded. 'Who told you this, when I've never mentioned it myself to another living soul?'

The old man smiled and the light grew stronger. 'Let me ask you something else, son of Laertes: when you were attacked by that boar on these very slopes so many years ago, do you recall how strong your arm felt when it thrust that spear into the animal's neck? How sure the aim was? Can you still remember the shadow that appeared at your side, scaring the animal so that it missed tearing out your intestines and gored you in the leg instead? And have you forgotten that The Lady visited you again in your dreams as you lay wounded, that she gave you strength to fight the darkness of approaching death?'

Odysseus fell to his knees and lowered his head to the dirt. His cracked voice was barely audible as he confessed that he could remember it all. In that very moment Eperitus looked from his friend to the face of the priest. A piercing light was coming from

Elatos's mouth, then from his nostrils, spilling out to fill the whole of the space between the circle of trees. Suddenly a white fire burst from his eyes and his arms flipped back in the throes of a metamorphosis too terrifying to watch. Eperitus threw his head into his hands in fear for his life, and twisted away from the brilliant radiance.

An instant later the light was gone and comparative darkness had descended on the quiet grove. He dared eventually to open his eyes and raise his head just enough to look through the gap in the leaves. Odysseus lay cowering on the floor, but it was no old man who stood before him now.

Eperitus had heard many tales about the gods appearing to men and women. The legends spoke of a time beyond the memories of the elders, when mortals and immortals walked the earth together, eating, drinking and even sleeping with each other. There were people he had spoken to, mostly travellers exchanging stories for food, who claimed to have met gods, and it was not uncommon for a woman in Alybas to explain an illegitimate child as the product of a god's attentions. But in the age of separation from the immortals such tales were doubted, if not mocked, and those who claimed such experiences were regarded as liars or madmen.

So who would have believed him if he had said he saw a goddess that evening? Tall as a young tree, strong-limbed with skin as white as marble, she shone with an inner light that he sensed was only a glimpse of a deeper brilliance. Her young face was lovely and yet stern, set with large grey eyes that were dark with the knowledge of many things. On her golden-haired head she wore a helmet fashioned of bronze, and in her right hand she carried a spear which, by its size and weight, Eperitus doubted any mortal could hope to throw. Over her shoulders and left arm she carried an animal's hide bedecked with a hundred golden tassels that danced as she moved. In the centre of the hide was a face, as repulsive as the goddess herself was awe-inspiring – the face of a gorgon.

She bent down and stroked Odysseus's hair for a moment, before seizing his arm and pulling him to his feet.

'Stop grovelling and stand up, Odysseus. If I was an assassin from Eupeithes you'd be dead by now.'

Odysseus dared to look at the goddess, briefly, before lowering his eyes again.

'Is this how you greet your favourite goddess? I have protected you for the whole of your short life and all you can do is look away in fear.'

Eperitus could hardly take his eyes off her, and yet even in the presence of Athena, the virgin daughter of Zeus, he found himself thinking about Odysseus. Why should a lowly island prince be honoured by one of the Olympians? Who was Odysseus that a goddess such as Athena would choose him above so many others?

As he watched in awe, pressing himself as close as possible to the branches of the bush, Odysseus looked up at the goddess and Eperitus thought there were tears in his eyes.

'My Lady,' he said, then fell to his knees and held the hem of her robe to his face. To Eperitus's amazement and disbelief she also knelt and lowered her lips to kiss his hair.

'I have been with you all these years, Odysseus, watching over you and protecting you until you were ready.'

'And am I ready?'

'Yes,' she said. 'Your time is near at hand.'

An owl hooted from the trees, startling Eperitus so that he caught his cloak on the branches, rustling the leaves of the bush he hid behind. Athena glanced briefly in his direction before turning back to Odysseus and pulling him to his feet.

'You must listen to me, Odysseus, and remember what I say. The trouble in Ithaca is closer than you have dared to think, but you must not be there when Eupeithes makes his move.'

'But my Lady,' Odysseus protested, 'I have to protect my father's kingdom. Anybody who tries to take it from my family will taste the point of my spear.'

'And you theirs.' Athena put an arm about him and led him

away from the pool, nearer to where Eperitus lay concealed. 'Eupeithes is a fool. I might even kill him myself one day, but until then if you are to be king in your father's place you first have to prove yourself worthy. The Pythoness wasn't wrong when she told you that you will be king; but there are journeys to be made and alliances formed before you can hope to take your rightful inheritance.'

Odysseus stopped close to Eperitus's hiding place and scratched his scar vigorously. 'But if Eupeithes strikes soon and I'm away from home, then Ithaca will be lost.'

'Don't forget that you are only mortal, Odysseus,' Athena warned him, rising to her full height. 'Only the gods know the future, and you must place your trust in them if you ever hope to be king. I tell you truthfully that if a man follows his own designs and doesn't place his fate in the laps of the gods, then his path will be dark, difficult and doomed to ultimate failure. I promise you my help, and you will receive it, but you must have faith. What is more, I want you to do something for me.'

'Whatever you ask, mistress,' Odysseus said, though with hesitation.

The goddess smiled. 'I need you to go to Messene. I have a temple there which has fallen out of use. Hera put one of Echidna's spawn there to spite me – a monster older than Python and greater in size. Now it's keeping my followers away and even my priests dare not tend the altar.' She slammed the butt of her spear on the ground in anger and spat. 'I want the creature dead, and I want you to kill it for me.'

'It won't be easy, my Lady,' Odysseus said, 'but I will go if you command me to. What shall I tell my father?'

'Let me take care of that. I promise you my help if you need it, too, though only once. You must test your own prowess, rely on your skill as a warrior and use the brains that you have in abundance. But there will be a time when even your art won't save you, and when that moment comes you must use this to summon me.'

Athena opened her hand to reveal a small clay seal. Odysseus took it from her and held it up. By the light of the goddess's radiance Eperitus, from his hiding place, could just make out that it was in the shape of an owl.

'Break this and I will come to you,' she instructed. 'But it can only be used once. After that you must rely upon your own resources. And those of your companions, for I will not send you out alone. First you must take this one with you.'

Suddenly she bent over the bush where Eperitus was crouched and lifted him effortlessly into the open. He fell to the ground between their feet and lay on his back, shocked and surprised, looking up at them as they stared back down at him.

'Eperitus!' Odysseus exclaimed. 'You're supposed to be at the camp.'

'And you're supposed to be buying meat,' he retorted.

Athena stamped the butt of her spear on the ground beside his head. 'Silence!' she commanded. 'The gods have killed countless men for spying on their practices. And I've a mind to kill you, too.'

Eperitus twisted over and threw his arms about her legs in supplication. 'Please, goddess, no! I only came to eavesdrop on Odysseus because he lied to me. It never crossed my mind to spy on you, your ladyship. Forgive me and I'll honour you all my days; I promise to hold you closer to my heart than any of the other Olympians.'

'That is only what I deserve,' she said in a harsh tone. Then, with a degree of softness, she prodded him away from her legs with her spear. 'Let go now, Eperitus. Let go and stand up.'

Reluctantly he released her legs and got to his feet, patting the dust from his cloak. He took a step back and lowered his head so as not to look directly at the goddess.

'And if I told you to follow Odysseus to the ends of the earth, would you honour my wish?'

'Yes, Mistress Athena,' he answered. 'My fate is already tied up with Odysseus. And I'm also sworn to follow the will of the gods. You can be certain I'll do as you say.'

'Good! Be true to your word and no ill will befall you, though I also offer you this warning: beware the charms of women. You have no experience with those vile creatures, Eperitus, and a wrong choice could be perilous. Odysseus, my parting advice for you is to be wary of your friends. And don't forget my temple at Messene.'

In an instant she was gone. Eperitus waved his hand through the air where she had stood, but there was nothing.

Though the party was awake before dawn and did not tarry, it took them most of the next morning to reach the port where the Ithacans' ship was harboured. The journey was uneventful as they descended towards the great gulf of water Eperitus had seen the evening before, though it was strenuous under the merciless leadership of Odysseus and Halitherses, who insisted on a quick pace with few stops. Despite this, their newest recruit was pleased to find that the other warriors had welcomed his inclusion in their ranks, albeit with coldness from Mentor.

As they marched Eperitus became aware of a strange smell in the air, which was neither pleasant nor offensive, simply alien to his nostrils. He also saw great white birds circling in the sky above them, the likes of which he had never witnessed until his arrival at Pythia. They had long, hooked beaks and wing spans large enough to cast shadows over the soldiers as they flew. He watched them riding the wind, swooping and rising in the bright sunlight, and felt an unfamiliar pang stir in his heart. He felt as if he was on the threshold of the new world he longed for, that soon now he would be able to shake off the rags of his past life and for the first time discover who he really was. He was turning a corner that would put Alybas and his father out of sight, and would set him on the path to his promised glory, where the bonds of the old world would no longer hold any power over him.

A transformation of spirit overcame his companions, too. They no longer seemed weary, nor stooped by the weight of their arms.

Instead, their sombre mood had been replaced by a chattiness and excitement that Eperitus had not before seen in them. Their conversation was no longer a string of muttered curses or an exchange of complaints, as it had been only the day before, but turned now to the subject of Ithaca. They spoke eagerly of their wives and families, home cooking and wine shared by their own hearths. They were also talking of the sea.

Already Eperitus had seen tantalizing glimpses of this mysterious entity in the great body of water that was visible from the slopes of Mount Parnassus. Last night it had shone like silver in the moonlight, and this morning it was a dark mass upon whose surface the sunlight had shattered itself into a thousand pieces. But he knew that even this was only a channel that led to the sea, little more than the least twig on a great tree.

He lost sight of the shimmering waters as the party reached the plain below Pythia. As they followed the course of a boulder-strewn river that grew steadily wider and noisier they passed several pilgrims on their way to the oracle, escorted by local peasants acting as guides. The first sign that they were approaching a town was a group of girls washing clothing on the other side of the river. Shortly afterwards they began to pass huts and a few larger dwellings. Gradually the path became a road, populated by water-carrying women and their grubby-faced children, who looked blankly at the strangers as they filed past. A goatherd called a cheery greeting as he took his flock to drink at the river, but nobody else spoke to them.

Before long they were in the town itself, and followed the river, to the harbour. The great spread of water that Eperitus had seen at a distance now lay hammered out before him, a dark, shining mass that heaved quietly beneath the shore wind. This was not the sea – he could see land on all sides – but Antiphus told him it was an entrance to the gulf that split northern Greece from the Peloponnese, and which ultimately led out to the oceans of the world.

Flocks of seagulls screeched and cawed as they wheeled in wide circles over the town. Crowds of them were focused above a boat moored beside a wooden platform that had been built to reach out into the water. Eperitus watched in fascination as the crew passed wooden crates down to people on the platform, who then took them back to the shore.

'What's the matter, Eperitus? Never seen fishermen before?'

Antiphus joined him where he had lagged behind the group. The Ithacan was in a carefree mood now that he was homeward-bound, and gave the young warrior a dig in the ribs with his elbow. Eperitus looked back at the fishermen as they passed more crates out of their boat, watching keenly as they tossed shining objects into the water, where gulls darted into the waves and plucked them out again.

'No,' he confessed. 'Not in Alybas. My home is many days' march from the sea.'

'Then you've never even seen the sea?' Antiphus asked, shaking his head and trying to imagine a life without sight of the ocean waves every day.

Before now Eperitus's only experience of the sea had come through the fantastic stories of bards, or the tales of the grizzled adventurers who now and then passed through Alybas. They told tales of a great bottomless lake with no end, filled with gold and silver fish that the people who lived by the sea ate. They described oceans as blue as the sky, or at other times as dark as wine, where the restless surface moved like the wind over a field of barley. Sometimes, they said, Poseidon would make the waters rise up in great walls to smash the ships that rode upon them, and because of this the sea people built their ships of such strength and size that they could withstand the anger of the god. There were small boats in Alybas, of course, but the few natives who had ever seen the sea declared authoritatively that ships were as large as two or three houses put together, and some could hold over a hundred men.

'Are the creatures of the sea really made of silver and gold?'

'Silver and gold?' Antiphus laughed. 'If they were, Ithaca would be the richest country in the world. Well, country boy, what are you waiting for? Come and find out for yourself.'

With that he strolled towards the fishermen. Eperitus, keen to see a fish of silver, followed close behind.

They made camp by the shore that evening, Odysseus having decided to wait until the next morning to make the voyage back to Ithaca. His ship was not as big as Eperitus's imagination had hoped – just as he had learned that sea fish were not made of silver or gold – but she was a beautiful craft and he could barely wait to board her. He helped make a fire on the beach while others prepared the food or fetched fresh water (to his surprise, they informed him that sea water could not be drunk), and as he collected wood his mind and eyes were on the vessel. It was sunset and the calm waters were ablaze, glowing orange-red like new bronze as the black silhouette of the ship lay at anchor amidst the gentle, fiery waves. Her hull was low and wide, with great wooden barbs rising at each end and a prow that would cut through waves like a spear point. The tall mast stood forward of the centre of the boat, carrying a furled sail on its cross-spar and strung about by a web of ropes.

Besides Odysseus and his ten companions, a further eight men had been left to guard the ship. They welcomed the newcomer from Alybas with genuine friendship, despite being greatly saddened by the loss of one of their comrades. They demanded the story of the fight and the visit to the Pythoness, and as his men gathered to eat and share wine Odysseus gave them the tale in full, with much embellishment and ornamentation. For a man with so uncouth an appearance, the prince's voice was as smooth and as sweet as honey. His words fell like flakes of snow in the mountains at wintertime, gentle and enchanting and irresistible. The men listened intently and without interruption, their minds filled with the images that Odysseus created before them. They listened as if under a spell until, eventually, the tale was done and the teller leaned back with a smile and sipped his wine.

At the men's request, Eperitus described his part in the battle and the encounter with Python. The wine had driven away his inhibitions, and even Mentor's scowls could not prevent him from telling them the predictions of the Pythoness for his future. It pleased him that his audience were impressed enough to ask Halitherses and Antiphus whether it was true; but when Eperitus offered to tell them of the oracle's prophecy for Odysseus, Halitherses raised his hand.

'Enough, Eperitus. That's for Odysseus to reveal to the council, and is best left unspoken until then.'

After that the conversation died down, and soon the men were laying out their cloaks and blankets in the sand. Eperitus lay awake for another hour, listening to the snores of his companions and looking up at the stars that pierced the darkness above. His thoughts lingered in the streets and palace of Alybas for a while, remembering the evil events that had overtaken the town and driven him away. But the dark loneliness of exile had been mercifully short and already the gods were sending him to Ithaca. He tried to picture his new home, piecing together an image from the fragments of information he had heard around the fire earlier – a sunny island with woods and springs, villages and farms; populated by a happy people, and yet threatened with rebellion. And the whole surrounded by the endlessly shifting sea. He turned his eyes to the ship – a black, formless shape now in the dark waters of the estuary – and soon fell asleep, dreaming of an armada of such vessels carrying an army of men too vast to be numbered.

Chapter Six

THE KEROSIA

Ithaca was the hub of a group of larger islands that lay north, west and south of it. It was shaped like two leather bags knotted together: both halves were hilly and wooded and did not suit crops, though corn and vines were grown there in small quantities; the southern reach had only a few farms and was mainly given to pasture land for goats, while the northern half was where most of the islanders lived, and where Laertes's palace was situated.

At first light that morning the ship's sail was set, and with the wind filling its belly the vessel slipped up the gulf that led out to the Ionian Sea. Damastor had volunteered to teach Eperitus some of the basic elements of seacraft, but spent most of his time asking unwelcome questions about his past and the visit to the oracle. He seemed especially keen to learn what had been said to Odysseus, but when it became clear that Eperitus would not reveal anything of significance – either about his reasons for leaving Alybas or the words of the Pythoness – the probing stopped and Damastor began to talk instead of his wife and young child. As they passed the final headland some hours later the crew could see the islands of their homeland dominating the horizon before them, but when they reached open waters the wind blew up and they were forced into a flurry of action. Damastor left his pupil to look on helplessly as he joined his comrades at the leather ropes.

The men who had accompanied Odysseus to the oracle were as much at home on the sea as they were on land, if not more so, and rapidly set the dolphin-motifed sail to take full advantage of the new wind. The ship surged forward over the furious waves at a pace Eperitus had never imagined possible on water, and before long was rounding the southern tip of Ithaca and cruising into the narrow channel that separated it from its much larger neighbour, Samos.

No longer required to man the sails, the crew idled on the benches as Odysseus steered the ship up the familiar strait. They watched happily as the features of their homeland passed by on their right. With no more lessons in seamanship likely, Eperitus sat in the ship's prow and looked down at her blue beak as it split the waves, sending the frothing waters up in great jets to fall across her red bow cheeks. A giant eye was painted on either side, staring down the waves as they ran before it. Since boarding her that morning he had become fascinated with the vessel and the medium that gave her such invigorating life. Never had he seen anything as graceful as Odysseus's galley, or as pleasing to the eye in form and motion.

As he sat there admiring her speed and power, he vowed to one day go on a lengthy sea voyage and travel with the wind behind him to places he had only ever imagined before. He would see cities of legend and places of natural beauty beloved of the gods themselves; but most pleasurable by far would be the sea itself. To a landsman who had spent his entire life on solid ground, the feel of an unsteady ship's deck under his feet had at first been terrifying, then disorientating, and ultimately exhilarating. To stand on a plunging deck with the wind in his hair and the snapping of a sail overhead was a thrill the like of which he had never before experienced, and could not wait to enjoy more fully at his leisure.

He joined Antiphus on the bench where he was watching the island go by. The lofty bulk of southern Ithaca quickly gave way to a small but steep-sided peak that saddled the two halves of the island. Ravens flew around its scrub-covered slopes and filled the air with their cawing, heedless of the beaked ship that slipped past them. Then a second hill, the largest on the island, presented its near-vertical flanks to them, basking like a giant beast in the rays of the westering sun.

'Mount Neriton,' Antiphus said, pointing up at the hill. 'Ithaca's chief landmark. It overshadows the palace and our homes in the north, and we use it to keep a watch for visitors. From its peak a keen-eyed man can see townships in the Peloponnese, so the sentinels will have seen us some time ago. The king's slaves will already be preparing a feast for our return, and when they hear of your exploits, Eperitus, you'll be an honoured guest.'

Eperitus steadied himself against a rope and looked up at the wooded hill, its sides turning pink under the late afternoon light. So this was his new home, he thought: a collection of rocky hills rising up from the sea at the edge of the known world. It was an alien sight, but although the landscape was new the island appeared familiar, a self-contained refuge that even a wanderer like himself could call home. Its borders were defined for ever by the unchanging sea and, once ashore, he would be in a land immune from the strifes of the outside world. Here a man could stay distant and free from the feuds and civil wars that had unsettled Greece for so long.

Odysseus began angling the ship towards the mouth of a small bay. Soon they were drifting into the peaceful inlet, which formed a mere pocket in the shoreline between the northerly slopes of Mount Neriton to their right and another sheer hill to their left. All around, the sailors were occupying themselves with the sail and the anchor stones, whilst Odysseus, still gripping the twin steering oars, leaned over the side to judge the clearance left between the hull and the bottom of the bay. He gave a nod, and the anchor stones dropped overboard with a splash.

A group of youngsters had gathered on the beach and were waving and shouting at the crew. Two of them boarded a small boat and paddled out to meet the moored galley. Eperitus watched with interest as Damastor and Mentor helped the occupants aboard, where they were greeted warmly by the crew.

'Eumaeus!' Odysseus said, coming down from the helm and crushing the youth into his huge chest. 'How are you, boy? Have you been looking after my sister?'

'She's here, my lord, safe and sound,' Eumaeus answered, indicating the beach where a bare-breasted girl in a short purple skirt was waving wildly at the ship.

Odysseus waved back, then leaned against the handrail and shouted in his booming voice to the indistinct figure on the shore. 'Ctymene! Put something on, you strumpet. You're not a little girl any more.'

He threw a cautionary glance at his crew, who busied themselves stowing the sail and making ready to leave the ship. Eperitus joined them, though he could hardly keep his eyes from wandering to the slim girl on the beach. Considering Odysseus's ungainly, triangular bulk he would not have expected any sister of his to be as shapely as she was. Then he remembered the words of the oracle and was amazed at how easily the warning could come true: here was his friend's own kin and he was already succumbing to his most basic instincts at the sight of her half-naked body. He determined there and then to have nothing but the most formal and distanced relationship with the girl. As a member of the palace guard he would no doubt find himself in daily contact with her.

'Eperitus,' Odysseus called, beckoning him over. 'This is Eumaeus. My father bought him as a small child and over the years he has become like a little brother to me.'

The slave was only slightly younger than Eperitus, handsome, with a ruddy complexion and dark, curly hair. Although he was lean, he had good muscles, the strength of which the warrior could feel as he gripped his hand.

'Welcome to Ithaca.'

'Thank you,' Eperitus replied, taking an instant liking to him.

Odysseus climbed into the rowboat, followed by Halitherses, and called for the two young men to join them. Eumaeus stepped from one vessel to the other with ease, then turned to help Eperitus as he struggled to avoid falling into the waters that sloshed between ship and boat. The laughter and jeers of the crew followed his exertions. More embarrassing, though, was the knowledge that Ctymene was watching from the shore.

They rowed to the beach and were soon knee-deep in water as they leapt out and hauled the boat up to lodge in the soft sand. A pair of young men left the group on the beach and rowed the boat back out to the waiting sailors on the deck of the galley.

'Hello brother,' Ctymene said, leaving her friends and walking tartly up to Odysseus. She was short, like him, with the same plain looks, though her nose was smaller and she had fuller lips. She also had long, dark hair that fell nearly to her breasts, and a commanding femininity about her that made her powerfully attractive. She might be thirteen or fourteen years of age, and Eperitus agreed with Odysseus's sentiment that she was no longer a little girl. Remembering his pledge, he fixed his eyes firmly on the damp, shell-smattered sand.

'Hello sister,' Odysseus returned her greeting, with similar aloofness.

Then, after a lingering pause, he snatched her up in his massive arms and hoisted her onto his shoulders. She closed her hands over his eyes and laughed hysterically as he horsed about, stumbling across the beach with his arms splayed before him.

'You can be Orion,' she cried, 'and I'll be Cedalion, guiding you in your blindness.'

'Lead me to the rising sun then, Cedalion,' Odysseus answered.

The other youths immediately spread out in a crescent about the beach, putting themselves at a good distance from the blundering pair at the water's edge. Eumaeus, Halitherses and Eperitus stood to one side and watched Ctymene shout directions to her brother as he chased her companions about the beach. Their efforts were fruitless, even though their targets were not allowed to run, but Odysseus persisted without showing signs of tiring. Gradually the pair edged closer to the little group at the water's edge, and Eperitus noticed Ctymene snatching frequent glances at him. Then, suddenly, she instructed her brother to turn right and go straight, and a moment later his large hands were upon Eperitus's shoulders.

'You've found the sun, Orion,' she announced, removing her hands from his eyes. Odysseus blinked at Eperitus and smiled.

'By the rules of the game it's your turn to be Orion,' he said. 'But my sister isn't as light as she used to be, and I doubt it would be the most appropriate form of introduction.'

Ctymene stared down at her captive with a shameless look in her eyes.

'Who's this?' she asked.

'Eperitus of Alybas,' Odysseus answered, unconscious of his sister's staring. 'He killed five men the other morning, so be careful not to make him angry.'

'Five men!' she cooed with sudden interest, clambering down from her brother's shoulders and threading her arm through Eperitus's elbow. 'Really? Five men?'

'Yes,' he answered, tensing at the feel of her warm flesh against his. He was unused to the close attentions of a female and did not know how to react to Ctymene's immature flirting, especially in front of Odysseus. The fact she was attractive was undeniable, with her soft skin and the aroma of flowers that hung about her, but he was also hotly aware of his recent resolve to maintain an entirely formal relationship with the girl.

The rest of the crew were ashore by now and were ready to make their way to the palace.

'Ctymene,' Eumaeus said, noticing Eperitus's discomfort with amusement.

'Yes,' she replied, without taking her eyes from Eperitus, who looked nervously back at her. She gave him a mischievous smile.

'Didn't you say that the king wanted to see Odysseus?'

'Does he? Oh yes! Odysseus, Father wants to see you the moment you arrive. He's convening the Kerosia and wants you and Halitherses to go there. Right now, I think.'

Odysseus took a bag from Antiphus and slung it over his shoulder. There was a sudden sense of urgency about him.

'You'll have to feast without me,' he shouted to his men, waving them up the beach. 'Mentor, see they don't get too drunk. Come on, Halitherses, we're required elsewhere. You too, Eperitus. And as for you, sister, if you had a mind for anything other than dancing and boys you might remember that the king's messages are a matter of urgency.'

With that he headed towards a wooded ridge that spanned the gap between the two mountains. Here a track led him into the trees, and Eperitus followed behind Halitherses, with Ctymene still on his arm.

The great hall was windowless and sombre, lit only by a fire in the central hearth. Smoke twisted up towards the high ceiling, where shadowy images of sun, moon and stars were all that remained of its once vivid murals. Four tall pillars stood like sentinels about the fire, half bathed in the light of the flames and half consumed by the encircling darkness. Barely distinguishable about their smooth circumferences were the faded outlines of birds, trees and flowers.

On every side the gloomy walls were hung with shields and spears, mostly of an antique style and in a state of disrepair, their bronze tarnished black by the smoke of many years. By the wavering firelight Eperitus tried to discern the spectral scenes of animal and marine life depicted on the flaking plaster, but these were several generations old and had diminished along with the glory of what was now an ageing and functional palace. Only the two painted lions flanking the unadorned granite throne, which stood against the east wall, retained any semblance of their former life and colour.

He sat on one of the seven wooden chairs around the burning hearth, set facing the vacant throne and an empty stool that had been placed beside it. Odysseus was next to him and Halitherses sat on the other side of the prince, both men staring thoughtfully into the fire. Eperitus's own eyes were upon the silent members of the Kerosia who occupied the other chairs. These were the king's most trusted advisers, men of seniority who would counsel him in times of need. Most were old or middle-aged, their features illuminated by the flickering flames, deep shadows etched into the creases and contours.

As he studied them through the distorting flames, the door behind him opened and the members of the Kerosia stood as one. A man and woman entered the hall side by side, without ceremony, and sat at the two vacant places. A pair of armed guards came with them and took up station by the door. They were followed by slaves carrying platters of drinks, which they served to each member of the Kerosia in turn.

'Remember you're the youngest here, Eperitus,' Odysseus said, leaning across and whispering in his ear, 'and that you're a stranger. Speak only if you are spoken to; otherwise follow my lead in everything.'

Eperitus lowered the silver goblet from his thirsty lips and watched the others, whose drinks remained in their hands. Despite the simple, unannounced entrance, Eperitus could tell by the continued silence that they were waiting for the newcomers to speak.

The man held a twisted staff of dark wood, almost as tall as himself, which would be given to each speaker in turn as the debate began – a sign of their right to speak without interruption. But if this was Laertes, king of Ithaca, Eperitus could hardly have imagined a man more unlike Odysseus. His grey hair, watery eyes and thin, drooping lips made him look old beyond his years. His body was wasted and bent and his thin, bandy legs were forced to support an oversized belly. The pallor of his skin suggested a life spent mostly indoors, and by the way he squinted across his hooked nose at the members of the Kerosia, Eperitus guessed that his eyesight was deteriorating.

In contrast, Anticleia, Laertes's wife, bore a strong blood-resemblance to Odysseus. She had the same green eyes, red hair and straight nose that her son possessed, with broad shoulders that echoed his physical presence. She looked much younger than Laertes and all eyes rested upon her as the royal couple sat before the council.

Laertes took his cup and sprinkled a few fingertips of wine into the flames – a libation in honour of the gods – before sitting down again to drink. The rest of the Kerosia stood and copied his brief gesture. Eperitus was notably the last to do this and caught the king's liquid eye as he retreated to his place, his glance lingering just long enough not to become a stare. Then he broke the silence by slapping his palm repeatedly on the stone arm of the throne.

'Now then, you all know each other, so let's do away with the formalities and start the work of the day. Halitherses, my friend, I'm glad to see you've brought my son safely back from the oracle. What news from the Pythoness, Odysseus?'

Odysseus stood and took the staff from his father. Their eyes met in silence: on one side the reigning king, small and frail, his head and nose raised slightly as if listening, his teeth resting on his lower lip in an unconscious sneer; opposite him, the future king, hugely strong, wearing the confidence of his youth like a rich, impenetrable cloak.

He recounted the events that had happened whilst he had been away, avoiding a repetition of the Pythoness's prophecy but emphasizing the role Eperitus had played in the fight against the deserters.

'In recognition of his courage,' he concluded, 'I've asked Eperitus to join the royal guard.'

'The king chooses his guard,' Laertes replied sternly, without looking at his son's guest. 'Both you and Halitherses know that.'

'His appointment is subject to your approval, Father, I grant you. But ask yourself if you can turn away a willing warrior who killed five men in his first combat.'

There was a stiffness in Odysseus's response that betrayed the silent contest between son and father, prince and king. Laertes bit back with the speed of a striking snake.

'Ask yourself if the king's life can be trusted to a stranger! Have you tested him?'

'More than enough, Father. He's fit to serve the king, and the Pythoness herself has promised him great things.'

'The oracle never promises anything, Odysseus,' Laertes retorted. 'You'll do well to remember that. Why did you aid my son and his men?'

It took Eperitus a moment to realize that Laertes was speaking to him. He looked at the king in surprise, suddenly at a loss for what to do or say. Then he noticed Odysseus beside him, discreetly tapping his knee. Eperitus knelt at once, and bowed his head.

'My lord, I saw brave men outnumbered and surrounded. It was easy to decide who needed my help most.'

'And if my son's men had been in the majority?'

Eperitus raised his head and met Laertes's gaze. 'In that case, my lord, I might have slain five Ithacans instead.'

The king smiled at his reply, but it was not a smile that brought any sense of warmth or relief.

'You are on probation, Eperitus of Alybas,' he told him. 'But I'll watch you.'

This time he fixed the young warrior with a stare that he would not release. Eperitus met his eye, but as he did so he felt the keen gaze stripping away the fragile barriers that concealed his innermost thoughts. Quickly he lowered his eyes for fear that the old man would follow the passages of his mind into areas he had not even dared to explore himself.

'Yes, I'll watch you like a hawk,' Laertes repeated, before turning to the others. 'Now, where are you, Koronos? Stand up so my old man's eyes can see you. I've called you all here because Koronos has news for us from Eupeithes's camp. Stand up, man, and take the speaker's staff.'

A middle-aged noble with pitch-black hair raised himself from the chair closest to the king and took the staff from Odysseus. Eperitus could see that he was wealthy by the quality of his clothes and his well-kept, well-fed appearance. From his confidence before the Kerosia he also guessed he was a man of position, used to deference from others.

'My lords, your ladyship, King Laertes is fortunate in having me as his close and faithful ally, for I bring news which those of us loyal to his rule must act upon immediately. Sometime ago a god put it into my mind to bribe one of Eupeithes's slaves into my service. This man has become my eyes and ears in the traitor's household, and there's little of that man's scheming that I don't know about.

'Eupeithes is an Ithacan and familiar to us all. But allow me to enlarge on what we know of this man, if only for the sake of our guest.' Koronos bowed briefly to Eperitus. 'Though he is a noble, a wealthy merchant, a powerful orator and a man of political ambition, he has never before sought to bring violence to these islands. For some time now we've been subjected to his speeches in the marketplaces, so we know he claims to be a patriot . . .'

'Patriot!' snorted one of the Kerosia, a man bent with age who could barely straighten his back to vent his disgust. 'He's a fat, pampered coward with no mind for anything other than increasing his own wealth! Who can forget how he sided with the Taphians when they raided our allies, the Thesprotians? Can a man who attacks his country's friends call himself a patriot?' The old man stopped to draw breath and, in honour of his age, nobody dared interrupt him. Not even Koronos, who held the speaker's staff. 'I was among the crowd of islanders who wanted to kill him for his treason. We chased him from his farm on the north coast all the way to the palace – you'd never have thought such a fat man could move so quickly.' He took breath again, wheezing in his excitement. 'Only Laertes had compassion on the man, and gave him sanctuary in this very house. He and the boy', he pointed his stick at Odysseus, 'held the gates, forbidding us entry and persuading us to return to our homes. And this is the family he wants to overthrow!'

After a respectful pause, Koronos continued. 'Thank you, Phronius. If we all bore grudges as tenaciously as you, perhaps

Eupeithes wouldn't have wormed his way back into the hearts of the people. But, nevertheless, he claims himself a patriot and a respecter of the gods, and he spreads his lies amongst those who'll listen to him. He claims Laertes is an idle king, an incompetent ruler who wants to keep Ithaca in stasis, never growing or rising to fulfil her potential. He tells us that, if he were monarch, he'd make our small knot of islands into a kingdom to be reckoned with. And the people are listening to him! They believe Eupeithes when he tells them he'll bring new wealth to their towns and farmsteads, when he promises to build a palace to rival Mycenae, and that he'll make powerful alliances with other states. And I'll tell you what's even more dangerous: he has the ear of many of the nobles of these islands.'

Koronos looked round at each member of the council, sliding his gaze from one set of eyes to the next, pushing home to them the prospect that Laertes was losing his grip on the populace.

'But for all his influence, for all his patience in stirring up the people, he doesn't have the majority of support. Perhaps a quarter of the people and nobles are for him.'

'Nonsense!' shouted Phronius. 'A tenth at the most.'

'Another quarter is sympathetic,' Koronos continued, 'but undecided. The remainder are loyal to the rule of Laertes and will never support a usurper, even if some of them agree with Eupeithes. Because he knows this, the traitor has changed his plans. And that is what brings me here.'

At this point Koronos signalled to one of the slaves, who came over and refilled his cup. He took a mouthful and looked around again.

'Eupeithes, for all his treachery, doesn't want to kill our great king. He still feels a debt of honour for the time that you shielded him from the mob, my lord. But he's also a politician, and fears your death would win him more enemies than friends. Therefore he'd rather see you retired with the agreement of the nobles than murdered like a dog. And yet he has gathered about him men who are not so discerning. These men, most notably the twins Polybus and Polytherses, are tired of waiting for public opinion to turn in their favour. They're pushing for action now, and they mean to have their way.

'Until recently, I've been content for my spy to report the daily goings-on: the name of any new nobleman won over to Eupeithes's cause; the travelling plans of the traitor; any new schemes he has dreamed up to oppose the rule of our king. These are the things that have been reported to me for months, but a few nights ago Eupeithes was visited by the twins and they spoke together long into the night. My man served them throughout and has relayed every word to me. These men don't care for their country – they want only wealth and power. They're also young and don't share their leader's patience in sowing dissent for a popular and peaceful removal of the king. They've spent the winter recruiting hard and raising funds, intent on recruiting a force of mercenaries. They even mentioned the Taphians, who their master still has secret connections with, and Eupeithes has agreed a plan to attack at the end of spring and take the throne by force. My lords, the time of political strife is passing. We must sharpen our swords for war.'

Chapter Seven

ODYSSEUS'S CHALLENGE

Tyndareus paced the floor of the great hall. Fired by his idea for gathering together the best of the Greeks, Agamemnon had sent mounted messengers to spread the word that Helen was to be married and her father was inviting suit from the greatest kings and warriors in all Greece. Perhaps fearing that the Spartan king would change his mind, he had dispatched the heralds that same evening. By now news would have reached every corner of the Peloponnese, whilst merchant ships would already be carrying messages out to the islands. Some horsemen might even have reached northern Greece, especially as this was a time of relative peace and the only trouble on the roads was the occasional brigand.

The king sighed. He might have a few days or even weeks of grace as Greece's greatest men made preparations to come, but he also knew how much these men hated each other and would not want their rivals to steal a march on them. Though they would want to come with a full retinue, they would also be keen not to waste time in getting to Sparta: each would want to stake a claim on Helen before some other suitor could work his way too deeply into Tyndareus's favour. He imagined that within a month the cold, echoing walls of the great hall would be filled with the clamour of many mighty voices.

He sighed again and tugged desperately at his beard. Though he admired his son-in-law, he was also frequently vexed by Agamemnon's ability to persuade him into doing things that he did not want to do. Helen was a good age for marriage, but he had not wanted her given to another man just yet. In truth, he had hardly put his mind to the matter before now, probably because he was too happy having her about his palace. No doubt she was a moody girl and not as disciplined as a daughter should be, but Tyndareus knew he was clay in her hands. She only had to bat her long-lashed eyelids or pout her full lips and he was helpless. Hence the thought of actually losing her, now that he had milled it through his mind for a couple of days, made him very unhappy.

If Agamemnon had not headed home at first light yesterday, to tell his brother Menelaus to make ready, Tyndareus would have confronted him on the matter. Losing his beloved daughter was one reason for concern; feeding the most ravenous appetites in Greece was entirely another. Sparta was a rich state, but he resented having to give one copper piece of its wealth for the sake of Agamemnon's grandiose strategies. For that reason he intended to make a full inventory of everything in the palace, from each head of livestock and bushel of corn right down to the smallest clay drinking krater.

'Tyndareus, are you in here?' asked a female voice.

'Yes, Leda,' Tyndareus answered, turning to greet his wife as she entered.

Helen was with her and together they crossed the floor to join the king. Leda was a tall and attractive woman, beautifully dressed and wearing her long black hair over her shoulders. The only sign of age, other than the wrinkles at the corners of her eyes, was the two thick streaks of grey hair that sprouted from her temples. She kissed her husband and took his big hands in her slender fingers.

'Are you busy?' she asked. 'Helen and I would like to spend some time with you before retiring.'

Tyndareus shook his head. 'I'll be grateful of your company, my dear.' He looked at Helen. 'Why the frown, daughter?'

'I'm saving my smiles for the best men in Greece,' she told him sharply.

'Then you're still unhappy,' he sighed. 'How can you be sad

when kings and princes from every city in the land will be coming to pay homage to you?'

The king looked at his daughter as she stood before the hearth. As usual she was dressed in white, and with the light behind her he could clearly distinguish her naked silhouette through the gossamer material. He shook his head, silently wondering how any man could ever hope to resist her. Agamemnon might not have considered it in his great plan, but Tyndareus knew there would be bloodshed as soon as a husband was picked, if not before. All those proud warriors! Did his son-in-law really expect them to form an alliance under his leadership, when any fool could see they would be at each other's throats within days?

'Father,' Helen said angrily, 'you intend to parade me like a prize cow before a pack of over-preened simpletons, and expect me to be pleased at the prospect?'

She forced a tear into each eye, which was easy to do considering the frustration she felt about the situation, and looked away from her foster-father.

Tyndareus was a great king and a formidable fighter, and as such he knew how to read most men. But about women he knew nothing. Although the rumour was well known amongst all ranks at the palace, never once in all the years since the birth of Helen and her twin brothers had he believed the children were not his own. Similarly, in his doting love for Helen he did not suspect that she considered him an old, dim-witted fool, or that she had very little genuine affection for him.

'Come and sit with me, daughter,' he offered, retiring into his large wooden chair. 'And will you sit beside us, Leda?'

Helen walked over to him, slipped off her sandals and curled up in his broad lap, pressing her long, white feet against the arm of the chair and laying her head against his shoulder.

She found herself thinking of Theseus, the Athenian braggart who had kidnapped her when she was a girl and taken her to Attica. She remembered his heavily built body, so close to her own, the hardness of his muscles and the smell of his sweat. How scared she had been, how repulsed, and yet how excited. Though she was afraid and knew that her brothers would be searching for her, she also wanted to remain unfound, wanted to discover love in his arms. But in some last act of heroic self-denial he had rejected her when he learned she had not yet become a woman, even when in her naive way she had offered herself to him. And so her brothers had found her safe, her virginity intact.

The experience had changed her. Helen had stepped beyond the safe confines of palace life and had grown conscious of herself and her effect on men. Though Theseus, whom she hated now with a passion, had resisted her, she knew that the decision had broken him. Even at the age of twelve, her beauty had destroyed the man who had once defeated the infamous Cretan Minotaur.

Of her own desires, she had learned that she did not want to be a pawn in a political game. Surrounded by walls, guards and the confines of palace life, Helen felt trapped. She wanted freedom, adventure – *love*. How could Tyndareus really expect her to be happy, exchanging her for political favours, selling her to a man who was not her choice? Where was the romance of escaping with a young lover, where was the danger and the scandal?

Helen was certain of one thing, though. If a man appeared who could love her for more than the fortune and favour she brought, then she would follow him to the ends of the earth. And she silently vowed that no power – of man or god – would come between them.

The debate in the Kerosia continued into the night, shuttling back and forth as the slaves brought more food, wine and torches. Eperitus watched as different options were discussed and plans put forward for defending Laertes's throne from the threatened rebel attack.

Some suggested taking a force to Eupeithes's manor house and arresting him for treason, but Koronos assured them the house was well defended and prepared for an attack. Any attempt would only spill Ithacan blood, and could even act as a call to arms for Eupeithes's supporters. In the end, Laertes insisted he did not want a civil war on his hands and quashed the idea.

Equally, Koronos's own suggestion of a meeting with Eupeithes was shouted down. Only when Odysseus insisted that he should be allowed to speak was Koronos able to propose placating Eupeithes with a place on the Kerosia and a promise to adopt his suggestions for generating wealth and forming alliances with other states. But Odysseus argued vehemently against the idea, refusing to reward a would-be traitor with the power he craved.

'Then what do we do?' asked Halitherses. 'We can't sit and wait for Eupeithes to attack us.'

'We won't.'

Eperitus looked at Anticleia, who had spoken for the first time. It was irregular in the extreme that a woman should be tolerated at a Kerosia, even if she was the queen, but the sight of a woman addressing a gathering of male elders was something he had never heard of. In Alybas no woman spoke when men were talking, unless specifically invited, but to his surprise Anticleia was permitted to continue.

'There's more than one way to string a bow. Eupeithes's power comes from the disaffection he spreads about your father. Fortunately for us, Ithacans are slow to react and their hearts are essentially true, which is why it has taken him so long to turn just a few of the people against Laertes. By lying and emphasizing minor misjudgements he has established a firm opposition to the absolute rule of the king, but if we can remove the foundation upon which he has built his popular support, then it will collapse.'

Laertes, who had been sulking quietly as his wife spoke, slammed the butt of the staff on the floor.

'What Anticleia means to say is I should hand over my kingship to Odysseus, and then there will be no uprising,' he said bitterly, staring with open animosity at his son.

'Eupeithes will have lost the very reason for his opposition to the throne,' Anticleia explained to him gently. 'His support will simply drain away.'

The other members of the Kerosia looked at each other in a startled hush, then as a single body looked at Odysseus. The prince leaned back into his chair and stared at his parents.

'The queen's wisdom is well known and highly regarded. But she is a woman and holds no power at the Kerosia. For myself I ask only this: what does the king say?'

Laertes looked at his son with sad, angry eyes, before lowering his gaze to the flames.

'It's the only way to defeat Eupeithes without bloodshed,' he sighed. 'If the Kerosia will support you, Odysseus, then you shall be announced king tomorrow. So speaks the king of Ithaca.'

There were murmurs of approval amongst the ring of counsellors. Eperitus looked at Odysseus and recognized that he would make a good king, for all his deception and trickery. He was young, strong and brave and Eperitus had seen with his own eyes that he was a talented warrior. More importantly, he had the support of a goddess and the blessing of the oracle.

'Forgive me, lord,' Halitherses said, bowing to Laertes, 'but I feel the time has come for Odysseus to take his rightful inheritance. I, for one, will support him.'

'Odysseus isn't ready for the responsibility,' said Phronius, waving his stick in a prophetic fashion. 'I tell you all that a king must have a wife, and she must be a woman suited to rule.'

'When Odysseus is king he'll have plenty of time to find himself a wife,' said Halitherses. 'The important thing is that he should become king now, before the rebels attack in the spring. That way he'll steal Eupeithes's thunderbolts from his hand. The people know and love Odysseus, and they'll follow him because he is Laertes's son. The blood of the king's line is in him, and that is something Eupeithes will never have. Given the full support of the Kerosia, he will be able to build on the strong foundations laid by his father.'

'I disagree,' said Koronos, his voice no longer smooth but suddenly harsh as stone. 'The majority of the people are for Laertes. If Odysseus takes the throne before the people are ready for him, then Eupeithes will exploit this to his advantage.'

He stood and held up his hand against the murmuring of Odysseus's supporters.

'Listen to me,' he insisted. 'If Odysseus becomes king now, Ithaca will be turned against him by Eupeithes's rhetoric. These are simple folk whose loyalties are bought slowly and grudgingly; though they know Odysseus the prince, what do they know of Odysseus the king? The first thing they'll look for is the stamp of his authority, and unless Fortune provides Odysseus with a chance to prove himself Eupeithes will be swift to spread dissent. What he has taken years to do to Laertes's reputation, I tell you truthfully he will do in days to Odysseus's.'

Koronos watched the effect of his words settling upon his audience before sitting and giving the arena to whoever should dare to challenge him. It was Odysseus who stood. Crossing to his father he took the proffered staff and turned to the Kerosia.

'Friends, beloved father, listen to what I have to say. It appears to me that the ultimate decision lies not with age, but with youth. I've listened to your counsels and feel like a rope between two teams of men, one moment pulled this way and the next that. I hear the words of my parents and feel the temptation of the throne. I see my friend Halitherses speak in my favour, and I feel that I could take on my father's yoke and bring these islands to even greater prosperity.

'And then I hear Phronius say that to be an effective king I need a woman who is worthy to become my queen. Most convincingly, I hear the argument of shrewd Koronos, a man with a god-given gift of intelligence, who is more familiar than any of us with Eupeithes's strengths.' He fixed his eyes on Koronos, who acknowledged him with a nod. 'His words stand fast against all counter-arguments. A young man cannot become king without first proving his worth to his people. Therefore, though I must accept one day soon, I cannot become Ithaca's king until I've earned the loyalty of the people.'

'And how do you intend to show the people you are fit to be king, Odysseus?' Koronos asked.

The prince confessed he did not know how to prove his worthiness to the people of Ithaca. A few hasty suggestions were made for quests that would test his abilities, but these were either too unimpressive or too ridiculous, and faded away with little or no further consideration. Then Koronos, who seemed to have been in control of the debate at every juncture, stretched out a hand for the speaker's staff.

'If you want to prove yourself, Odysseus; and if you must have a wife; and if we all want Laertes's son to reign in his father's place and to defeat Eupeithes, then I have news which will solve all our problems. Only this morning I returned from a visit to the Peloponnese, where I occasionally travel on business. While I was busy discussing the price for a batch of oil yesterday evening, a herald arrived in the marketplace announcing that the king of Sparta is inviting the nobles of Greece to pay court to his daughter, Helen. I've never seen her, but we've all heard she's the most beautiful woman alive.'

Odysseus laughed out loud. 'And you're suggesting, Koronos, that I march halfway across the Peloponnese to beg at the tables of the rich and famous for a few weeks, before being turned out on my backside like a dog.'

'You haven't allowed me to finish, my lord,' the noble answered stiffly. 'The man who is chosen to become her husband will inherit King Tyndareus's throne – whoever gains the hand of Helen also gains the might of Sparta. If you came back to Ithaca with Helen as your queen all our problems would be solved: you'll have proved your worthiness to rule; the people will love you; and Eupeithes will wither from their minds like a cut flower in the sun. And should he decide to make a fight of it with his Taphian mercenaries, then he'll have our Spartan allies to reckon with.'

Odysseus merely shook his head and smiled. 'It's a preposterous suggestion, Koronos, especially for you. Greek laws don't allow a man to rule two nations, so eventually I would have to choose between Ithaca and Sparta – not that it will ever come to that. Besides, I'd rather risk the throne now than waste my time strutting around Sparta like a peacock, all for the pleasure of a girl whose future husband was probably chosen long before this suit was offered. There's more to this than meets the eye. I won't go.'

'Why not?' Eperitus blurted without thinking. For a painful moment all eyes were upon him. 'Besides, if Eupeithes intends to attack in the spring, what alternative do we have?'

Halitherses added his voice to the young warrior's. 'Don't be frightened of a woman, Odysseus. A man of your calibre can achieve anything he puts his mind to. That's the mark of a true hero.'

Laertes nodded his agreement. 'Succeed or fail, it's clearly the will of the gods that you go. Never has there been a man of our family so blessed with good fortune as you, so I agree with Koronos that you should go to Sparta, even if only to test your luck in the wider world. One thing is true about this whole affair: the answer doesn't lie within these islands.'

Odysseus shook his head. 'I'd need at least half the palace guard as escort and to provide a statement of my rank when I reached Sparta. We would be away for six months at least, by my reckoning, and with half the guard and the heir to the throne gone, why would Eupeithes need to wait until the spring? We would be splitting our forces and inviting trouble. It would be madness.'

Eperitus slumped dejectedly back into his chair, convinced that nothing was ever decided at an Ithacan council. The only debate he knew how to handle was the kind that was decided with sharpened bronze. But at that moment Koronos stood again, still clutching the speaker's staff, and looked directly at Odysseus. Something burned in his eyes that was not anger, but amusement.

'You sit there, Odysseus, and talk of proving yourself. I wonder, as the opportunities come and go, will you continue to sit and talk?'

Odysseus covered the space between them in the blink of an eye. Eperitus watched him wrench the staff from Koronos's fingers and fully expected him to dash the man's brains out with it. But within the same instant that his anger had flared, Odysseus controlled it again and forced the staff to his side with a trembling hand. They faced each other and, to Eperitus's surprise, the older man did not flinch before the terrifying gaze of the prince.

'You're fortunate this is the Kerosia,' Odysseus hissed, before forcing a smile to his lips. 'Here I can accept your criticism without feeling insulted. And perhaps you're even cleverer than you seem, my friend, for you must surely have wanted me to go to Sparta from the beginning. And I accept your challenge.'

Chapter Eight

FAREWELL TO ITHACA

Eperitus leapt from his bed and dressed as quickly as he could. Outside, the dark streets of Alybas were filled with the din of fighting – men shouting, the scrape and clatter of bronze on bronze. He could smell smoke and a flickering orange glow shone through the high window of his room onto the ceiling.

Moments later he was rushing down the steps to the ground floor, pushing the household slaves aside and ignoring their urgent pleas as he ran to arm himself. There was no time to fit breastplate or greaves, so he crammed his bronze cap onto his head and pulled his shield from the wall. One of the newer slaves, whose name he could not remember, followed him in and handed him his sword.

'What's going on out there?' Eperitus demanded.

'Looks like rebellion, my lord. A group of soldiers set a few of the houses alight to draw the guards from the palace. Now there's hand-to-hand fighting and the streets are littered with corpses.'

'You seem to have your wits about you,' Eperitus said. 'Find what weapons you can and arm the male slaves, then lead the women up into the hills until the fighting is over.'

'What about the house?'

'Don't worry about the house. Have you seen my father?'

'No, sir. He could have been in the palace until late, as usual, or perhaps he left as soon as the trouble started.'

Eperitus patted the man's arm and ran out into the street. A house was burning further up the hill, filling the night air with sparks that spiralled up towards the black clouds above. There was an awful stench of burning flesh and Eperitus could see several lifeless shapes lying in the mud of the street. The sounds of battle continued, but had moved away in the direction of King Pandion's palace.

Eperitus set off at a sprint, driven by fear for the king's life. He passed several more corpses and only stopped as he approached the gates. These were guarded by four members of the guard, who lowered their spear points as they recognized him.

'What's happening?' he asked, relieved to see the gates held by the king's men, but concerned to still hear the sounds of battle within. 'Is it a rebellion?'

'Your father has everything under control,' one of them answered. 'They're just finishing off the last of the survivors now. You'll find him in the great hall.'

Eperitus ran through to the small courtyard beyond, where yet more bodies littered the ground. Even in the reflected glow from the clouds he was able to recognize many of their faces, the light absent from their eyes and their features frozen in the agony of death. Knowing his spear would be awkward in the narrow corridors, he threw it aside and drew his sword as he hurried over the threshold and into the palace.

Torches sputtered in their brackets, casting a dull, pulsing light over the passage that led to Pandion's throne room. The sounds of fighting had all but disappeared, leaving only the clashing of swords from beyond the doors at the end of the corridor. Eperitus had a sudden feeling that the king was in danger and that only he could save him, but as he prepared to join the fight he was stopped by a sight that drained the energy from his limbs. Lying on the stairs to the women's quarters were his older brothers. One lay face up, his throat open and dark with blood; the other lay across him, the broken shaft of a spear protruding from his spine.

As he stared at their corpses, feeling empty and emotionless, the clamour from the throne room stopped. Eperitus felt a rush of fury and ran the length of the body-strewn passage determined to avenge his brothers. He shouldered the doors open and stood with his legs apart and his sword and shield at the ready. But he was too late. The king lay slumped across the floor, one hand still clutching a sword whilst the other reached towards the throne. His dead eyes stared accusingly at Eperitus.

Standing over him was a tall figure, wiping the king's blood from his blade. Eperitus stumbled and lowered his sword.

'Father?'

A part of him understood what had happened, but the greater part would not accept it.

'It had to be done, lad,' his father replied calmly. 'I would have told you before, but I was afraid you'd give my plans away. You have too much of your grandfather in you – I knew your loyalty would be to the throne. Well, now *I* am the throne.'

As if to emphasize his point, he stepped over Pandion's body and sat in the stone chair.

'What have you done?' Eperitus asked, only then noticing several members of the palace guard standing on either side of him.

'Pandion was a fool and a weakling, Eperitus. Under his rule Alybas was becoming a feeble and insignificant city, so some of us,' he raised his sword point and indicated the surviving guards, 'decided it was time for a change.'

'No king is weak who has the full loyalty of his followers,' Eperitus responded, gripping his sword and taking a step forward.

Instantly the guards formed a circle about his father, who laughed as if drunk.

'Gods! You remind me so much of my father – that rigid sense of honour and devotion to duty. But that's what I want, Eperitus. I'm king now, and I need someone trustworthy to succeed me. Your brothers died fighting at my side like true sons; now you must decide where your loyalties are. If you swear allegiance to me, we'll make Alybas a city to be proud of. And when I die, you'll become king in my place. What do you say, son?'

He leaned across the arm of the throne, offering his hand. Eperitus ignored it.

'Once I loved and respected you. I obeyed your every wish freely and willingly. But now you've brought dishonour on our family. I can't forgive you for that.'

His sense of disbelief had not disarmed his anger, and with a curse on his lips he lunged at his father with the point of his sword. Two of the guards threw their shields before the new king, whilst another knocked the weapon from Eperitus's hand with a swift stroke of his own blade. Two others leapt on him and pinned his arms behind his back. They dragged him before his father, whose smile had been replaced with an angry scowl.

'You disappoint me, lad. I should kill you, but I've lost enough sons already today. You can have your weapons and that old shield you're so proud of, but from this point on you have no home, no possessions and no family. You're an exile, and if you ever set foot in Alybas again I'll kill you myself.'

❦

Eperitus sat up, gasping for breath and clutching at his blanket. He wiped the sweat from his brow and looked about at the unfamiliar surroundings. A grey light was seeping into the window-less room, revealing the rows of large clay jars along the walls. With a sense of relief he realized he was in one of the storerooms in the palace at Ithaca, where he had been quartered after the Kerosia three nights ago.

As he allowed the emotions of the dream to fall from him and his eyes adjusted to the pre-dawn light, he became aware of sounds from within the palace. The kitchen slaves would be busy lighting fires and cooking breakfast, whilst others would be making prepa-rations for Odysseus's journey to Sparta.

After Koronos's public challenge to the prince's courage, which he had little choice but to accept, there had been another lengthy debate between the elders. One wanted Odysseus to travel light with only two or three companions, but this was quickly dismissed by the other members of the Kerosia. Some valued his life too highly and did not want him to travel to Sparta without a full escort. Others pointed out that he would need to impress King Tyndareus, and to do this a more substantial guard would be required.

They finally reached a compromise. Half of the thirty-strong palace guard would accompany Odysseus, led by Halitherses himself, whilst the remainder would be left under Mentor's charge. This force would be bolstered by a hastily assembled militia that would be sufficient to defend the palace, until Odysseus returned in the spring.

With that point grudgingly settled the debate focused upon what gift they should offer. It was the height of good manners that a guest should take a present, and it was customary to give something that reflected the suitor's standing, as well as the degree of respect with which he regarded his host. Therefore, despite Ithaca's comparative poverty, the Kerosia agreed to send a gift beyond their means. Laertes's second-finest sword would be sacrificed – a weapon with an ivory handle and pommel, gold inlay on the blade, and a gold-filigreed leather scabbard. Anticleia also offered three of her finest dresses for Helen (there was not enough time to make new garments), along with the finest jewellery that could be plundered from the palace stocks.

Odysseus took a surprisingly small part in the discussions, allowing the elders to decide his fate for him. He appeared to have his mind on something else – Helen perhaps – and only spoke to ensure that his father would be adequately protected whilst he was gone. However, it was at his suggestion that the elders agreed to waste no time, and that the expedition to Sparta should set out before dawn on the third day after the Kerosia. A quick departure, unannounced, would draw minimal attention and catch Eupeithes off balance. The recruitment of the militia would then be completed within a few days, before the rebels could muster their forces and threaten the undermanned palace guard.

By the amount of light that was now suffusing the gloomy interior of the storeroom, Eperitus judged that dawn had already arrived. He picked up his cloak and threw it about his shoulders. As he finished tying on his armour Eumaeus arrived, looking sleepy and dishevelled, to inform him that breakfast was being prepared in the great hall. Eperitus followed him out and joined Odysseus and a handful of his men, who had finished eating and were discussing the arrangements.

'We need fifteen guards, Antiphus, not five,' the prince said. 'I don't care what they're doing or where they are. Search every house in the town if you have to.'

The archer turned and gave Eperitus a brief nod before running from the palace. Odysseus ordered Eumaeus to chase the head steward about the provisions for the journey, then turned to Eperitus and gave him a weary smile.

'So much for leaving before first light, eh? No food, no gold, gifts mislaid and most of the guard haven't even reported in yet. Still, I should consider myself lucky: it took a week to organize the visit to Pythia. How about you? Sleep well?'

'Yes, my lord,' Eperitus lied, not wishing to share his nightmares with the others. 'Can I help?'

The prince placed a huge hand on his shoulder. 'I doubt it – you'll only get lost in all the chaos. The best thing you can do is sit down and eat a good breakfast, as you'll be lucky to eat again before we make landfall.'

By mid-morning the dresses were packed in a chest, along with the jewels Anticleia had chosen. Laertes's sword had eventually turned up beneath a pile of mildewed shields and was stowed with the other gifts. The other members of the guard had been located and were assembled on the grassy terrace before the palace walls, sweating in their full armour. Some of them had been in the group that escorted Odysseus to Pythia, others he had met in the three days since the Kerosia, but most were strangers to Eperitus.

Scattered around were small groups of slaves, gathered ready to carry the gifts and provisions down to the galley. The crowd was further swelled by the remainder of the household, who had left their tasks and come out to see the party off. Finally, the goings-on at the palace had also excited the interest of the towns-folk, who had come to watch the expedition leave.

'There goes our plan to slip away unnoticed,' said Halitherses, standing beside Eperitus and Damastor. 'We might as well have invited Eupeithes in person to wish us a safe journey.'

'Perhaps we've played directly into his hands,' Eperitus replied, cynically. 'This may be just the opportunity he needs.'

'Whatever happens, lad, it'll be according to the wishes of Zeus. He is the unseen mover in the affairs of men.'

'Where's Odysseus?' Damastor asked anxiously. 'We should be going.'

'With his father and mother,' Halitherses answered. 'They're making sacrifices for the journey to Sparta. What about Koronos? I haven't seen him since the Kerosia.'

'He returned home after the Kerosia,' said Damastor. 'His wife is due to give birth.'

'A midwife is he?' Halitherses sniffed, making no effort to hide his dislike of Koronos. 'Clearly a man of many talents.'

At that moment Ctymene appeared. It was the first time Eperitus had seen her since his arrival on Ithaca and he was relieved to see her fully covered, wearing a clean white dress clasped at one shoulder and carrying a basket of flowers on one arm. As she crossed the grass in her bare feet she was the very image of childish innocence.

'Good morning, Damastor; Uncle Halitherses,' Ctymene said, her voice like sunshine on that cloudy, rain-threatened morning. 'Good morning, Eperitus. Have you killed many men today?'

'No, Ctymene. Have you?'

She laughed and shot him a mischievous look, then linked her arm through his. 'I have a gift for you,' she announced.

He watched as she untangled a single pink bloom from the mass of flowers in her basket. The smell of perfume that hung about her was delicate in comparison with the sharp tang of sweat that clung to Halitherses, Damastor and himself.

'Here,' she said, handing him a flower. It had been plucked and dried in the sun to preserve its beauty. 'We call it chelonion, because its root is shaped like a turtle. See? Wear this to remind you of your new home when you're far away. I've prayed to Aphrodite that it will protect you from harm and bring you safely back to Ithaca.'

Eperitus slipped the stem of the flower through a loop in his leather belt, then bowed silently. Ctymene squeezed his hand before slipping her arm from his and offering flowers to Halitherses and Damastor. They accepted the reminders of their home with cheerful words and kisses. Then she left them and went over to share the remainder amongst the other members of the escort. As Eperitus watched her, Odysseus walked out from the palace gates and joined the guards. The men shared a joke and a few words, then the prince turned to his sister and embraced her. She held him tightly, throwing her arms as far as they would reach about his muscular chest, but neither said a word. When they finally parted there were tears glistening in Ctymene's eyes. She kissed him on the cheek then ran back into the palace.

'I've said my farewells to the king and queen,' Odysseus announced as he came over to the others. 'They won't be here to watch us depart. The men say they are ready, Halitherses.'

'As ready as they'll ever be, my lord. There are oarsmen waiting in the galley below, and we have a good crowd to ensure our departure is known by the whole island.'

'I share your worries, old friend,' Odysseus said, looking at the number of townsfolk who had come to see them off. 'But our anchor ropes are cut and we must see this thing through to the end. I only hope I have a kingdom to return to when it's all over.'

'There'll be a strong militia in place before the news spreads to Eupeithes,' Damastor assured him. 'Everything will be safe and secure.'

'All the same, I pray the gods will watch over the place in our absence,' Odysseus replied. 'And may Mentor and the others have the good sense not to underestimate their opponents.'

At his signal the escort picked up their shields and spears and the slaves hoisted their burdens onto their shoulders. The expedition formed up in two files and set off, the townsfolk parting to let them through.

Odysseus walked beside Eperitus and they looked about themselves at the cheering crowds. The people called out Odysseus's name again and again, honouring their prince as he set out upon whatever new mission his father had assigned to him. Eperitus caught the scent of the chelonion in his tunic and thought how little time he had had to get to know his new home. The Ithacan faces were unfamiliar and their voices strange compared with Alybas. He knew little about them or their island, where the hills were called mountains and the alien sea lay all around. And yet here he was, venturing into the unknown for the sake of a country and people not his own, but which he hoped one day would be.

He had spent only three days on the island, and with Odysseus as his guide had trekked its wooded hillsides and dusty cart-tracks by mule. The prince had shown him many of the caves and bays along the rocky coastline, where the high cliffs were thick with gulls. He named each different hill, copse and spring in both halves of the island, and pointed out the numerous little farms that they passed. Often, when they were hungry, the prince would stop at one of the farms and be welcomed with warmth and good food. He seemed to know everyone by name – including many of the children – and was greeted lovingly wherever he went. And the people had treated Eperitus with kindness and respect – partly because he was Odysseus's companion, but also out of their naturally contented and welcoming natures.

He quickly came to understand Odysseus's love of his home, and appreciated the time he spent showing him the island. But he also realized that the prince was not simply expressing his pride; he was saying goodbye to the place he loved. No one knew what the expedition to Sparta would bring or how long they would be away, so Odysseus was spending the final days before his departure with the place and people he loved above all things.

Eperitus wished he were not leaving Ithaca so soon and that the Fates had been kind enough to give him just a few days more to enjoy its hospitality. But the gods had other uses for him and he supposed that, like Odysseus, he must earn his place in the hearts and minds of its people if he was to establish himself amongst them.

As the group passed the outskirts of the town and left the crowds behind them, all bar a few children, they passed a group of young men standing by a spring. It was here, surrounded by tall black poplar trees, that the townspeople fetched their water. To Eperitus's surprise the men greeted them with mocking jeers. One of them, a handsome man with close-cropped black hair and fine clothes – noticeably missing the whole of his right ear – was more abusive than all of his companions put together. Eperitus left the file with every intention of knocking the man's teeth into the grass at his feet, but Odysseus stopped him with a hand on his shoulder.

'I'm surprised you have the courage to leave your master's side, Polybus,' he said. 'And where's Polytherses? Your sneering face seems incomplete without your brother's alongside it.'

'Keep your charm for the beautiful Helen, oaf-prince,' Polybus replied. 'The sooner you and your clowns are gone the better we'll all feel around here.'

'Which Helen is that, Polybus?'

For the briefest instant the other's composure wavered, but he was quick to gather his wits about him again. 'The whole of Ithaca knows you're off to Sparta, expecting to bring back Tyndareus's daughter as your wife. News spreads quickly on a small island, Odysseus, and the crew of Koronos's ship was full of it. Your dim-witted guards may not know it yet, but it doesn't take an oracle to guess what you're up to.'

Eperitus realized the braggart was one of Eupeithes's twin henchmen, mentioned at the Kerosia. As he had listened to the debate about these would-be usurpers, he had felt his hatred growing with each mention of their names. A man must be loyal to his king, his grandfather had taught him, or social order falls into chaos. Only by accepting authority can a man receive the rewards of order and peace. That is why his grandfather had told him to obey three things unfailingly: his gods, his oaths, and his king. Without these principles the world of men would fall into the abyss.

Eperitus's eyes narrowed with anger. He shrugged off Odysseus's restraining hand and advanced on Polybus. The sneering braggart looked at him with disdain, as if offended that he should dare approach him, but soon retreated as he realized his intentions. An instant later Eperitus swung his fist into Polybus's face and watched with satisfaction as he fell backward into the waters of the spring, blood pumping from his lips and broken nose.

'That's what I think of traitors,' he spat. 'Tell Eupeithes that Laertes will remain king of Ithaca, and if anyone is to replace him it will be Odysseus, the only man who can claim that right.'

Polybus scrambled out of the pool, helped by his friends. He was incandescent with rage and in a deft movement whipped out a dagger from beneath his tunic.

He lunged with the weapon, but Eperitus brought his shield round and knocked him to one side. Quickly stepping back, he pulled the sword from his belt and faced Polybus's six companions, who held daggers of their own. In the same moment he was joined by Odysseus and the rest of the guard, spears and shields at the ready.

Now they were seventeen fully-armed men against Polybus's seven, carrying only daggers. It did not take them long to see the futility of the situation.

'There'll be no bloodshed here, Polybus,' Odysseus said, his voice as calm and commanding as ever. 'Not if I can prevent it. So put your toys away and go about your business.'

They had no choice but to do as they were ordered, but as

they slunk off Polybus could not resist turning and having the final word.

'We'll settle this matter another time, you bronze-haired buffoon, when the odds are more equal. And as for you,' he said, spitting on the ground at Eperitus's feet, 'I pray to all the gods that you and I will meet again. Then I'll teach you to respect your betters before I send you scuttling off to Hades.'

'I've been waiting a long time to see that arrogant swine made a fool of,' Antiphus said, slapping Eperitus on the back with a laugh as they watched the group of youths retreat up the road to the town. 'He docked my bow fingers when I was a boy, after he and his father caught me hunting on their land. I'm indebted to you for the show, Eperitus.'

'We all are,' Halitherses agreed. 'But he'll want his revenge. We haven't seen the last of him yet.'

'I'm more concerned that he knows we're going to Sparta,' Odysseus added with a frown. 'He says he worked it out for himself, but I think someone in the palace has told Eupeithes. A traitor – maybe someone within the Kerosia itself.'

'There's nothing we can do about that now, Odysseus,' said Damastor, appearing at his side. 'The council has decided this is the only way to save Ithaca from rebellion, so we'd better go and pray that the gods protect our homes and families until we return.'

A short time later they passed over the wooded ridge and headed down to the small harbour where the galley was bobbing gently on the waves. Mentor was there to meet them and Odysseus immediately took him to one side. Eperitus did not hear what was said, but assumed that the prince was warning Mentor of the possibility of a traitor. Mentor nodded and set off up the beach, but as he passed Eperitus in the file he stopped.

'I'm left behind to nursemaid the king while you get the privilege of escorting Odysseus to Sparta. Well, at least you won't be hanging around in the palace, because . . .' He drew closer and lowered his voice. 'Because I don't trust you. We don't know you or your family, so if anyone is spying for Eupeithes it's a foreigner like you. And I've told Odysseus as much, so you won't catch him off his guard either.'

'I'm no traitor,' Eperitus spat, but Mentor was already striding down the slope to the bay.

book
TWO

Chapter Nine

IN THE LAND OF THE WOLFMEN

The north wind was full in the galley's sail and drove the vessel irresistibly forward across the waves. It ploughed great furrows into the sea and made the going particularly rough, though it was not enough to hamper the speed with which the gods had blessed them after their late start. Eperitus stood at the prow of the ship, fighting for breath in the teeth of the gale. The Peloponnese flanked him on the left, its mountains silhouetted blue in the afternoon haze, whilst beneath his feet he could hear the waves slapping against the thin planking of the hull.

Sensing a presence, he turned to see Odysseus standing at his shoulder. The prince's arms were behind his back and his gaze was fixed firmly ahead. It was the same look that he wore when at the helm, observing the wave caps for the best currents and watching the distant clouds for warnings of a change in the weather, whilst keeping an eye on the shoreline for safe anchorages along the way. He looked as strong as a bull, his burly frame unfazed by the blustering wind that had been tearing the air from Eperitus's lungs. One could almost believe there was no wind, were it not for his narrowed eyes, the flapping of his red hair and the billowing of his great black cloak.

'You know, Eperitus,' he said, his smooth voice perfectly audible in the wind, 'I wish I wasn't here. Not very heroic, really, am I? Not for a prince of his people.'

'What do you mean?' Eperitus asked.

'I mean that to be great a man must leave his home and family and go out into the wider world, seeking to carve a name for himself in the ranks of his enemies.'

'I suppose it's hard to win fame by staying at home.'

'But that's exactly what I'd rather do,' Odysseus sighed. 'Part of me dreams about slaying monsters, sacking cities, ravishing beautiful maidens and coming home laden with gold. What man doesn't? And yet in my heart I could wish for nothing more than sharing meat and wine with friends in the great hall at home, talking about the local girls, the harvest and fishing. The closest I like coming to adventure is listening to a good story around a blazing fire.'

Eperitus envied Odysseus his contentment in such things, but never having experienced a true sense of happiness in his own home he could not understand it. All he wanted was to see the world and write his name into one of the tales that Odysseus liked to hear beside the hearth.

'So why leave Ithaca?' he said.

'For the same reason that you left Alybas, I assume,' Odysseus replied. 'To prove myself! To achieve something that will allow me to go home to my people and hold my head up high.'

'That isn't why I left Alybas,' Eperitus muttered.

Odysseus seemed not to hear. 'Of course, it's unlikely Helen will choose me above her wealthier and more powerful suitors, and it's probable Tyndareus has already chosen her a husband. Which makes me wonder what the idea is behind this gathering of kings and princes – it's a lot of trouble to go to for nothing. But either way, I may be able to form friendships and alliances that will carry weight back home. That's the real reason my father sent me on this journey. But tell me this, Eperitus: do you think the most beautiful woman in Greece might choose me for a husband?'

Eperitus considered the possibility, matching what he knew of Helen's legendary beauty to the little he had learned about Odysseus. 'You're as likely to be chosen as any other suitor. You're a prince, soon to become a king. You have wealth and power, and you're a great warrior – any sensible woman would be out of her mind to reject you.'

A great shout followed by laughter came from the benches. Some of the escort were playing a game with marked ivory cubes, and their constant chattering and clamour had become a feature of the voyage. The game would shortly be broken up, though, as the sun was already dipping beyond the island of Zacynthos to the west and the helmsman would soon be seeking a convenient landfall.

'The problem is that a woman as desirable as Helen can afford to pick and choose between suitors,' Odysseus said thoughtfully. 'Have you ever been to another palace outside of Alybas?'

'Of course,' Eperitus confirmed. 'Your own.'

Odysseus laughed. 'Well-travelled indeed, I see. And how does the palace at Ithaca compare to the one in your own city?'

'They're about the same. Yours looks older, but has more servants and guards.'

Odysseus nodded sagely. 'Well, my friend, the nobles that we'll meet in Sparta come from much grander places than you or I. They have wealth beyond your most fantastic dreams. My beloved Ithaca is little more than a hovel compared to the cities they rule. Wait until you see Tyndareus's palace – that'll give you an idea of the power and wealth of the men I'm competing against, and why it's likely Helen will choose another before me. In truth, the odds are too heavily stacked against me.'

'You must believe you have a chance, though, or why would you go?' Eperitus insisted.

'In the hope of forming alliances, as I said, and perhaps of bringing something back that will make the journey worthwhile. And also for my father's sake. It's his command, and a father must be obeyed, don't you think?'

Eperitus shifted uncomfortably under Odysseus's searching gaze. 'That depends upon what your father expects you to do.'

'Then can a man have more wisdom than his father?' Odysseus challenged, his voice firm but no less persuasive. 'Can any son rightfully contest his father's authority and expect his own children to obey him?'

'My father tested my loyalties to the extreme,' Eperitus responded sharply, 'and I responded in the way that I believed was right. I disobeyed his will, yes, but I'd do it again. The choice he gave me was absolute, and I chose the only option that a man of honour could take. I proved myself better than he.'

Odysseus looked at him seriously. 'A man doesn't become great by overthrowing his father, Eperitus. It's unnatural and opposes the will of the gods.'

Eperitus stared fiercely at his captain. 'Answer me this, my lord: does Eupeithes have a son?'

'Yes, an infant named Antinous.'

'And when Antinous becomes a man, would you expect him to support his father against the king? If you were Antinous, what would you do?'

Odysseus shook his head and sighed. 'So, at last I understand,' he told Eperitus, patting his shoulder reassuringly. 'Ever since we first met, I've been wondering why you won't name your father. He betrayed your king, didn't he, and you had no choice but to disobey him.'

'It's worse than that,' Eperitus said. His face was ablaze with shame as he recounted the awful events on the night his father had killed King Pandion and seized the throne for himself. It was a story he had not wanted to share: ever since his banishment from Alybas he had wanted his ignominious past to remain unknown. There was something about Odysseus, however, that invited confidence, and Eperitus felt the better for sharing his story.

'So you see, I won't let Eupeithes take your rightful place as king,' he said ardently. 'Not whilst there's breath in my body. I hate a usurper before everything else, and my father put a stain of dishonour on our family that only I can remove. If I help you to defeat Eupeithes, then I feel I'll have done something to restore pride to my family's name.'

They sat silently for a while, watching the gulls riding on the wind. Then the helmsman called out for a change in the sail. He had spotted a bay that would suffice for the evening, and with the westering sun threatening to leave them with only a failing light he chose to make harbour now. There was a flurry of activity as everyone moved to help, and the frenetic action left Eperitus no time to mull over his revelations to Odysseus.

Eperitus was woken before dawn by Odysseus holding his foot up by the big toe.

'I'm sending the galley back to Ithaca,' Odysseus told him. 'We're going overland, so I need you to help unload the galley. Halitherses has gone to buy mules from the village above the bay.'

The news brought dismay to the other members of the expedition, who had expected an easy sea voyage around the Peloponnese. Odysseus explained that he and Halitherses had decided that the remaining crew – all young, able-bodied men – should return home and bolster the militia, but it did not make the news any easier. Now the men would be required to walk for several days across unknown terrain to the palace of Tyndareus. In one sense Eperitus was disappointed not to have more time on the galley, but in another he was also pleased at the likely prospect of adventure on the way.

'Besides which,' Odysseus added as his men sat before him on the beach, 'I've a mind to visit Athena's temple in Messene. We need her support in our quest, and we should pay her our respects. Don't you agree, Eperitus?'

Eperitus remembered their encounter with the goddess at Pythia, and the duty she had charged Odysseus with. Now he realized it had always been the prince's plan to make landfall on the first day and go overland from there. Even the urgency of their mission could not come before the command of a goddess.

The crew's complaining was cut short by the braying of mules. As Halitherses led them along the track that fed in from the fields, it did not take long for Odysseus and his companions to realize that they were sorry beasts indeed. All three had great running sores on their backs and flanks and didn't look strong enough to walk, let alone to carry the bride gifts and supplies, but Halitherses explained they were the best he could find.

After loading the mules and watching their ship head back to Ithaca, the band of warriors began their own journey across the Peloponnese. They were in the southernmost part of a country called Elis, and the going was slow due to the rocky terrain and the poor condition of the animals. They followed the line of the coast south, heading in the general direction of Messene, and cut across the spur of a headland that jutted out into the great expanse of sea. By late afternoon, however, they found themselves stuck on one side of a broad, fast-flowing river that did not appear to be fordable. They trudged further upstream, but found no sign of a possible crossing point.

Frustrated, Odysseus ordered his men to make camp whilst he and Halitherses went looking for a ford or bridge. Before long they returned with news of a ferry not far downstream. There was no sign of a ferryman and the craft was in poor repair, but it could float and would be able to take them a few at a time across the broad river. However, with twilight already upon them it was decided to wait until daylight before making the crossing.

Eperitus found a patch of comfortable ground by the bole of an old tree. Shortly afterwards he was joined by Damastor and Halitherses. For a while they discussed the river and the crossing of it, then turned to their impressions of the country itself. It seemed to be sparsely populated, despite being a pleasant land with plenty of streams and meadows for keeping livestock, as well as good soil for growing crops. It would be a place worth settling, were it not for the strange tales they had all heard about Elis and the larger region called Arcadia, of which it was but the north-western part. Even in faraway Alybas there were stories about the wolfmen of Arcadia, prowling the hills and pastureland at night in search of victims. Under the light of the sun or the moon they could not be told apart from another wolf, except that they hunted alone and were not afraid of anything. But in the twilight of early evening or the dusky period before dawn they regained human form, at which times they would seek out human company to ease the suffering of their loneliness. Yet the host of such a beast would become its victim once the sun or moon was in the sky again.

It was said they were descendants of an ancient king who had practised human sacrifice. When he tried to offer one of his own sons to Zeus, in his anger and disgust the father of the gods had turned the king into a wolf. The curse had been passed to the sons of the king as well, and the only way they could ever return to their original form was to abstain from human flesh altogether. That being impossible for a wolf, they were doomed to wander the earth in a state lost between man and beast.

After they had finished sharing their tales, the three men agreed that the mules should be kept closer to their camp for the night, rather than leaving them tied to a tree far from the safety of the fire. They also discussed the wisdom of setting a guard in this strange, underpopulated country, and to Eperitus's relief Halitherses split the watch between two of his men.

Eventually, they pulled their blankets over themselves and lay down to sleep. There were no clouds or moon in the sky above, but the stars were like the grains of sand on a beach and their pale light made everything about the men clear. The cold air carried every sound clearly: the rush of the river over the rocks that were scattered along its banks, the snorting and stamping of their mules, even the cry of owls hunting in the darkness. Eperitus fell asleep listening to the noises of the night and thinking about the wolfmen of Arcadia. He dreamed he was in the great hall in Alybas, where a giant wolf was crouched over the dead body of King Pandion. The king's blood dripped from its jaws, and as it looked at Eperitus it seemed to grin.

They stood in a circle about the raft. Eperitus could not imagine how it was supposed to carry them across the foaming waters that separated them from the next stage of their journey. The wood was rotten, broken in places and bound together by leather ropes that were cracked and splitting. Although the rectangular deck would fit six men and a mule, he doubted whether it would take their combined weight. Another problem was the strong current. The raft must usually have been pulled from one side of the river to the other along a rope, and though the stumps were still there the rope itself had gone. Because of this it would take two or three men using poles to get the raft across safely.

Despite these problems, Odysseus wasted no time in sending Antiphus out to trap a wild animal for sacrifice, whilst ordering others of the party to repair the ropes that held the raft together. The islanders were skilled seamen and, using a combination of axes and some rusty tools from the deserted ferryman's shack, were soon busy replacing the worst of the wood. Before joining them in their work, Odysseus sent Eperitus on a chore of his own, to find and cut lengths of wood to act as staves in punting the raft across the river.

By the time he returned with four long poles the work on the raft was finished. Replacement wood had been taken from the contents and walls of the shack to repair the worst of the damage, whilst the ropes that lashed it together were the original cords reinforced with strips of cloth, leather or the intertwined branches and stems of plants.

Last of all, Antiphus arrived carrying a squealing goat over his shoulder. He handed the struggling animal to Odysseus, who carried it under his arm to a large rock by the river. Close by, a fire had been lit using the oddments of wood that had been discarded in repairing the raft. Odysseus took a dagger from his belt, whisked off a tuft of hair from the goat's head and threw it into the flames. Then, offering prayers for safe passage to the god of the river, he picked up a stone and gave the animal a swift blow to the forehead, killing it at once. Quickly laying it on the flat-topped rock, he slit the animal's throat and let the blood gush out onto the earth. A couple of the men stepped forward to help him dismember the carcass with easy and practised movements. The meat from the thighs – favourite of the gods – was cut out and covered in a layer of glistening fat before being thrown on the fire as an offering. The remainder of the beast was dissected with speedy efficiency and was soon being roasted on spits over the flames.

Odysseus left his men to finish the bloody work and went to wash his hands in the cool, clear water of the river. His men made quick work of the sacrificial meat, downing the scraps with a few pieces of bread and the water from the skins they carried. By that time it was already late morning, so without further delay they shoved the raft into the fast-flowing river and Odysseus led the first party across. Keeping the mule still proved the most difficult task, unused as it was to floating on water, but after the prince threw his cloak over its head and assigned two of the guards to hold the animal steady they were able to cross without mishap.

The two men who had not been on the poles began the return journey as Odysseus and the others stood ready with their shields and spears, remaining vigilant whilst their force was divided and at its most vulnerable. Soon they were joined by four more of their comrades, who arrived with the second mule, and not long after that the third crossing brought another four, the provisions for the journey and the gifts for Tyndareus and Helen.

Eperitus had been left with Halitherses and a few others to take the final load across, and as the raft struggled back towards them the landsman from Alybas suddenly felt nervous at the prospect of crossing the torrent. Although he had learned to swim in the mountain pools and streams of his own country, he was not confident in water and muttered a hurried prayer to the god of the river.

The boat thumped against the bank and the two men leapt off and pulled it safely up on to the pebble-strewn ground. As Eperitus considered how to get the last of the mules aboard – a docile creature that he hoped would give little trouble – he noticed that the condition of the raft was deteriorating rapidly. Already some of the hastily repaired lashings had frayed to the point of snapping and a hole had been punctured in the centre of the raft, where a mule had put its hoof through the old wood. But there was nothing for it now but to load up and set off.

He helped push the raft into the water again, then led the mule up onto its ramshackle planks. Wrapping his cloak around the head of the beast, he began talking softly into one of its hairy, oversized ears. Meanwhile Damastor stood against the animal's flank and signalled for Eperitus to take up position opposite him. Together they took a firm hold of the beast as Halitherses and the last two men of the escort splashed aboard and began to push them out into the rapidly flowing waters. The force of the river hit them straight away, sweeping the raft into an eddy that momentarily spun the flimsy vessel out of control. The men on the poles strove with all their might, their muscles tensing and straining as they fought to steady the fragile platform. For an anxious moment they looked to be lost, but finally managed to regain control of the craft and straighten it back on a course to the opposite shore.

The roar of the water raged in their ears so that they could hardly hear the shouts of encouragement from the far bank. The raft began to ride the strong current, almost bouncing along the surface as the men on the poles fought against the pull of the river. Eperitus watched Halitherses's ageing face, contorted with the exertion of battling against the current, and debated whether to leave hold of the placid mule and help with the spare pole. Then everything went suddenly and terribly wrong.

With the mule still quiet beneath its cloak and the shore looking temptingly close, Damastor released the animal and shook the stiffness out of his aching limbs. But before he could take hold again, a sudden blast of wind tore the cloak from its eyes. Seeing the rushing water on either side it panicked and kicked out with its strong hind legs. There was a splash and a shout behind Eperitus; in the same instant one of the planks cracked and gave way beneath the stamping hoofs of the mule, tipping it headlong into the water and beyond any help the men could give it.

'Halitherses is in the river!' shouted Damastor.

The captain was already being dragged away by the strong current. Pausing only to slip his grandfather's shield from his shoulder and the sword from his belt, Eperitus dived into the water after him.

Exhausted as he was by the day's work and the struggle against the river, the freezing cold shocked him back into total wakefulness. The roaring waters threatened to pull him under, but he fought to keep his head above the surface. As he was swept rapidly away from the raft he turned to see the remaining men straining at the poles, still fighting to haul the damaged craft to the opposite bank.

Flailing against the current, he caught sight of Halitherses ahead of him. The old man appeared to be drifting, rather than struggling against the current, and Eperitus realized he must have been caught by the kick of the mule and was unconscious.

With a renewed sense of urgency, he summoned all of his strength and began to swim with the boisterous flow of the river. At first it was hard to control his direction, but by trying to pull ahead of the current he found he was able to angle himself towards the old warrior, who was drifting out into the middle of the river. Deafened by the rushing of the water and buffeted by its constant motion, he could barely stay afloat, let alone keep sight of Halitherses. Then, over the tumult of foam, he caught sight of dark shapes in the water ahead.

Rocks. They rose like broken teeth from the river, each one surrounded by a head of foaming water. Eperitus tried shouting to his friend over the roar, but knew it was useless. He hauled himself forward with all his might, desperate to gain precious moments over the current that was sweeping Halitherses to certain death. All the time he willed his captain to return to his senses, if only briefly, and realize the peril he was in.

Fortune carried Halitherses unscathed between the first two rocks. A moment later Eperitus plunged between them himself. Three more rocks rose up ahead of them, evenly spaced like the prongs of a fishing spear. Then Halitherses woke from his stupor and turned to see the murderous doom he was being swept towards.

With whatever wits and energy were left to him, Halitherses fought against the current and won Eperitus the fragment of time he needed to catch hold of him. He pulled him just wide of the boulders and kicked for the bank. His lungs on fire and his body numbed with cold, he angled towards a smooth rock that jutted out into the river like a jetty, offering them their only hope of shelter before the current carried them to their deaths. Though stunned and weak, the old captain had enough sense left to realize where Eperitus was aiming at and kicked out with him.

As they swept by it, Eperitus reached out and caught hold of the rock. It tore the skin from his palms, but he got a firm grip and pulled on it against the fierce current. Half senseless with exhaustion, he hauled them both to relative safety behind the shelf of smooth stone. At that same moment something reached down and touched his shoulder.

'Take my hand,' a voice shouted. 'Quickly.'

Looking up, he saw Odysseus silhouetted against the bright sky. Eperitus shook his head and indicated Halitherses. 'Take him first. I can hold on a while longer, but he's weak.'

With what little strength he had left, Eperitus lifted the old man out of the swirling water and within reach of Odysseus, who caught him under the shoulders and hauled him up as if he was a baby. Moments later Eperitus felt a hand close around his wrist and Odysseus's immense strength pulling him free of the river. He slumped onto the broad, flat top of the rock and vomited the liquid he had swallowed.

'No, I didn't use it,' Odysseus answered when Eperitus asked him about the clay owl Athena had given him. He glanced about himself to ensure that nobody could hear. 'It's safe in my pouch. I'll only call on her if Ithaca itself is threatened.'

They were drying themselves around a fire by the bank. Miraculously, Halitherses had only been stunned by the kick of the mule, and now sat opposite them eating barley broth from a wooden bowl, seemingly unaffected by his trials. The mule had been dashed to death in the rapids. Despite the fact that its load would now have to be shared between them, the men were all happy to be across the river alive and together.

It was early afternoon already, but they could not afford to waste time recuperating from their ordeals. The urgency of their mission forced them to strike their makeshift camp and march south again towards Messene. The land was becoming hillier as the eastern mountains rose beside them and they found very little sign of human life in the curiously deserted land. By last light they had not seen a single person and decided to find shelter in a small grove of trees on a conical foothill, where they made a fire. As the evening drew in and the men got weary of talk, Halitherses thanked Eperitus for saving his life and promised to return the gift.

'Until I have that chance, though,' he continued firmly with a smile, 'you are still under my orders and will be accorded no special favours. Therefore I have to remind you it's your turn to take first watch tonight.'

'Keep an eye out for werewolves,' Odysseus added unhelpfully, curling up under his cloak and closing his eyes.

Eperitus did not welcome his joke as he picked up his shield and spear and trudged out alone to the edge of the ring of trees. Sitting down at the top of the rock-strewn slope, he looked out at the land before him. To the south rose the mountains that lay between them and Messene. Not far to the west was the coast, and beyond it the sea. The sun had long since sunk behind the horizon, leaving the land between mountains and ocean in a stagnant twilight. Although they had met nobody on their journey to this place, Eperitus now saw that here and there in the quiescent landscape lights were beginning to show. There were not many of them and he was unable to see whether they marked farms, homesteads or whole villages, but at least he knew they were not alone in that strange country.

Suddenly a howl broke the stillness of the evening. Startled, he jumped up and looked about himself. Another call came in answer and he realized they were distant, far away from where he stood guard. Nevertheless, he longed for company and hoped that one of the others might join him.

They did not, and he was left alone in the deepening darkness. The wolves, if that was what they truly were, did not call out again and the unsettled landscape began to reclaim its serenity. Above him the stars shone bright and sharp, as if newly created, and an owl hooted as it hunted in the dales below the hill. Then a sudden noise broke the stillness.

Eperitus seized his spear and stood up, squinting into the darkness. There before him stood a man. Eperitus could make out nothing of him in the darkness, only that he was groaning as if in pain. Suddenly he stumbled forward. Eperitus raised his spear to defend himself, but at the last moment recognized the handsome features of the man's face. Throwing the weapon aside, Eperitus reached out and caught him.

It was Mentor.

Chapter Ten

THE FALL OF ITHACA

The first of the suitors had arrived.

Helen lay on a couch that had been draped in the finest purple cloth. A slave girl was busy trimming and polishing her toenails, ready to be painted. Beside her waited a small jar of plant and berry juices, mixed by the slave earlier that morning to make a thick red pigment.

Her maid raised one foot and started carefully applying the pigment. 'What do you think of Menelaus, my lady?'

Helen smiled, knowing her answer would be spread rapidly through the servant's quarters, if not the entire palace. 'Tell me what you think, Neaera.'

The slave girl blushed. 'Well, he's handsome and strong with beautiful auburn hair . . .'

'Which is thinning on top,' Helen added.

'I don't have your height, my lady, so I can't tell. But he's a fine-looking man nonetheless, very wealthy, and he treats everyone as if they were royalty. Even slaves.'

Helen withdrew her foot and sat up, sighing with frustration. 'Yes, he's all of those things. Although I've only met him once, he also seems a kind-hearted, thoughtful man with good manners and a love of the simple life. And if Agamemnon is to be believed, I won't find a man amongst his peers who has such fairness of mind, modesty of character, depth of intelligence or courage of spirit.'

'Oh, my lady,' exclaimed the slave with excitement. 'Then you *will* marry him?'

Helen shook her head. 'No, I won't. Menelaus doesn't inspire the least morsel of desire in me.'

The slave girl looked deflated. 'Then who will you marry, my lady? Diomedes is coming. And Ajax, they say.'

'That oaf!'

'I've even heard that Achilles will come,' Neaera persisted. 'Surely you can't turn down someone as handsome as Achilles?'

'How do you know how handsome Achilles is?' Helen scoffed. 'Besides, don't you know that Achilles is little more than a boy? How can I fall for a boy, whatever his pedigree?'

'Then who, my lady?' Neaera implored. With all the bets that were being placed in the palace, the slave who managed to obtain the secret of Helen's true desire could win enough money to buy their own freedom.

'Do you really think I'll be allowed to choose?' Helen asked bitterly. 'Tyndareus is only interested in Agamemnon's favour, and Agamemnon is only interested in a marriage of power. He knows that whoever wins me inherits my father's throne. That's why they will choose Menelaus, because Agamemnon's brother will eventually become King of Sparta and the Atreides will be the most powerful dynasty in Greece.'

The slave girl looked at the princess for a moment. The politics of power meant nothing to her, but she recognized the sadness beneath her mistress's anger. 'Then who do you like most?'

'None of them, Neaera,' Helen said, throwing herself back onto the couch. 'Does that win your wager with your friends for you? There isn't one of those supposed noblemen who inspires *any* passion within my heart. What would I want with an overdressed, obnoxious, arrogant buffoon, however pretty he is or how nice he smells? I don't care how many men they've killed or how many cities they've plundered: I want a man who makes me feel my heart beat in my throat when he enters the room. I couldn't care less if he's ugly, or even if he's poor, within reason, as long as he takes me away from all this . . .' she swept a white arm through the air, 'paraphernalia. Find me a real man who doesn't give a damn for power or the glory of the Greeks, and who can take me from this palace, then I'll tell you who I really favour.'

Neaera looked down, ashamed. Despite her mistress's wilful and often petulant nature, she loved her with all her heart and was sorry to have upset her. It was a slave's privilege to be burdened with a mistress's deepest worries, so Neaera knew how much Helen despised the idea of becoming the prize of a wealthy prince. For all her beauty and wealth there was still one thing beyond Helen's grasp: freedom. It was a desire the slave girl understood fully.

'Do you never wear any clothes when you're in your room, sister?'

A young woman stood in the doorway eyeing Helen's nakedness with undisguised amusement. She was tall and lean with pale skin and long, red hair, which swept around her protruding ears to fall down to the middle of her back. She had an attractive face with thin lips and staring eyes, but was dressed all in black, as if in mourning.

Helen smiled knowingly. 'If my body repels you, Clytaemnestra, you shouldn't come here unannounced.'

The woman entered anyway and, indicating to Neaera that she should leave, sat down next to her sister. They had not seen each other for over a year, but Clytaemnestra had decided to come to Sparta with Agamemnon and Menelaus to visit her family.

'I've been listening from the doorway, Helen. You should be more careful of who's eavesdropping when you speak disparagingly about my husband.'

'I don't care who hears me,' Helen replied, sitting up and taking her sister's hand. 'I'm speaking the truth, after all. You know Agamemnon thinks of nothing else but power and ruling the whole of Greece.'

'He will rule Greece,' Clytaemnestra stated simply. She stroked her sister's hands affectionately and sighed. 'He always gets what he wants, as I've found to my loss. But he also wants peace. He's sick of the constant wars – I think they all are – and the only way to achieve that is to unify Greece.'

Helen stood and picked up a piece of clothing from the floor, draping it about her flawless body. The white cloth was so fine that it hid nothing of her nakedness.

'How convenient that Greece should be unified under Agamemnon, though,' she insisted.

'I'm sure he would gladly serve under somebody who he thought was more capable of rule than himself,' Clytaemnestra added calmly, used to her sister's outbursts. 'But like all of his kind, Agamemnon just feels there *is* nobody more capable.'

'You sound like you agree with him!' Helen said angrily. She strode over to the window that overlooked the courtyard, where a group of guards stared up at her. Their eyes lingered for a brief but longing moment, then as one they switched their gazes to the ground, unable even to meet each other's eyes with the vain desires that lay behind them. She turned to look at Clytaemnestra, shaking her head bitterly. 'How can you even sympathize with what he thinks and what he wants? It was want of you that made him murder your first husband and butcher your baby as you held it against your breast! They were the only living things you've ever really loved. How can you stand that monster?'

Clytaemnestra glared at her younger sister. 'What choice do I have? Agamemnon is the most powerful man in Greece, and I'm just a woman. And what is a woman without a man, Helen? We can't bear arms or declare ourselves kings. We've both seen what happens to wives who lose their husbands and have no sons or married daughters. If they're young enough they can sell their bodies; otherwise they're abandoned and forced out of the community to scratch a living in the hills, or to die. A slave is better off than a freeborn woman: at least she has food and a roof over her head.'

'It wouldn't matter to me,' Helen insisted. 'I would never forgive. Never! And I'm surprised at you, Nestra. You were always the strongest of us all, even the boys. You should have been born male.'

Clytaemnestra laughed and allowed herself to relax. She beckoned her sister over and embraced her tightly, turning her face away to hide her tears. 'I may endure him, Helen, but I've never forgiven him. Agamemnon still thinks I wear black in mourning for my first husband, but he has faded now in my memory, along with all the good things. I wear black because it angers him, and reminds him I'm not his in my heart. Every breath I take fuels my hate for him. My only joy is in knowing that, as his wife, I can deprive him of the love he should otherwise have received from another. He took my love, so I will deny him his. It's the same when he comes to me at night. I don't give myself to him, Helen, only my body. Do you understand?'

'Not really,' Helen answered, kissing the tears from her sister's cheeks. 'I understand the hate, but I don't comprehend how you can give your body and not yourself.'

Clytaemnestra held Helen at arm's length and looked straight into her eyes. 'When Theseus took you, did you give yourself freely or did you divorce your spirit from the physical act? Either way, you'll understand what I mean.'

'Then I can't understand,' Helen answered, blushing and avoiding her sister's eyes. 'I'm not yet a woman in that sense.'

Clytaemnestra looked at her in disbelief. 'And all this time I thought we shared the same scars. Oh, dear sister, I pray you will get the husband you deserve, and not be struck by the curse that has destroyed me.'

She wept again. Helen held her close and swore to herself she would never let any man hurt her in such a way.

❦

Eperitus watched Mentor with concern as he ate a bowl of warm porridge and drank fresh water, trying to regain some of his strength before recounting his ordeal. The others were desperate to hear his news, concerned as they were for their families and homes, but Odysseus insisted that the exhausted man's wounds were dressed and he was fed before being forced to relive the events on Ithaca. Despite his calming voice and forced smiles, though, Odysseus was unable to disguise the anxiety that stiffened his features and set his mouth in a tight line.

Eventually Mentor laid the wooden bowl aside and looked around at his comrades, who sat in a crescent about him and waited silently for him to speak.

'Ithaca is lost,' he began, and as he spoke tears filled his eyes. 'Laertes has been taken captive and Eupeithes has declared himself king.'

Mentor looked up and met Odysseus's hard eyes. 'Go on,' the prince said. 'Tell us everything you know and don't spare us the worst of it. Leave nothing unsaid.'

§

It had rained in Ithaca after Odysseus and his men left her shores. In the afternoon the clouds came and hovered low over the island, their great bellies threatening to crush it into the sea from which it had sprung. They poured down endless torrents of water, blotting out the moon and stars and leaving the town in a stifling darkness.

Mentor had ordered the usual guard of one to be tripled. One of the sentries peered out through a viewing slot in the thick wooden gates, but all he could see was an impenetrable curtain of rain obscuring everything beyond a stone's throw from the walls.

As he watched a figure came into view, struggling against the lashing rain and the howling wind. 'Let me in, man,' he shouted. 'I have urgent news.'

Recognizing Koronos, the guard hurriedly unbolted the gates and pulled them open. The merchant rushed inside the shelter of the walls and immediately swung the gates shut behind him.

'Make sure they're bolted. I was followed here,' he said, removing his hat and shaking the water from the brim. 'A force of

Taphians has arrived on Ithaca and joined Eupeithes. They're marching on the palace as we speak.'

Koronos possessed a natural air of authority and the guardsmen were quick to obey as he ordered one of them to wake the king and another to fetch Mentor. The remaining warrior looked out into the rain-filled darkness again.

'Sir! I can see somebody. No! No, there are a few of them out there.'

'Yes, I know,' Koronos answered, pulling his rain-black cloak to one side and feeling along his belt. 'Tall men with long hair and spears as high as these gates. They're Taphians, and there are around four score of them.'

The dagger in his hand shone blue in the darkness as he walked towards the stooping guard. The man turned his head in time to see the blade flash before him. A moment later he fell dead at the merchant's feet, the blood swilling out from the gash in his throat.

Koronos dragged the body away from the gates and slipped the bolts aside. The doors were at once thrust inward by Polytherses, who walked in with confidence and looked quickly about himself. 'Well done, Koronos. We shall not forget your loyalty.'

A seemingly endless stream of heavily armed men poured through the gates after him. Koronos, who had sold his king in exchange for a promise of money and power, stood aside to let the mercenaries pass.

At that moment one of the guards returned with Mentor at his side. They halted just beyond the threshold of the great hall, hardly able to believe that the gates had fallen and their enemies were already filing into the courtyard. Then they heard a shout and saw Polytherses leading a group of Taphians towards them at a run. Several more of the enemy were pulling bows from their shoulders and fitting arrows.

Shocked into action, Mentor and the guard ducked back inside the palace, slamming the doors shut behind them. Arrows thumped into the great wooden panels as they barred the door against the invaders.

For a short while the two men struggled to catch their breath as they stood in the small anteroom to the great hall. But there was no time to spare: there were other ways of getting into the palace from the courtyard now that the outer walls had been penetrated, and unless they acted at once the building would be overrun.

'Go to where the militia are billeted and wake them,' Mentor ordered. 'Quickly!'

The guard ran across the hall and disappeared through a side-entrance. Moments later, Mentor sprinted across to the far wall of the great hall where a hunting horn had hung for as long as he could remember. Pressing it to his lips, he blew hard and a clear and piercing note thundered out into the still air of the hall, blasting beyond the walls and high ceiling to echo about the whole palace.

He blew again, then tugged the sword from his belt and fled through the side entrance into a corridor that skirted the great hall. He heard voices approaching from around the next corner, whilst behind him something heavy crashed against the palace doors, coughing splinters into the great hall. After two more blows the doors burst inwards and the flames of the hearth flickered with the fresh night air. Figures entered and gathered in the shadows, three or four of them, their foreign voices filled with threat. Taphians.

Mentor turned and ran. Arrows bounced off the walls about him as he cleared the corner, only to find himself faced by a hedge of spears. He stopped short and looked into the confused faces of half a dozen Ithacan guardsmen. They had thrown their armour on in a hurry, but they were armed and ready to fight.

'Taphians,' he warned, pointing back down the corridor. 'They're inside the palace.'

As he spoke, three of the mercenaries came rushing round the corner and almost impaled themselves on the wall of spears. The guardsmen reacted quickly, spitting the invaders upon their sharpened spear points. All three fell in a groaning mass, their stomachs gushing dark blood onto hands that tried desperately to stem the flow. The victors wasted no time in dispatching their souls to the Underworld.

'They'll be coming in through every door and window by now,' Mentor told the bloodied guards. 'Our only chance is to get to the upper level and defend Laertes. The stairs are narrow and we'll be able to hold them until the townsfolk come to our aid.'

'The king's gone,' one of the men announced. 'He took the other guards and went to alert the militia; he ordered us to stay here and defend the way to the upper levels.'

Suddenly the whole palace erupted with noise. A loud shout from the great hall announced the arrival of more Taphians. From the corridors surrounding them they heard more shouts and the ringing of weapons, whilst on the upper levels there was screaming from the women's quarters. And now the first party of Taphians from the great hall turned the corner and faced them, their swords at the ready.

Mentor struck quickly, swinging his sword to slice open the neck of their leader. A mist of blood sprayed over the knot of soldiers behind him, who fell back as the body drove a wedge into their tightly packed ranks. A moment later the Ithacan guardsmen rushed into the gap, sinking their spear points into two more of the tall warriors.

The remainder turned and tried to push the weight of men behind them back into the great hall. Mentor picked up a spear and thrust it into the back of one man, then trod his body down into the dirt of the corridor floor as he hacked down another. His companions managed to gouge the life out of a further three before the mercenaries escaped back into the open space of the great hall.

Their victory had filled them with confidence and a fierce lust for more slaughter, but Mentor knew the Taphians would quickly return in more strength. Realizing that their best hope was to defend the upper levels, he ordered them back. Upon reaching the stairs they paused before a dead female slave who lay across the broad steps like a toppled statue, her arms hooked above her head and her eyes shut as if sleeping. Only the dark stain of blood still spreading through her clean white dress indicated there had been any violence. The guardsmen recoiled briefly at the sight of her, but Mentor waved them up the steps.

'Protect the queen,' he ordered, knowing that at least one of Eupeithes's men had already found his way to the female quarters. 'I'll try to find Laertes. May the gods protect you!'

The men sprang up the steps while Mentor set off down the corridor, past the storeroom and the slaves' quarters to the door that opened onto the courtyard. The dull clash of arms was audible through its thick panels.

Nervously, and hastily in case of pursuit, he opened the door and stepped out into the courtyard. The clouds had now dispersed to reveal sable patches of night sky and a curved splinter of moon. Spread across the courtyard, individually and sometimes bunched into small knots, were the dark shapes of numerous corpses, the debris of a battle that was now concentrated on the left-hand side of the broad enclosure.

There were around thirty men still standing, but the majority were Taphians, led by Polytherses. At their rear, running about on his spindly legs and shouting encouragement to his men, was Eupeithes. He was a fat, arrogant-looking man in his late middle age, with white hair and pale, mole-strewn skin that looked translucent in the weak moonlight. His clothing and armour were luxurious, reflecting the expensive taste for which he was well known, but remained unsoiled by battle. Although his home was filled with images of heroes and wars, his own bravery was nothing more than imagined and he had no nerve for the filth, the exertion, or the risk of battle.

As Mentor watched from the shadow of the palace walls, the two sides parted and he saw Laertes standing in the midst of five remaining Ithacan guardsmen. The old king raised his spear and invited Eupeithes to decide the fate of Ithaca by single combat. A number of the warlike Taphians murmured their approval and looked at their leader.

The merchant faced the challenge with a smile. 'Laertes, my friend, don't be angry. I haven't forgotten the time you saved my life from the mob, or that you were once king of these islands, so I have no wish to see you harmed unnecessarily. And why should you and I fight each other for the throne? These Taphians have battled bravely to win liberty for their Ithacan allies – to save them from *your* folly, Laertes – and there can be no dispute who is ruler here now.'

Laertes stared at the merchant with disdain. 'You'll never be ruler, Eupeithes. Betrayal begets betrayal and your actions will only earn you treachery in return. Kneel before your rightful king now, and pray to the gods he'll have mercy on you.'

Eupeithes stepped forward and waved his hand dismissively. 'A king is but a representative, the bearer of a title and a position, but he is nevertheless a man who will ultimately die. A nation, however, is something which surpasses the individual. It outlives us all and must be honoured above any one man. I act for our nation and that's why I must replace you, Laertes. You have failed your people with idle hands and a self-regarding mind.'

'You see things with the eyes of a merchant, Eupeithes,' Laertes replied. 'You don't see there are other things in this world beyond how much a man does or does not possess. You were born into a wealthy family who trained you to think about the acquisition of riches, to know what to buy and where to sell, and you have spent your life as a trader in goods. That makes you an excellent man to trust when it comes to money and making a profit.

'I, on the other hand, was born into a ruling family. I was trained to think about the welfare of my people, to provide for them and protect them. From boyhood I was taught to fight and to lead troops; I was told how to take from the people in times of plenty, so that I could give to them in times of hardship; I was shown how to watch every part of my kingdom, from the harvest, to the work of the craftsmen, to the trading of the merchants and the scheming of the nobles, so that there was balance and harmony.

And that's how I've spent my life, be it for better or worse. But whatever truth there is in your accusations, I have kept this nation together. It's only through *you* that Ithacans have spilled each other's blood on the soil of their homeland. Only *you*, Eupeithes, have divided these islands and destroyed the one thing that has kept them together and at peace for so long. In your very first act you have invited our oldest enemies onto our shores, killed your compatriots and put the future of these islands into question. The biggest mistake *I* made was in allowing you to spread your lies amongst the people.'

As both groups listened to the king, his voice filled with authority despite his tiredness and wounds, Mentor heard the sound of others coming down the corridor behind him. Looking about himself, he snatched a long Taphian spear and a shield from one of the many bodies in the courtyard and retreated back into the shadows, pressing his body as close to the wall as possible. Just as he did so, Koronos walked out into the courtyard, followed by Polytherses and the remainder of the Taphians, who had broken in through the great hall.

Laertes saw the approaching reinforcements and knew that the battle was lost. Realizing their desperate situation and not wanting to waste more lives, he threw down his weapons in surrender and ordered his men to do the same.

Eupeithes had won a stunningly quick and complete victory. By clever deceit and ruthless determination he had overthrown the king and taken power. And as Mentor slipped away unnoticed through the palace gates, he knew that only the return of Odysseus could save Ithaca now.

Chapter Eleven

THE ROAD TO MESSENE

Mentor raised his head and looked at Odysseus. 'There's something else,' he said. Despite his hardships, he sat tall and as straight as a spear. 'The fishermen who helped me escape told me a galley had already left for the mainland. A force of Taphians was aboard, led by Polybus. Eupeithes knows that until you're dead there will always be hope and resistance amongst the Ithacans. He also knows from the crew of your ship where you landed, so he intends to hunt you down while you're still within his reach.'

After breakfast, they gathered in the shade of the trees where Odysseus had called them to council. Other than Eperitus, every member of the expedition had family and friends back in Ithaca. However, it was so incredible that their homeland could now be under the rule of Eupeithes that for a while nobody knew what to say.

It was Damastor who broke the silence. He had a wife and infant son at home and did not want to leave them to the mercy of Taphian pirates. There was no choice, he argued, but to go to the nearest coastal town and take a ship back to Ithaca. They knew the countryside better than the Taphians and could observe their numbers and defences from the hills surrounding the town. If they sailed by night the invaders would not even be aware of their return, and then they could gather an army of the people and wrest the island back from Eupeithes.

There were murmurs of agreement, but little enthusiasm. Laertes's defeat had lowered their spirits and put doubt into their minds. Eperitus could see from the lifeless expressions that they questioned their chances of defeating Eupeithes's much stronger force. Even Halitherses looked sullen and dismayed. Only Odysseus seemed unbowed by the news. Instead, his eyes were fixed on the distant shoreline as he pondered what to do.

After a few moments he stood and looked at his men, their dirty, tired faces raised in expectation. If they hastened back to Ithaca now, he explained, they might catch Eupeithes unprepared and the islanders angry enough to fight. But it was more likely their small force would be massacred, gifting Ithaca to their enemies for ever. The alternative was to continue to Sparta, where they might gain powerful allies and come back with a force that could optimistically challenge Eupeithes. And yet that would also give the usurper time to establish himself and strengthen his position.

'Whatever we may think,' said Halitherses, 'the decision has to be yours, my lord. We all have homes and families on Ithaca, but you are the heir to the throne. You know what's best, and we'll commit ourselves to your judgement.'

'Then I'm going to pray on the matter,' Odysseus announced. 'If you're wise you'll do the same. I'll decide when I return.'

He turned to go to the other side of the hilltop, and as he did so gave Eperitus a long look and nodded his head for him to follow. The young warrior waited a short while then went to find him.

Odysseus sat on his haunches, his elbows balanced on his knees and his hands wilting at the ends of his outstretched arms. He was looking out towards the sea. Though winter had begun the sky had few clouds and the sun was bright as it climbed towards its apex, enabling a keen-eyed observer to see for great distances. The prince did not look at Eperitus as he joined him.

'You wanted me, my lord?'

'No formalities here, Eperitus. Sit down.'

Rocks were scattered everywhere, none of them flat or smooth enough to sit on, so he squatted next to Odysseus and faced the sea. The landscape was typical of southern Greece – hilly, boulder-strewn, punctuated with scrubby plants and olive groves – but it felt an empty and lonely place.

'What will you do?' he asked.

'That isn't my decision,' Odysseus replied, opening his hand to reveal the small clay owl that Athena had given him. 'She told me to go to her temple at Messene.'

Eperitus looked at the object resting in the palm of his friend's hand and recalled the goddess's instructions, as well as her promise to help Odysseus at the time he needed her most.

'That's why I wanted you to follow me, Eperitus,' Odysseus continued, looking at him with his intelligent green eyes. 'You were there. You saw her and heard what she said. I can't share that with Mentor or Halitherses, so I need you to help me decide.'

'We won't be able to defeat Eupeithes without using the owl to call on Athena's help,' Eperitus began. 'But she won't come unless you honour her command to go to Messene first.'

'Even with the help of a goddess it'll be a difficult task,' Odysseus said. 'We're too few in number. But you're right either way: we must at least rid her temple of the serpent, as she has commanded. We can decide between Ithaca and Sparta then. And yet . . . and yet I fear for my parents. My every thought burns with anxiety for them! Ithaca will still be there if we return tomorrow or in ten years, but I can't delay if by doing so I risk the lives of my father and mother.'

'From everything I've heard it seems that Eupeithes is a coward,' Eperitus said. 'Surely he wouldn't dare murder Laertes?'

'No, he wouldn't. But he has Polybus at one ear and Poly-therses at the other, and the Taphians may yet decide to do away with them all and take Ithaca for themselves. They wouldn't spare its king and queen.'

'I can't make that decision for you, Odysseus,' Eperitus replied.

'But if you want the opinion of an outsider, then go to Messene first. That's the sum of my wisdom on the matter. And now I should go back, before Mentor suspects me of being up to mischief.'

As he rejoined the camp, he saw Mentor sitting on a rock and staring at him. His arms and legs were tied with fresh bandages – replaced that morning – and the few hours sleep he had gained during the night had eased his look of exhaustion. Eperitus was about to look away and find a friendlier face, when Mentor rose to his feet and walked towards him. The man's accusations of treachery were still fresh in Eperitus's mind, and the ordeals Mentor had been through did not lessen his anger towards him.

'What is it?' he said, sharply.

Mentor stared at him for a moment, then offered his hand. 'I owe you an apology, Eperitus. I judged you too harshly when we first met, and I haven't made things easy for you since. But the events at the palace have changed me, and I just want to say I was wrong to speak as I did.'

Eperitus held Mentor's gaze for a moment longer, then forced a smile to his lips and took his hand. 'I'm glad we can be friends, Mentor.'

Odysseus returned shortly after and wasted no time in informing the men of his decision. They would head for Sparta, travelling via Messene to buy new supplies. Even those who were eager to return home and fight it out did not question his decision, and Eperitus sensed the prince's authority grow then. Before, he felt that the men followed Odysseus because he was the son of Laertes; now it was because they were learning to trust him. The only voice of dissent belonged to Damastor, who still insisted they should return to Ithaca. But his protests were short-lived in the face of Odysseus's silence and he resigned himself to the long journey ahead of them. And so they marched late into the evening, following the coastal road and hoping to put some distance between themselves and any pursuit.

They made camp away from the road on an outcrop of the eastern mountains. It was similar to their resting place of the previous night, with steep slopes facing the sea and a crown of olive trees upon its summit. They made as large a fire as they dared, which hardly merited the title, and Antiphus sang them an ancient tale from Ithacan legend. It was not a story Eperitus had ever heard in Alybas, as it told of sea gods tormenting shipbound mortals and keeping them from their homes, but it was familiar to Odysseus's men. They nodded in sad recognition of each element or in anticipation of the next, and the subject of the cursed wanderer struck their mood. But it was also a short song, the sort that can be easily learned and which men will sing to their comrades when they have no bard, and so it was soon the turn of others to sing. They all knew the tales that were shared because they had heard them so many times before and the words had been embroidered into the fabric of their minds. Even Mentor, who was still tired and sore from his wounds, gave them a song in his deep and musical voice.

Then it was the turn of Odysseus. The songs that had come before had gently drawn them away from their self-centred, individual patterns of thought, their insignificant anxieties about food, sleep and tomorrow, and knitted them slowly together into a single entity that fed on words, unconsciously transforming them into a smooth succession of shared emotions which in turn became the heartbeat that unified them. When Odysseus spoke his smooth voice mastered them entirely, reached into their mood and gripped them, leading them, lifting them. He did not sing, but spoke the words of his tale, clearly and rhythmically, mingling their thoughts and emotions into a stream that flowed directly into him and back out again to them. He told them of the gods and the ancient things that preceded them, of battles fought before man's creation that tore up the mountain tops and burned the oceans, and when, eventually, he stopped telling the tale their minds did not stop hearing it, could not stop, but poured back over it and around it until the night breeze tugged at their cloaks and pinched their skin, slowly clawing them back to the world of the hilltop, encircled by the age-old trees and observed by a raven sky filled with stars.

One by one they turned away into their blankets and tried to sleep, pondering the great world that they were but a small fragment of, not needing to comprehend it or their part in it, simply accepting once again their own mortality. And as he saw his true self, a brittle, finite thing, Eperitus did not sink resigned under a sense of fatalism but felt himself lifted, his spirit rising to claim the infinitesimal spark of life that the gods had granted him. He was such a throwaway thing of no importance, and yet he existed and would make that existence worthwhile.

They were woken before dawn by the smell of smoke and the crackle of fire.

Eperitus lifted his head from his rolled-up cloak and at first thought his dream had taken a bizarre twist. Then he saw Damastor running through the camp and shouting.

'Fire! The trees have caught light! Wake up!'

Eperitus leapt to his feet and looked about with a horrified realization. Two of the trees that circled the camp were now blazing brightly, forming a raging beacon against the fading darkness. The others stumbled from their blankets, bleary-eyed and dishevelled. Eperitus saw Halitherses amongst them and ran to him.

'We must find some water,' he said urgently. 'If Polybus is anywhere nearby he's bound to see this.'

'It's too late for that, lad,' Halitherses said, pointing towards the raging inferno. 'See how the flames are spreading from tree to tree? Even if there was a river here and we had something other than our helmets to fetch the water in, we could never douse these flames. I only pray to the gods that there are no Taphians within sight of this.'

Eperitus remained anxious to do something, but the truth was that the fire would be visible to any watching eyes for miles around, and when dawn came the smoke trail would be obvious to all. So they watched helplessly with the heat drying their eyes and warming their faces, and wondered whether matters could get worse. Then Damastor appeared at his side and seized his arm.

'Eperitus, where are the mules? They were picketed over there last night.'

He looked at the place where the beasts had been when he fell asleep, but they were not there. They must have broken free, panicked by the flames, and bolted into the night. With them they had taken the last of their provisions and, what was worse, the gifts for Helen.

Odysseus came running towards them. 'Get some men together and search for the mules, Damastor,' he ordered, clearly angry with the guardsman. 'Halitherses, see that the escort is ready to march before sun-up. I want to get away from here as soon as possible and continue to Messene.'

'How could this have happened?' Eperitus asked him. 'And why didn't the sentry see anything?'

'Damastor was asleep again,' the prince replied, tight-lipped. 'And as for the blaze, it was probably an ember from the fire, caught by the night breeze.'

'Sabotage is a more likely explanation,' Eperitus replied, but Odysseus was already hastening away to issue more orders to his men.

Damastor's search for the mules was unsuccessful and they were forced to leave with nothing but the food they had in their pouches. Soon afterwards it began to drizzle, and they cursed their bad luck that it had not rained the night before. At least then the trees would have been too wet to catch light, and they would not have needed to leave the road and cut across country to avoid pursuit.

Nobody spoke. They followed a route that kept them out of sight of the road. It took them through valleys and along the reverse slopes of hills, through woods and along riverbeds so that they were not seen by unwelcome eyes. Without the road their going was slow and Odysseus would occasionally climb a hill to check their position in relation to the road south. By afternoon the men were tired, being generally unfit and unconditioned to long marches. They also began to find that they could no longer continue south and remain invisible to anyone using the road.

Odysseus, Halitherses and Eperitus made their way up to high ground and saw that the road had now split in two. One route followed the coast as it bent outwards and then plunged south again; the other curved away from the coast and turned inland, heading east through the mountains.

'Which way now?' Eperitus asked.

'Using the coastal road will take us days,' Odysseus answered. 'It circumvents the southern mountains, then angles back up to reach Messene. I've sailed around that cape many times and know it would be a long journey on foot. But if we take the road through this valley,' he added, pointing east, 'it should lead us to the northern end of a broad plain. From there it forks again: south-west to Messene, or east over the Taygetus Mountains to Sparta. Polybus would expect us to head through the valley, but he wouldn't anticipate us doubling back to Messene. I think we should take the risk and hope to lose him there, if indeed he is following us. What do you say?'

'I wouldn't want to follow the coastal road and lose the cover of these hills,' Halitherses said, stroking his beard and looking across at the open stretch between their hiding place and the junction below. 'At least if we head east we can keep ourselves concealed a while longer. There's still the open plain to come, where we'll have to take to the road again for a time, but we can deal with that when it comes to it.'

By last light, after pursuing another skulking course through the foothills and woods that skirted the main road, they finally emerged from the other end of the valley. There before them lay the open plain of Messene. Only the northernmost reaches were visible – the remainder obscured by a last spur of the mountains to their right – but they could see that it was a broad and fertile place. There were fields and orchards, and quiet villages that lay dozing beneath the shadows of the hills. And there, just beyond the rocky spur, they could see the road splitting again. One branch continued south-east towards the Taygetus Mountains and eventually Sparta, whilst the other veered south to Messene.

They increased their pace to a run as Odysseus led them out of hiding and into the vulnerable open spaces about the road. The sun had set, but until they passed the rocky spur it was still light enough for them to be seen from the steep hillsides to the west. Eperitus was at the back of the group, and as he reached the fork in the road he noticed something shining in the dirt. He paused as he reached the object, and looked down to see a dagger in the damp mud, the blade pointing south in the direction they were running.

'Come on, Eperitus,' Odysseus shouted. 'This is no place to rest.'

Shamed by the insinuation that he was tired, Eperitus sprinted to catch up with the rest of the men. Whoever had dropped the dagger would have to do without it.

They did not push on towards Messene that evening. Visitors in the night are rarely made welcome in a town, so they made camp in the foothills of the western mountains. It was a grim and cheerless assembly, without the warmth and light of a fire and with nothing but the meagre rations in their pouches to provide a meal. The watch was tripled and nobody enjoyed an unbroken night's sleep.

Woken by a grey light distilling through his eyelids, Eperitus opened them to see a cold and cloudy sky overhead. All night the winter chill had been eating away at his flesh and burrowing into his bones, leaving him stiff and awkward as he stood and began shaking the blood back into his limbs. They ate a cold and lifeless breakfast of bread with strips of dried fish, washed down with icy water. Amongst the whole group only Odysseus had any cheer, which he tried to spread by reminding his men they were only a morning's march from Messene. As for Eperitus, the prospect of finding Athena's temple by late morning did not encourage him. He had no appetite to face a creature akin to that which protected the Pythoness. But he also knew that to win glory he must face his fears and overcome them.

They took to the road again and marched in a double file. Eperitus walked beside Antiphus and for a while they shared their knowledge of Sparta, swapping tales they had heard of its wealth and the splendour of its palace. But after a while Antiphus began pointing out the signs left by what appeared to be a large group of travellers: recently trampled mud, crusts of bread or olive stones, and even a leather sandal-strap tossed away at the side of the road. Then, as the road slipped between two steep hills on its route south, he called out to Odysseus and pointed out a clump of bushes at the side of the road.

'Somebody's ahead of us, my lord. These bushes have been hacked with a sword, and that means they're armed. I think we should send out flanking scouts, just in case Polybus and his Taphians have overtaken us in the night.'

Odysseus shook his head and pointed to the crests of the slopes on either side of them. 'It's a little bit late now for that, I think.'

They turned to see both sides of the narrow gulley lined with tall, long-haired men. They held spears almost twice their own height and some of them had bows at the ready, arrows primed and pointing directly at them.

Chapter Twelve

AMBUSH AND PURSUIT

·

The Taphians surrounded them like a ring of hunters, but Eperitus felt no fear. He believed in the promise of the oracle and knew his time to die had not yet come. He also trusted in the years of training he had received at the hands of his father and grandfather, both of whom had expected him to one day become captain of the palace guard at Alybas. Since boyhood they had worked on his physical strength, his fighting technique and his reactions, and the fruit of their efforts had pleased them both. As Eperitus crouched behind his ox-hide shield and looked up at the fearsome mercenaries, he knew that his aim with a spear was deadly and his skill with sword and shield second to none.

He touched the flower Ctymene had given him, which he wore in his belt, and prayed to Athena for protection. The Ithacans were surrounded on both sides and whichever way they faced their backs were exposed to the archers on either slope. Their inexperience had allowed them to walk into a trap, and he knew they should have been more cautious. Like the others, he had not expected the Taphians to follow them to Messene, let alone pass them in the night and set up an ambush, but the more he thought about it the more his mind focused on the dagger in the mud. He felt sure it was a sign, left by the same person who had torched the olive trees. Clearly, Koronos was not the only traitor.

The fighting, when it commenced, would be quick and bloody. But as they waited for the first arrow to be loosed, the soldiers around him filled with anticipation and fear, Eperitus looked at the tall men on the hillsides and felt only excitement at the thought of pitting his fighting skills against theirs. His imagination tasted the prospects for glory, whilst feverishly planning how to turn the trap. But even if Odysseus's men were able to escape the well-laid ambush – and he saw no way out other than to hack themselves free – they would leave most of their number dead behind them. Their foes outnumbered them and had the advantage of archers and the high ground. They could pick the Ithacans off at their leisure, forcing them to take the fight up the rocky slopes to the Taphians, by which time the enemy arrows would have reduced them to half their own number.

With the bad news from Ithaca and the loss of their precious baggage, the expedition to Sparta was already in a precarious position. On the other hand, Eperitus had confidence in the men who were with him: the level heads of Odysseus and Mentor; the experience and strength of Halitherses, the bow of Antiphus; the loyalty and comradeship of the others. They also had the happy advantage of being in a tight group, whereas the Taphian leader had spread his force out to prevent the men below escaping. This meant he would have difficulty in keeping control of the warriors furthest from him. Eperitus knew this instinctively, and within moments of the ambush being sprung was searching for a weak spot, a place to launch an attack at and drive the surrounding foes apart.

He looked from position to position, counting each man and eyeing the terrain, remembering the lessons in tactics his grandfather had given him and hoping to identify where they were most vulnerable. It seemed to him that about two-thirds of their force were spread across the wider, steeper hill to their right, whereas the easier slope to the left was more lightly defended, a mere barrier to slow them down if they chose to escape that way.

'There's one of the twins,' Mentor announced, pointing a thumb up the hill to their right. 'You've got good eyes, Damastor: is he missing an ear?'

Damastor squinted over his shield. 'Yes – it's Polybus.'

Antiphus, who crouched next to him, spat over his shield. 'Good. I've got an old score to settle with him.'

Eperitus looked up and recognized the arrogant braggart he had knocked into the pool back on Ithaca. His handsome features were out of place beneath the bronze helmet he wore, and his clumsy shield and spear were even less becoming against his elegant, well cared for physique. He looked as if he had just stepped out of his bath, been oiled by slaves and dressed in the finest armour wealth could buy. But none of the accoutrements of a warrior could make him look like a true fighting man. Judging by the way he had spread his men so thinly, Eperitus did not think he was a talented commander of soldiers either.

As he watched, Polybus stood on a large outcrop of rock and put his hands on his hips.

'Greetings Odysseus,' he shouted down to them. 'I hope you like the little surprise I've prepared for you. The last time we met I told you we would continue our discussion when the odds were more equal. That time has come, I think.'

'Our spears will speak for us,' Odysseus replied, his deep voice reassuring to the men around him.

In answer, Polybus shouted to one of his archers and the first arrow flew. It caught an Ithacan in the chest and threw him back on to the road, his armour crashing about him.

The lull was over.

More bowstrings twanged from the hillsides, arrows splitting the air about them. One pierced Eperitus's shield, the point stopping a finger's breadth from his face. He stood and looked about himself, but by good fortune or the protection of a god only one man had fallen to the first volley. He leapt over the prostrate body as more arrows whistled about them and joined Odysseus, who stood with his shield held up against the deadly rain.

'Polybus has spread his men too thinly,' Eperitus suggested. 'He's left himself vulnerable on the left-hand slope. There are fewer Taphians there and the approach is less steep. They should break easily if we attack, and we can escape with only a few losses.'

'What glory is there in escape?' Odysseus smiled. 'Besides, Polybus wants us to retreat that way so he can pursue us across the plain towards Sparta. He's placed most of his archers on the right to fire at our backs, and just enough men on the left to hold us until his main force can attack our rear. It's clever, but obvious. But if we kill Polybus, we break them as a force and gain victory against the odds. So we go right, where they least expect us.'

'But if we fail, you lose everything.'

'The gods will be with us, Eperitus.'

With that Odysseus let out a great cry and called for his men to follow him up the hill towards Polybus. They obeyed without question, lifting their shields before them and advancing in a steady line up the slope. Forgetting any thought of escape, Eperitus followed close on the heels of Odysseus.

Arrows fell into them from behind and two men went down before they were more than a few paces up the hill. Damastor turned in a mixture of surprise and anger, but caught his foot and fell, striking his head against a boulder. He did not get up again and his comrades were forced to leave him as they drove on into the rain of missiles from above.

Despite the early casualties, Polybus had kept the balance of his fifteen or so archers on his own side of the ambush, as Odysseus had pointed out. This made the threat from behind less effective, and all the time the Ithacans were moving out of the effective range of the smaller group of archers. Also, by holding their oversized shields before them they made the shots of the men on the slopes above ineffective, and were able to steadily close the distance on them. And yet the hill was steep and their careful approach, with shields held out as they scrambled around boulders and over loose rocks, allowed the Taphians to pull back before them and tighten their ranks.

'Eperitus!' Antiphus called over to him. 'Stay here and protect me with your shield while I take some shots at them. I'm sick of not being able to fire back.'

Eperitus ran across and fixed the point at the bottom of his shield into the dust. It was tall and broad enough to provide cover for both himself and Antiphus, who slipped his bow and quiver from his shoulders and knelt down. Having no natural skill with the weapon, Eperitus watched with impressed satisfaction as his companion flipped the lid off the quiver, laid a handful of arrows down in his upturned shield and fitted one to the string. He stretched it back with his left hand, resting the shaft on the knuckles of his right hand where his index and forefinger had been severed by Polybus, then steadied his breathing and took aim.

Eperitus peered around the other side of the shield. The Ithacans were clambering more slowly up the hillside now, but still maintained the even dispersal of their line. Odysseus was at their centre, undeterred that he was the target of most of the Taphian archers. It was he who kept the advance steady, ensuring with booming commands (which Halitherses reinforced) that no warrior outstripped his comrades. He controlled them like a man reining in a chariot team, keeping each horse in check until the final burst of speed is required.

Then Antiphus's bowstring twanged loud in Eperitus's ear and he saw one of the tall archers flail backwards, caught in the eye. With amazing speed, Antiphus fitted a second missile, took a moment to aim, then let it fly towards a second Taphian, who folded as the point pierced his stomach. Moments later, a third man was hit in the shoulder, and at this the enemy gave up their bows and withdrew behind the safety of their shields. Eperitus saw Polybus then, moving between his bewildered men and marshalling them into a line to meet Odysseus's advance. Either through stupidity or a complete lack of fear, he walked with his shield slung over his shoulder, unconscious or dismissive of the danger from the slopes below.

Seeing the opportunity, Eperitus touched Antiphus's shoulder and pointed at the easy target. 'Revenge for losing your fingers?'

Antiphus saw Polybus, who he could easily have slain, but shook his head. 'His life isn't mine to take. Odysseus wants him. I have a different revenge in mind.'

As he spoke an arrow passed between them and tore a channel of flesh from his left shoulder. He cried out in pain and surprise, and clapped a hand to the wound. Together they turned to see that the Taphians from the hillside behind them had left their positions and were closing on their rear, threatening to cut off their retreat and trap them. Eperitus looked up at Odysseus, but he and his guards had restarted their advance on the now fixed line of mercenaries before them, ignorant of the new danger. He shouted to Mentor, who was nearest, and pointed to the ten or so enemy warriors below.

More arrows fell around them and Antiphus called for Eperitus's shield again. He swung it about to face the archery from below and immediately caught two of the lethal shafts in its thick hide, where they joined the earlier shot that was still buried there. Antiphus moved around behind his companion and knelt down to his right. He drew back the string, despite the pain in his shoulder, steadied his breathing and took aim. This time, though, the arrow went wide and bounced off a rock, provoking jeers from its intended target.

Antiphus cursed and, almost in the same breath, called on the help of the gods. He did not miss again. His next arrow pierced the cheek of one of the attackers, whipping his head to one side and sending him rolling back down the hill. His comrades stooped and found what cover there was amongst the boulders, propping their shields before them. But they were not quick enough. Antiphus's next arrow went straight through a man's thigh, sending him stumbling back down the slope, shouting with pain. A further arrow finished him, piercing his exposed back and dropping him face-first amongst the rocks.

Mentor hurried down the slope to join them, bringing two others who had received light arrow wounds.

'Can you keep them off our backs?' Mentor asked.

Antiphus's reply was distracted as he searched for a target amongst the broad shields before him. 'There are already two fewer than before, and I count only eight men left. I've enough arrows for the remainder, but if they press hard they'll overwhelm me. So you'd better stay.'

At that moment they heard shouts and the clash of arms from above, signifying that Odysseus and his eight remaining men had brought home their charge on Polybus's score of Taphians. Eperitus was torn between rushing to their aid and waiting for the smaller group to attack. Then the weight of the decision was taken from him as the remaining Taphians began their advance, emerging from the cover of the boulders with their shields held before them.

The situation reminded him of the first skirmish at Parnassus, except that this time he was not an outsider: their prince was now his prince; their home was his home. Antiphus's bowstring sounded and another Taphian fell, screaming with agony as he clutched at the arrow in his foot. Realizing their vulnerability, his comrades broke into a run, frantic to cover the remaining distance before the deadly accuracy of the Ithacan archer could take a further toll of their numbers.

Anxiously, Eperitus glanced over his shoulder to the battle on the slopes above. Mentor did the same and they exchanged worried glances. The situation was desperate and they knew that even Odysseus could not defeat a force twice his own number.

'We've got to finish these Taphians now,' Eperitus said, motioning down the slope with his head, 'or Odysseus is going to be overwhelmed.'

Mentor balanced the bulk of his shield on his arm and raised his spear point. 'Form a line,' he ordered. 'Shields and spears at the ready.'

Antiphus fired one last shot, which bounced harmlessly off the helmet of one of the Taphians, then took up his shield and spear and joined his comrades. Eperitus led the attack, closely followed by the others. The enemy were only seven spears strong now, compared to their five, and the slope gave the Ithacans' charge momentum as they rushed at their foes.

The foremost Taphian offered little resistance as the metal boss of Eperitus's shield smashed through his own. He tumbled backwards before his assailant, the look of shock on his face changing to pain as his head fell against a rock. It was the matter of a moment for Eperitus to push his spear into the man's soft stomach, tug it free and look for another victim.

Taphians were a confident breed by nature and remained sure of victory over the smaller Ithacan band. Yet this self-assured reliance on their own brute ability in combat was also the key to their defeat. It made their defence ragged as each man fought his own ground, opening up gaps that the Ithacans exploited with ruthless efficiency. As Eperitus turned to face the next warrior, he saw that Mentor and the others had already attacked the two foremost Taphians in pairs: one forced a parry from his opponent's shield while the other closed in on the man's exposed flank, bringing him down with an easy spear thrust. It looked a practised tactic.

Seeing that the Ithacans' first onslaught had sent three more of their comrades to Hades and had robbed them of the advantage in numbers, the courage quickly drained from the other Taphians and they fled down the hillside. Only the warrior who faced Eperitus remained, a giant who stood a full head and shoulders above his opponents. He showed no fear as he faced the five Ithacans. Throwing his spear contemptuously to one side, he drew his sword and beckoned Eperitus to attack.

The young warrior did not disappoint him. Confident after the swift defeat of the others, Eperitus stabbed his spear forward to penetrate the man's guard. But, though huge, he was not as slow as Eperitus had hoped and easily deflected the spear thrust with his shield. In the same move he brought his sword down upon Eperitus's shield in a crashing blow that sent him reeling backward with his left arm numbed. Eperitus looked up from the shock of the attack and saw the Taphian raise his arm for a second swing.

Often the gods will give a man the power to think faster than the chaos and confusion about him, sharpening his awareness and enabling him to react with the speed of instinct. As the giant warrior brought his sword down in a deadly arc, his guard opened. Without thinking, Eperitus twisted aside and pushed his spear into the gap. He felt the elastic resistance of the man's skin popping beneath the sharpened bronze, followed by the slippery welcome of his stomach as the weapon buried itself in his innards. The Taphian's sword left his hand and bounced off Eperitus's shield. He fell sideways and his great weight almost tugged the shaft of the spear from his assailant's grasp. Then with a snap the intensity of the moment was gone. Eperitus pulled the spear from the twitching body and turned to the others, who were already running back up the hill to join their prince.

He looked up the rocky slope. The battle now raged at its summit, which was a small knoll on top of the larger mass. It would take them only a little while longer to skirt the mound, giving it a wide enough berth not to be noticed by the Taphians, and then climb up behind them.

'Wait!' he said, catching up with his comrades. 'If we rush straight into the fight the Taphians will still have the advantage of the higher ground; if we go around and attack them from behind we'll throw them into panic.'

Mentor looked up the hill, weighing up the suggestion as he watched the tight skirmish in which his lord and friend was fighting. 'Then we'll need to be quick. Come on.'

Carrying their spears at their sides they set off at an even run. A goat track led around to the other side of the hill and made the climb much quicker. Soon they were ascending from the other side of the hill and forming a line behind the Taphians.

The sight that greeted them was a desperate one. The Ithacans had by now been encircled by the greater mass of their foes, and bodies and broken or discarded weapons lay strewn all around. Odysseus's squat, muscular form stood out in the centre of his men, fighting off two Taphians as if he were fresh to the battle. At his side was Halitherses, straining shield-to-shield against another of the mercenaries.

As he had done at Parnassus, Eperitus launched one of his spears into the back of an enemy soldier, then charged at the remainder. Another warrior turned in shock at the death of his comrade, only to receive Eperitus's second spear point in his throat. The momentum of the thrust snapped the man's head back and broke his neck, killing him instantly and toppling him to the ground. On either side more Taphians fell to the spears of the others. Still more were killed by Odysseus and his group as they broke through the circle of their stunned foes.

The effect of the attack was devastating. The brief and chaotic butchery that followed left only seven opponents standing, including Polybus, and these withdrew steadily before the Ithacan onslaught.

Polybus raised his sword and ordered his men forward. They were the last and the best of the Taphians and obeyed the command without compunction, whilst Polybus turned his back on them and ran. Halitherses and Mentor stood at each end of the rank of Ithacans and ordered them to stand firm and meet the attack. But as the two lines met a hand fell on Eperitus's shoulder and pulled him out of the battle. It was Odysseus.

'Come with me. We still haven't finished that discussion with Polybus yet.'

Antiphus was next to them and heard the prince's words. 'I'm coming too,' he said.

Odysseus did not question him, but simply turned and set off at a run in pursuit of Polybus. They followed him down the reverse slope of the hill, instinctively finding their footing amongst the treacherous boulders and rocks. Already Eperitus could see their quarry before them, running beside the course of a small stream that cut between large, steep hills. The narrow valley was green with the recent rains, and as they reached the swollen watercourse they found a level footpath that gave them more speed. Ahead of them they could see that Polybus had cast off his spear and shield and was stretching the distance between himself and their pursuit. They followed his lead, retaining only their swords and Antiphus's bow.

Despite the heavy fighting, Odysseus showed no sign of fatigue and soon began to close on Polybus. Eperitus had never seen a man so short and stocky run with such speed, and he and Antiphus had to keep up as best they could. The stream wound its way between the spurs of the hills, which sometimes hid Polybus from sight, only to reveal him again as they passed each bend. Then, just as Eperitus's legs were tiring beneath him, he saw Polybus head uphill. Odysseus mustered fresh energy and sprinted to where he had left the path, but there he stopped. By the time they had caught up with the prince, Polybus was nowhere in sight.

'Where did he go?' Antiphus asked, his hands on his knees as he struggled to catch his breath.

Odysseus pointed up the hill. 'He's in there.'

They looked up. Another path led to the summit where, surrounded by olive trees and overgrown with scrub, a large stone building stood. Judging by its stern silence it was disused.

'What is it?' Eperitus asked.

Odysseus smiled and, as if to himself, said, 'The temple of Athena.'

Chapter Thirteen

THE TEMPLE OF ATHENA

The temple was larger and more impressive than any Eperitus had ever seen before. In Alybas they worshipped at natural places associated with the gods: groves of trees, caves or mountain springs. The only man-made objects were altars and statuettes, perhaps the occasional hut, but nothing so awe-inspiring as this. And yet what had once been a place of beauty and reverence was now a scene of waste and devastation.

They stood by a painted statue of Athena, its once rich colours faded by the sun, and looked through the entrance of the walled compound that surrounded the temple. The decorated wooden doors had been thrown down and lay shattered amidst a chaos of other debris and destruction in the courtyard beyond. Parts of the wall were staved in and the rubble was strewn about at random, punctuated by broken vases, upended tripods, clothing and even an overturned cart. Who, or whatever, had caused such damage had immense strength, and clearly did not fear the wrath of the gods. They drew their swords from their belts and walked in.

Inside the compound they could see the greater extent of the desolation. Half a dozen olive trees – sacred to Athena – had been wrenched out of the ground and left to wither in the sun. There were innumerable shards of pottery spread about, the tatters of ornamental drapes that must once have hung inside the temple itself, and dozens of clay figurines. It looked as if a whirlwind had sucked out the contents of the temple and regurgitated them over the courtyard, then resumed its chaotic path of destruction until there was nothing left to ruin but the plastered stone walls of the building itself.

The temple entrance had once consisted of a pair of doors approached by four broad stone steps. The doors had long since been burst open, while on the steps lay the skeletal remains of a human being. The rotted clothing hanging about it could once have been a priest's robes, but such was the decay that they could not tell. The body had long since been picked clean of flesh and the bones bleached by the sun, but there was something in those empty eye sockets that retained an unspeakable terror, something about the open jaw that still cried out in silence.

As they stared at the chaos a hideous scream rang from the temple. It rooted them to the ground with its despairing horror, then it was suddenly silenced. Eperitus's blood ran cold and the hair on the back of his neck was stiff with fear.

'Goodbye Polybus,' Odysseus said grimly, staring at the shadowy entrance.

So the serpent was still there, jealously guarding the temple against any who dared enter. Perhaps it had relieved them of the need to take the pursuit any further, but Odysseus would want to make sure that Polybus was dead. He would also want to honour his promise to Athena, though Eperitus hoped he had the good sense to go back for the others first; the thought of encountering another serpent in the darkness, without his spear, his shield or the aid of his comrades, made him sick with fear.

Odysseus, however, had no intention of waiting. He led the way up the steps and into the shadowy interior of the temple, beckoning for the others to follow.

'What could have made Polybus scream like that?' Antiphus asked quietly, unslinging his bow and readying an arrow from his quiver. 'If it caused all that damage back there, it can't be a man.'

'It's a serpent. The spawn of Echidna,' Odysseus answered, though he offered no account of how he knew.

Antiphus looked at Odysseus in horror. Echidna was a monster of legend, half woman, half snake. A child of hers would be the stuff of nightmares.

They edged further into the shadows, where for a few tense moments their eyes struggled to adjust to the gloom. They had come to the head of a long aisle, flanked on either side by two rows of pillars. The rank-smelling air was thick and oppressive and their limbs felt suddenly heavy with the toil of the battle they had just fought. Then they heard something heavy slithering across the dusty floor at the far end of the temple.

Antiphus leaned his weight against one of the pillars and sought a target for his bow, but could see nothing in the weak light that suffused the interior. Odysseus drew his sword and walked cautiously towards a stone dais at the back of the temple, watching for movement as he passed between the rows of columns. Anxiety for the prince made Eperitus follow closely behind, his sword held before him. Never had he felt so vulnerable, or so naked, without his grandfather's shield on his arm.

Something glinted on the broad flagstones a few paces ahead of them.

'Odysseus!' he hissed, afraid to disturb the sinister silence. 'Polybus's sword.'

Odysseus saw the discarded weapon and stopped.

'The beast must have snatched him out of the darkness,' he whispered, turning slightly to face Eperitus. 'He couldn't have known . . .'

Suddenly the great bulk of the serpent lashed out from the shadows. Eperitus flinched and this was the only warning Odysseus had of the doom that was closing rapidly behind him. In that splinter of time he turned and swept his sword up to defend against the terrific force of the monster's attack. The blade thumped into its thick neck, but the blow was thrown back without effect. The open jaws and long fangs would have bitten the life out of Odysseus in a moment, had not an arrow from Antiphus's bow taken the creature in the eye and sent it lashing back into the shadows, hissing with pain.

Eperitus's shock at the speed of the attack and his companions' reactions did not hold him for long. Nor did his fear of serpents. In an instant he became a warrior again, aware that death was upon them and his friends were in danger, and without thinking he charged after the retreating coils of the great beast. It sped away as fast as it had come, but in its half-blind confusion smashed into one of the painted pillars, splitting the wood and stalling its flight.

He was upon the monster in an instant. His sword flashed down upon its glistening hide, but just as Odysseus's blow had bounced off, so did his, unable to pierce the hideous skin. Its scales were like flaps of hardened leather, overlapping each other to form an impervious armour. Eperitus struck again, numbing his arm as the force of his blow was returned twofold by the creature's defences.

The pain from Antiphus's arrow had caused the serpent to momentarily forget the men who had invaded its lair, but as Eperitus's second blow rebounded from its hide it drew back and cocked its ugly head at him, surveying him with an evil intelligence in its eye. It was bigger than Python and, unlike in the pitch-black cavern at Pythia, there was just enough light to see the monster in its full, terrifying hideousness. It raised itself to the ceiling of the temple – the height of two tall men – but even this represented only one quarter of its full length.

It gave Eperitus no time to recoil in disgust or horror, but darted towards him with the swiftness of an arrow. He could not even raise his sword in defence before its bony head punched the breath out of him and tossed him against one of the pillars like a child's toy. The impact left him dazed, his senses reeling.

Odysseus leapt to his defence, standing before him and slashing at the giant creature with his sword. At the same time Eperitus heard the twang of Antiphus's bow and saw the arrow, a speeding sliver of light in the shadows, skitter off the monster's armoured neck. It had drawn its body up into a coil now to give more force to its attacks, and swayed before Odysseus as it sought the chance to launch itself upon him. In response the prince sought to edge close enough to use his sword on the beast's softer underbelly, but was repeatedly forced back by its cautious repositioning.

Antiphus knelt to Eperitus's right and drew his bow again. He wasted another arrow on the tough skin before sweeping out his sword and rushing forward. But before he could reach Odysseus's side, the serpent flicked its giant tail and threw him back against a pillar, where he lay unmoving. Seeing his comrade dashed aside, Odysseus called on Athena's name and charged beneath the looming head of the creature. With a huge thrust of his muscular arms he planted his sword in its neck.

The ages-old monster bellowed with rage and pain. It slithered back across the floor to the rear wall of the temple, wrenching the deeply buried weapon from Odysseus's grasp, and as it moved a large swelling was visible in the middle of its body, slowing it down. So this had been the fate of Polybus, Eperitus thought groggily. Then he heard Mentor behind them, calling Odysseus's name from the doorway. Eperitus had never taken pleasure from the sound of his voice, but now he rejoiced at it. He only hoped he had brought the others with him.

Looking back at the serpent Eperitus realized that it was not retreating to die from the wound inflicted by Odysseus, but was manoeuvring itself to strike again. He gripped his sword and struggled to his feet, feeling sick and disorientated. His instinctive reaction was to run to Odysseus's defence, but he was too late. The creature opened its slavering jaws to reveal fangs as long as spears, shining blue in the fading light from the temple's entrance, then hurled itself at the unarmed prince. Odysseus was swept from his feet by the force of the attack, yet somehow managed to seize hold of the brute's head and hang on to it.

For a moment Eperitus could do nothing but watch as the serpent tried to free itself of Odysseus's grip, shaking its head like an untamed horse trying to throw its rider. But the man's strength would not succumb, even when it butted him against the pillars, dislodging showers of dust from the ceiling. And then Eperitus's fighting rage took him. His repugnance at the sight of the great snake was forgotten and he rushed in to the attack once more, leaping onto its back and forcing his blade between the tight-knit scales. His anger gave him strength and the blade slid between the overlapping plates into soft flesh, releasing a gush of black blood to erupt over his hands and forearms.

Just then he heard a crack and saw Odysseus tossed across the temple, still holding on to the fang which he had torn out of the monster's jaw. He fell against the stone dais and moved no more. Eperitus tried frantically to drag Polybus's blade free again to inflict further wounds, but the serpent took no further notice of him. It was intent now on the man who had twice wounded it, maddened to vengeful lust by the pain that swept in great waves through its body, from its dimmed eye to the barbs that had pierced its previously impenetrable flesh. Eperitus's eyes were fixed on Odysseus, knowing he could not save him now from the serpent, and in that moment he realized all his hopes were about to die with him. Then he heard a cry of anger and Mentor came running out of the shadows.

In an instant he had placed himself between the beast and Odysseus. Dropping his shield, he slammed the butt of his spear into the ground by the prince so that the point faced directly up into the path of the monster's head. Hardly noticing the newcomer in its rage and pain, it launched its full weight against Odysseus. The force drove Mentor's spear point up into its brain and out through the top of its skull, killing it instantly.

Eperitus fell from the back of the slain beast and crawled to where Odysseus and Mentor lay flattened by the weight of the fallen creature. With Antiphus still unconscious, it took all of Eperitus's remaining strength to lever the heavy head from the two men and topple it over to one side.

Fortunately neither man was badly hurt, and for all the violence Odysseus had suffered his only wound was a slight cut above his eyebrow, which was bleeding freely. They found Antiphus returning to consciousness, but he too had not suffered beyond a few bruises and cuts.

'Where do you think Polybus is?' he asked, looking at the dead monster.

'There,' Eperitus answered, pointing at the pregnant bump in the animal's stomach.

Antiphus walked over to it and drew a dagger from his belt. While they watched him he punched it into the soft underbelly and, using all his strength, forced open a great tear in the stomach. Suddenly a huge volume of liquid burst across the temple floor, spattering Antiphus with gore and almost knocking his legs from beneath him. In the midst was a slimy parcel of meat, spilling out like offal from a sacrificed heifer. Fascinated, Eperitus took a step forward, but instantly leapt back in horror as a great horde of lesser snakes came rushing out of the rent in their mother and squirmed their way to freedom in the shadows of the temple.

The sight turned his muscles to water and he had to close his eyes and fight down nausea. He wanted to run as he felt scores of them sliding in cold masses across his feet, but the fear of dishonour was greater and he stood his ground. Only when the sound of them had disappeared did he dare open his eyes again. The larger object was Polybus and Antiphus had hold of his right hand. Using the blood-stained dagger, he sawed off the dead man's bow-fingers, first one and then the other. When he was done, he dropped the limb back into the mess of gore and stowed his trophies in his pouch. He had a right to those fingers, Eperitus thought, and nobody questioned him.

Their task had been completed and Odysseus's promise to the goddess fulfilled, so they recovered their weapons and walked out into the twilight of the winter evening. The heaviness had lifted from the temple and Eperitus, breathing the clean air, was suddenly overcome by a sensation of relief, even joy, at being alive. He realized that the worry of facing the serpent had made him tense for days, but from now on he would be able to enjoy the prospect of Sparta, where they would be feted in luxury by one of the richest kings in Greece.

Then a sound behind him made him turn, and he saw Polybus staggering down the steps towards him, dripping with the serpent's bile and reaching out his maimed hand in a plea for help. The others turned also, as shocked as Eperitus to see the hideous ghoul who had somehow survived being devoured by the monster. Gone were his arrogant sneer and his self-confidence. Now his eyes were wide with terror, his mind lost for ever.

As he came closer Eperitus could see him mouthing something, one word over and over again. At first he could not hear him, then suddenly his ranting grew more audible.

'Fingers. Fingers,' he groaned as he reached the young warrior. Then with a scream of loathing: 'Give me my fingers!'

At the last moment, he snatched the dagger from Eperitus's belt and thrust it at his stomach. Eperitus instinctively caught Polybus's wrist with his left hand and turned the blade aside, then swung his right fist into his jaw, toppling him backwards into the dust. Odysseus stepped forward and brought his sword down upon Polybus's neck, severing his head with a single blow.

Chapter Fourteen

THE BOW OF IPHITUS

Eperitus reached down to retrieve his dagger from Polybus's death grip and, without a word being spoken, they walked free of the courtyard. The day's fighting had left each of them spattered with gore, so they headed back downhill to the stream, where they stripped off and washed themselves in the cold, refreshing water. Mentor informed them that the last of the Taphians had been slain quickly, but as Halitherses had sent him to find Odysseus he did not know the full tally of their own casualties. The only thing he knew for certain, he said, was that he was hungry and wished there was something to eat.

As he spoke, a fat sheep appeared on the opposite bank of the stream, its fleece shining like silver in the twilight.

'Well, if that isn't an answer to prayer,' Mentor said, drawing his dagger from his belt and wading into the stream.

'Leave it alone,' Odysseus cautioned. 'I don't think we should touch it.'

They heard bleating from further along the path. More silvery shapes were picking their way over the fallen rocks and through the scrub on either bank of the gurgling waters. A creeping, impenetrable mist followed them, its foremost fronds curling between their fat bodies and reaching towards the four men. Soon it was all about them, so that the only thing Eperitus could see was Odysseus sitting next to him on a rock. They heard the bleats of the sheep and saw their shadows in the fog, but their companions were lost from view.

Then a voice spoke out of the haze. 'Very wise of you to keep your friend from my sheep. I wouldn't have wanted to kill him after he spiked that serpent for me.'

They looked up and saw a young man standing before them. He was tall and carried a silver sheepskin draped across one forearm, whilst in his free hand he held a long crook. He had golden hair and huge grey eyes that looked at them sternly and expectantly. Odysseus was quick to recognize Athena and slumped to his knees before her; Eperitus followed his example and bowed his head so as not to look at the goddess.

'Mistress,' Odysseus said. 'The beast is dead and the temple clean.'

'I would hardly say clean,' Athena complained. 'But just to show you that the gods reward those who obey their commands, I'm going to tell you two things in return for ridding my temple of Hera's pet.' She put a smooth white hand under each of their arms and lifted them to their feet. 'First thing, Odysseus: Tyndareus has already decided that Helen will marry Menelaus.'

'Then I should return to Ithaca at once,' Odysseus said.

The goddess ruffled his red hair affectionately. 'Not so hasty, please. It's Zeus's will that Helen be given to Menelaus – he's planning something big, but won't let anyone know about it. You must still go to Sparta, though. A man of your charms will find important friends there, and perhaps something else, too. But I shan't spoil things for you.'

Odysseus seemed restless. 'You said there were two things, mistress.'

'Yes: go to Messene and restock your provisions. There you'll meet a man fording a stream. He will be carrying a large horn bow, which the god Apollo gave to his father. You must use your wits to get the bow from him, as he won't be needing it for much longer himself. How you do it is up to you, but you will be ill advised to leave Messene without it. Do you understand me?'

'What's the importance of the bow?' Odysseus asked.

But the goddess was gone, swallowed up by a billow of the fog. The gentle bleating of her sheep faded away and the mist evaporated about them to reveal Mentor and Antiphus, looking around themselves in surprise.

'Where in Hades did that fog come from?' Mentor said. 'And where did those sheep go?'

Antiphus walked over to them. 'You had a lot to say for yourselves, didn't you? Chattering away in the mist.'

It was clear neither man had been aware they had been in the presence of an immortal. Odysseus and Eperitus made no answer, but instead headed back upstream to retrieve their shields and spears.

※

Three Ithacans had died in the battle. Eperitus had expected there to be more casualties, but the islanders were tougher men than they looked. From their outward appearances he had first thought them simple folk with little inclination to fight and no stamina for battle. They seemed to him men who preferred wine and the song of a bard to adventure and hardship. And so they were. But there was something about their island identity that gave them a toughness and spirit excelling anything he had encountered before. Again and again they proved themselves against every test. And only slowly, through listening to them tell stories over the camp fire each night and hearing them grumble on the long marches, did he realize the source of this strength. It came from their love of Ithaca and the simple freedom they had always enjoyed there. They would do whatever was needed of them to regain the idyllic world Eupeithes had stolen.

Eperitus only knew the dead men by sight, though they were obviously sorely missed by their comrades. They buried them together on the hill where they died. The place was marked with a mound of rocks, and when the last stone was laid they shouted three times over the grave of their comrades. After that Eperitus did not hear their names mentioned again for many months.

Damastor had been found still unconscious at the foot of the slope. He suffered a large bruise on his forehead and a headache that did not leave him until the next day, but was more dismayed at having missed the battle. Eperitus tried to reassure him that there was no shame attached, and yet he understood Damastor's disappointment at missing the glory his comrades now enjoyed.

By good fortune they found the Taphian mules tied up at the foot of the slope, and amongst them their own animals, complete with the rich gifts for Tyndareus. As many of the Ithacans had received injuries that needed tending, Odysseus ordered the fine dresses to be torn up for bandages. The wounded men were ridiculed by their comrades for the pretty yellows and blues, of course, but this soon stopped when Odysseus tied a bright purple bandage around the wound on his forehead. Grateful for the clean material, which was far better than the dirty cloaks and tunics of the dead, they were nonetheless concerned that Odysseus had chosen to use Helen's bride gifts in such a manner. Eperitus wondered how many other nobles would put the care of their men before their own gain.

They slept that night on the threshold of the temple. At dawn they returned to the hill and dug a large grave for the Taphians they had slain. It took much of the morning to make a pit big enough. Many had been put to death as they lay wounded on the ground after the battle, pleading for mercy from the men whose homes they had taken. But they received none, unless it was to save them from the carrion birds that circled above.

And so it was that by noon they started for Messene, saddened by the deaths of their fellow warriors but lifted by their victory over Polybus. The gods had been with them on the battlefield and they were encouraged by their protection. There were many, though, who pointed at Odysseus as he led the march and said it was he whom the immortals favoured. A handful of Taphians had escaped and would eventually reach Ithaca with the news that the prey had turned on the hunter, but by then Odysseus and his men would be guests at the palace of Tyndareus and safely beyond the reach of Eupeithes.

The chariot of the sun had not travelled far in its course through the dull and cloudy sky before they could detect animal dung and smoke in the air, the familiar smells of a township, and knew that Messene was just beyond the hills ahead of them. Odysseus, standing with Mentor at his side, called Damastor, Antiphus and Eperitus over to join them.

'I was a fool to march us straight between those hills yesterday, so this time I'm sending you four to scout ahead. If you meet any trouble, send someone back to warn us – we'll be close behind.'

They had no difficulty in outstripping the rest of the party, who were slowed down by the mules and the wounded men. Soon they reached the hills that separated them from Messene and stood in the road that wound its way between them. The boulder-strewn slopes rose steeply up on either side, providing another easy site for an ambush. With Polybus's force destroyed and their leader dead it was unlikely they would meet more Taphians, and yet travellers in Greece – even armed warriors – were always at risk from bandits. So Mentor suggested they split into two groups, one to flank the road on the left and the other on the right.

'Eperitus and I will go left,' he said. 'You two go right, but don't wander from our view.'

With that he began to climb the scree-covered flank of the steeper hill, followed closely by Eperitus. Clambering over the small rocks and struggling through thick bushes quickly brought them out in a fresh sweat, despite the cold of the day and the fine drizzle that had started. This made the stones wet and their progress more treacherous, but eventually they reached level ground again and looked across to see Damastor and Antiphus picking their way along a rough track on the other side of the road.

Larger hills loomed ahead of them now, blocking everything

that lay beyond from sight. They continued between outcrops of rock and boulders that had toppled from the peaks above, until before long they could hear the sound of flowing water. It came from a low valley that intersected the road and lay between themselves and the larger range of hills. Mentor ran ahead and was soon calling for Eperitus to catch up with him.

'A river,' he said. 'The road starts again on the other side.'

Eperitus looked down into the valley. The waters were wide and fast, swelled by the recent rains falling in the mountains to the east, but nothing like the obstacle they had encountered a few days before. At least it was shallow enough to ford and would not delay their progress. Then, as his gaze crossed to the opposite side where the road to Messene continued, he noticed a lone figure crawling about amongst the stones. Ducking behind the bole of a weather-beaten olive tree and signalling Mentor to get out of view, he looked across to see if Damastor and Antiphus had seen the man. To his dismay they had not, and were already making their way down to the ford.

'There's someone on the other side of the river,' he told his companion. 'I think he's alone, but can't be sure – and the others haven't spotted him yet.'

Mentor nodded. 'I'll go and warn Odysseus. In the meantime, see if you can stop the others giving us away.'

'Tell Odysseus he's carrying a bow,' Eperitus shouted after him as he sprang off in the direction by which they had come.

Seeing that the mysterious figure was still on his hands and knees, searching for something in the mud of the road, he began the descent as quickly as he could. The scree slope was treacherous, made more slippery by the rain. He had no hope of reaching the river before Damastor and Antiphus, but in his haste sent a cascade of small rocks tumbling down to the road below, catching the attention of the man on the opposite bank. He stood and looked across the flowing waters, just as the others reached the road. They were as surprised as he was to find anybody else in the small valley.

Eperitus sprang down the last stretch of the hill to join his comrades, where they stood eyeing the young man with silent curiosity. He was small and pale with hardly the bulge of a muscle upon him, looking more like a living skeleton than a human being. His head was crowned with a sheaf of black hair, and a thin, juvenile beard sprouted from his bony chin. He wore no armour and his only weapons were a dagger that hung loose in his belt and a bow of white horn slung across his back.

The magnificent bow was much too big for such a skinny lad, and Eperitus knew it must be the weapon Athena had told Odysseus to make his own. He walked across to Antiphus and asked what he thought of the stranger.

'A child with the weapon of a god,' the archer replied, eyeing the horn bow greedily.

Damastor agreed. He raised his voice above the cacophony of the river and called out to the stranger, who had been looking back at them with wary interest.

'What's a boy doing with a man's bow? Did you steal it from your father, or did he give it to you in the hope it would make you a man?'

'What would a bastard such as you know about a father's gifts?'

The young man looked so meek and pathetic that Eperitus was shocked, as well as amused, by his feisty retort. For a moment Damastor was flabbergasted at the youth's audacity, but when he realized he had been humiliated his temper quickly got the better of him. He set his jaw and narrowed his eyes, then advanced into the river with his spear levelled above his shoulder. Mirroring his advance, the archer on the far bank unslung his bow, fitted an arrow and waded out to meet him. Unless the younger man was an appalling shot, there was little doubt about the outcome of the fight. Eperitus even felt concern for Damastor, though the Ithacan's rudeness had deserved an insolent reply. In contrast, Antiphus was laughing at his friend's vexation and appeared completely unfazed by the encounter.

'Give me the weapon, lad, and I promise not to kill you,' Damastor shouted.

His answer was the twang of the great bow. Antiphus choked on a new wave of laughter as the arrow plucked Damastor's bronze cap from his head and carried it clean beyond the river to clatter amongst the rocks behind them. Damastor was so shocked that he fell back into the water with a great splash. This brought tears of laughter to the eyes of his comrades on the river bank, followed by more shouts of laughter from the road behind. Eperitus turned to see the rest of the party arriving, led by Odysseus and Mentor, of whom only Odysseus was not touched by the hilarity of Damastor's situation.

Instead he threw down his weapons and waded out into the water, past his floundering comrade and out to the young man with the bow. A new arrow was already primed and aimed at his chest, but Odysseus showed no fear. He stopped a spear's length from the stranger and looked first at the lad, then at the tall weapon in his hand.

'My name is Odysseus, son of Laertes of Ithaca,' he said, looking the archer in the eye and smiling. This surprised Eperitus, as he had expected his friend to announce himself as Castor, son of Hylax of Crete. However, he was not to be wholly disappointed by Odysseus's deceptive nature. 'I've come to Messene to recover three hundred sheep stolen from my islands, and I'll reward any help you can give me.'

The man wavered in thought for a moment, then, to the relief of all, lowered his weapon and stepped forward to offer his hand in friendship.

'I am Iphitus of Oechalia. My father is Eurytus the archer, favourite of Apollo. As for your sheep, well,' he shrugged his shoulders and spread his hands apologetically, 'I've never seen a country with so few of the creatures. But maybe you can help me?'

'If I can,' Odysseus replied, placing one of his oversized hands on Iphitus's bony shoulder and leading him across to the far bank of the river.

'I've lost some horses.'

'*Lost* them?'

Iphitus smiled. 'Not exactly. My father and brothers think Heracles stole them.'

At that point Damastor regained his feet and came splashing through the river towards the young archer. Iphitus saw him and, with a quickness of mind that echoed his earlier sharpness of tongue, waded out to meet him. He thrust out his hands, palm forward.

'My apologies, friend. I'm sorry for our misunderstanding, which was entirely my fault. I took you for a brigand without realizing you must, in fact, be a man of noble birth.'

Damastor was taken aback by the unexpected show of friendship, but after a moment's thought chose to accept the apology. The incident was laughed off in a face-saving show of camaraderie.

The others waded across, leading the mules with their loads of supplies. Mentor handed Damastor his cap and returned the arrow that had plucked it from his head to Iphitus.

'Is it true you're hunting Heracles, lad?' he asked, proving that rumours were already spreading amongst the men of what they had overheard.

Iphitus was about to reply, but Odysseus spoke first.

'If there's a tale to be told, and there surely is, then let's hear it in full and in the right place. For now we should find an inn at Messene where we can eat and restock our provisions; our friend can tell us the whole story then. And perhaps he will tell us about this bow – I've never seen its like before. What do you say, Iphitus?'

'The trail's already cold,' he answered, 'so perhaps I can find some inspiration in a cup of wine. I'll come.'

Messene was a city hidden in the foothills of the western mountains, lying on the opposite side of the plain from the more lofty Taygetus range. It consisted of a collection of unimpressive hovels on the outskirts, followed by an inner ring of better-made crafts-men's houses, which in turn encircled a core of progressively larger, more substantial homes belonging to the merchants and nobles of the town. Its crooked streets were muddy with the rain and deeply rutted from the heavy goods carts that occasionally creaked their way up or down the narrow thoroughfares. Despite the chill, naked infants ran about between the houses, happy to be free of their homes again now that the rain had stopped. Mostly their mothers ignored them, preferring to gossip with neighbours in doorways or too busy with the daily chores to concern them-selves with noisy children. And everywhere the air smelled of cooking fires, food and dung, the comforting aroma of civilization that reminded the Ithacans of their own distant homes.

The sight of armed men was not uncommon in Greek town-ships. However, the wounds the newcomers bore showed they had been in a recent fight, and the locals eyed them with suspicion and hostility. Nobody spoke to them, and if they approached them they would either turn away or tell them they could not help. Despite this they eventually found their way to an inn, where the patron was happy to sell them food and wine, and for an additional price provided them with a large room with straw mattresses for all. They gave the mules into the care of the innkeeper's son, then returned to the main room of the house.

In the late afternoon the inn was empty but for themselves and a few old men, left there by their families to sup wine and keep warm by the large hearth in the centre of the room. It was a low-ceilinged place lit only by the fire and the last of the afternoon light slanting in through the open doorway. Noisily, the Ithacans crowded onto the benches and began discarding their armour and weaponry like snakes shedding skin, leaving great flakes of leather, ox-hide and bronze about the floor. The old men broke off from their story-swapping and watched the newcomers with silent interest, perhaps recalling the days when their own bodies were filled with enough youthful strength to carry breastplate, spear and shield.

By the time they had settled down a huge woman brought in two earthenware bowls filled with cold water, followed by the innkeeper with two more. Moments later, as they were cleansing their hands and faces of the day's dirt, the couple returned carrying a large krater of wine between them which had already been mixed with two parts of water. The soldiers wiped their hands dry on their tunics and filled wooden bowls with the wine, drinking deeply to slake their thirst whilst baskets of bread were passed. These were followed by plates of tough goat's meat and dishes filled with salad and pulse. There were large numbers of tasteless barley cakes too, the likes of which had formed the mainstay of their rations on the journey to Messene.

There was no ceremony about the meal and they did not hold back in satisfying the hunger that days of marching, fighting and hard rations had inspired in them. There was very little conversation as they filled their ravenous stomachs, until finally they were using the last wafers of bread to wipe up the grease and fat from the plates. Then Mentor demanded more wine and the talk began to flow as their tongues were loosened.

At first they were polite to Iphitus, asking general questions about his home and his family. But the subject was turning with slow certainty to Heracles. They had all of them heard the youth tell Odysseus he was hunting horses allegedly taken by the most famous warrior in Greece, and there had been an undercurrent of excitement ever since the name of Heracles had been mentioned. Eperitus had already heard endless tales of his unmatchable strength, his prowess in battle and his seemingly endless sexual conquests. Some said he had diverted rivers with his own hands, others that he had slept with fifty maidens in one night, and all that he had killed a gigantic lion with his bare hands. These tales made the man a living legend, though until Iphitus's brief mention of him the warrior from Alybas had no idea he was still alive. His nurse had told him stories about Heracles when he was a mere infant, so to him he was a figure more from myth than reality, a man from a past age who could hardly belong in their own fallen era.

But live he did, or so Iphitus testified. Neither did he need their encouragement to tell them the full story of Heracles's visit to his home in Oechalia. The wine encouraged openness to their questions and soon the words were tumbling from his lips, which the Ithacans drank up like cattle at a trough. Even Odysseus leaned in over his cup to hear what their new companion had to say, though Eperitus noticed that his eyes continuously strayed to the bow leaning against the wall.

Long ago, Iphitus's father Eurytus, king of Oechalia and a renowned archer, had offered his daughter in marriage to any man who could outshoot him. As Apollo himself had tutored Eurytus in archery he had every right to be confident of his marksmanship and was justly proud of his skill with the bow. Indeed his reputation was so widespread that few had bothered to take the challenge and his beautiful daughter, Iole, was in danger of becoming a spinster.

At that time Heracles was the king's friend. Eurytus had taught him to shoot when he was young, and their bond of friendship had remained. But Zeus's wife, the goddess Hera, bore a grudge against Heracles and induced a madness in him that caused him to slay his own children. When he regained his sanity he rejected his wife Megara and, upon the instruction of the Pythoness, served penance as a slave to King Eurystheus of Tiryns.

It was whilst he was Eurystheus's bondsman that Heracles decided to challenge his old friend for Iole's hand in marriage, seeing her as a potential replacement for the unfortunate Megara. Eurytus had no choice but to accept the challenger as a matter of honour, though he had misgivings because Heracles's arrows were reputed to be magically guided to their target. And so they were, making Heracles the first man to defeat Eurytus in an archery contest.

But the king also knew of Heracles's womanizing and his

treatment of Megara. Friend or no, he loved his daughter too much to give her in marriage to the worst husband in Greece. So, Iphitus explained, his father declared the contest void because of Heracles's magic arrows and threw him out of his palace. Iphitus alone complained at the treatment of their famous guest, goaded by his strong sense of fairness under the heroic code and the friendship which had formed between them during Heracles's short stay.

'It stung me to see a man as mighty as he thrown from the palace like a beggar,' he said. 'And when a few days later twenty-four of our prize horses were stolen, I was the only one who would not believe Heracles had taken them. Such a petty act of revenge is below him. It would have been more in keeping with his character to storm the palace single-handed and lay us all out on the flagstones, like so many fallen leaves in autumn.'

They pictured Heracles in their minds, a huge man, bigger even than Odysseus and half again as tall, smashing down the palace doors with one blow of his fist and then carving up Eurytus and his guards as if they were nothing more than a herd of goats. He crashed through their imaginations like a whirlwind until, finally, they noticed that Iphitus had stopped talking.

'And what do you believe now?' Mentor asked, the first to speak since Iphitus had begun his tale.

'There are rumours amongst the people I've spoken with. They say a large number of horses were herded north to Tiryns by a lone warrior dressed in a lion's skin, a huge man bound with muscles the size of boulders. That's what they say. As for me, I left the trail to come south to Messene, in the hope that my father's horses would be hidden here by thieves other than Heracles.'

Now Halitherses spoke: 'And do you still refuse to believe your friend stole these prize horses? It seems clear to me he did. After all, everybody knows Heracles is a slave in Tiryns and wears the skin of the lion he slew in Nemea. To my ears the things you've heard aren't rumours, but news.'

'Yes, old man,' Iphitus conceded. 'Only a fool can deny it – or a friend. But even loyalty can't stifle suspicion, and for a long time now I've known I must confront Heracles.'

Damastor sat back and gave a whistle, expressing the thoughts of them all. Eperitus looked at Iphitus in a new light. How could a mere youth even contemplate matching himself against Heracles? Only a man of extraordinary courage would seek out a fight that would end in his own ignominious death.

The band of soldiers looked at their guest in silence.

'And how can you hope to get your horses back if Heracles has taken them?' Odysseus asked. 'You're not unaware of his reputation.'

'I have my bow. Here, take a look for yourself.' Iphitus handed the curved weapon over with pride, taking satisfaction from Odysseus's close and knowledgeable inspection of it. 'Heracles may have magic arrows, but this bow was the gift of a god. Apollo gave it to my father, and he in turn to me, so you see it has divine powers. It can hit a hawk in the eye at twice the distance of any mortal's weapon. And it can only be strung by the man to whom it is given freely. If Heracles himself were to find this weapon, for all his great strength he would not be able to fit a bowstring to it. So I tell you in full confidence that if my father's horses are in his possession and he will not return them to me, then I will use this bow to mete out justice to him.'

Eperitus liked Iphitus, but for all the divine origins and powers of the bow he had little faith in the lad's ability to kill Heracles – especially if Odysseus fulfilled the command of the goddess and took it from him. He watched the prince admiring the weapon in which Iphitus had placed his faith, running his fingers over its smooth surface of crafted horn and admiring the skill that had shaped it. He stood and tried the string, finding that the bow bent to his will as if it had been made especially for him. And Eperitus could tell that he coveted it, that he wanted it with all his heart, as a man would want a woman.

'Innkeeper!' Odysseus shouted. 'Bring more wine in here. My men want to get roaring drunk.'

Another krater was brought in to the cheers of his guards, but Odysseus did not stop to taste it. He announced he was going to check on the mules and, taking the bow with him, went through the door that led to the stables. Iphitus became fidgety without his prized weapon. Unable to let it out of his sight for a moment longer he stood and, excusing himself politely and promising to return, followed the prince. Eperitus waited a short while then followed in his wake.

He reached a doorway onto the courtyard and heard their voices coming from the stables on the other side. Waiting in the shadows, he heard Odysseus explain the real reason for their journey across the Peloponnese.

'And when will you leave for Sparta?' asked Iphitus.

'We won't delay any longer than we have to,' Odysseus replied. 'Perhaps tomorrow, if the men's wounds show signs of healing and they feel fit enough. And what about you, Iphitus? When will you head to Tiryns?'

'Messene holds no attraction for me,' he replied. 'Tomorrow will be as good a time as any. Already the trail is fading, and yet my mission won't allow me to delay. I have to find Heracles.'

Eperitus crossed the courtyard. It was lit only by the glow of the moon, an eerie light that reflected in the dozens of small puddles on the muddy ground, which was still sodden from the day's rain. The mules were huddled together in the darkness, where Odysseus was stroking their long noses and ugly, twitching ears. Iphitus was in the corner of the stable, once more in possession of his bow.

'Hello Eperitus,' Odysseus greeted him.

'My lord.'

'Not interested in getting drunk then?'

'Not really. I thought I'd join you and see if I could dissuade Iphitus from pursuing Heracles.'

'I'm afraid not,' said the young archer. 'I feel honour-bound to find my friend and prove the rumours wrong.'

'Or right.'

'At least travel with us, Iphitus,' Odysseus said. 'Sparta is on the way to Tiryns. We can share the road together and keep each other company. The men like you.'

'It's true,' Eperitus agreed. 'Who can forget the way you shot Damastor's cap off with that arrow? And even *he* has come to forgive you for it. You should join us.'

As Iphitus shook his head resolutely, Odysseus moved towards the baggage that had been stowed in a corner of the stable, knelt down and untied one of the leather bags.

'Your decision makes me sad,' he sighed, standing again. In his hand was his father's sword, the guest-gift for Tyndareus. He pulled it from its scabbard and the ornately carved blade glinted in the silvery light, each tiny detail pin-pricked by the moon as Odysseus turned it this way and that. Eperitus had never seen a weapon so intricate in its design, so rich in the quality of its workmanship, or so dreadful as it sat poised in Odysseus's hand. For a moment he feared his friend would strike Iphitus down in cold blood and take the bow from him. Iphitus, too, looked uncertain and took a step back, gripping his bow tighter. But as he did so the prince slid the sword back into its scabbard and offered the hilt towards him.

'If you won't accompany us to Sparta, then you must visit me when I've restored Ithaca to my father's line. There I will receive you with fair words, have my slaves bathe and clothe you, and we'll eat together as old friends. That's my promise to you, Iphitus, and before Zeus I offer you lifelong friendship, an honourable alliance that will hold for me and my descendants to you and yours for seven generations. And until we meet again in Ithaca I offer you gifts to seal my oath of friendship. I give you this sword of my father's, which was to be our guest-gift to Tyndareus.'

Iphitus took the weapon and looked closely at the gold filigree on the leather scabbard. He drew the sword and studied the ornamentation on the blade, felt with his thumb the carving on the ivory handle, then held it above his head to watch the moonlight trickle off its glistening edge. Even though he was the son of a king, he had never seen such beauty in a man-made object.

As he admired its workmanship, Odysseus turned to Eperitus and told him to fetch one of his spears. 'My *finest* spear, Eperitus. Be quick.'

Eperitus ran to where the others still sat, drinking from a fresh krater of wine. They hailed his arrival and asked where Odysseus was, but he made no reply other than to say the prince needed his spear. Halitherses handed him the great ash shaft and followed him back out into the courtyard, where Odysseus and Iphitus still faced each other.

'This, too, I give to you,' Odysseus said as Eperitus arrived, taking the spear from his hand. 'The spear which Ares gave to my great-grandfather, and which has been passed from father to son since then. Take it, Iphitus, in sign of our friendship.'

Eperitus looked at Halitherses after hearing Odysseus's extraordinary claims about the ordinary-looking weapon, but the old warrior screwed his lips to one side and gave a slight shake of his head.

'Your generosity astounds me, Odysseus,' Iphitus said, taking the spear and feeling its balance in his right hand. 'Truly you are a great friend and a noble ally, a man of virtue and nobility. And you do me great honour with your words and these gifts.' He looked again at the things Odysseus had pressed upon him in the ages-old custom of *xenia*. As a man of royal birth who had already proved himself to be honourable and true, Eperitus knew Iphitus would accept and return Odysseus's oath. He watched him take the prince's hand and look him sternly in the eye.

'Odysseus, I give you an oath of my allegiance, before the all-seeing eyes of Zeus. When our separate missions are completed I'll visit you in Ithaca to confirm the words we've spoken here. And then you shall visit my father's palace in Oechalia and be our most honoured guest. This is my promise, true for seven generations.'

Then he stopped and withdrew his hand. Iphitus was required

to give a gift in return, a token to seal his side of the alliance. And yet he had nothing to give beyond his travel-worn cloak and the plain dagger tucked into his belt. His only other possession was the bow, the one weapon with which he could defeat Heracles.

He looked at Eperitus, who could not return the Oechalian's gaze. He felt ashamed for his simple part in Odysseus's trick, even though he had not realized it until the last moment. Then Iphitus looked at the sword again and tucked it into his belt, smiling with what seemed a mixture of pleasure at the richness of the gift, and resignation at the knowledge that he must give the bow to Odysseus. Everything, after all, was the will of the gods, and they clearly favoured the Ithacan prince.

'This is my gift to you. It's a great weapon, Odysseus, made by Apollo himself. It'll respond to you like a lyre in the hand of a skilled bard. You'll never miss your target with any arrow fired from this bow, and only you or the one you give it to will be able to string it. I give it to you freely and happily in token of our friendship.'

Odysseus took the bow from Iphitus's hand. It was clean and smooth and sat in his palm as if it had been purposely crafted for him alone. Then they all looked at Iphitus and knew he would never now feast with them in the great hall in Ithaca, for when he found Heracles he was certain to die.

book
THREE

Chapter Fifteen

SPARTA

They stood in the foothills of the Taygetus Mountains and looked across the wide valley to the city of Sparta. It lay wedged between the river Eurotas and a lesser tributary, strung like a gold medallion on a silver necklace. It was a wealthy place, home to a numerous, warlike and proud people who had made themselves rich by conquest and trade. They were further blessed with rolling, fertile plains for the growing of crops and the breeding of horses, for which the Spartans were famous throughout Greece. The Eurotas flowed freely down to the coast, enabling their merchants to reach the sea with ease. And by the same route goods came in to Sparta from the rest of the world, providing Cyprian copper for her armourers, Nubian gold and Attican silver for her craftsmen, and a wealth of ivories, textiles, pottery and other luxuries.

The city was larger than anything Eperitus had ever seen before or had dared to imagine. There were the usual hovels of the poor on the outskirts, but these eventually gave way to the magnificent homes of the richer classes, whose lime-plastered walls staggered upwards like giant steps towards the city's acropolis, the hill upon which sat the royal palace.

The morning had been a dull one – cold and threatened by rain – but as he caught his first glimpse of Sparta, set against a backdrop of steep mountains, the clouds parted and broad fingers of sunlight reached down to lift the city from the greyness. It glowed golden-white under the scintillating rays as wall followed wall, gate led to gate, and roof overlapped roof, creating an awesome edifice that dominated the whole valley.

The group of dusty warriors looked on in silence. In comparison, Ithaca was nothing more than a poor, unsophisticated island with a few ramshackle towns and villages. There were no glorious buildings or awe-inspiring palaces to impress visitors; no battlements or soaring watchtowers to deter invaders; no paved streets filled with wealthy merchants or bronze-clad soldiers. All that their homeland could offer were dusty cart tracks that led to simple dwellings surrounded by pigs, chickens and dogs.

Eperitus glanced across at Odysseus. After Messene, the men's spirits had lifted; they knew that once they had passed the Taygetus Mountains and reached Sparta they would find food, drink and plenty of rest. In contrast, Odysseus had grown quiet and withdrawn. On the night before they entered the mountain passes that would take them to Sparta, he had invited Eperitus to join him as he went into the hills to hunt food. Whilst the prince had an arrow fitted to the great bow he was happy again, shooting rabbits at great distances and exulting at the magical accuracy of his new weapon. Often he would comment upon what a match there would have been between Apollo's bow and the arrows of Heracles. But as they headed back to camp his despondency returned and the prince began to talk about Ithaca and his concerns for his countrymen under the yoke of Eupeithes and his Taphian army. He longed to return and fight, especially now he knew Helen's husband had already been chosen, but Athena had told him to go on. Yet what would he find there? And what if he failed in his task and returned to Ithaca empty-handed, to lead the last of the palace guard to certain death against Eupeithes's army?

'I feel helpless, Eperitus,' he said, kicking out at a pile of dead leaves and scattering them across the path. 'I may be known for living by my wits, but I prefer to know where I'm going. I'd happily exchange places with you or any of the others. You're soldiers and your job is to follow orders. If your captain says, "Slay that man," then that's what you do. But I have the fate of a whole people on my back. If I fail, Ithaca fails. And *my* captains are the gods — a more heartless and fickle bunch you couldn't ask for. What matter if their earthly schemes don't come off? They return to Olympus and forget their sorrows with ambrosia and nectar, whilst mortal corpses lie piled on the ground, their souls shepherded off to eternal misery in the halls of Hades. But what choice do we have but to obey their whims? I tell you in truth, I'd give *anything* to overturn my fate and dictate my own destiny.'

Talking about it put him in an even blacker mood, and when they returned to the camp he placed himself on guard duty and spoke to nobody for the rest of the evening. His silence continued throughout the next morning as they marched over the mountain passes to the Eurotas valley. But as Eperitus looked at his friend now, with the city of Sparta gleaming in the valley below, his stern expression had gone. He looked at the city as if he were sizing up an opponent. Here was the challenge that would require all of his wit and resources, and it was a test that he could not afford to fail. Suddenly his features were transformed by a smile.

'Halitherses! See that the men are looking their best. We don't want the Spartans mistaking us for a bunch of brigands, do we?'

Halitherses made himself busy inspecting their armour, making sure it was laced up tightly and sitting properly on their torsos. Then he tugged their shield straps and belts into place, checked that they still wore their little sprigs of chelonion — to remind them of their homes when they were tasting the delights of Sparta — and finally had them take out their whetstones from their pouches and sharpen the blades of their weapons so that they gleamed with a killing edge.

'When you march through those gold-paved streets,' he said, manhandling them into a double file, 'I want you to walk with your chins held high and your eyes straight ahead. No looking at the pretty young Spartan girls, do you understand? Remember who you are, where you're from and why we're here.'

When they eventually reached the city, there were no pretty

girls to be seen. In fact, other than a number of soldiers in various styles of armour and dress, they saw very few people at all. But the empty streets did not detract from the wonder of Sparta. Every wall was high and well built, each strong door ornately carved, and almost every house possessed a second floor. Empty windows stared down on them from every side as they marched up the steep and winding road towards the palace, and Eperitus marvelled to see such beauty and magnificence.

Eventually they reached the palace gateway. The doors were twice as high and twice as wide as their counterparts in Ithaca and were covered in beaten silver that gleamed dully in the watery afternoon light. As they arrived a soldier in full armour emerged from a large guard hut built against the wall to one side of the entrance. He looked strained and tired.

'State your name and your business,' he said, with a voice that sounded weary of dealing with foreign nobles.

'I am Odysseus, son of Laertes, king of Ithaca. I've come to pay court to Helen of Sparta, by reputation the most beautiful woman in Greece.'

This last was added by way of a compliment to Sparta as a whole, but the guard captain remained unimpressed.

'I'm sorry, my lord, but I have orders to permit entrance only to those who have been invited by the king. As I've never heard of Ithaca or any of its princes or kings, you'd better turn about and return the way you came.'

When Eperitus heard his words and thought of the hardships they had endured to arrive at these gates, only to be rejected like a pack of mere beggars, he felt the fighting rage come rushing into his veins. By the murmurs of his comrades he could tell they were angered too. One nod from Odysseus and they would happily have killed the guard and stormed the palace gates. But the prince was more patient than his men, and showed no sign of anger as he walked up to the Spartan.

'I've travelled for many days to come here, have fought two battles and lost three men. If you don't wish to earn your master's wrath, then I suggest you ask him to come here so he can tell me himself to leave. As I told you, I've come to see the daughter of Tyndareus, and see her I will.'

'Then you've found her,' said a voice from behind them. They turned to see a tall woman dressed all in black, escorted by four slave girls and two guards. She was tall, handsome and elegant, and had a commanding femininity about her, but Eperitus could not help but feel disappointed. He sensed the same reaction from Odysseus, whose eyes lingered briefly on the woman's harsh and reproving mouth and the ears that stuck out like the handles on an amphora.

Recovering from his surprise, the prince stepped up to her and bowed. 'Your reputation does not do you justice, Helen of Sparta.'

She arched an eyebrow. 'And your reputation does not exist, Odysseus of Ithaca. But let's not get muddled about identities. For one thing, *I* am Clytaemnestra, daughter of Tyndareus and wife of Agamemnon. Helen – my sister – is within the palace, so if you're here to join the general rabble you'd better follow me.'

At her command the massive gates were swung inward by invisible hands to reveal a spacious yet crowded courtyard within. They followed Clytaemnestra into the compound, which was surrounded by the magnificent stonework, high walls and countless windows and doorways of the palace. There were stables filled with scores of splendid horses, a dozen or more ornate chariots propped up against the palace walls, a host of richly armoured guards, and countless slaves rushing to and fro on untold errands. They had entered a city within a city, a place that teemed with people and yet was perfectly ordered.

'Things are usually busier,' Clytaemnestra commented. 'Especially since the other suitors have been arriving. But today the mighty warriors are all out hunting boar. Things have been getting a little . . . shall we say strained? . . . in the palace of late, with all those former enemies living together under one roof. I'm sure that, as men, you'll understand. So Tyndareus has taken them out into the hills for the day.'

She turned about and placed her hands on her hips, staring at them one after the other and assessing the state of their shabby clothes and battered armaments.

'I apologize for the guard,' she said, a hint of genuine kindness entering her voice for a brief moment. 'He probably thought you were brigands. He *does* have orders to keep out the more general riff-raff, but he isn't very bright in distinguishing between a commoner and a well-travelled nobleman. But the invitation was a general one and, if you truly are a prince, Odysseus of Ithaca, then you are welcome here. I'm also sorry you have to endure the welcome of a mere woman in my father's absence, but you can rest assured that both he and my husband will want an audience with you this evening. There'll be a banquet, of course, to feast on the boars they kill today, and you will all be guests of honour. But until then I'll do what I can to see you are well housed.

'The chief steward will take your guest-gifts, or you can wait to give them to Tyndareus in person if you prefer. Most do, though it makes little difference to him. He has so many swords, spears, daggers, tripods and the like that he doesn't know what to do with them any more. And nobody ever brings anything for Helen herself, poor sister. I suppose you're the same?'

'I regret to say we haven't brought any gifts at all,' Odysseus answered, his tone even and pleasant.

'Not even for the king?' Clytaemnestra asked, momentarily shocked. Then her growing look of impertinent boredom was swept away and she stared at Odysseus with a new-found interest. 'Well, that's certainly different. What strange customs you must have in your part of Greece.'

Odysseus shrugged complacently. 'We had many adventures on our journey here and, regrettably, our gifts were lost on the way. So we come empty-handed in the hope that your father will accept, in place of gifts, our services and lasting friendship.'

'We'll see,' she replied. 'But you interest me, at least, and I think Helen might find some of your qualities more than interesting.' Her eyes shot a glance at one of the windows that overlooked the courtyard, but an instant later she looked back at Odysseus as if her gaze had never left him. 'I wouldn't call you handsome, but what's one more fine figure amongst a host of fine figures? Now, I'll arrange for you and your men to receive baths and new clothes, as well as something to eat. Then you'll be taken to your rooms.'

'You still have rooms left?' Eperitus asked.

'You're not in Ithaca now.' She smiled at him. 'This is Sparta, and you're in the palace of its king. Tyndareus could house an army of suitors before he worried about having enough rooms, as you will see.'

And so, like a pack of obedient hounds, they followed the princess across the busy courtyard. The servants and soldiers barely noticed them as they entered the stream of activity, a mere ripple in the already choppy waters of palace life. But, despite their indifference, Eperitus felt that he and his comrades had crossed the threshold of a world much wider and deeper than anything any of them had experienced before, and from which none of them would emerge the same again.

Chapter Sixteen

THE GREAT HALL

Odysseus did not tell the others that he was fated to fail in his mission. Athena's words were not for their ears, he told Eperitus, and it would only demoralize them to know that Menelaus had already been chosen as Helen's husband. What would they care for alliances with other princes and kings, when they believed that Ithaca's only salvation lay in his marrying Tyndareus's daughter?

They were walking the clean, well-built corridors of the uppermost level of the palace, where the Ithacans had been assigned two rooms between them and a thick straw mattress for each man. People were everywhere, even on the upper floors — mostly household slaves or soldiers from various Greek states. The former went about their duties with vigour and concentration, owing to the large number of duties that had been imposed on them with the coming of the suitors. The latter idled about singly or in pairs, admiring the palace, stopping the overworked servants with requests for food or drink, or trying to find female slaves with time on their hands and a mind for some private relaxation. Nobody carried weapons. It was a rule of the king that all arms were to be handed in at the armoury and stored there whilst their owners remained in the palace. The chief armourer, a man of many words, told them of the near-fatal arguments this had caused, so attached were the many warriors to their weapons. But compared with the bloodshed that would have

180

occurred in the palace had Tyndareus not ordered this precaution, the price was a small one.

Eperitus sat with Odysseus on the wall of one of the third-floor balconies and looked down at the city of Sparta. They were joined by a warrior who introduced himself as Peisandros, son of Maimalos of Trachis. He was a spearman in the army of the Myrmidons, a name which he explained meant ants and was given to them for their hard-working nature. His captain was Patroclus, who had come to Sparta as the representative of Achilles.

'Why doesn't Achilles come himself?' Eperitus asked.

Peisandros laughed heartily at his question. He was a barrel-chested man with a huge beard and a roaring guffaw that shook the air.

'Why doesn't he come? Because he's still a child, that's why.'

'A child!' Odysseus exclaimed. 'But I've heard he has the respect of kings and fame that extends throughout Greece. How can a *child* exceed his elders in glory?'

'He has a great lineage,' Peisandros explained. 'His father is Peleus, whom these lands are named after, and his mother is Thetis, a sea-nymph. It's said she took him as an infant to the river Styx that flows from Hades itself, and dipped him in its waters to make him immortal. No arrow's point or sword's blade can harm him, no spear pierce him or axe slice his flesh. His tutors were Phoenix, the wise king of the Dolopes, and Chiron the centaur, so he has education beyond his years. They also taught him to fight and, my friends, if you could see him wield a spear and shield, child though he is, you would never again scoff at his age.'

'But how can a child expect to marry Helen? Why would the most beautiful woman in Greece choose him over grown men?' Eperitus asked.

Peisandros slapped a hand on his shoulder. 'Since when has marriage between royalty been for anything other than power? Achilles could still be in his mother's womb for all they care; it's his parentage and his prospects that count for them. And there are all sorts of prophecies about his future greatness. At least when we lesser nobles marry there's something more than alliances and wealth involved. Take my wife for example.' Here he paused and ordered a girl carrying a basket of barley cakes to come over. He helped himself to a handful, gave Odysseus and Eperitus a few, then sent the slave on her way with a pat on the backside. Peisandros stuffed one of the wafers into his mouth and continued. 'Now, my wife can cook, which is the most important thing, but she's a handsome lass too. She isn't a Helen, of course, but . . .'

'Tell us about Helen,' Odysseus interrupted, biting into one of the cakes. 'You must have seen her by now. Is she as beautiful as they say?'

Peisandros thought for a while in silence, looking across the valley to Mount Taygetus. 'No, she's not as beautiful as they say, because they can't describe her kind of beauty. Helen's got the best of everything a man could want, of course, and rumour has it that her real father is Zeus himself. But there's a spirit in the girl that can't be captured by words. She's too . . . *free*, I would say, though that falls short too. Even the poets tear their beards out in frustration when they see her. New words would need to be thought up, and even they would only have any meaning to those who'd actually seen her.'

'She must be wonderful,' Odysseus said, 'if she can make bards out of the toughest warriors.'

'She is, my friend, and she does. I'm no man of words – my spear talks well enough for me – but even the simplest soldier has to spend hours and days trying to dress her up in words. All of us fail, of course, and our princes and kings fare no better; but if we don't try to comprehend her in some way – to contain her within words if you like – then we'd lose our minds.'

Eperitus thought of Athena in her full immortal brilliance as he had seen her by the moon-silvered spring, and wondered if Helen had a similar effect on mortal eyes. Although he had not thought of Athena as beautiful, this was only because he did not consider the physical aspect of her being. As a goddess she was but one thing and one thing only: glorious. He had hardly been able to look at her, because in her was the immeasurable, unattainable, incomprehensible essence of perfection. She had lacked only the one shade of absolute supremacy, which belonged to Zeus himself, whom no mortal can witness in his true form and live.

'You might be fortunate enough to see her this evening,' Peisandros added, 'and then you can judge for yourselves. I've discussed her with others in my troop and we all see something different. For me she has something of the moon in her: a hard, cold, ageless beauty, aloof and alone in a world of darkness. *You* might see the brilliance of the sun, the source of the rest of your life. Or she may remind you of the sea – she does others – with a beauty that goes on for ever and is too deep to fathom. She's all of these things, I can tell you, and much more beyond your understanding. But I warn you, too: to see her is also a curse. I'll never forget her, not even when my tortured soul is sent to the halls of Hades, where they say everything is forgotten. It makes me sad to know the world I once loved will never hold the same wonder as it did before, because *she*'s taken its place in my heart. There's some kind of witchcraft in her to do that in a man.'

He fell silent and looked out over the valley again. Could Helen really have that effect on men? Eperitus wondered. Part of him did not want to find out – would rather he walk out of that palace of the damned before it was too late. But the stronger part was intrigued by Peisandros's words.

'Come now,' Odysseus said. 'Surely you don't mean the girl practises the dark arts.'

Peisandros cocked an eyebrow at him. 'Maybe she does, maybe she doesn't,' he said, 'but there's no doubt it runs in the family.'

'What do you mean?' asked Eperitus, leaning forward.

Peisandros turned to the two men and gave them a dark stare. 'I mean there are a lot of rumours about Leda, Helen's mother, and even more about Clytaemnestra. I've heard it said all Leda's children were born from eggs, and that's strange enough, but few question that Clytaemnestra is a follower of the old gods. She and Helen are as different as night and day, of course, but it doesn't mean Helen doesn't have something strange in her blood. It would explain the way she can bend any man to her will.'

Eperitus looked at Odysseus, who returned his gaze but revealed nothing of what was in his mind.

'Then let's talk no more of women, Peisandros,' the prince said. 'Tell us about the other suitors – who they are and where they've come from.'

'There's already too many to remember,' Peisandros laughed, 'and more arrive every day. But I'll name the most famous – all powerful and from good stock. First to come was Agamemnon, son of Atreus and king of Mycenae. You've met Clytaemnestra, so you already know he hasn't come as a suitor: he's here to support his brother's claim.'

'Menelaus? I already know about him,' Odysseus murmured.

'And a fine man he is, too. Rumour says he's already been chosen as Helen's husband. But that's just gossip between the men, of course,' Peisandros added, remembering Odysseus was a suitor. 'What would we know of politics, after all?

'Then there's Nauplius's son, Palamedes. He has a face like a rat, but Helen couldn't wish for a more intelligent and inventive husband. Then there's Idomeneus, king of Crete and son of Deucalion. He has all the attributes a woman could want: strength, courage, wealth and power. Good looks, too. Next comes Menestheus, son of Peteos. His father made him king of Athens at a young age and now he's come here to find a wife worthy of his position. Athens is an ambitious state, and he's confident Helen will be his.

'The most recent arrival, other than yourselves, is King Diomedes of Argos, Tydeus's son. He arrived this morning, refusing refreshment or rest so that he could join the boar hunt. When I saw him walk through the gates, I thought a god had come to preside over the festivities. I tell you now, if he isn't chosen as Helen's husband – if you'll forgive me saying so, Odysseus – then Tyndareus has already made up his mind and this whole gathering is a charade.'

At that point they heard the sound of horses' hoofs in the streets below, accompanied by the shouts and laughter of a multitude of men. The hunters were returning in good spirits.

'Roast boar tonight then,' Peisandros said, leaning over the balcony and trying to catch a glimpse of the returning warriors.

'I'd expect no less,' Eperitus commented, joining him. 'If the best warriors in Greece can't spear a couple of boars, then who can?'

The Myrmidon laughed. 'Just as long as they aren't trying to spear each other, that's all I care about.'

&

The great hall of the palace at Sparta dwarfed Laertes's throne room back on Ithaca, easily accommodating the hundreds of guests and slaves who were busy with the night's feast. At its centre were four painted columns of wide girth, supporting a ceiling so high that it was almost lost in shadow. A great pall of smoke gathered there from the central fire, curling about the rafters like a serpent upon the branches of a tree.

Every room in the palace complex was clean, roomy and magnificently decorated. The walls abounded with an endless variety of animals, birds, fishes and plants, skilfully depicted in vibrant colours that made the creatures seem alive as they stalked each other between bushes and trees, lakes and rivers. But these were only the commonplace designs, used to enrich the hundreds of functional rooms that filled the palace. The more important rooms such as the great hall and the royal quarters were decorated with scenes from legendary battles or stories concerning the gods. Some pictured mythical creatures, whilst others showed human figures at work or play: there were naked boys running foot races; others wrestling or boxing; yet more competing with javelin or discus. It was a place of such wealth and luxury that the halls of Olympus itself would have struggled to surpass it.

The hunters' return had filled the palace with the hubbub of many people. Odysseus kept his men confined to their rooms on the upper floor, but outside they could hear the many kings and princes disperse to their separate quarters to bathe and put on fresh clothing. Only when Clytaemnestra, still dressed in black, came to bid them join the feast at her father's request did the Ithacans leave and descend the broad steps to the floors below.

Filing out across the central courtyard towards the entrance to the great hall, they passed the carcasses of scores of bullocks, sacrificed to bring the blessings of the gods and feed the many revellers whom the four or five roasted boar would not. The blood ran down in thick rivulets across the muddy floor and gathered in pools of deep red. The smoke from the burned thigh-bones and fat which the priests had offered up to the gods choked the air and put a pall over the face of the early evening moon.

Before Odysseus and his men had even left their rooms the sound of the feasting had been like the hum of ten thousand bees in their ears, but as they stepped into the great hall the full force of it burst upon them like a roaring sea. Wine-lubricated tongues fought to gain ascendancy over each other as well-fed, big-voiced men shouted to be heard by their neighbours amongst the drunken cacophony. Laughter, music, excited voices, arguments and shouts from one side of the room to the other filled the air, and the babble of sound was matched by the chaos of movement. For each guest there must have been two slaves, rushing here and there with kraters of wine, baskets of bread, platters of meat and small tables on which to set them; unarmed warriors leaned across each other in vociferous debate or lolled about arm in arm, seeking either wine or women amongst the busy slaves; there were stewards and squires chasing the servants or running after their noble masters, and the whole chaotic scene moved with an instinctive, flowing rhythm that sucked the Ithacans in and dragged them inevitably towards its natural vortex.

Suddenly a man appeared from the milling crowds. 'Lord Odysseus? Tyndareus and Icarius, kings of Sparta, invite you to join them.' He pointed across the low flames of the hearth to a group of men seated together at the far end of the hall. They were locked in conversation, and paid no heed to the new arrivals. 'Food and wine is being prepared for your men, if you will follow me.'

While the others were taken to a cluster of vacant chairs guarded by three slaves, Odysseus skirted the fire and walked up to the group of kings and princes that the chief steward had indicated. As his party sat and drinking bowls full of wine were pressed into their hands, Eperitus could not help but watch his leader as he stepped proudly up to the most powerful men in Greece and stood before them until, one by one, they stopped talking and looked at the newcomer. Never in all their trials together had Eperitus felt so anxious for him.

'I am Odysseus,' he began, his voice even but audible amidst the din. 'My father is Laertes, king of Ithaca. I have heard that King Tyndareus is inviting suitors for his daughter, Helen, and I have faced many hardships to come here and name myself amongst them.'

For a while they looked at him, silently observing his ungainly bulk, poised awkwardly on his short legs, and noting his drab clothes and plain looks. But whatever his outward appearance they, more than any others in that vast room, were able to distinguish the noble look in his eyes and sense, as if they could smell it, the royal blood in his veins. The oldest and largest amongst them stood, a man whose strong presence was not due merely to his solid gut and wild black beard.

'I'm King Tyndareus,' he said. Despite the noise he did not need to raise his voice to be heard. 'You wear the signs of your travels, though any man can see you aren't of low birth – only a fool would judge a man's character by the quality of his clothing. You are welcome here, Odysseus, son of Laertes, and I don't need to remind you that you are amongst exalted company.' The king briefly named the dozen or so men who sat on either side of him, whose reputations and lineage were for the most part well known by all Greeks. 'Now, sit between Agamemnon and me and give us the story of your journey. It'll interest us to set your tale against our own adventures on the hillsides this day.'

A slave brought a high-backed chair and placed it between Tyndareus and Agamemnon, who scraped his own chair reluctantly to one side. Odysseus took his seat under the cold, appraising stares of the dozen or so high nobles from states infinitely more powerful than his own. These were the men who, if anybody could, would help him save Ithaca from Eupeithes's clutches. It was for their power and not the beauty of a girl that he had marched across the Peloponnese. Unless he was at his most persuasive now, his home, his family, his position and his renown would all be lost. So he gripped the arms of his chair and looked at the stone floor for the space of a breath, before raising his eyes to the faces of the company he had been invited to share.

Tyndareus returned his gaze in a friendly enough manner, but beside him Agamemnon remained reserved and neutral, allowing nothing of his true self to show in his eyes. His outward appearance suggested a man obsessed with detail: his white tunic was immaculate; his blood-red cloak perfect; his few adornments opulent but not excessive; his auburn hair and beard long but neatly trimmed. Power and majesty resonated from him, and yet in his practised reserve there was a deliberate, well-trained masking of the passions that burned within. Agamemnon was not a man to expose his strengths, weaknesses, thoughts or ambitions to anyone without need. But when he chose to draw away the screen, the man beneath was driven, quick and uncompromising. He had not become the most powerful man in Greece by birthright alone.

For all that, Odysseus instinctively identified something of himself in the king of Mycenae – a leader's natural insecurity and desire for control. Though he was unsure whether he liked Agamemnon, he sensed a mutual admiration that he hoped would turn to friendship.

On Tyndareus's right was Icarius, who smiled briefly and without warmth at the new arrival. Next to him sat Diomedes, the Argive prince who had recently destroyed the city of Thebes.

Like Agamemnon's, his hair was long and brown with a hint of red, but unlike the Mycenaean he did not hide his good looks behind a beard, leaving his strong jaw clean-shaven. His clothes were expensive but not showy, unlike most others gathered in the group, and despite his handsome appearance he had an aggressive, hard-bitten mien that Odysseus approved of. A long pink scar stood out on his tanned cheek, running from the top of his ear down across his jawline. He acknowledged Odysseus with a nod before beckoning to a slave for more wine.

'Aren't these islands you name in the Ionian Sea?' asked a short, black-haired man with a pinched nose and small black eyes. 'Full of rocks and sheep and little else, I'm told.'

Palamedes laughed at his own sally and looked about at the others, laughing at each one in turn until their silence quietened him.

'Yes, there are rocks and sheep,' Odysseus answered. 'Rocks and sheep, sea and fish, flowers and women, homes and families. We left all these things many days ago to witness the glory of Sparta and marvel at its most blessed child. But our journey hasn't been easy.'

And so he told the kings and princes of the hardships he and his men had faced in reaching Sparta. His voice was calm and smooth, instantly washing over them and stilling their minds. Those that were already talking fell silent and turned their heads towards him, quickly forgetting their own adventures in the boar hunt as the other sounds in the great hall faded and they heard only his words. He spoke passionately of the river, of Mentor and the news from Ithaca, of the burning trees, the battle with the Taphians, the slaying of the serpent, the death of Polybus and the meeting with Iphitus. Only one thing remained unmentioned, but Odysseus was clever enough not to make reference to his patron goddess or the things she had told him. It was enough that these men knew of his country's plight without him having to plead its cause like a beggar.

His words commanded their silence, though there were

occasional grunts of approval or noises of disgust as each event was unfolded before them. At the mention of Laertes's throne being forcibly taken from him there was even an angry murmur, but when Odysseus had ended his tale at the Taygetus Mountains, looking down over the Eurotas valley, there was no more mention of the subject. Odysseus was not disappointed. He understood that the nobility of Greece were no ordinary audience; when they spoke, lives were changed, and so they knew when to reserve their comments and when to voice them.

'You impress me, Odysseus,' Tyndareus said. 'You're a worthy suitor, even amongst such men as these. And you have my sympathies for the loss of your father's throne, which is your birthright.'

More food and wine were brought by the slaves and, with Odysseus's tale finished, the noise of the feast swept back in on them like a wave. Agamemnon leaned towards Odysseus.

'You seem like a resourceful man, friend, and not without your share of protection from the immortals. Perhaps we can test your judgement also: will you settle a small debate for us?'

'If I'm able.'

'Good. We were discussing the question of continued peace between Greek states.'

'Peace?' Odysseus replied, as if the word was new to him. 'How can there be peace when the Epigoni are making war on Thebes?'

'The war is over,' said Diomedes. 'We defeated them and took their city. Our fathers have been avenged and now there is peace.'

Odysseus looked at the scar-faced warrior, who had a clear sense of honour to his father and showed a warrior's pride in his achievements. 'It's a privilege to meet the son of Tydeus, whose fame threatens that of his own sire. And I thank you for making my point for me. Have you asked yourselves when this cycle will stop? Won't the next generation of Thebans want revenge for their dead fathers? Doesn't each of us have family feuds that began before the times of our grandfathers? I've heard that even Agamemnon and Menelaus seek the death of Aegisthus for murdering their father. This is the barrier to peace amongst our states. We're so busy avenging the transgressions caused against our forefathers that we'll never be able to live side by side ourselves. Greece is held back by the grudges of its warrior families.'

'What did I tell you?' boomed Tyndareus, triumphantly. 'Hey, Agamemnon? And you, Diomedes, echoing all this talk of unity across Greece. It's a nonsense, and you know it.'

'I didn't say it was nonsense, my lord,' Odysseus added carefully, taking a krater of wine from a passing slave. 'Warriors have always fought whomever they chose, and our fathers made their fortunes and their names by the spear and the sword. Yet the times are changing. Trade flourishes throughout Greece and across the seas to other nations, and it seems to me that the era of military expansion is being replaced by a time of consolidation. Our enemies are now our neighbours, whether we like it or not.'

'So will there be peace, even with the feuding?' asked Menelaus. He was a young, well-built man with red-brown hair, thinning on top, and a black beard. His pale face was authoritative but kind, and yet his brow was furrowed as he addressed Odysseus. 'I for one will never forgive my cousin for killing my father, even if my brother could countenance it. It dishonours my family and it dishonours me.'

'That's a question for yourself, Menelaus,' Odysseus answered. 'But for me, I think there *is* one thing that could bring the Greeks together.'

Agamemnon folded his hands in his lap and retreated behind his neutral, unimpassioned look. 'What's that?'

Odysseus did not answer immediately, but picked up a slice of boar from the platter in front of him and crammed it into his mouth. He chewed it and washed it down with wine before looking into the cold blue eyes of Agamemnon.

'A mutual enemy will unite Greece. We share a common tongue and follow the same gods as each other, so what Greece needs is an outsider who doesn't. Any gibberish-talking foreigner who gives us a reason to fight would suffice. That and an oath between kings, the most sacred and binding oath ever taken.'

The Spartan wine was strong and had already worked its way to Eperitus's head. All around him his companions were adding their own noise to the general cacophony as the wine oiled their tongues. Hard-worked slaves brought them a constant supply of meat and drink, and with much-tested patience did little more than grin or nod apathetically at the drunken suggestions and comments that were offered them. The women in particular had grown used to the lewd attentions of the hundreds of men in the palace; they smiled and flirted their way free of their embraces and like a mountain breeze were heading back to the kitchens, larders or wine cellars before the soldiers knew it.

They were soon engaged by the group of warriors next to them, who came from Lindos on the island of Rhodes. They were fascinated with the tales of the Ithacans' adventures, and sympathetic to the point of anger when they told them their king had been overthrown in their absence. It was an outrage to them that Ithaca, a place they had never heard of before, should be ruled by foreign invaders. Being islanders themselves, they understood what it was like to have a border set by the sea, where the sense of belonging to a homeland was so much stronger. From that point on they adopted the exiled Ithacans as their own, and both parties sought each other every night in the great hall throughout the months they remained in Sparta.

The Rhodians had been amongst the very first to arrive and had already been in the city for several days. Their second-in-command was a brash, fierce-looking man called Gyrtias, who quickly became good friends with Halitherses due to the rank they shared.

'There he is,' he announced to Halitherses, though loudly enough for all of the Ithacans to hear. He pointed a thick arm that was stiff with muscles at a slight figure seated behind the higher nobles. 'Prince Tlepolemos of Rhodes. A more handsome and worthier Greek has not yet been born. *That* is the man who will marry Helen.'

Eperitus looked and saw a baby-faced youth who was struggling to grow a beard and had not yet developed any muscles to speak of. He simpered at the back of the group with his pale brown locks falling in front of his eyes, and Eperitus could only wonder at how out of place the young prince looked amongst such proud men.

Gyrtias went on to name the other kings and princes who had arrived so far. Never before had Eperitus seen such a magnificent assembly of men. It was almost unbelievable, he thought, that in so short a space of time he had risen from being an outcast from his own land to become an attendant to the highest royalty in the Greek-speaking world. Here before him were men whose collective power was beyond belief. When the assembly was complete they would represent almost every nation and dynasty of importance in the whole of Greece. Most had fathers whose fame was legendary, but many were great warriors in their own right. More significantly, they represented the ripening youth of Greek nobility.

Before Gyrtias could finish naming each man and his lineage, a new group of men entered the hall. They were dressed all in black and all eyes turned to watch them as they approached the twin thrones where Tyndareus and Icarius sat.

'Myrmidons,' Gyrtias grumbled as Eperitus recognized his friend Peisandros amongst them.

They halted before the grouped kings and bowed, before dispersing into the crowd. This impressed him, as good manners were a sign of honourable men, and so he could not understand the hostility in Gyrtias's voice. Only one man remained, standing stiff and awkward before the twin thrones. From behind, Eperitus guessed he was the same age as himself, though he was taller and more sinewy, and as he had been at the head of the Myrmidons he also assumed him to be their leader, Patroclus. Tyndareus beckoned him to join the royal gathering and a slave brought a stool for the newcomer, but to Eperitus's surprise it was placed on the floor before the raised dais upon which the other leaders sat.

'Why doesn't he sit with the others?' Mentor asked, echoing Eperitus's thoughts.

'Because he isn't high-born,' Gyrtias answered, staring scornfully at the new arrival. 'He's just a commoner like you or me, here to represent Achilles. Thinks he's better than the rest of us though, the arrogant bastard. They're all arrogant, Myrmidons.'

Patroclus sat and Eperitus saw his face for the first time. He had a large nose and high cheekbones, set in a triangular, clean-shaven face. This was balanced atop a scrawny neck that was dominated by the boulder-like lump in his throat. He had an affected expression of disdain which was made more hateful by his half-lidded, disapproving eyes, though whether he disapproved of the rabble of common soldiers to his right or the elitist kings to his left was not clear.

'Now there's a sight for men who've marched halfway across the Peloponnese,' said Damastor.

Eperitus followed his gaze to where a young woman had entered the great hall. Her dark brown hair was long and tied up in a tail that dangled from the back of her head, flicking about gaily with every movement. She was tall, perhaps only a little shorter than himself, and her slim body was hidden by a green dress that fell to her ankles. Her assured self-confidence marked her out as a member of the ruling class, though she lacked the arrogance and disdain common to others of her rank.

'So that's Helen?' he said aloud, to nobody in particular.

'Helen?' Gyrtias scoffed. 'That's not Helen, lad. That's Icarius's daughter, Penelope.'

Odysseus looked up as Penelope approached the dais and his conversation with Agamemnon and Diomedes fell away. He could scarce take his eyes from her as she moved through the press of men, entranced by the beauty of her movement and the perfect, calm symmetry of her face. If this was Helen, he thought, it would have been worth the journey just to set eyes upon her. As she reached the raised platform, he stood and quickly patted the creases from his drab clothing.

'Tyndareus, your daughter's reputation is well deserved,' he began, bowing low but unable to take his eyes from her intelligent, pretty face. 'No wonder the best men in Greece are flocking to Sparta.'

Penelope put her fists on her hips and tilted her head, frowning at him from beneath her smooth brow.

'Fortunate, isn't it, that intelligence isn't a requirement amongst the best men in Greece,' she said. Then, having dismissed the newest of Helen's suitors, she turned to Tyndareus. 'Uncle, your queen sends her apologies and asks me to tell you that Helen will be here shortly.'

Tyndareus nodded. 'Can't she find the right dress again?'

'Perhaps she has too many, uncle,' Penelope replied. 'But I think the dress she has chosen emphasizes her best features.'

'Good! That's what my guests are here to see.'

'You may not be so pleased when she arrives.' Penelope smiled wryly. 'But all will be revealed.'

She bowed her head and turned to go.

'Penelope!' Icarius said sternly. 'I didn't bring you up to be rude to strangers. Perhaps you should be less harsh in future to Prince Odysseus.'

With her back still turned she took a deep breath and closed her eyes. 'I'm sorry, my lord,' she said, though it was not clear to whom she was apologizing. Then she looked at Odysseus and added sincerely, 'I hope I didn't cause offence.'

Odysseus still smarted from the humiliation, which was made worse by his attraction to the woman.

'It would take more than your low wit to offend me,' he replied.

Penelope shot him an angry look before turning on her heel and marching off into the crowd of revellers.

'You were saying about King Priam,' Odysseus reminded Agamemnon, his eyes following Icarius's daughter into the mass of slaves and warriors.

Agamemnon, whose own gaze had also been fixed on Penelope, nodded and placed a finger to his lips. 'Already I can see we share similar views, Odysseus, so I'll bring you into my confidence. But these things aren't for all ears. Not yet.'

Together, he and Diomedes explained in hushed voices how Troy was demanding tribute from all merchants passing through the Aegean. Not only was it an affront to all Greeks, they said, it also threatened to become a stranglehold on the trade that the Greek states depended and thrived on.

Odysseus drained his cup. 'So what do you propose?'

'Anything necessary to keep the peace here,' said Diomedes. 'We're considering a combined raid on Ilium, the land around Troy, to sack a couple of Priam's allied cities. Something to give the Greek states a common purpose. But we need to have all the kings on our side, or else who would take their armies across the Aegean if there were enemies still at home? This gathering is an ideal chance to hold a council of war.'

'I'm all for an alliance between the Greek states,' Odysseus began. 'Especially if it keeps peace between us all. But putting this idea into practice is another matter altogether.'

The others were no longer listening. Instead their eyes were looking past him to the open portals of the great hall, which had fallen suddenly silent. Odysseus turned.

Two women stood at the entrance. One was tall and slim with long black hair, streaked grey at the temples; only a few wrinkles at the corners of her eyes marked her age. She would have dominated the gathered warriors with her powerful beauty, were it not for the presence of her younger companion.

Helen of Sparta had arrived.

Chapter Seventeen

DAUGHTERS OF LACEDAEMON

A hush spread across the hall as Helen stood before the gathered warriors. The words died in their mouths and the drinking cups froze in their hands. It was as if Medusa herself had entered, and with one look turned them all to stone.

She was tall with long black hair and white skin that looked as if it had never seen the sun. Her eyes were like burning ice and as she looked about at the crowded hall they set a cold fire running through the veins of every man. Peisandros was right, Eperitus realized: the words did not exist that could describe her. She was like a mountain that a man sees from afar and wants to climb, so he can tell himself he is better than the mountain. But Helen possessed no fault in which a man could gain a foothold. There was no blemish or imperfection with which the spectators in the great hall could pull her down to their level. She soared above every warrior, every prince, every king, until it was an agony for them to look at her, knowing they had been defeated by a woman's looks.

And yet, if her beauty cut deep into their souls, she had other weapons that struck at their corporeal natures. Though only a girl of seventeen years, she was fully a woman and had the ruthless confidence to display it. She had come barefoot into the great hall and wore only a white dress of the thinnest material, which hid little of the naked body beneath. No man in that room was left in any doubt of what Helen had to offer her chosen husband.

Eperitus's sense of honour told him that the mind of a better man would dwell upon her perfect face and not upon her perfect body, and yet he was a slave to his animal nature. By her mere presence she had made pigs of every man in the room, exposing their high ideals and their heroic codes and letting them feed in the troughs of their base natures. Eperitus felt ashamed, but could not avert his eyes.

Then the older woman threw a cloak about Helen's shoulders and released the assembled warriors from the fierce grip of her spell. Men looked at each other and spoke in hushed voices. More wine doused dry throats and sluggish movements returned to the organism that had taken possession of the great hall. But the noble suitors, the men who had come to claim her, remained in silent thrall as Helen approached the dais where her foster-father sat. The older woman followed, like a tutor presenting her prize pupil.

'She isn't interested in any of them, you know.'

Gyrtias sat down next to Eperitus and held out a platter of bread and meat.

'What do you mean?' he asked, taking a handful of each.

The soldier from Rhodes took some of the food for himself and washed it down with a slop of wine that spilled over his beard. 'I spoke with one of Helen's slave girls this morning and asked what her mistress thought of Prince Tlepolemos. It took a bit of persuasion, but the girl's a bit simple so I got what I wanted in the end. She told me Helen isn't interested in Tlepolemos or any of the suitors. She thinks her father and King Agamemnon will choose her husband for her, so she's planning to run away!'

Eperitus laughed at the suggestion. 'Does she really think she can just slip off into the night? Every man in Sparta would be hunting for her, and with a face like that she wouldn't be hard to follow. Besides, she should be happy to have any of Greece's finest men for a husband.'

'She isn't, though,' Gyrtias assured him. 'She detests being a pawn in Agamemnon's political games, and doesn't have much love for Tyndareus either. She believes her real father to be Zeus, so the will of Tyndareus means nothing to her. The maid claims she would even run away with a common warrior, just to spite him. Can you imagine it, a commoner?'

Eperitus looked over at the princess as she stood tall and proud amidst the throng of nobles who had stepped down to meet her. Her chaperone – who he assumed was Leda – had joined Tyndareus and looked on approvingly as her daughter stood like a white candle in a crowd of moths. Did any of them realize she was simply mocking their attentions? Suddenly, insanely, Eperitus imagined Helen and himself escaping through the darkness of the night, over the passes of the Taygetus Mountains to freedom. Visions of her perfect face and godlike physique electrified his mind and he felt excited at the incredible thought. But as quickly as the fantastic notion had seized him, it faded away again. His grandfather had told him many times that the greatest enemies of a fighting man were death and women. And the oracle's words provided a much greater warning: 'The hero should beware love, for if she clouds his desires he will fall into the Abyss.'

2

Odysseus looked at the crowd that stood about Helen. How could they ever hope to possess her? he thought. But as he watched her receive their praise, her even and faultless features meeting their words with little more than a nod or a wry smile, even a yawn, he could not blame them for wanting her. There was something magical about the princess that surpassed the purely physical beauty she had in abundance. Some of this allure lay in the elusiveness with which she taunted their ambitions, challenging them to claim her for themselves. Some looked on her as a boar to be hunted or a horse to be broken in, whilst others simply despaired. But none received anything more than her contempt, and of them all only Odysseus knew beyond the slightest ember of a hope that she would not be his; and so he sat back and watched the others expend themselves upon her.

Until her bored gaze wandered beyond the group that imprisoned her and fell unexpectedly on him.

In an instant, Odysseus was pierced to the core by the sudden shock of her beauty. All his plans to ignore her and seek alliances amongst her suitors trembled about him. In the lingering moment that her clear blue eyes probed his he looked into his heart and questioned the things he valued most. Would he give up Ithaca for her sake, she seemed to ask? Would he forget even his family and friends to be with her?

And he knew the answer was no. The spell was broken, the challenge met. Helen had tested him, damaged him, almost defeated him, and only his love for his home saved him from her. But he understood now what was most powerful and dangerous about this woman. In that brief instant he realized she must have looked at each of her suitors in the same way, questioning their individual values and breaking each of them in turn. He freed himself from the gaze that had locked them together and scanned the hall for his countrymen. He finally found them in the throng and was surprised to see the wilful daughter of Icarius, Penelope, standing before them.

'You're a curious man, Odysseus,' Tyndareus said beside him. He, Icarius and Odysseus were the only three who had not risen to greet the princess. 'You travel halfway across Greece, facing all manner of dangers to see my daughter, and now you sit by without a word to say. You must have strange customs on Ithaca.'

On hearing her husband's words, Leda looked at Odysseus with mild amusement in her eyes. 'What kind of a suitor ignores the woman he longs to marry?'

'Maybe he does not want to marry me,' Helen said, stepping onto the broad dais to stand before Odysseus.

'Why else would I be here, my lady?' he replied, bowing his head.

The suitors resumed their places without removing their eyes from the princess. Only Agamemnon remained standing, sending furtive glances across the room at Penelope. Helen took his seat and faced Odysseus, her cloak falling open to reveal the gossamer-thin dress beneath. It was a wonder that human hands could make material so fine, yet Helen was more than worthy of its craftsmanship. It was like a thin mist that gave tantalizing glimpses of the naked form beneath. But at the same time she fixed him with her eyes, offering him the agonizing choice between her face and her body. He chose neither, and instead beckoned a slave to refill his drinking cup.

'Where do you come from, Odysseus? Are you powerful and rich like Diomedes?' At the mention of his name – Helen's first recognition of him – Diomedes sat up. His noble nature did not begrudge Odysseus the princess's attention, though he envied him for it. 'Or are you one of the lesser royals, hoping to increase your country's might by marrying the daughter of the Spartan king?'

'Co-king,' Odysseus reminded her, sensing every eye was upon them. 'In answer to your first question, I'm from Ithaca; in answer to your second and third, I am very much a lesser royal. As for seeking a marriage of power, I doubt that a man of my standing would get very far with the great Helen of Sparta.'

As he spoke, Helen touched her foot against the thick calf muscles of his leg, rubbing her toes briefly and seductively against his skin. The cloak opened further to reveal more of her perfect body, and Odysseus recognized that her provocative manner was practised and compelling. But he sensed this was a façade, not the real Helen.

'Then why would a man travel all the way from an island in the Ionian Sea to pay court to a princess in Sparta, whom he had never seen before and had no hope of marrying?'

Surprised that she knew of Ithaca, Odysseus was even more intrigued by her shrewd insinuation that he had not come to Sparta for her. He was suddenly aware that, though young, Helen had an intelligence to match her outstanding looks, and that he must be careful around her. More importantly, he had to be mindful not to fall for the charms of a girl whom Zeus had already decreed should marry another. Whatever her reasons for flirting with him, whether they were born of genuine attraction or of more deceitful motives, he could not allow her to distract him from his mission.

'My country is humble and distanced from the central powers of Greece,' he replied. 'Our life is simple and carefree. But in a land of ease a man must go beyond his home borders to experience the world. When I heard the most beautiful woman in Greece was to be married, I thought I should like to see her for myself. That she could show any interest in an island prince was beyond my expectations, and still is, but it does no harm to worship an earthly divinity.'

'Your rough looks belie a fine character,' Helen remarked. 'I think I should be happy on Ithaca, if it produces such a breed of well-spoken men.'

Odysseus was about to say she would be welcome there, and that her presence would turn every Ithacan into a bard, but as he opened his mouth to speak Clytaemnestra joined them.

'Always dreaming of running away, sister. Isn't it a shame you're a woman, and your destiny is ever in the hands of others.' She looked about at the seated nobles. 'Where's my husband?'

'Where do you think?' Helen answered. 'Snooping after Penelope, as usual.'

Eperitus looked up at Penelope as she stood before the seated soldiers with her hands on her hips and a smile upon her face.

'Welcome to Sparta, men of Ithaca,' she greeted them. 'I am Penelope, daughter of King Icarius. I hope your needs are met, but if not I'll do what I can to help you feel more at ease in our home.'

'You can tell us whether Odysseus will win Helen's hand in marriage,' Damastor asked, to the cheers and laughter of the others. Gyrtias and his Rhodians jeered mockingly and received a hail of bread and barley cakes in response.

'Is he the red-haired one with short legs and arms like tree trunks?' Penelope replied. 'Then I hope his clumsy charms are more effective on my cousin than they were on me.'

There was another roar of laughter. Warming to the young woman in their drunkenness, the warriors offered her wine and a seat, which she accepted.

'And what about you, my lady?' Eperitus asked. 'Are you married?'

She looked at him and grinned. 'Are you suggesting I should be?'

'I am,' he said, encouraged by the wine.

'Yes,' Antiphus added with a laugh. 'To him!'

'Are these men bothering you, Penelope?'

'No, Lord Agamemnon,' she answered stiffly, as the Mycenaean king appeared beside her.

He slipped his hand about her slim waist, his thumb almost touching her breast. The soldiers fell silent as he stood before them in his immaculate clothes and golden armour (which he wore at all times for fear of assassination). Eperitus felt a strong dislike for him, irked partly by the king's arrogance and partly by the arm about Penelope's waist. He noticed her flinch slightly as Agamemnon's arm encompassed her and felt a surprising urge to defend her from his possessive touch. He could not understand why she did not remove herself from the king's embrace, though perhaps she knew better than to resist the advances of the most powerful man in Greece, who rumour said would frequently take lovers from slaves and nobility alike.

'These are Odysseus's men,' Penelope explained. 'I was simply welcoming them and trying to make them feel more comfortable. The palace can be an overawing experience for those who haven't been here before.'

'I've heard of the fate of your home, and you have my sympathy,' he said. The men grunted, approving of Agamemnon's recognition. 'Who's in charge here?'

Halitherses stood and took a step forward.

'I am, my lord. Halitherses, son of Mastor.'

'Tell me, Halitherses, if Ithaca went to war how many men could it muster? How many ships?'

Agamemnon had already put the same question to Odysseus, but to ask the captain of his guard would let him know whether the prince had been honest or was hiding his real strength. It would also make the men think he cared about their opinion, which would earn their loyalty if they were ever to fight under his command.

'Nobody really knows, my lord,' Halitherses answered. 'We've never had to summon every man to war before. But I should estimate that from all our islands we could fill twenty galleys with men able to fight, whilst leaving enough men to defend our homeland in our absence.'

'Over a thousand warriors,' Agamemnon said, nodding. 'And how many men could be sent on a prolonged campaign, keeping sufficient at home to carry on normal life?'

'Perhaps ten galleys, sir.'

At that moment Penelope saw Clytaemnestra approaching and released herself from the king's grip in a quick, graceful movement. Agamemnon acknowledged his wife's presence with a cold nod, but no familiar arm was placed about her hard, thin body.

'Thank you, Halitherses,' he continued. 'You should know I have every respect for Odysseus. He and I are like-minded men. Now, carry on your drinking and find yourselves some willing girls to warm your beds tonight.'

The men cheered his words and there was a riot of speculation amongst them as he led the two women back to their fathers. Eperitus and Halitherses, disquieted by his questions, exchanged concerned looks.

Eperitus was the first of the Ithacans to leave the feast. He sat on the balcony adjacent to his quarters and looked out over the city of Sparta and the plains beyond, where the clear moonlight reflected from the winding course of the Eurotas river. His mind was full of the events of the evening, when from the corner of his eye he saw a young girl approaching and turned to face her. She bowed and asked if he was one of the party of Ithacans.

'I am with them, though not an Ithacan,' he replied. 'Who are you?'

'My lady sent me – she must speak with you about an urgent matter. Meet her in the temple of Aphrodite tomorrow night, after the evening's feast has begun. Come alone and tell no one.'

Her errand accomplished, the slave did not stay to be questioned. She ran off into the shadows at the end of the corridor and disappeared down the steps to the second floor.

Chapter Eighteen

SECRET LIAISONS

The streets of Sparta were quiet and dark. The moon had not yet risen, and when it did would remain hidden behind the thick rain clouds that were filling the sky. Several times Eperitus stumbled in the deep wheel-ruts that numerous wagons had carved into the road, and though the palace armourer had given him directions to the temple of Aphrodite he felt sure he was now lost in the eerily empty streets. The only sounds came from the palace at the top of the hill, where the feast he had just left was at its height.

He clutched the hilt of his sword, comforted by its presence. These past two days, since arriving in Sparta, he had felt naked without his weapons. Only his mission outside the palace walls had given him the right to have his sword returned, and now he felt whole again and capable of taking on any enemy who dared confront him. But the safe streets of Sparta posed no threat, beyond the danger of being endlessly trapped within its unlit labyrinth of thoroughfares. The only encounter he expected was in the temple, though he could not guess who would want to speak with one of Odysseus's men, or why.

He turned a corner and saw a flickering pool of light cast across the road, coming from an open doorway. Bats squeaked over his head as he approached. Soon he was able to see that the building was not a dwelling but a temple. Even if this was not the temple of Aphrodite the attendant priest would point him in the direction of his goal so, loosening the sword in his belt, he went in.

The two wooden doors were wide open. They led into a chamber that was a little smaller than the hall in the palace at Ithaca. Its floor was paved with evenly cut flagstones and a row of painted wooden columns reached from either side of the entrance, forming an aisle that led to a sacrificial altar. This had been plastered with white clay which, in turn, was marked with dark stains that could not be identified in the gloom. Fixed into the wall behind the altar were two torches, the only sources of light in the shadowy temple. These stood on either side of a raised platform, on which stood the clay figurine of a goddess. It was as tall as his sword, with voluptuous curves and large breasts, but as Eperitus stepped closer he could see that the face was grotesque, deliberately distorted into a demonic expression.

He shook off the feeling of unease it put into him and looked about the temple. In one corner were an empty mattress and a heaped blanket where the priestess usually slept. He had brought a few barley cakes with him, taken from the feast to give as an offering to the goddess, so in her absence he slipped these from his pouch and placed them on the altar. When she returned the priestess would keep some for her own needs and see that the rest were offered to the deity.

There were alcoves in the walls that housed smaller but equally ugly figurines, their features leering out into the chamber. The shifting orange light of the torches showed only small details, but he was also able to catch glimpses of the murals that decorated the temple walls. These showed images of men and women copulating in every position imaginable – and some unimaginable – confirming beyond doubt that he had found the temple of Aphrodite, goddess of love. Being inexperienced in love-making, some of the pictures confused him, and the bodies of the lovers needed unravelling before he understood what they were doing. Others he found disturbing, but whether mystifying or sickening all were intriguing.

Some of the murals depicted women being raped by gods, well-known tales from the lost era when mankind and immortals intermingled freely together. Almost without exception the god or their victim would be transformed into some variety of beast, bird or plant, and the different metamorphosis in each mural identified which story was being explicitly recalled. Only one was unknown to him: a painting of a great swan standing over a naked woman, who writhed in ecstasy beneath its broad wingspan.

As he looked, a shape broke free from the shadows below the mural. It moved towards him, causing him to jerk the sword free of his belt and hold it out before the approaching phantom. Sensing danger, he watched the figure emerge into the light. Then he saw the long hair, the curve of her hips and the press of her breasts beneath her cloak. It was Helen.

'Put down your weapon and explain yourself,' she commanded. 'Who are you and what are you doing here?'

Even in the shadowy gloom of the temple her beauty was stunning; standing only a sword thrust away from her, it turned Eperitus's limbs to stone and stole his thoughts. Strangely, in this place dedicated to lust and carnality, the girl looked fresh and young, a vision of purity and innocence. There was no trace of the Helen who had stunned the great hall into silence only the night before. But she remained powerfully enchanting, so much so that he had to force himself to summon a response to her questions.

'I am Eperitus of Alybas.' He put his sword back into his belt, aware of how ridiculous he looked pointing it at her. 'I received a message to meet someone here.'

'Some common whore, no doubt,' Helen said, disdainfully. 'Anyway, she isn't here so you can go.'

'I'm going nowhere,' Eperitus insisted, angered by the girl's arrogance. Despite her divine beauty, she reminded him of a spoilt child too used to getting her own way.

'Do you know who I am?' she spat. 'Now, leave at once or I'll have my father throw you out of the city!'

'Not before I've told him you've been leaving the safety of the palace. He wouldn't like that, would he, with all these great warriors around?' Eperitus caught her hand as it swept towards his cheek. 'So why don't you tell me what it is *you're* doing here, Helen of Sparta?'

She shook herself free of his grip and glared at him with furious eyes. 'I'm here to meet one of Odysseus's men, if you must know.'

'Then it was *you*?'

Helen looked at him with equal surprise. 'You mean to say *you're* the one my maid spoke to? Neaera!'

A figure emerged from the shadows behind the open doors of the temple and came to stand at Helen's shoulder. Eperitus recognized her as the same young girl who had spoken to him the night before. She peered at his face in the wavering torchlight and nodded.

'It's him, mistress – the one I gave your message to.'

'Very well, Neaera,' Helen said. 'You can wait outside now – but stay close.'

Once the slave had moved out into the narrow street – where her cloaked form could still be seen in the darkness – Helen returned her gaze to Eperitus, scrutinizing him closely.

'Why did you say you were from Alybas, not Ithaca?'

'I was exiled from my homeland,' Eperitus explained. 'Odysseus recruited me into his guard. Now perhaps you'll tell me why you want to speak to a mere soldier?'

'Why not?' she answered, playfully raising an eyebrow. 'I like your prince, and who better than one of his men to know whether *he* likes *me*?'

'Who better?' the warrior replied, shocked that the most beautiful woman in Greece could find the curious, ungainly bulk of Odysseus attractive. 'Why not Odysseus himself?'

'Because he would have been followed,' Helen answered. 'Tyndareus is paranoid; he likes to keep an eye on all the suitors. But he doesn't care about soldiers like you. You can roam around with relative freedom.'

'All the same, I can't say what Odysseus's feelings for you are, my lady. But he *is* here to pay court to you, so that must mean something.'

'It means nothing. We both know these suitors are here as much for the chance to inherit Tyndareus's throne as they are to win me. I doubt whether any of them could give me true love, and I certainly couldn't love any of *them*. But Odysseus might be different: he comes from the other side of Greece, a poor island with no ambitions about war or trade. Someone like him might love me for who I am, not what I am. *Could* he love me, Eperitus?'

Her fingers reached out and gripped his arm, as if trying to squeeze an answer from him. Eperitus thought of Athena's words by the stream and wondered whether the goddess could have been wrong about Menelaus. 'Would you marry him if he could?'

'Not in Sparta,' Helen said. She turned away and walked over to look at the mural of the giant swan and its human lover. There was something familiar about the features of the woman, Eperitus thought, following the princess's gaze. It was difficult to say in the half-light, but it was as if the artist had tried to make the depiction individual, to stand out from the generic portrayals of the other figures.

'Tyndareus wants me to marry so that he'll have a successor. But I have no respect for Tyndareus or his ambitions. Does that shock you?'

'Not all fathers deserve respect.'

Eperitus looked again at the mural. The swan stood over the naked woman, who lay below it with her knees raised and her legs apart, her head thrown back in profile so that the long hair cascaded onto the floor. The hair was black and streaked with a band of white that sprouted from her temple. It was Leda.

'To marry in Sparta would be to honour his wishes,' Helen continued, looking over her shoulder at him. 'So I want to run away. I want to escape from this palace, all palaces, and live a simple life. If Odysseus took me to Ithaca I would marry him.'

In his amazement Eperitus forgot the mural of Helen's mother and looked into Helen's eyes. He also forgot that Ithaca no longer belonged to Odysseus. At that moment he could think only of them stealing away the most beautiful woman in Greece to live on an island in the Ionian Sea.

'But could you love him?' he asked.

'I don't know. I would want to, if he took me away from the clutches of powerful, ambitious men. But tell me, are there bays and secret coves on Ithaca, where a woman can swim alone without being followed by a dozen admirers and twice as many slaves?'

'Lots, I think,' Eperitus said. 'I know there are plenty of caves to hide in. And hilltops where you can see people coming from a long way off.'

She smiled and touched his cheek, and he understood then how a man could willingly die for her. Despite her arrogance and her impenetrable allure, there was a girl beneath it all who would make the perfect queen for Ithaca. Or perhaps she would consider the exiled son of a nobleman, from a place even more remote than Ithaca. Gyrtias had said she would run away with a common warrior, and what Eperitus had heard from her own lips did not discourage the idea. Would she elope with a man who had neither wealth, home nor family? The light in her eyes told him that anything was possible.

'Oh, it's you,' Penelope said. She sat on a stone bench in the palace gardens, where it was her habit to come every night before going to her bed. This part of the palace was often deserted in the evenings, especially when a feast was being held, so it was with surprise that she saw the Ithacan prince come strolling across the lawn towards her. 'The gardens are usually quiet at this time of night.'

Odysseus looked at the princess and felt again the attraction that had struck him the night before. He had regretted his reaction several times since then, and though he still smarted from her insult he was nevertheless pleased to find her alone in the quiet gardens.

'I've come to escape the clamour of the great hall,' he

explained. 'It's not what I'm used to. But I'll be happy to return and leave you to your thoughts, if you wish.'

'Do as you please, my lord. With feasts every night and guests everywhere it's been difficult to find time to oneself, but if you insist on staying . . .'

'Well, if you insist on asking,' he said, sitting down beside her and looking up at the cloud-filled sky. Penelope moved to the far edge of the bench. 'Are the feasts always this grand?'

'Grand? Well, I suppose they look that way to simple folk. They get much bigger when there's something to celebrate. If you're invited to Helen's marriage banquet, you'll see what I mean.'

Odysseus knew exactly what she meant, but took no offence. Her sharp wit and intelligence were appealing, even when directed at him, and he knew it must be difficult for the young woman when her cousin was the centre of attention all the time.

'Talking of Helen,' he said, looking about himself once more. 'I notice she isn't at the feast tonight. Do you know where she might be?'

'No. She only comes to a few, and then not for long. I would imagine she finds all that attention nauseating. Most evenings she remains in her quarters with her slave girls, or with her mother.'

'And what do you do?'

'Me?' Penelope replied, surprised that he should ask. 'Sometimes I sew. Sometimes I visit Helen's tutors – she has the finest in the Peloponnese, though she hardly appreciates them. Other times I just sit here and enjoy the quiet.'

'And the feasts?'

'Not if I can avoid them,' she admitted with a reluctant laugh. 'But I'll come if new guests have arrived. You princes and kings are always well met, but your men are given nothing more than a cup of wine and a place to sit. That's why I make it my job to welcome them. It may have been my curse to be born a woman, but where men fail to show true hospitality our sex must do what honour requires. I can say with pride that no man shall leave Sparta feeling they didn't receive the right words of welcome.'

'It's good to honour the traditions of *xenia*,' Odysseus agreed. 'The gods demand it of us. My men . . .' He paused, wondering whether to make the admission.

'Yes?'

'My men have spoken highly of you today.'

They looked away from each other, Penelope smiling with pleasure while Odysseus frowned with embarrassment. He turned back a moment later, but could think of nothing to say. In the face of Penelope's prickly attitude he wanted to offset his compliment with a barbed comment or, at worst, a thinly disguised insult, but the words would not come. Instead he found himself looking at the back of her head, its long brown hair tied up in a tail on top. The skin of her neck and arms was unfashionably tanned and he could see the fine hairs bleached a light colour by the sun. Her clothes were plain, as was her face, though in a pleasant, faultless and undemanding way. No, the insult that excused his earlier praise of the woman would not come.

'So you won't join the feast tonight?'

'No.' She turned back to him and, pulling a disapproving face, shook her head so that the tail of hair frisked about behind her.

'Afraid of the attentions of all those men?'

'Pah! They're not here to see *me*. It's Helen or nobody for them.'

Odysseus wondered at the stupidity of men. While Penelope might not possess the untouchable beauty of her cousin, she was warm where Helen was aloof, quick and clever where Helen was selfish and irritable; it was like comparing the glacial beauty of winter with the freshness of an autumn day.

'Are you disappointed?' he asked with curiosity.

A large spot of rain slapped onto the stretch of stone bench that separated them, causing them both to look up at the swollen sky above.

'Of course not,' she said, defensively. 'I don't rue her the attentions of that pack of oafs.'

'Oafs?' Odysseus scoffed. He put a large hand down onto the bench, narrowing the distance she had put between them. More spots fell onto the flagstones at their feet, whilst others bounced off the leaves in the shrubs and bushes of the garden. 'Surely a princess like you must see good qualities in some of them. And there'll be a whole host of disappointed princes when Helen is married.'

Penelope conceded him a nod. 'Maybe I was a bit harsh. Menelaus is kind-hearted, but . . . But not for me.'

'Idomeneus is wealthy,' Odysseus suggested.

'And what would I want with wealth? No, if I had to choose, I think I would like Diomedes.'

Odysseus removed his hand with a frown. 'Diomedes, eh? Yes, a good choice. He's a fine man. Just as Helen is a fine-looking woman. Of all the women I've seen in Sparta, I would choose her every time.'

Now it was Penelope's turn to withdraw. Her cheeks flushed red.

'Well, Odysseus of Ithaca, I doubt very much she'd be interested in *you*.'

'Do you?' he replied tartly. 'Then why was I the only suitor she spoke to last night?'

'Perhaps she finds your peasant wit amusing.'

Odysseus scowled. 'Maybe if your tongue weren't so sharp you'd have your own suitors, instead of having to disparage Helen's. It sounds to me like jealousy!'

Penelope stood and glowered at him. 'How dare you, you . . .'

Unable to finish her sentence, Penelope stormed back into the palace. Odysseus watched her go, feeling the impact of the raindrops increasing on his skin and hearing the growing hiss as they fell into the foliage about him. After a while he stood and left the lonely gardens, stirred by a blend of anger and regret.

The days passed with a feast each night. The Ithacans were quickly drawn into a routine of idleness during the day and drinking themselves senseless in the evening. Whereas they would normally wake at dawn to go about their daily chores, in Sparta they were waited on by the hundreds of slaves at the palace and had little to do for themselves. So they awoke later each day, and if the previous night's feasting had been particularly heavy then they would not rise until after noon.

Then Halitherses, who was concerned for their fitness and battle-readiness, began to order weapon practice, rousing them at first light and taking them into the courtyard with wooden sticks to rehearse a number of drills he had thought up. It kept them busy. At first the other warriors would come and watch them, standing about in groups or leaning out of the many windows that overlooked the compound. They would cheer and jeer, shout useful advice and suggestions or mock them.

But soon the numerous captains from across the mainland and islands of Greece began following Halitherses's example. They would drill their men along the lines the Ithacans had adopted, adding or leaving out various moves as befitted their own weaponry, armour and style of warfare. Eventually they practised against each other, until every day the courtyard was filled with men fighting mock battles with lengths of wood.

At other times Halitherses would take his men on marches through the Eurotas valley. They would climb hills or follow small ravines into the mountains, returning each time just before sunset. At first they would rush to have the slaves bathe them before going down to the evening's feast, where they would meet with Gyrtias and his men, and the others with whom they became familiar during their shared drills. Eperitus would often have a drink with Peisandros, who introduced him to the other Myrmidons so that they became fast friends over the days and weeks. But as Halitherses's drills and marches became a daily ritual and they struggled to be fit enough for the physical demands they made of them, Odysseus's men began curtailing their eating and drinking and would usually leave the great hall by the middle of the night to be ready for the following dawn.

Whether it had been part of Halitherses's plan or not, Eperitus watched with amazement as the band of amateur soldiers became a close-knit unit. Odysseus was always with them during drill and the marches – though he spent the evenings in the separate company of his peers – and he soon became a leader to whom they responded naturally and without question. The authority of Halitherses and Mentor also became more firmly established as the guardsmen learned to react to their orders. Even Eperitus, who had earned the respect of the Ithacans through the battles and hardships they had shared, began to discover his own aptitude for leadership and took on various responsibilities in the training of the men.

It was a role the young soldier enjoyed, a role that was reinforced by the unique confidence Odysseus had placed in him. Not only was he the one man amongst the troop that the prince had not known since childhood – and hence he retained a certain neutrality on any issues concerning Ithaca – he was also the only one of Odysseus's companions whom Athena had allowed to know her plans. Because of this the two men would often walk together in the evenings, through the garden and sometimes out into the streets of the city to share the dilemmas that faced the prince. At these times Eperitus would listen as Odysseus confided in him about the intrigues, plans and petty squabbles that were an everyday part of the life of the Greek elite. Odysseus would give him his opinions of each man, telling him their backgrounds and their strengths and weaknesses, as he perceived them, and ask for Eperitus's own observations and what he had heard from the soldiers. One evening he even revealed the secret plans that Agamemnon and Diomedes had for a council of war, which only awaited the arrival of one particular prince, Ajax of Salamis. He was a ferocious giant of a man who, Odysseus said, had been covered with Heracles's charmed lion-skin as a baby, making him invulnerable to all weapons.

Eperitus was fascinated to hear of this indestructible warrior and plagued Odysseus with questions that he could not answer. But there were other things the prince told him of, personal revelations about his feelings for a woman in the palace. He would not share her identity, and Eperitus did not ask, but as he often spoke of Helen by name it became clear that the woman he loved was not Tyndareus's matchless daughter. The only thing he would say about her, in a tone that wavered between frustration and despair, was that she disliked him; indeed, she would not even honour him with the briefest glance or a single word beyond the formal requirements of palace life. From these few clues, Eperitus eventually guessed that he was talking about Penelope. He remembered how the cool and intelligent princess had spoken harshly about Odysseus on the Ithacans' first evening at Sparta, and since then he had noticed how she made a point of avoiding him at the nightly feasts. Eperitus had also seen the prince's eyes seek her out amongst the crowds. Indeed, he would have felt pity for his friend had he not also noticed how Penelope's gaze would occasionally linger on Odysseus when he was not looking.

But Odysseus's was not the only confidence Eperitus shared.

Helen would often arrange to meet with him in the temple of Aphrodite, where she came disguised in Clytaemnestra's black cloak with the hood pulled over her face. Careful of her mistress's reputation, Neaera would always accompany her and remain just beyond the temple doors as they spoke. Although Eperitus knew his life was at risk if he were to be found in such a situation, he could no more resist Helen's pleas to meet than he could stop the sun from rising. At first her intoxicating beauty drew him, but it did not take him long to see past her physical attraction to the young, frustrated woman beneath.

Amid the shadows cast by the torchlight, Helen would ply him for news of Odysseus, talk with him about the Ithaca he hardly knew and share with him her dreams of fleeing Sparta. Then she would press him to tell Odysseus that she would marry him, if he would help her to escape.

This forced Eperitus into an ever-narrowing corner. Knowing the gods had decreed she be given to another – and that Odysseus was falling in love with Penelope – he was forced to rely on the excuse that Odysseus could not return to Ithaca whilst it remained in the hands of Eupeithes. But he also realized that to run away with Helen would estrange her from her family and lose Odysseus the power he needed to win back his homeland. As the prince was already forming strong friendships, especially with Agamemnon and Diomedes, Eperitus was not prepared to make him choose between the unrivalled temptation of Helen and the possibility of an alliance with one or more of the other nobles.

His only hope was for Ajax to arrive so that the planned council could take place, after which Helen's husband would be chosen. What would happen then was in the hands of the gods, and beyond the influence of lowly warriors like himself. Just how Tyndareus and Agamemnon had planned for that day he could not guess, though he hoped the friendships that had formed between the nobles and warriors alike would prevent a quarrel in the palace. Despite this, many of the common soldiers were already predicting a split amongst the suitors, and that war between the Greek states would surely follow. All for Helen's sake.

At first, Neaera would tell him when to meet the princess, but one day it was Clytaemnestra who sought him out.

'Where's Neaera?' he asked, suspicious of the sudden change in messenger.

'Don't be concerned,' Clytaemnestra replied, guessing his fears. 'I know all about Helen's foolish desire to run away with Odysseus. Do you think she'd be using my cloak as a disguise if I hadn't allowed her to?'

Eperitus looked at her coldly. 'I hadn't given it any consideration,' he said. 'But you still haven't answered my question.'

'If you must know, I volunteered to take Neaera's place. Does that surprise you?'

'It surprises me that Agamemnon's wife is acting as a go-between for Helen's private affairs,' Eperitus responded. 'I know your husband intends to hold a council of war, and it wouldn't help his plans if the bait disappeared before all the fish had been caught.'

Clytaemnestra's nostrils flared briefly, but she was quick to control the flush of anger she felt at Eperitus's suggestion. 'Then you presume to know too much, soldier,' she said. 'If you think I would dream of spying for Agamemnon, you're gravely wrong. Do you know that he murdered my first husband and our child, just so that he could make me his own? I find the man detestable, and if I can spite his plans by helping my sister to run away, then so much the better.'

The Mycenaean queen's features grew hard and cold as stone and it seemed as if she no longer looked at Eperitus, but through him. Then she saw the muted shock on Eperitus's face and her icy expression was thawed by a warm smile.

'But do you want to know the real reason why I'm here today? Curiosity! To see you, Eperitus.'

'Me?' he replied, surprised by the admission. 'Why would you want to see me?'

'Why not?' Clytaemnestra laughed. 'Helen speaks almost as highly of you as she does of Odysseus. I wanted to see what sort of a man would risk his life just to entertain a girl's fantasies of escape and freedom.'

She had a knowing look in her eyes that made Eperitus think of her reputation as a witch – did her ancient gods give her an inner knowledge of things? he wondered.

'And what do you think, now that you've seen me?' he asked.

But she simply smiled again, then turned and walked away.

Clytaemnestra continued to bring her sister's messages to him over the ensuing days and weeks, and their brief parleys evolved into longer and ever more personal conversations. She was always friendly and polite, but Eperitus quickly realized that, like her sister, she was lonely. Little by little her hatred of Agamemnon revealed itself more openly, until eventually the passion of her frustrated emotions flooded out. She despised his mighty plans and ambitions for Greece, and derided his pathetic affections for her; she hated him for killing her first husband and their child; she wished him dead, over and over again, making Eperitus recoil at the thought of living with her wrath. But beneath the anger he could sense her feeling of helplessness, trapped in a marriage to a man she loathed. Once, as they spoke in the solitude of the gardens, she had flung her arms about his neck and buried her face into his chest to hide the tears. He had tried to comfort her then, though he did not know how to soothe such torment.

Whilst besieged by the concerns of others, Eperitus was also worried to see the Ithacan soldiers becoming at ease in Sparta. On their journey to the great city their talk had always been about their families and homes, but now Ithaca was mentioned only occasionally and in the guise of a distant memory. As the feasts continued and some of them formed relationships with Spartan slaves, and as they no longer needed to provide for themselves, so their homeland seemed to fade from their minds. The thought of returning to their little island and fighting the Taphians was far off, and in time even Halitherses and Mentor stopped planning how they would retake Ithaca.

Eperitus thought of mentioning his observations to Odysseus. He also considered telling Helen that Odysseus loved another. He even wondered whether to tell the Ithacans that the gods had forbidden their prince to marry Helen. But, for good or ill, he did none of these things. He was the linchpin between them all, holding secrets that none of the others were party to, and yet he was bound by oaths and loyalties that did not permit him to share his knowledge. It was a difficult time, in which his only guides were his sense of honour and his loyalty to Odysseus.

Then, when his burdens were becoming too much to bear, Ajax arrived.

Chapter Nineteen

AJAX OF SALAMIS

'Odysseus has told you about the planned council, then.'

Agamemnon looked at Eperitus with his passionless blue eyes, hiding all thoughts and emotions behind their impervious gaze. He stood before him in the feasting hall, having descended with Diomedes and Menelaus from the dais where the nobles ate and ordered him to one side, away from his comrades. Eperitus saw Odysseus with the other suitors, talking with Clytaemnestra, and he felt abandoned and vulnerable before the awesome presence of the three men.

Sensing his uncertainty Menelaus placed a hand upon his shoulder. 'It's all right. Odysseus has already told us you are in his confidence, so if he has faith in your discretion then so do we.'

'Yes, I know about the council,' Eperitus admitted, reluctantly. 'You want to unite the Greeks against Troy.'

'And what's your opinion on the matter?' Diomedes asked. 'As a soldier, I mean.'

The Argive prince looked him straight in the eye, with neither the coldness of Agamemnon nor the friendly charm of Menelaus. But for all his apparent interest in his thoughts, Eperitus was not fool enough to believe that he or the Atreides brothers were really concerned about the opinions of a lowly spearman. Again he looked over to Odysseus, who by now had spied them at the shadowy edges of the hall and was watching them keenly. Did the prince know why he was being singled out by his high-born friends?

Eperitus wondered. He appeared suspicious and for a moment it looked as if he might join them, but any intentions he had of this were checked by Clytaemnestra, who held him fast in conversation. Eperitus returned his gaze to Diomedes.

'All I know about Troy is that it lies on the other side of the world. But I'm a fighting man, and what warrior doesn't yearn for the chance to test himself in battle? If you go to kill Trojans, then my spear will be right beside yours.'

Though little more than twenty-five years old, Diomedes was already a seasoned warrior, and Eperitus could see by the slight arching of his eyebrows that his answer had earned his approval. Agamemnon, however, was not so easily won. Unlike most men in the warrior classes of Greece he did not lust after the physical and emotional joys of war, or even the attainment of honour. His focus was ever on the greater issues and he rarely stooped to the urbanity of human feelings. He reminded Eperitus of a mortal Zeus, watching over all things whilst the lesser gods squabbled about trivialities.

'Why? For glory?' Agamemnon said, disdainfully.

'Yes, for glory. And for Odysseus.'

'Your devotion is commendable,' Menelaus complimented him. 'I can see why Odysseus speaks so highly of you. In time your loyalty will find its rewards.'

'Yes, if you aren't undone by your own treachery first,' Agamemnon said, fixing him with a determined stare. 'We know you've been meeting with Helen.'

Eperitus's instincts had warned him he was being manoeuvred into a trap, and now he was caught. Someone had told them about Helen, and he did not possess a devious enough character to wriggle free of the predicament. Odysseus would have escaped the ambush with ease, but he could only choose between the truth and silence. He chose the latter.

'You don't have to protect her, Eperitus,' Agamemnon continued. 'No harm will come to the princess, after all, but *you're* a different matter. Did you know the punishment for sleeping with an unmarried Spartan woman is death?'

The king's words were not meant as an idle threat.

'I haven't so much as touched her, my lord,' Eperitus told him with dignity. 'And by accusing me of such behaviour you also accuse the princess, though neither of us deserves such suspicion. Ask Helen's maid; she was with us every time we met.'

'We know,' Diomedes said. 'The girl has a loose tongue amongst her friends, and when news of these meetings worked its way up to us that was the first thing we made sure of.'

'But Tyndareus needs only to suspect and he'll kill you, Eperitus,' Menelaus interjected. 'There's too much at stake here. On the other hand, if you can explain to us why you've been meeting with Helen then it's unlikely this matter will go any further.'

Eperitus wondered how much Neaera had already revealed, though it was clear the three men did not yet know everything. It was likely she had told them of her mistress's wish to escape Sparta and avoid the marriage that was being imposed on her, but had Helen even told the girl about her desire to flee to Ithaca? He looked across at Odysseus, but the prince was still talking to Clytaemnestra.

'Don't look to Odysseus for salvation,' Agamemnon said, noticing his glance. 'We know Helen plans to run away, and Odysseus is just as keen as we are to prevent her. Tell me honestly, has she asked you to help her? Was that why she arranged to meet you?'

Relieved that they did not yet know everything, Eperitus told them Helen had not asked him to help her escape from Sparta, which was the truth. Menelaus seemed happy to accept his word and looked at him with all the earnestness he could muster in his honest heart.

'I'm glad to hear it,' he said. 'But if you won't reveal why she meets with you, then we want you to do something else for us.' It was clear he loved the princess deeply and it made Eperitus glad that he would be chosen to marry her. 'Watch over her for us, Eperitus. I don't ask you to betray her confidence, just keep her from leaving Sparta.'

He offered him his hand. Diomedes, whose affections for Helen were no less than those of Menelaus, looked at him and nodded that he should accept the role that was being forced upon him. Eperitus took the proffered hand.

At that point there was a loud bang and the doors of the great hall burst open, sweeping broad arcs through the crowded revellers. He was unable from where he stood to see who or what had hurled the massive portals open with such force, and his view was further obscured as a press of guests and slaves stood to see what was happening. Then Diomedes and Menelaus cleared a passage through the throng and Eperitus followed Agamemnon in their wake.

Three men stood in the aisle that led to the twin thrones of Sparta. On the left stood a skinny youth with a hooked nose and a twitch. To the right was a short man with an evil look to him; about his shoulders, much to Eperitus's disgust, was draped an enormous brown snake. This alone would have been enough to cause a stir amongst the crowd, but instead all eyes were fixed on the third man.

Eperitus had never before seen anyone as tall or as broad as he was. He stood head and shoulders above everybody else in the room and looked about himself with long, slow sweeps of his head, shrivelling people with fear as his eyes fell upon each of them in turn. That he was a handsome man who wore a smile behind his black beard was no comfort, for his looks were hard and the smile was a mocking one, completely without fear. It came from an overwhelming confidence in his own prowess – a knowledge that nobody in the room could match him: few of them reached higher than his chest, and even Odysseus's massive build was dwarfed by the titanic muscles on the man. Although he carried no weapons and wore no armour, everybody felt vulnerable before him.

'I am Ajax, son of Telamon,' he boomed. 'I have come to marry Helen of Sparta and take her back with me to my kingdom of Salamis. When I want something I get it and not even the gods can stop me, so the rest of you fools may as well go home. Now, which of you is Tyndareus?'

'I am,' Tyndareus admitted, cautiously. Despite his own fierce looks, the king was clearly nervous in the presence of the bearded giant who had burst into the heart of his palace like a thunderbolt. 'Welcome, Ajax. We have been awaiting your arrival for some time.'

'We expected you to wait,' said the short man, stepping in front of his companions. All three men carried the dust of the road on their clothes but, unlike the other suitors, there was no sign of an escort or retinue with them. 'I am Ajax of Locris, son of Oileus.'

'As nasty a brute as you'll ever meet,' Diomedes confided to Eperitus in a whisper, all his previous hostility forgotten. 'They call him Little Ajax to distinguish him from his colossal friend, though some call him Ai for short.'

Ai was an exclamation of woe, and looking at the man Eperitus could guess why he had been given the nickname. He stared about at the watching crowd with insolence in his dark, closely set eyes, and though he was hardly much older than Eperitus his look of fearless arrogance warned of trouble to come. His features matched his fearsome manner: a single eyebrow ran in an unbroken line across his forehead, his nose was squashed flat from fighting and his thick black beard could not hide the scars on his disease-ravaged cheeks.

'This is Teucer, youngest son of Telamon and half-brother of my namesake,' he continued, pointing at the third member of the party, who fidgeted nervously and lifted his head as if sniffing the air, then looked back down at his feet so as not to meet the eyes of the onlookers. 'We've come to support Ajax's claim to the princess Helen.'

'Then step forward, all of you, and refresh yourselves after your travels.' Tyndareus walked down to meet them, while a flurry of slaves brought food, wine and chairs to the dais for the latest of Helen's suitors. But the men remained where they stood.

'Where is Helen?' demanded the greater of the Ajaxes.

'Sleeping,' Tyndareus answered. 'There will be time to see her tomorrow, but for now you should eat and drink and tell us the tale of your journey here.'

But Ajax was impatient, as if he expected the girl to marry him before the night was out. 'Then wake her. Should I be kept waiting for the sake of a woman's sleep?'

'Her beauty will not diminish overnight, Ajax,' Agamemnon said, leaving the crowd to join the newcomers. 'Take your seats and join the feast.'

Little Ajax's snake flicked out its tongue and hissed as he approached, but the king of Mycenae had a commanding presence that seemed to silence even the irrepressible Ajax. The three men allowed him to shepherd them to the places set out by the slaves.

But if Agamemnon was pleased to receive the latest suitor, happy that his planned council of war could now go ahead, there were others among the noble guests who were not so pleased at the giant's words or the insolent presence of his lesser namesake. Palamedes and King Menestheus stood as the trio stepped up to the dais and walked to the opposite side. Patroclus, who sat on a chair at the foot of the dais, also stood and walked away. Seeing this, Little Ajax draped his pet snake over the twitching Teucer and followed the Myrmidon.

'You!' he said.

Patroclus turned and sneered down at the Locrian prince, who now stood threateningly before him.

'You've no royal blood in you. Who are you and what are you doing here?'

Patroclus wrinkled his pinched nose at the stench of the man's breath. 'My name is Patroclus, representative of Achilles.'

'Achilles?' Little Ajax scoffed. 'Do you hear that, lads? He says he's here to represent Achilles! But everybody knows Achilles is just a boy. He *is* just a boy isn't he?'

'Yes, of course,' Patroclus replied, testily.

They were the two most disliked, arrogant and mean-looking men in all of Sparta, and it surprised nobody to see them already at loggerheads.

'Then he must be,' Little Ajax persisted, like a boarhound on a scent, 'because I'm sure *you'd* know if he had hair on his balls yet.'

Suddenly Patroclus dropped his natural reserve and seized him by the throat. He was not a well-built man but his sinewy muscles were deceptively strong. He also had the reactions of a cobra – Peisandros had boasted that his captain was the most accomplished fighter amongst the Myrmidons – and Little Ajax could do little more than try to pull the strong, long-fingered hands from his neck.

An instant later Ajax himself leapt down from the dais and with one blow from his massive fist knocked Patroclus halfway across the hall, where he landed at the feet of his own men. They took one look at their leader, unconscious and bleeding, and with a great shout of anger rushed as one towards the giant.

Peisandros was the first to reach him. He slipped inside Ajax's guard and punched him in the stomach. It was as hard a blow as he could give, but his fist rebounded as if he had slammed it into an ox-hide shield. Ajax roared with joy and hurled Peisandros into the crowd of onlookers. An instant later he threw himself into the rest of the Myrmidons, tossing them about the great hall like dolls. He was joined by Little Ajax, who was always looking for the opportunity to fight. But unlike his companion, who simply enjoyed beating his opponents, the smaller man was driven by a constantly simmering hatred for all mankind. He went for the tallest warrior he could see and jumped up to hit him full on the jaw. The man fell back and took no further part in the fight.

Despite being knocked this way and that, the Myrmidons were proud fighting men and would not give up the fight until the last man was beaten. They launched themselves in numbers at Ajax, though with no more effect than the sea crashing against a great rock. But the more badly mauled amongst them now saw an opportunity for revenge against Little Ajax, and Peisandros and two of his comrades crowded about him and began to give him a severe beating.

Eperitus, Diomedes and Menelaus had stood by in the crowd, enjoying the spectacle of Ajax fighting off a dozen men whilst his colleague took a much-deserved battering. Agamemnon and Odysseus seemed to be watching the spectacle with equal satisfaction from the royal dais, whilst beside them Tyndareus looked on aghast, imagining similar scenes when he eventually chose a husband for his daughter. But as Eperitus watched Little Ajax reel away from his attackers with a punch to the side of his head, he saw him snatch a knife from one of the meat stewards and immediately go running back into the fray, straight at Peisandros. Instinctively Eperitus stepped forward and called out to the Myrmidon, who turned to see the Locrian running towards him, a sneer of hatred on his battered lips. In the same moment Teucer stood up on the dais and called out frenetically to his half-brother.

Ajax was still fending off the other Myrmidons, but turned as he heard Teucer's voice and saw the blade glinting in Little Ajax's hand. In a moment he had bounded across the floor and smashed his fist down upon the head of his companion, crumpling him in a heap. The knife skittered across the flagstones and came to a spinning rest at Peisandros's feet.

The Myrmidon signalled for his comrades to stop the fight. Immediately he walked up to Ajax and offered his hand in thanks for saving his life. Ajax enclosed it in his own and nodded curtly. The fight was over as quickly as it had begun.

§

Neaera stood at the entrance to the temple of Aphrodite and glanced shamefacedly at Eperitus as he arrived. The interior was lit by a solitary torch and he could see Helen waiting for him by the whitewashed altar.

She looked even more beautiful than usual tonight. Her hair

was worn loose to frame her face and emphasize the features that the warrior had come to know so well during their many meetings here. He had often thought of how he could be happy spending hours just looking at her, absorbing the gentle lines of her face and the full curves of her body. A man could die for that pleasure, he thought, but would he ever be happy? The suitor who finally won Helen would never be able to possess such beauty and would spend his whole life jealously guarding her from the attentions of other men. He felt sorry for her – her delicate femininity and spellbinding looks were as much a curse as a blessing.

As he shook the late winter rain from his cloak, she came up to him and kissed his cheek. Up until that point she had barely touched him in all of their secret liaisons, which was a painful irony in view of the news he had to bring her. And yet the touch of her soft lips on his stubbly cheek, with the faint hint of perfume in her hair, was exquisite.

'What's wrong, Eperitus? Are you shocked that I should kiss you? Well, you shouldn't be. If I wasn't the plaything of the powerful, who knows that I wouldn't be happy to spend my life with a handsome warrior like yourself?'

'You're kind, my lady,' he replied despondently. He knew she wanted to repay him for being her one friend during the long weeks of her courtship by so many men, but he could not bring himself to match her cheerfulness, weighed down by the guilt of what he had to reveal to her. 'But you truly *are* the plaything of the powerful, to use your own words. I'm afraid you will always be a prisoner of Tyndareus and Agamemnon.'

She laughed. 'I'll be free when you convince Odysseus to take me away from here.'

'You don't understand me, my lady. Helen. I'm trying to tell you that they know.'

She froze and the playful smile fell from her lips. 'Know what?'

Eperitus could not bring himself to say it in full, but Helen knew anyway. She closed her eyes and seemed to crumple under the realization. Tears collected beneath her long, dark eyelashes and began to roll down her cheeks to fall in large, fast drops to the floor. He watched her as she stood there, silent and unmoving, the tears shining on her proud face, and he wanted to touch her but could not. She was the loveliest creature he had ever seen and it was like a sword through his heart to see the sadness of despair hurt her so deeply. Then he gathered all his courage and stepped up to her, daring even to hold her and let her fall against his chest, where the warm dampness of her tears seeped into his rough woollen tunic.

She put her arms about him and held him tight. Her face was buried into his neck, hidden beneath her dense black hair, and he looked down at the top of her head. Something told him to kiss her, a sudden, unexpected urge that threatened to take control of him. But the urge became a voice, the mocking voice of Gyrtias, and the beautiful, daring thought was soured and fell away. Then she spoke in a hoarse whisper.

'How do they know?'

Eperitus thought of the frightened young maid confronted by the most powerful men in Greece and could not blame Neaera for her betrayal. 'Agamemnon didn't tell me.'

'Oh, what does it matter any more?' Helen said bitterly, her wet cheeks shining in the torchlight. 'They'll be watching me now. Everywhere I go and everything I do. There'll even be somebody in the street now, hiding in the shadows and waiting for me to leave. Oh, it's terrible.'

This pained him even more, knowing he had agreed to be their watcher for them. Surely he could do something for her? Was he so weak that he could not help a girl in need? Then she looked at him again and a new light of desperate determination was in her eyes.

'I know a secret way out of here, Eperitus. We could leave together without being seen. You could take me away over the mountains to your homeland. I could marry you and we could live a simple life together. If you take me away now, I promise myself to you. Please, Eperitus.'

As she uttered these words to him the feasting hall on top of the hill was filled with warriors from almost every kingdom in Greece. The kings and princes of its nations and islands were gathered together in honour of this girl, the greatest assembly in Greek history. Each man was high-born. They were the sons of heroes, the leaders of their people, and each had the right to believe they could win the hand of Helen. Yet she had offered herself to him.

For a brief, wild moment Eperitus thought his heart would smash itself free of his ribcage, so fast did it beat. Helen had offered him everything he could ever want, and his head was dizzy with the thought of her, of having her for himself. All he needed to do was take her by the hand and slip out of the darkened streets of Sparta into the Eurotas valley. Men would come after them, following every conceivable route of escape, but he felt sure they could evade any pursuit.

But he knew it could not be. The oracle had warned him of the dangers of love, but worse still he would be abandoning Odysseus and Ithaca, whom he had sworn to protect. He had also given Menelaus his hand and obliged himself for the sake of his honour to see that Helen did not escape from Sparta.

The blood began to cool in his veins. Besides, where would they go? Where *could* they go that news of their arrival would not reach the ears of Tyndareus and Agamemnon? There was nowhere that Helen's beauty could escape notice. They would remain wanderers, roaming from place to place to escape the far-reaching wrath of Sparta and Mycenae. What sort of life would that give them, and how long before Helen despaired of a nomadic existence and returned to her father? No, he was a fool even to imagine such a thing.

He looked at Helen and she knew his answer.

'Of course not,' she said, forcing a smile.

'They made me swear to watch over you,' he admitted. 'They told me to see that you did not escape. I'm sorry.'

'Don't be. I know you won't break your word, and one day

that will make you into a great man.' She released herself from his arms and stood tall once again before him. 'I think better of you for your decision, my friend, not worse. But now I must face up to the destiny the gods have chosen for me.'

It was a destiny about which Eperitus knew more than he could say. But despite Athena's words he dared to believe there could be a different course, an alternative that might suit Helen and Odysseus both.

'Maybe there's another way.'

'Is there? I don't think so now,' she said.

'You could compromise. Although you hate being a piece in the power games of your father and Agamemnon, perhaps you could consent to marry a man of your own choice. Since we've been meeting here, your talk has always been of running away with Odysseus and living a simple life on Ithaca. Well, why not talk to Tyndareus about it? If you marry Odysseus at least you'll be able to leave Sparta and live out a quiet existence away from all this. And that way, Tyndareus can lend Odysseus all the soldiers he needs to win back his kingdom. Even Agamemnon will have had his council of war, which you say was the whole point of inviting the Greek nobility to Sparta. Everybody will be happy, except for the other suitors, of course. What do you say?'

'I say you're an optimistic fool, Eperitus. Don't you know my future husband will have been carefully selected before the first heralds were sent out to invite all these suitors?'

'But you've such charm, my lady. And I've seen the way your father looks at you. He's not such a puppet of Agamemnon that he can't have his mind changed by the most beautiful woman in all Greece, is he?'

She smiled warmly and gave Eperitus a look he would never forget. There was a magic about Helen that could drive men insane, and though he liked Menelaus he felt he could happily kill the Mycenaean prince to release her from her divinely decreed fate.

'You're thinking of my charm as a woman. It's different

between daughters and fathers – but perhaps it can be more effective. A few tears, the odd sigh here and there. I'll see what I can do, and for your sake I won't give up yet. Even though you only care about soldiers for Ithaca rather than what happens to me.'

Eperitus tutted at her suggestion. 'All I want is you to be queen of Ithaca, my lady.'

❦

Odysseus and Tyndareus walked through the gardens in the light of the early morning. The discordant clacking of wooden sticks could be heard from the courtyard where the warriors of the different states practised their battle drill.

'They're becoming very good soldiers,' Odysseus commented. 'All this practice has given my men a new edge, though I wonder how it will translate to swords of bronze instead of wood.'

'That's my worry,' Tyndareus said. He picked a pink flower and crammed it under his nose, inhaling its sweet aroma.

Odysseus guessed his meaning, having thought on the situation much himself. 'You're concerned about what will happen when Helen's husband is announced.'

'Exactly. You saw them the other day, brawling like commoners,' Tyndareus said glumly. 'And with so many warriors here, can you imagine what'll happen if there's a dispute about the choice? I must be getting old, Odysseus, because I'm losing sleep about the thought of a battle.' The Spartan king looked about himself and plucked another flower for Odysseus. 'Smell this. Wonderful, isn't it? Only grows here in Sparta.'

Odysseus's sense of smell had been weak ever since boxing lessons as a boy and he was barely able to appreciate the aroma from the tiny petals.

'Why don't you stick it in your belt,' Tyndareus suggested, 'and get rid of that dried-up husk you've been wearing since you got here.'

Odysseus patted the chelonion gently. 'I couldn't do that. My sister gave me this as a memento of Ithaca while I'm away. I keep it to remind myself that my people are suffering under a false king, and I must one day return to free them. All my men wear a sprig as a reminder of home.'

'You've been here for some time now. You must worry constantly about your homeland.'

Odysseus frowned. 'Constantly, but it's the burden of nobility, Tyndareus. What about your problem: have you thought of a solution yet?'

The king laughed. 'Solution? Only one springs to mind, but dividing Helen into thirty pieces would be a waste of a beautiful daughter.'

'Maybe I can help,' Odysseus offered nonchalantly, trying once more to detect an aroma from the flower.

'You've hinted as much on several occasions, my friend. But for all your cleverness I don't see how you can prevent them from slaughtering each other. They're all proud, and with Ajax and his vicious little friend amongst them I fear the worst.'

Odysseus cocked an eyebrow at Tyndareus. 'What will you offer me if I can give you a practical answer?'

'What's the price of peace to an old man?' Tyndareus replied. 'I'll give you anything that it's in my power to give.'

'Anything?'

'Yes: gold; women for you and your men; even land if you want it. But only if I agree to your idea, and it works.'

Odysseus offered him his hand, which Tyndareus took. 'That's settled then. I shall take your offer of anything I wish, but first I'll honour my half of the bargain. Agamemnon's council of war will take place in two days' time, when he expects your guests to support his raid against Troy. It won't work of course, but that's another matter altogether.

'When the suitors are gathered together, and before any disagreement can begin, you must demand that they take an oath. As you said, they're proud men and therefore you can be sure an oath will bind them. And to ensure they consent to the oath, tell them you won't consider any man as a husband for Helen unless he agrees.'

'But *what* oath?'

'Simple,' Odysseus smiled. 'You must make them swear to protect Helen and her husband against anyone who would come between them. That's the only way you can ensure they don't fight each other for her, now or in the years to come. And if anyone breaks the oath, the others will be compelled to protect your daughter and the winning suitor. It'll need to be accompanied by the most compelling sacrifice that your priests can devise, of course, but you shouldn't have any problems after that.'

'Yes,' Tyndareus agreed as the easy brilliance of Odysseus's suggestion grew on him. 'Yes, that should do it. Even Ajax will obey an oath, for all his brute strength and his confidence about Helen. I can't believe I didn't think of it myself. You're cleverer than you look, Odysseus.'

Odysseus smiled benignly. 'Thank you, my lord. But what about my price?'

Tyndareus gave him a cautious look. 'Well, I'm an honourable man, what do you want? You've sorted my problem out, so let me sort yours. Is it the land you want – you'll be welcome to settle in Sparta.'

'No,' Odysseus said. The thought of not returning ultimately to Ithaca had never crossed his mind. 'My price is a woman in your palace.'

'Any woman?'

'No. A princess.'

'I thought you might say that,' Tyndareus sighed, realizing he had been outmanoeuvred. 'Well, you might be surprised to know she's attracted to you, too.'

'I am!'

'No offence, my son, but so am I. Apparently she's been thinking about you since she first saw you. Wants a simple life on Ithaca, she tells me. My only problem is how to explain it to Agamemnon. We had an agreement, you see.'

Odysseus had no idea why Tyndareus and Agamemnon should have an agreement about Penelope, but he was more surprised to learn she reciprocated his own feelings. After they had fallen out in this very same garden she had shown him nothing but hostility, even contempt, and he expected to have to drag her kicking and screaming from Sparta. He had long ago struck on the idea of an oath to keep the peace between the suitors, and soon after had thought of using it to employ Tyndareus's influence in winning Penelope. But he had also lost sleep over the thought of marrying her against her will. It was customary that women were given away by their parents, to men they either did not know or did not have any passion for. For the most part they came to accept their lot and got on with their lives, and in the majority of cases familiarity bred love. But Penelope was different. She had an independent character that, he guessed, would not easily be tamed to love. So the news that she already loved him was a revelation and a wonderful blessing.

He smiled broadly. 'And what about Icarius? What does he say?'

'Icarius? What in Hades does he have to do with it? Helen's *my* daughter, and if she wants to marry you, Odysseus, then you should thank the gods and take her.'

Chapter Twenty
THE GREAT OATH

The Ithacans were training as usual when Odysseus came striding across the broad courtyard, shouting for Halitherses. Eperitus glanced across whilst fending off blows from Damastor's mock wooden sword and received a painful blow in the ribs for his lapse of concentration.

'Never drop your guard, Eperitus,' Damastor admonished him, before stepping back to prepare for another attack. But before he could renew their contest Halitherses called a halt to the drill. The two lines of sweating soldiers lowered their sticks and sat down in the well-trodden dirt.

'Mentor, Eperitus, I want you too,' Odysseus said, waving them over. He appeared unusually concerned. 'The gods have shown me their favour, at last, but I need your counsel.'

Halitherses put Antiphus in charge and went to join the huddle about Odysseus. The prince folded his arms and gave them a sober look.

'I needn't remind you that we came here for Helen,' he began.

'We came here to win friends and make alliances,' Mentor corrected. 'We all know the prince of a small kingdom doesn't stand a chance of winning Helen, not against men like Menelaus, Ajax and Diomedes.'

'Maybe so, but things have changed. Tyndareus has offered me Helen for my wife.'

They looked at him in disbelief and for a moment nobody

knew what to say. Then Halitherses cocked his head to one side and narrowed his eyes at the prince.

'Is this another of your tricks?'

Odysseus smiled. 'I can understand your disbelief, old friend, but I'm telling you the truth. Ever since the Ajaxes arrived Tyndareus has been worried. He thinks a fight will break out between Helen's suitors when he announces her husband.'

'Oh, I see now,' Mentor said. 'He'll announce you as her husband so the rest of the suitors can kill you first.'

'I'm serious, you idiot. He came to me for advice; he's at a loss about how to stop them killing each other, and in return for a solution he offered me anything it was in his power to give. The answer was an easy one, of course – I simply told him to make the suitors swear to protect Helen and her husband from anybody who would come between them.'

Halitherses nodded. 'An oath? That's clever. No man of honour will break his sworn promise, however deeply hurt his pride may be.'

'And you chose Helen as your payment?' Mentor asked. 'I'll wager a gold piece he wasn't happy to hear you say that.'

'That's what's so strange,' Odysseus protested. 'Even I wouldn't be so bold as to ask for Helen's hand in marriage. *He* offered her to me! And the most ridiculous thing about it is that she told him she wanted me.'

'By the gods,' Eperitus exclaimed. The blood turned cold in his veins as he realized Helen had acted on his suggestion and somehow convinced Tyndareus to choose Odysseus as her husband. The others looked at him expectantly. 'What Odysseus says is true,' he explained. 'She told me she wanted to run away with him and live on Ithaca, so I said she should speak to her father about it.'

Odysseus, Mentor and Halitherses stared at him with incredulity. Behind them another round of sword practice had begun, but as Damastor no longer had a partner he had left the group and was sitting nearby. Eperitus thought of moving out of earshot, but Halitherses interrupted his thoughts.

'And why would the most prized woman in Greece discuss her marriage with a soldier? Are you dreaming, Eperitus, or just drunk?'

'I swear it by the gods,' he answered sternly. He explained to them the circumstances of their meetings. 'It's nothing physical, don't fear. She just wants a friend to talk to, someone from outside her normal life.'

'So she does want to marry me,' Odysseus mused. 'But why?'

Eperitus shared with them the things Helen had said to him, how she hated palace life and longed for a less complicated existence. He felt like a traitor as he revealed the secrets of her heart to his friends, but was consoled by the knowledge that his words brought satisfaction to Odysseus, whose previous doubts were now washed away by understanding. However, he remained unusually solemn.

'I've told Tyndareus I need a short time to think it over,' he announced.

'What are you waiting for?' Mentor laughed. 'Marry her! That's why we came here.'

'What's to think about?' Eperitus agreed, smiling along with Halitherses and Mentor. 'Accept the offer and ask Tyndareus for a Spartan army to escort you back to Ithaca. Eupeithes and his Taphians will die of fright before we can put a foot on shore. And if anyone ever tries to take your rightful place again, you'll have the word of every lord in Greece to come to your protection.'

Halitherses shook his grey head. 'I never thought there'd be an end to all this feasting. And I never, ever thought the final feast would be in your honour, Odysseus. Do you realize this means we can actually go home? I was starting to believe we'd never see our own hearths again, but now we can do it. Zeus's beard, I still can't believe it.'

Odysseus sighed. 'The problem is, I don't love Helen.'

Mentor rolled his eyes heavenwards. 'Since when were you a follower of Aphrodite? I remember you used to despise the Cyprian and all her arts. But if love is a condition of your marrying Helen, I'm certain one evening with her will satisfy you of that. That girl could overcome any man's shyness.'

'What I mean, Mentor, is that I don't love Helen because I love another.'

The smiles fell from the faces of Mentor and Halitherses. Even Eperitus, who already knew of Odysseus's other love, was surprised the prince seemed ready to abandon his mission for her sake.

'Who?' Mentor said, a hint of impatience in his voice. 'No, don't tell me. Just answer me this: can marrying this girl give us an army, or friends enough to win back Ithaca? Can it? Or are you prepared to sacrifice your home — our home — for the sake of a woman? Be reasonable, Odysseus. I don't think Helen is a bad second best. Do you?'

'It's Penelope, isn't it?' Eperitus said.

Odysseus smiled wryly. 'Yes, Eperitus, it's Penelope.'

'Penelope?' Mentor echoed. 'But she's . . . She's hardly Helen, is she? Odysseus, my friend, I implore you in the name of the people of Ithaca to accept the generous offer of Tyndareus. Penelope is a fine woman, but Helen is like a goddess.'

'I don't even know whether Penelope would have me,' Odysseus replied, annoyed by Mentor's reaction. 'Up until now she's been as cold as a mountain stream, so perhaps I don't have a choice in the matter anyway.'

'Then marry Helen so we can go home to Ithaca,' Mentor said.

'Ithaca?' Odysseus scoffed. 'I haven't heard any of you mention Ithaca for weeks now. You were all so busy eating Tyndareus's food and drinking his wine that I thought you'd forgotten about our home. And yet I've wrung my heart out over that island every moment of each day since we left her shores. Don't any of you speak to me of home when you've already pushed it out of your own hearts.'

Mentor's face darkened with anger, though he did not refute

the indictment. 'I can bear your accusation, Odysseus, because you're my friend and will one day be my king. And there's truth in your words, which no Ithacan can deny. But here's another truth: your choice is not between Helen and Penelope, but between home and love. We act only to fulfil the destiny set out for us by the gods, but as long as that remains a secret I advise you not to decide too hastily.'

With that he turned and crossed the courtyard to the palace. Halitherses patted Odysseus's arm, then went to rejoin the men, calling Damastor back to his feet on the way. Eperitus made to follow him, but Odysseus put a large hand on his shoulder.

'Stay a moment, Eperitus.'

'What is it, my lord?'

'You stayed quiet whilst Mentor did all the talking, but I want to know what you think. Would I be mad to turn Helen down?'

Eperitus looked across the courtyard as Halitherses barked a series of orders. The Ithacans threw their wooden swords into a pile and formed a double line behind their captain, before following him out of the palace gates at a gentle run. Part of him wanted to be with them, to enjoy the simple pleasures of physical exercise and escape the burdens that weighed on him. But he also sensed Odysseus's internal struggle, and had to earn the trust the prince had placed in him.

'If you marry Helen, your fame will spread across Greece,' he began. 'You'll have powerful allies and the means to win back your homeland.'

'But if I choose Penelope,' Odysseus picked up, 'and can persuade her to marry me, then our ability to win back Ithaca will be limited to whatever power Icarius holds. Even assuming it's enough, I'll return to being an obscure prince, eventually to rule over a small kingdom of poor islands. Not much of a choice, is it?'

'She'd make a wonderful wife though,' Eperitus said.

He liked Penelope, who had always made a point of talking to him whenever they met, whether it was in the palace grounds or at the nightly feasts. At first she had been polite and somewhat formal, but that was just the veneer she applied in public and it soon wore off as their conversations became more frequent. Underneath he had the pleasure of discovering a woman full of active emotions and animated thought processes, constantly observing and digesting her surroundings. She was also witty and clever, even to the extent of being cunning. Eperitus had watched with pleasure how, on several occasions, she had skilfully repulsed the attentions of Little Ajax, who had developed a liking for her. She would frustrate his advances with tricks and deceptions that would always allow her to escape from his odious clutches – a characteristic that was suited to Odysseus's quick mind.

'And didn't the oracle say you should marry a Spartan woman to chase the thieves from your house?' he continued. 'Penelope is a Spartan, too, though you might have to equip her with a shield and a spear if marrying her is to free Ithaca from Eupeithes.'

Odysseus smiled. 'That's why I place so much trust in you, Eperitus. You say the things I want to hear. But you forget Athena said Helen would marry Menelaus.'

'Then all the more reason to choose Penelope. If Tyndareus is prepared to offer Helen to you, I'm certain you could ask his help to marry Penelope instead.'

'That isn't my point. Don't you see, Eperitus: I have the power to break my own destiny. The goddess says I'll not marry Helen, and that Zeus himself has decided she will be given to Menelaus. And yet Tyndareus offers his daughter to me, and Helen is willing! What if I accepted his offer?'

The thought hit Eperitus like a bolt of lightning. It made his flesh creep and the hair on his neck stand up because the consequences were too frightening to contemplate. He looked at Odysseus and found his intense eyes staring straight back at him.

'You do understand then?' he said. 'Imagine it: I could do what I wanted. No oracle or prophecy of any kind would ever restrict me again. Take the words of the Pythoness: she said that if I go to Troy I wouldn't return for twenty years, and even then I'd come back destitute and without friends. But that would have no hold on me any more. If Agamemnon persuades the Greeks to sail against Troy, I could sail with them and have no concern about returning in my own time and with all my companions beside me.'

'But if you marry Helen you'll have defied the will of Zeus himself,' Eperitus warned. 'Are you so great that you should dare challenge the father of the gods?'

'But if the will of Zeus is defeated, what power does he hold? It's within my mortal grasp to lead my own life, be free to make my own choices without pre-ordained consequences. Why should I throw that chance away?'

'And have you ever thought this might be a test?' Eperitus responded. 'Until Helen stands beside you on your wedding day and is declared your wife, then, as I see it, Zeus's will is still firmly in place. If you accept Tyndareus's offer you set yourself in open opposition to the greatest of the Olympians. Do you think you'll win glory fighting the gods? You won't; it can only lead to oblivion.'

'The only power Ajax acknowledges is his own,' Odysseus protested. Then he ran his hands over his face and looked down at the floor. 'But he's a fool, and who knows what sort of end he'll come to? Perhaps you're right, Eperitus – perhaps I want too much. Maybe I'm like Ajax, wanting all the honour and renown for myself, without acknowledging that it's only by the will of the gods I come out alive after a battle.'

'It's because you're an intelligent man, my lord,' Eperitus said. 'I don't have that problem: I trust my heart before my head. But a clever brain can deceive its master, and that's when a man needs the counsel of his friends. So I say you should fear Zeus and submit to his will, and then you'll have as much honour and glory as you could wish for.'

'And a wife I can love,' Odysseus added. He put an arm about Eperitus's shoulder and led him towards the palace. 'I only wish I knew why Penelope dislikes me so much.'

'She either thinks you're an oaf or she's hiding her true feelings for you.' Eperitus grinned, slapping his friend on the shoulder. 'If you ask me, I'd say she thinks you're an oaf.'

❦

Damastor lay on his back, looking up at the ceiling. Neaera lay in his arms with her head resting upon his hairy chest.

'Penelope can be very stubborn,' the slave girl said. 'You can't force her to like Odysseus.'

'Doesn't she find anything attractive about him?'

'Not that I've ever heard. I know her maid, Actoris, but she never reveals anything about her mistress. Besides, I've never known Penelope to take much interest in men. She's too busy with other things. But I think it's nice you want to help him.'

Damastor gave a silent sneer and continued to look up at the ceiling. The only help he wanted to give Odysseus was a dagger in the back. Ever since Eupeithes had bought his loyalty with gold and a promise of rank amongst the new nobility of Ithaca, his mission to kill Odysseus had been beset by failure. Although he had helped Polybus and his Taphians to find the prince – with the fire and the dagger beside the road – the badly planned ambush had ended in defeat. Since then Odysseus had barely been alone for a moment: at the feasts he was always with the other suitors; at night he slept in the same room as his men; and in the day he spent most of his time with Mentor, Halitherses or the foreigner, Eperitus. It was far too dangerous to risk an attempt on his life, especially as Damastor had no intention of getting caught, so he had been forced to bide his time.

But now, against all expectation, he had overheard the prince say that Helen had been offered to him. Even if Damastor could not kill him, he must at least prevent him marrying Tyndareus's daughter. If that happened, his dreams of wealth and nobility were over, so his only hope was to encourage Penelope to return Odysseus's affections.

'I suppose you could always ask Clytaemnestra to help you,' Neaera said, nonchalantly.

'Go on.'

'Well, they say she's a witch.'

'A witch indeed!' Damastor scoffed. 'So what will she do? *Scare* Penelope into marrying Odysseus?'

Neaera propped herself up on one elbow, her large breasts hanging down across her rib cage. They lay upon a straw mattress in one of the palace's dozen or so armouries, surrounded by bundles of spears and rows of shields, stacked one upon another. A thick woollen blanket covered them, keeping the chill of the night air from their naked flesh. Her face was a blur in the darkness.

'*I* would never cross her. Her maids say she has an ancient knowledge that gives her terrible powers. She can make a mother's milk sour in her breasts or ruin a man's crops for a whole year. Some say she can kill animals by cursing them – even small children, too. And if she chooses to, she can make a woman love a man against her will.'

Damastor put a hand upon her waist and squeezed her soft flesh.

'And do you think Clytaemnestra will perform her magic so that Penelope falls in love with Odysseus?'

'If I can convince her it's for the good of her cousin,' Neaera said, kissing him on the cheek. 'I'll visit her after breakfast tomorrow.'

❦

Agamemnon had called his council of war. The kings and princes came as invited, bringing only their senior captains and advisers with them. Eperitus, Halitherses and Mentor accompanied Odysseus, and each felt the privilege of being there among so many great names. These were the elite of Greece, the pride of its young nobility, and in them burned the hope for its future.

No slaves were in attendance, as the meal that evening had

been a frugal one, so with only a handful present from each suitor's entourage the great hall was almost empty. Now, in the echo of their footsteps as they entered, they were able to appreciate the full size of the place. Without the distractions of food, wine or women the guests began to notice the splendid murals that decorated the walls, columns and ceiling, telling in vivid colour and larger-than-life imagery the rich mythology of Sparta's past.

The air buzzed with their hushed voices as rumour spread her evils amongst the gathered warriors. They were excited by the prospect of war, though they did not yet know who or where the threat was from. But the thought of taking up their arms again in anger, after several years of relative peace on the mainland, excited everyone.

Foremost among them was Ajax, standing an imperious and awe-inspiring head and shoulders above everyone else, his eyes alight with the prospect of bloodshed. He was accompanied by his twitching half-brother, who had a habit of hiding slightly to one side of his giant sibling and peering out from behind his elbow. There also was Little Ajax, wearing his snake about his shoulders. His eyes were blackened and puffed up from the fight of the other day, but this did not prevent him from staring about himself with aggressive malice.

Diomedes saw the Ithacans enter and came over to greet them.

'Magnificent, isn't he?' he said, indicating Ajax. 'Can you imagine him in battle? Even the gods would fear such a man.'

'That's what he claims himself,' Halitherses replied. 'I've heard him bragging that he could defeat Ares and Athena put together, with his bare hands if he chose. That sort of talk will only bring trouble.'

Diomedes nodded. 'It's true he's no respecter of the gods, but he's still a man of honour and someone I'd be happy to count as a friend and ally. Agamemnon and I have spoken to him about the coming war and he's taken the idea to heart. We didn't give details – that's for the council to reveal – but he'd go today if he could. He lives to fight and is totally without fear; if he's afraid of death at all, it's because he'll no longer be able to fight and win glory for himself.'

'There isn't a man here like him,' Eperitus said. 'But his pride is dangerous. I hear he came without an escort because he resents the idea of needing protection. Apart from those two creatures that hang about with him, he fights alone. I even heard him say the rest of the suitors were little more than worried slave women, bringing so many soldiers with them. But I tell you truthfully, that kind of fearless independence makes a man unreliable and dangerous.'

'Maybe so, Eperitus; but he's also our greatest weapon. If you can believe it, they say his skin can't be penetrated by any weapon, ever since Heracles's lion-skin was laid over him as a baby. It's also said that Heracles is the only man he respects. Can you imagine if those two ever came to blows? It'd be the war of the gods and the Titans all over again.'

Diomedes was clearly obsessed with the martial prowess of the king of Salamis. Having seen Ajax swatting aside the Myrmidons like ants, Eperitus shared his admiration of the man. However, he had always been taught to fight as part of a unit and remained naturally suspicious of anyone who fought alone.

They were joined by Menelaus, who greeted them in a friendly manner and said that things would begin shortly. Then, as he glanced about at the gathering, mentally counting off each of the suitors, something caught his attention.

'Who's that wearing the sheepskin vest?'

He pointed to a young man lingering in the shadows at the back of the hall. He was handsome but clearly of low birth; he had the appearance of a shepherd by trade, except that in place of a staff he carried a gigantic bow. It was even larger than the bow Iphitus had given to Odysseus, and Eperitus was relieved to see that the lad did not carry any arrows.

Suddenly there was a loud rapping as Agamemnon, carrying a long wooden staff, struck the stone floor and called for silence. A pause followed in which every eye was fixed upon the king of

Mycenae, dressed in his immaculate white tunic, golden breastplate and red cloak. He looked back at them as the co-kings of Sparta took their seats beside him, waiting patiently for everybody to follow their lead. Then, when all were settled in the chairs provided, he spoke.

'Nobles of Greece! Suitors to the princess Helen! I have called you to this council to discuss matters of war, but first it is right to weigh upon you the exalted company you are in this day. You are the pride of Greece; its highest-born. Some of you are the sons of gods; others accompanied Jason on his voyage to Colchis, or have fathers who were Argonauts; a few have recently returned from the siege of Thebes. And except for that unfortunate city and a handful of lesser states, every nation in Greece is represented here. Never before has such a wealth of rank and glory been brought together under one roof, and for that you should be proud.

'Men will speak of this assembly for generations to come. But it's not because of who we are that our children's children will preserve the memory of this day. No, I tell you truthfully that we shall be remembered for our own deeds, for today we can forge an alliance of nations that will endure for ever. If you will accept my counsel you have the opportunity to bring peace to our homeland, and unify the Greek-speaking peoples in arms against the growing influence of the perverse East!'

They cheered his words until the rafters of the hall were filled with their shouts. Even though Agamemnon lifted his staff for silence they still cheered, standing up and raising their fists at the promise of war. Then, as the last echo of their approval finally died, he looked at each of the suitors in turn and spoke their names, some resounding with fame and greatness, others yet to earn the trappings of glory and honour.

At the mention of his own name, Ajax stood and held up his hand. Eperitus saw the anger flicker across Agamemnon's brow, but in a moment he had controlled it and signalled for the man to speak.

'You talk of war,' he said, his great voice booming around the hall, 'and you declare that these men are the greatest in the land, but you are wrong. How can you say this is an assembly of the finest warriors of Greece when its greatest hero has not even been invited? Where is *Heracles*?'

Murmurs of agreement came from the gathered warriors. At this, Tyndareus stood and moved to the front of the dais.

'I wouldn't want that wife-killer paying court to *my* daughter! His outrages have made him unwelcome wherever he goes, and if he came here I would send him back beyond the borders of my country.'

Ajax laughed. 'You'd presume to send Heracles away from the gates of Sparta? Tyndareus, your words stand tall in his absence, but Heracles could take your daughter by force if he chose to. He may be old, but there's no man here beside myself who could hope to match him.'

As he spoke there was a jostling in the crowd of warriors beside him and the shepherd boy stepped into the open space before the hearth. He stood there and looked about at the staring faces, yet said nothing.

'Who in Hades are *you*?' boomed Tyndareus, his anger at Ajax's words venting itself upon the newcomer.

Though there were tears in his eyes the boy displayed no fear. Instead he lifted the gigantic bow above his head and showed it to the assembly.

'This is the bow of Heracles,' he said. 'He gave it to me before he died.'

Suddenly there was a pause, a silent, collective intake of breath; then the hall exploded in uproar. As if with one voice, the guests let out a great cry and filled the room with their shouts of dismay. Ajax took two strides towards the boy and picked him up by the throat, shaking him like a toy and cursing him for a liar. Odysseus and Mentor rushed to rescue the stranger from the clutches of the giant. Behind them Agamemnon slammed the butt of his staff upon the dais and shouted for order, but it was not until Ajax controlled his anger and in his roaring voice commanded silence that peace was restored.

With a look in his eyes that threatened instant death, he leaned over the boy and ordered him to speak. But despite being strangled almost to death, the boy returned Ajax's gaze without fear.

'Heracles is dead,' he confirmed. 'His wife gave him a tunic rubbed with a poisonous ointment. It gave him so much pain that he built a funeral pyre for himself and ordered me to light it. I was tending sheep on the hills nearby and, as nobody else dared put a flame to the stack, he offered me this to put him out of his misery.'

The shepherd held up the bow again and everybody knew that he spoke the truth. It was of such a monstrous size that even Ajax would have difficulty in handling it, and in the boy's grip it looked comically large.

'I recognize it,' the giant warrior said, putting a hand on the weapon. 'Many times in my youth I saw Heracles using this bow. They say the arrows are charmed and cannot miss their target. It's a great gift, boy; you must guard it well. What's your name?'

'I am called Philoctetes, sir. My father is Poeas of Malia.'

Ajax put a hand on the boy's head and thumbed his scruffy, badly shorn hair. Then, taken by an overwhelming sadness at the news of Heracles's death, he lowered his eyes to the flames that jigged happily in the hearth and fell into a deep silence. The rest of them turned to face the royal dais, still shocked to hear that the most renowned hero of their age had died. Most had thought it was not possible, but from that day on nobody ever saw or heard of the great man again, and so Philoctetes's report became more widely accepted. But for those of them present the bow itself was proof enough, as they knew no man could forcibly take the weapon from such an owner.

Agamemnon handed the staff to Tyndareus and retired to his seat, where he also slumped into contemplative silence. The king of Sparta, however, stood before the assembly with a look of defiance on his face. He rapped the staff once to demand their attention, then declared in a loud voice, 'Helen is my daughter. Any man who wishes to marry her will first obey me, as his host and as the girl's father. The time is coming soon – very soon – when I will make my choice. But before I do so I have one demand of all present. This demand is made of suitors first and foremost, but also of those men of power and influence who have come here as advisers, escorts or representatives. Any man who refuses to obey my wish is welcome to do so, and will not earn my enmity, but he must agree to leave Sparta this very day and not return without my permission. He can take with him any gift that he brought and go back to his home with my blessing.

'To those of you who choose to stay I say this: when my decision is made almost all of you will be disappointed. Some of you may even be angry and might resent the good fortune of the chosen suitor. But know this also, that I will not tolerate argument or bloodshed in Sparta. Therefore my demand is that you take an oath, a sacred promise amongst you all to defend Helen and her husband against any who would threaten their happiness. Only when each one of you has given his word will I be satisfied; only then will I announce my choice.'

Tyndareus left a long pause but nobody spoke. They were proud men who knew the power of an oath, and they considered the king's words in stern silence.

'Is there any man here who refuses the oath?'

Again silence.

'Then if you are sure in your minds and hearts that you will make this promise and honour it, stand up.'

There was a loud shuffling and scraping of chairs as the assembly rose to its feet. In the same moment the massive portals of the hall swung open, revealing the stars in the black sky above the courtyard. The night air came rushing in, filling their nostrils with its smell and prickling the skin on their arms and legs. The flames of the hearth leapt momentarily, then subsided again.

Two priests entered, leading a horse behind them. It was a beautiful beast, as tall as Ajax and blacker than Hades. Its coat shone blue as it stood in the doorway, washed clean by the light of the moon, but changed quickly to a fiery orange as it was walked into the great hall and up to the central hearth. Like a shadow plucked from the deepest hollow of the night, there was not a blemish of any other colour upon the animal. It stopped and tossed its head, snorting at the crowd of great men and confident of its own noble presence amongst them.

'Lord Zeus,' Tyndareus thundered, breaking the spell the magnificent beast had cast over them. 'Father of the gods, great ruler of the heavens and the earth, bear solemn witness to the oath we now take.'

He nodded to the priests. One of them eased the animal's head back, careful not to startle it, whilst the other slashed open its throat. The strong smell of horse was suddenly blotted out by the stench of fresh blood. Bright gore pumped from the open wound and onto the stone floor, splashing back up onto the watching suitors. An instant later the animal's lifeless body collapsed into the pool of its own blood.

The priests knelt to joint the corpse with deft movements, tossing parts of the body to each of the surrounding warriors and ordering them to place a foot upon the joints. Soon there was little left of the horse but its head and hide. This looked curiously shrunken and matt-coloured as it lay between the priests. Finally they rose from their labours and raised their arms to the heavens in prayer. Eperitus placed his left foot on the broken rib bone that they had thrown towards him and watched Tyndareus come to the front of the dais again. This time he was accompanied by Agamemnon.

Eperitus glanced across at Odysseus. The spectacle of the bloody sacrifice had awed the young warrior and the muscles of his face were strained with tension, but Odysseus simply grinned back at him and winked. Eperitus was taken aback by his cool, slightly amused indifference, but before he could react further Tyndareus spoke.

As he held the staff before him, he asked them whether they

promised to protect the husband of Helen against anybody who should wish Helen for himself. The words were not elaborate or extensive, as a Greek warrior will always obey the spirit of an oath, even those like Odysseus who could twist words like blades of grass. Every voice answered in agreement and thus the fateful oath was sworn.

A moment later one of the priests clapped his hands and a host of servants rushed in, carrying vessels of water to wash clean the floor of the hall. More servants brought bowls for the oath-takers to cleanse the blood from their skin, and soon they were seated again with food and drink set before them. Then Agamemnon stood and received the staff once more from Tyndareus.

The council of war had begun.

Chapter Twenty-one

ODYSSEUS AND PENELOPE

Fearing her cousin was already overripe for marriage – and would remain as little more than a maid to her demanding father if she did not force her hand – Clytaemnestra agreed to Damastor's plan and immediately made an ointment for the purpose. She gave it to Neaera with instructions to rub it on the clothing of both Odysseus and Penelope and arrange for them to meet shortly afterwards. As long as they were together when the ointment began to take effect, she assured her, they would be unable to resist each other.

When Neaera asked how she was to apply the ointment to the princess's clothing, Clytaemnestra handed her a vial filled with a pleasant-smelling liquid.

'Give this to Penelope's body slave, Actoris,' she instructed. 'It's a mild poison. Put it into her drink and she'll be paralysed with illness for a few days. Then you can volunteer to take her place, and after that you'll have every opportunity to rub the ointment into Penelope's clothing before dressing her.'

And so Neaera was able to prepare one of the plain woollen dresses that Penelope favoured and spread it out over the princess's bed while she bathed in an antechamber. Satisfied that the first part of her task was done, she picked up a soft brush and went to scrub her mistress, who lay stretched out in the heated water with only a few wisps of steam to cover her nakedness. Her breasts and stomach had retained their natural pink hue, but the rest of her flesh was burned almost to the colour of a common slave's, causing Neaera to frown disapprovingly. Helen, by whose standards Neaera measured everybody, kept out of the sun to preserve her pure white complexion; her cousin hardly seemed to care.

'Not so rough with that brush,' Penelope chided her. She stepped from the bath to drip on the stone floor, where Neaera at once began to dry her off. 'Are you this brutal with Helen? She told me you had a delicate touch.'

The truth was that Neaera was nervous. First Clytaemnestra, then Damastor, had instilled in her the vital importance of getting Penelope to the feast at the same time as Odysseus. Damastor would apply the charmed ointment to his master's tunic and ensure he was by the double doors of the great hall just before the food was brought in to the guests; Neaera was to do the same with Penelope, or risk Odysseus reacting to the first female he saw. But unless she could persuade Penelope to be a little quicker, they were going to be woefully late.

'Give me that, you clumsy girl,' Penelope said, taking the towel and drying herself. 'Bring me my best robe – the purple one. I feel like a change tonight.'

'But my lady . . .' Neaera stuttered.

'Stop flapping, Neaera. It's in the basket by the wall. Hurry up and fetch it for me.'

Why tonight, of all nights, did she have to be fussy about what she wore? The slave girl ran past the dress she had prepared and began looking through the large woven basket by the wall, all the time thinking about what she should do. There was not enough ointment left and no time to apply it anyway. Then, as she found the neatly folded dress in the basket, she heard Penelope pad barefoot into the room behind her.

'Come on, then. I'm dry,' she said, holding out her arms for Neaera to slip the dress over her naked body.

Neaera stood up, clutching the dress to her chest, but as she did so she felt it snag on the weave of the basket and tear.

'Oh, my lady! I'm so sorry,' she said, tears rimming her eyes.

She was too shocked to realize that her clumsiness had solved her dilemma.

Penelope sighed at the sight of the rip.

'Never mind, Neaera. Don't cry, now: I can mend it after the feast. I suppose I'll have to wear this old thing you've laid out on the bed for me instead.'

Suddenly, as if Penelope might change her mind, Neaera ran over to the bed and held the large oblong of cloth before her. 'This is just fine,' she said, turning the simple garment this way and that as if it were an item of great beauty. 'You'll look wonderful in it, my lady.'

'Of course I won't, and you know it. And just for once I wanted to look attractive.'

Neaera sensed something in Penelope's tone and enquired whether she wanted to catch the eye of anyone in particular.

'Perhaps,' Penelope answered. 'But it doesn't matter. Like most men here, he's much too besotted with Helen to look at any other woman. Now, put that dress on me before I catch cold, and then you can put my hair up. Assuming you can do that without mishap?'

Neaera was embarrassed but managed to return the princess's well-meant smile. She took the dress, folded it once and wrapped it about Penelope's body. With the deft skill of one who had dressed women all her life, she pinched the upper corners of the cloth over her mistress's left shoulder and fastened them together with a golden brooch. She then used a second clasp to secure the garment over the other shoulder. This left the left side of Penelope's body exposed, but the slave girl quickly fastened the two open halves of the dress with a cord about the waist. Then, remembering the ointment, she drew the woven material closer together so that it rubbed against Penelope's skin, ensuring that Clytaemnestra's potion was brought into contact with it. The adjustment also left less flesh exposed so, keen for Penelope to look as alluring as possible for Odysseus, Neaera arranged the material to fall open about one of her long, smooth legs, exposing it almost to the buttock.

Pleased with the effect of this, she proceeded to bunch Penelope's hair above her head with all possible haste, conscious that the feast would already be starting in the great hall below them. Despite this, Neaera risked precious time to make the princess look as attractive as she could. For someone who was used to the obsessive demands of Helen, the task was an easy one to execute. As a final touch, Neaera applied a little fine soot to darken her eyebrows and the transformation was complete. Penelope no longer looked like the plain and simple daughter of Icarius, whom only the most discerning men ever noticed for her natural beauty; now every feature of her femininity had been emphasized for all to see. Penelope asked Neaera how she looked, and was told she could not fail to catch the eye of every man in the hall.

'Hmmm,' Penelope purred. 'I feel good, too. Despite your hasty manner, Neaera, I think you've worked wonders with those clumsy fingers of yours. For the first time in ages I actually *feel* attractive. It's like I've had too much wine, but instead of going to my head it's worked its way under my skin. I'm tingling all over.' She looked down at herself and ran her hands over her stomach and thighs. 'You've done me up a little tight, though,' she added, and proceeded to loosen the cord about her waist so that her bare ribs and the swell of her left breast fell open to view. 'That's better. Now, let's go to the feast.'

As usual, the great hall was filled with suitors, warriors and slaves. Some of the guests were seated about a bard who sang a song on a lyre, recalling the feats of ancient heroes. Others were filling themselves with food or sharing wine with the friends they had made during the seemingly endless weeks spent at the palace. But as Penelope arrived their heads began to turn, in ones and twos at first until, eventually, every man was looking at her. She returned their lascivious stares, delighting in the feel of the air fanning across her bared flesh. She felt drunk with her own sensuality, and as her skin crawled with peculiar sensations she looked about the crowds of revellers, seeking one man in particular.

Neaera felt awkward beside her adopted mistress. They were only slightly later than the appointed time, but Damastor and Odysseus were nowhere in sight. This made her nervous, as she did not know what to do if one of the warriors should approach Penelope. Clytaemnestra had warned that Penelope's intensified affections could easily be directed to any man, and unwanted attention could prove fatal to her lover's plans. Then her fear became a reality as one of the men left his seat and walked over to them.

'You look even more magnificent than usual tonight, Penelope,' Little Ajax said, his small, closely-set eyes roaming up and down her body. He licked his thin lips and the snake about his shoulders did the same. 'Maybe you'd like to join me for a little wine?'

Neaera looked at the man with distaste, repulsed by his broken nose and pockmarked cheeks. The snake about his shoulders had more charm than its owner, and so the slave girl was terrified to see Penelope look down at the man with something akin to desire in her expression.

'If this man's bothering you, mistress, I can fetch your father. He's only over there.'

The warrior laughed. 'As if a mere serving girl would dare approach the royal dais. Besides,' he added, placing a hand on Penelope's exposed thigh, 'your mistress doesn't appear to be complaining.'

'Yes, Neaera,' Penelope agreed, 'there's no harm in spending time with such a strong, good-looking man, is there? Why don't you go back to my room and see if you can mend that dress.' She turned back and ran a hand along the neck of Ajax's snake. 'Go on now.'

Everything was falling down around Neaera's ears. This was not how things were supposed to have happened, but what could she do? She was only a slave, and not a very intelligent one at that. Feeling the panic growing inside her she glanced around the hall again. And there, finally, was Damastor.

❧

'Here, my lord, put this on. It's a gift from the lady Helen.'

Damastor handed the tunic to Odysseus as he was about to throw on his usual clothes after bathing.

'Her maid gave it me. She feels your old clothes are becoming a bit threadbare.'

And so they were, after so long away from home. Odysseus took the proffered gift and tossed his usual faded and repaired garment into a corner of the room. He had been so involved with Agamemnon's plans during the past few days that he had almost forgotten Helen wanted him as her husband. She must be confident of his acceptance though, he thought, to be sending him gifts before he had confirmed his decision to Tyndareus.

He pulled the tunic over his head and felt it settle against his skin. Already he could hear the noise of the banquet on the ground floor of the palace and began mentally preparing himself for the questions that Agamemnon would push at him. The council of war had been a disastrous failure, as Odysseus had expected. Some openly accused Agamemnon of wanting to weaken their strength at home, thus making them vulnerable to Mycenaean armies. Beset by such paranoia, it had not taken long for the council of war to slip into chaotic farce, with its members shouting at each other or walking out. Now the Mycenaean king was desperately trying to restore the situation. Impressed by Odysseus's suggestion of the oath, he had asked him to come up with a similarly shrewd idea for unifying the Greeks against Troy.

Despite the honour, Odysseus's heart was not in it. Much though he admired Agamemnon's character and shared his aspirations, his thoughts were focused on returning to his homeland and saving his people from Eupeithes's reign. He missed the sight of the sea every morning, the smell of the salt water in the air and the cry of the gulls on the wind. He longed to see his father and mother and their faithful servants again. More than anything, he wanted to leave this world of political intrigue and power games and go back to the simple life he had always known.

Had he dared to, he could have returned months ago and used the clay owl Athena had given him. Breaking the tablet would have summoned the goddess, and with her beside him few could have withstood his vengeful fury. But his doubts had prevented him. What if he had broken the clay tablet and Athena had not come? What if it was just another trick of the gods? His lack of faith made him seek out more certain methods of recovering his father's kingdom, and as a consequence he now faced the dilemma of choosing between Helen and Penelope. Between home and love. But whatever force he came away with from Sparta, be it the might of Tyndareus's army or the reluctant loan of Icarius's personal guard, and whatever strategy he devised for retaking Ithaca, in his heart he wondered whether he could achieve anything without the help of his patron goddess.

'My lord?' Damastor said, standing by the door. 'Shall we go? The men have already descended to the feast.'

Odysseus tied the straps of his sandals and followed Damastor out into the empty corridor. There was a curious new sensation in his flesh as he anticipated the night's banquet, lifting his spirits and sending his mind racing towards Penelope. He pictured her tall, slim body in his mind's eye and could hardly believe the feelings of physical desire that were coursing through him. His imagination was filled with her, recalling every detail of her physique from her long feet and shapely legs to the swell of her breasts and the curve of her brown shoulders. Would she be there tonight? He hoped so. Though he still feared her rejection, which would compel him to accept Tyndareus's offer of Helen, he drew renewed courage from the thought of being in her presence. Boldness won battles, not timidity, and tonight he knew he had to approach her or lay all hope of her aside. Just the thought of her made his skin tingle with anticipation, and suddenly he was grateful for the new tunic Damastor had given him.

'Perhaps Penelope will be there,' Damastor said, as if reading Odysseus's mind. 'If you don't mind me saying, my lord, you seem to have an eye for her.'

Odysseus nodded. 'She's a real beauty, Damastor, and she's got a quick mind, too. I intend to make her mine.'

Damastor smiled with secret satisfaction, hardly noticing the young slave girl who passed them by on the steps. Odysseus, however, stared after her with a grin on his face.

'Or any girl, for that matter.'

Damastor put a hand on the prince's shoulder and led him quickly away from alternative temptations, down into the maelstrom of the great hall. Almost at once, through the crowds of warriors and attendant slaves, he saw Neaera. Her eyes met his with helpless pleading.

Only then did he notice Little Ajax conversing with Penelope, and to his dismay he saw that the princess's attitude was not one of coldness. Suddenly he saw his plans slipping out of his grasp in the most unexpected of manners.

'My lord,' he said, grabbing Odysseus's elbow and pointing urgently at the group. 'If you want to speak to Penelope, you've got to do something quickly. That Locrian troublemaker is talking to her.'

Odysseus looked over at the woman he loved. For many evenings he had watched her at the nightly feasts, a distant figure who had dismissed him contemptuously from her company, which was in contrast freely given to others. But never had she looked as alluring as she did tonight. The tail in her hair had gone and the long, dark strands were tied up in a loose coil above her head, baring her exquisite ears and neck to the hungry eyes of the men around her. It set Odysseus's flesh alight to look at her, creating a vacuum that only his other senses could fill: the sound of her voice; the smell of her clean, feminine aroma; the feel of her smooth skin; the often imagined taste of her lips. The pricking in his flesh that had been stirring in him ever since he left his quarters became a frenzy of desire, aggravated further by Little Ajax's interfering presence. Instinctively he clutched at his belt, where his sword would normally hang. Recalling its absence, he clenched his massive fists and walked towards the Locrian.

Little Ajax seemed to sense his approach and turned. The flatterer's smile fell from his tight lips to be quickly replaced by the usual sneer of hatred, rucking up the side of his face as he stared at Odysseus.

'What do *you* want? Can't you see we're talking?'

Odysseus smiled coldly. 'So can everyone else. Penelope's a valuable prize, and some people here have an interest in who talks with her.'

The princess looked at him. Her usual hostility was strangely absent, making the desire in his flesh burn more fiercely.

'Go tell them to find another woman,' Little Ajax responded. His pet snake hissed, flicking its tongue menacingly at the intruder. 'There are plenty of slaves about, so stop wasting my time.'

'Icarius doesn't concern himself with slaves, but he *does* want to know what your interest in his daughter is. He sent me to tell you as much. If you're wise you'll go to him now, or it's my guess you'll be observing Penelope from the other side of the palace walls.'

The Locrian swore and spat onto the stone flags. Even he could not refuse the summons of a king or delay the matter for longer than Icarius's patience would last. Reluctantly he turned to go, nodding tersely to Penelope and promising to return as soon as he could. He shot Odysseus a suspicious glance and shouldered past him into the crowd.

Odysseus seized Penelope's arm and pushed her ahead of him to a corner of the great hall, out of the sight of Neaera, Damastor and the lustful eyes of the men who glanced at the princess.

'What do you think you're doing?' she demanded. 'Am I

forbidden to speak with noble-born men? And besides, my father wouldn't care *who* showed an interest in me.'

She shook his hand loose but her feeble anger could not disguise the deeper, more compelling feeling beneath. It showed in her dilated pupils and the colour in her cheeks. Her breathing became slightly heavier through her nostrils, so that she had to slightly open her mouth to steady its rhythm. Her nipples stood up beneath the woven material of her dress.

'Why do you avoid me?' he asked her, urgently.

'I don't know what you mean. You don't have exclusive access to my company, Odysseus of Ithaca. And what does it matter whether I talk to you or not?'

Odysseus looked at her and knew that, for all his wit and guile, he could not lie to her – and would never want to.

'Because I love you.'

Penelope looked at him with wide eyes, shocked by his admission. She continued to look at him, and as if for the first time took in the details of his face, his hair, his awkward, muscular body. The crazed tensions that had been crawling through her flesh since dressing became more fluid, running throughout her body with a wild abandon that loosened every nerve and made her horribly, frighteningly weak before him. The noises of the room were stilled by his heavy breathing, the light of the many torches dimmed by his green eyes as they searched into hers. She had wanted him before, but now it was as if she no longer had control of her truest desires. Her emotions had taken command of her body, foremost amongst them the dominant, all-consuming compulsion to be with him and to give to him everything that had been her own for so long.

'Isn't that why you've rejected me?' Odysseus persisted.

He placed his hands on her sides, a presumption that she did not resist. The palm and fingers of his right hand parted the split in her dress and shaped themselves to the curve between her hip bone and lower ribs. His touch made her almost frenzied with the need of him.

'Because you're afraid of your own love for me, aren't you? Tell me, Penelope. Say it.'

'I don't know. Yes. Yes, I want you.'

As the words forced themselves free from her lips she heard a voice calling her name. It was harsh and driven with anger; Little Ajax had discovered Odysseus's trick and was forcing his way back across the great hall at that very moment. His shouts urged her to desperation.

'I must go. Come to my room tonight – soon! There's an olive tree opposite my window where you can enter without being seen by the guards. I'll be waiting for you.'

Suddenly Damastor found them.

'Little Ajax knows he's been fooled, my lord. The runt is looking for a fight.'

'I haven't got time to give him that satisfaction tonight,' Odysseus answered as he watched Penelope disappear into the throng. '*She* wants me. Quickly, Damastor, do you know an olive tree opposite the women's quarters?'

A hazy sliver of moon slumbered beneath a thin veil of cloud, its half-lidded eye illuminating each swirl and eddy of the dark vapours as they were fanned across the night sky. By its dim light Odysseus picked his way up the twisted bole of the old tree, slipping dangerously in his haste to be with the woman he loved. His mind whirled with the excitement of knowing she returned his love and would very soon be his. Helen, the beacon that had drawn him to Sparta and the prize that would give him back his homeland, was forgotten.

He crawled out to the end of a long branch that pointed with forlorn rigidity towards a window in the palace wall. Leaning across, he seized the lip of the window and hauled himself over the ledge to land in a heap on the bedroom floor. He lay on his back and looked up at the plain but spacious room. Its high ceiling loomed above him, whilst by his head was the foot of a large bed.

As he looked, Penelope's face appeared over the edge and peered down at him.

'Are you all right?'

'I think so. Isn't there an easier way to reach you?'

'I'm afraid not,' she answered, watching him rise to his feet and stand before her. She sat up and the split in her dress fell open over her thigh. 'Unless you want to fight your way through the guards.'

'You'd be worth it.'

She tossed her head back and untied her hair so that it streamed down across her back. Taking a deep breath, she leaned back and closed her eyes, feeling again the desire for Odysseus that had gripped her in the great hall. A spasm of sheer lust ran from her groin up into her breasts and down again to her stomach, flowing out into the very tips of her toes and fingers. Nervously, her hand wandered to the cord about her waist, fumbled with the knot and released it. The clinging dress drifted free of her arched back and buttocks, letting in the cool air of the moonlit room to play freely over her flesh.

She sensed the man watching her every move and, enjoying his attention, lifted her hand to the brooch at her shoulder. Her eyes remained closed as she undid the two pins, allowing the dress to slip down over her smooth skin to reveal her nakedness. For the first time in her life she had exposed her natural state to a man, and yet nerves and inexperience could not subdue the lust within her. Opening her eyes, she lay back on the bed and held out a hand to him.

'Come here, Odysseus.'

In the corridors below them Damastor approached an officer of the guard, who barred his way with a spear.

'No men beyond this point. Women only.'

'But there's an intruder in the women's quarters. One of the slave women has just told me.'

The soldier looked at him puzzled. 'That's impossible, or I'd have seen him myself.'

'Well, he's up there. In Penelope's room. Do you want to risk the wrath of her father?'

The guard did not seem frightened by the threat, but knew the duties laid upon him. 'All right then, we'll have a look. And you'd better return to the feast.'

Damastor headed back to the great hall, smiling to himself. The moment he realized Odysseus was intending to climb up to Penelope's room, he had remembered that the punishment for entering the women's quarters was death and seized his opportunity. At last, it seemed, the gods were on his side.

Behind him, the guard officer turned and called back along the corridor. Two men emerged with spears in their hands and came running towards him. One of them was directed to fetch King Icarius, whilst the other accompanied the officer up the steps that led to the next floor. They rushed along the torch-lit corridor that linked the many rooms of the women's quarters, shouting the princess's name as they ran. Turning a corner they were suddenly at the door to her room, where they paused momentarily to listen for any suspicious sound beyond the thick wood. Then they heard voices, hushed and urgent. The door burst open with one kick and they ran into the darkened room.

Penelope fell back onto the bed, clutching a blanket to herself. By the window, where the thin light of the moon infiltrated the shadows, they saw a naked man. He took one look at them, then plucked up his clothes from the floor and dashed to the window. They were after him in a heartbeat, but to their shock he leapt out into the night air, heedless of the drop two floors to the ground.

'Help me!' Penelope called behind them.

Turning they saw her kneeling naked on the bed, the blanket in a pile at her knees. For a moment all thoughts of the intruder were forgotten.

'He attacked me,' she pleaded. Having stolen their attention away from the escape of her lover, she pulled the cover back over herself again. 'He was here when I returned from the feast.'

'Did he . . . touch you?' asked the officer.

'Do you know him, my lady?' added the other guard in the face of her silence.

'No. It was dark and . . . and he covered my face with this blanket so that I couldn't see him.'

There would be trouble from this, the soldiers knew, but for now they had to see that Penelope was safe. The officer went to the window and looked down. Nothing. Then he looked at the tree and an explanation dawned on him.

Suddenly there were more voices in the corridor outside and a moment later Icarius burst in with three guards at his heels. He took one look at his daughter and with a sinking heart knew that what he had been told was true. Seizing a torch from one of the soldiers, he held it before her as she hid her nudity behind the flimsy covering.

'Who?' he demanded.

When she did not answer the officer repeated what she had told him. 'Shall I send the men out and call for a slave, my lord?'

'No! Let her squirm in her own infamy. Did you see the man?'

'We saw him, but it was dark and before we could do anything he leapt out of the window and escaped.'

'What do you mean, you idiot? How could anyone jump out of the window and run off? He'd break his legs, if he didn't break his neck first.'

'He must have got in by climbing up the tree, father,' Penelope offered, still kneeling on the bed. The lascivious urgings had faded and she tried harder to conceal her nudity behind the blanket.

Icarius ignored her and went to the window. After thrusting his head out and assessing the means of entry and exit he turned back to the knot of guards in the centre of the room. They were trying desperately not to look at the naked princess or her incensed father.

'Have you looked to see if he left anything behind? A sandal or a piece of clothing? Anything?'

They shook their heads, but as they did so Icarius suddenly shot out an arm and pointed at the floor.

'There!' he exclaimed, and leaned down to pick something small and delicate from the bare slabs at the feet of his soldiers. He held it up like a prize, turning its delicate form before their eyes. It was a dried sprig of chelonion, the badge of the men from Ithaca.

The feast was stopped immediately and every man – noble or commoner – ordered back to their quarters. Eperitus and Peisandros had already quit the festivities for the night, preferring instead to walk through the gardens and swap stories of the battles they had been through. Eperitus was recounting the fight with the serpent when armed guards approached and escorted them back to their rooms. He found Odysseus already there, looking breathless and dishevelled with scratches on his arms and legs. As the prince offered no explanation for his condition, or his absence from the feast, Eperitus knew better than to interrogate him about it.

They remained under strict guard until first light, when a herald visited each suitor and his men with a summons to assemble in the courtyard. There was a great press on the stairs as the Ithacans descended, swapping keen gossip with the friends they had made amongst the warriors of other Greek nations. Speculation was rife. Some said Helen's husband would be announced, whilst others declared it would be war with Troy. But nobody suspected that the true reason for the summons would prove much more sensational.

In the meantime Odysseus was curiously withdrawn from the excitement that gripped his men. His absence had been noticed from the banquet the night before, but when the men questioned Damastor about it, knowing he had remained with the prince until after they had gone down for the feast, he dismissed them with impatient gestures. Instead, he preferred to spend his time looking about the courtyard in a distracted manner.

So as they waited, watching slaves cut down an old olive tree close to the palace walls, they remained in ignorance of the reason for the muster. Then Agamemnon, Tyndareus and Icarius appeared and walked across the compound towards them. That they were escorted by two dozen heavily armed guards brought new questions to the minds of the waiting men and made them shift uneasily, conscious that their own weapons were locked in the palace armoury.

Agamemnon stepped forward, glowering at the assembly with a ferocity none of them had ever witnessed in him before. 'Whilst most of us were feasting in the great hall last night,' he began, 'someone entered the women's quarters and assaulted the princess Penelope. It's beyond any doubt in my mind that a man here, be he king, prince or soldier, has violated the trust of his hosts. Such an act is a vile abuse of the customs of *xenia*. That Icarius is angry is his right; and both Tyndareus and I support his demand for justice under Spartan law.' Agamemnon left a pause, in which Icarius stood erect and cast his glance across the silent files of men, his eyes lingering meaningfully on Odysseus. 'You all understand the Spartan punishment for any man who sleeps with an unmarried noblewoman?'

Death was the punishment, and every man knew it. They stood more stiffly now, staring directly ahead without turning to look at the faces of their colleagues. The news left a bitter taste in Eperitus's mouth, not only because of what had happened to Penelope but also because their period of happiness had ended in such a dishonourable way. He sensed the three men already knew who had committed the offence, or why else would they have ordered them to the courtyard? It could only be to make a public show of the culprit, and the prospect turned his stomach. He dared to glance sideways at Odysseus and noticed that his friend's head hung down and his eyes were closed.

Tyndareus now stepped forward, his grim face dark with emotion.

'Shame has been brought not only upon this house, but upon every man here. I intend to see the perpetrator found and punished, not only with death, which is the law, but also with disgrace. His name will be cast down into ignominy where it belongs; a name to be despised, hated, and then forgotten; a punishment befitting a true coward, a man without honour or glory. And don't think we are in ignorance of who did this, for the man who invaded the privacy of the women's quarters last night left a clue to his identity. Odysseus!'

Tyndareus pointed directly at the Ithacans, sending Eperitus's heart beating hard against his chest. Odysseus lifted his head and looked back, but said nothing.

'Odysseus,' the Spartan king repeated, his voice trembling with rage. He held up a small, fragile flower in his great fist for everyone to see. 'You once told me your men wear these flowers as a reminder of their homeland. This one was found on the floor of Penelope's room!'

Suddenly there was uproar amongst the gathered soldiers. The warriors on either side of the Ithacans stepped back as if they were diseased. They looked at them with anger in their eyes, and some shouted abuse at them for bringing dishonour on every man there. The crime itself was nothing compared to the shadow of shame that had touched upon them all.

Meanwhile, Odysseus's men frantically checked their clothing for the dried flower that each wore as a badge. Upon finding them still attached – to their relief – they glanced about at their companions to see whose was missing. Eperitus was comforted to see his own sprig of chelonion secured in his belt. Then a sense of foreboding made him look at Odysseus, who remained staring at Tyndareus. He did not move, though Eperitus saw his vast bulk wavering in a strange manner, as if he were about to step forward but a greater will restrained him. Then his fears were confirmed: the flower that the prince usually wore with such pride was gone.

Eperitus's first reaction was one of shock and sickened horror. He could not believe Odysseus was the man who had assaulted Penelope, though his eyes and heart told him it was true. Even then he trusted him not to have stooped to rape and knew he would not have hurt the princess. But that would not save him from public execution for his crime. Worse than death, though, was the dishonour that would destroy his name. To a warrior such a punishment was unthinkable, and Eperitus was repulsed by the thought.

Then he remembered his duty of honour to Odysseus. The prince was a great warrior and the best man he had ever known, someone whom he had come to love. He knew he could neither see him shamed nor killed.

So, as Odysseus took a step towards Tyndareus, he caught one of his large hands and pressed his own sprig of chelonion into his palm, then walked out to accept his friend's punishment.

Chapter Twenty-two

THE EXECUTION

'I'm the man you're looking for,' Eperitus said. He opened his cloak so they could see he no longer wore the badge of Ithaca. 'It was I who dropped the flower in Penelope's room last night.'

Shouts of abuse erupted from the crowd of warriors. Agamemnon and Tyndareus looked at him with disdain, and even his comrades took a step back as Icarius came purposefully towards him. Eperitus knew he would have to accept the king's hatred without complaint, along with public execution and the dishonour that would accompany it. These were the consequences of his sacrifice. Not that death scared him, but the shame that would attach to his name was worse than a hundred deaths. And yet as the son of a traitor, he thought, he should have known the gods would not choose him for glory. The Pythoness had lied; his father's curse had been passed down to him.

Icarius stepped up to him and spat in his face. Eperitus felt the spittle running down his cheek, and then Penelope's father punched him with all his strength. It was not a hard blow, because Icarius was not a strong man, but he felt his nose break and tasted the blood running onto his lips and into the back of his throat. For a moment he was glad for the king that he had drawn blood, as it might slake some of his thirst for revenge. But then he sensed the crowd of warriors gathering around him and knew that public humiliation and execution were not enough for them, who believed he had brought dishonour on them all.

The first soldier hit him and sent him spinning backwards, where he was caught by one of the other men in the circle closing around him. Then he received the full force of their collective anger. Fists came at him from all sides. They hit him in the stomach, kidneys, face and head so that within moments he was on the ground, consciousness slipping away from him as he impulsively curled up in a ball to resist their blows. Blood ran into his eyes and mouth and he was barely able to see as his senses folded in upon him. As blackness tunnelled his vision, he looked up and recognized Little Ajax amongst the snarling faces.

Then the blows and kicks receded. Through his throbbing ears he heard the voice of Odysseus. He blinked the blood from one of his eyes and saw the prince dragging his assailants off him, helped by Menelaus, Halitherses and Gyrtias the Rhodian. Somebody pulled him to his feet and he recognized Mentor's voice whispering encouraging words in his ear. He supported Eperitus until he regained enough strength to stand unaided, then withdrew to leave him alone with Odysseus before the kings of Sparta and Mycenae.

Odysseus looked long at Tyndareus before speaking.

'This man is no criminal,' he began. The sound of his voice was smooth and calming, countering the rage that was all about him. 'Though he confesses to the crime, he doesn't deserve death. In my company he has always proved himself a man of honour; a warrior whose bravery is second to none, and whose skill with the spear has laid many of my enemies in the dust. Were it not for his courage and self-sacrifice I might not be standing before you now, pleading for his life. So I beg your mercy, and Icarius's, whose daughter's honour has been offended by the rash act of a foolish man. The shame of dishonour is enough for any warrior: let that be sufficient.'

'There's nothing I can do,' Tyndareus replied. 'The decision is not mine to make.'

'I've helped you ensure peace will be kept in your palace, and for that you promised me anything it was in your power to give. I ask you for the life of Eperitus.'

Tyndareus was surprised that Odysseus should be prepared to exchange Helen for the life of a mere soldier, but he kept his wonderment to himself. 'Only Icarius can make that choice, Odysseus. You must ask him.'

'My answer is the same,' Icarius said, coldly. 'The man must die.'

'Then if you won't give me Eperitus's life, at least offer me his death. Allow me to be the executioner.'

Icarius laughed at the suggestion. 'No. He raped *my* daughter, and I'll be the one to put him to the sword. The right of revenge is mine.'

'He's my friend and, what's more, he's an Ithacan warrior. If a man is to die, let it be by the hand of one of his own countrymen.'

Tyndareus sighed loudly. Taking a sword from one of the guards, he handed it to Odysseus. 'Be quick,' he said. 'I'm already sick of this whole affair.'

Odysseus took the weapon, but made no move to carry out the king's request.

'Not before the eyes of all these onlookers,' he announced. 'Let me take him down to the orchard by the bridge and carry out the sentence there, privately and with respect for the service he has given me. I give you my word Penelope's attacker will receive his just rewards.'

'No – do it here,' Icarius demanded. 'Where there are witnesses to the act.'

There were murmurs of agreement from the crowd. They had already come to regard Odysseus as too clever for the absolute truth, and though they respected him few trusted him. But at that moment Peisandros stepped from the ranks of the Myrmidons and joined Odysseus.

'I'll see that it's done. Permit Odysseus to take this man to the orchard he talks of, the one by the tributary that runs into the Eurotas. I will be your witness. This is an evil business and, by the gods, I want to see it over.'

'I agree,' Menelaus said, his face full of disgust at the proceedings and Icarius's lust for revenge. 'Let Odysseus kill his friend and let Peisandros act as witness. He's of noble birth and we can trust what he says.'

The early spring sky had filled with grey clouds and a wind was blowing across the courtyard now. Agamemnon and Tyndareus exchanged hushed words then quickly nodded their approval. Odysseus and Peisandros bowed low before them, then, as the first dollops of rain began to sink pits into the dust, they led Eperitus across the courtyard and through the gates.

For a while they walked in silence through the town, Odysseus on one side of Eperitus and Peisandros on the other, looking in every respect the escort that they were. The rain shower had been brief and as the townsfolk emerged from the shelter of homes and doorways they stared at them because of the prisoner's beaten and bloodied state. A few children dared follow in their wake to throw sticks and stones at his back – instinctively identifying him as some form of criminal – but were chased angrily away by Peisandros.

Before long they reached the city walls and could see the bridge and the orchard only a short walk further on through the arched gateway.

'Wait here and keep watch, Peisandros,' Odysseus commanded, handing him the sword. 'I'll be back shortly.'

With that he sprinted back up the hill at a speed that belied his heavy bulk. They watched him out of sight, wondering what had brought about his sudden desertion, and then Peisandros turned to the young soldier.

'What's all this about, Eperitus? I was with you last night before they sent everybody back to their quarters, so I know you couldn't have been in Penelope's room. You're covering for someone, aren't you?'

Eperitus remained silent.

'Was it Odysseus? You can trust me not to say anything. If

you're standing in for the prince then I honour you for your sacrifice, but I'll not see you murdered for something you didn't do.'

At that point Odysseus reappeared, carrying a struggling goat under his arm.

'Come on,' he told them, and marched through the gate at a pace which they struggled to keep up with.

'He's keen to see you dead, my friend,' Peisandros muttered as they dropped behind. 'Perhaps he doesn't want you changing your mind. But don't forget who's carrying the sword now.'

Although his name was now a thing to be despised, Eperitus felt a glimmer of hope that the Myrmidon spearman did not want him dead. How he planned to save his life he did not know, though if it meant Odysseus would be found out he would freely have chosen death again. Either way, if he lived he knew that his time in Sparta was over and the life of an outcast lay once more before him.

They reached the orchard and sought the shade of the apple trees. Here Odysseus passed the restless goat to Peisandros and turned to Eperitus.

'Come to the river bank,' he ordered, and led him down to the water. Here he made him kneel and began scooping up handfuls of the cold water, pouring them over his friend's head to loosen the caked blood. Then he removed his own cloak and, dipping a corner in the gurgling waters, began to gently dab the blood from Eperitus's skin. If he winced, Odysseus tried again with more care, and did not stop until every bit was gone.

'You're a fool,' he said, shaking his head at the numerous cuts and swollen bruises that decorated Eperitus's body. 'But a noble one, and I thank you for your loyalty. I was an idiot to be in Penelope's room, though it was at her invitation and not my own imposition; but to have openly admitted it would have meant not only my death, it would also have heaped shame on the woman I love and brought an end to our mission! And nothing must stop me from restoring Ithaca to my father's rule, even if it means allowing the death of my closest friends. Maybe you understand?'

Eperitus looked at the eddies flowing past on the surface of the tributary and wanted to ask Odysseus if that also meant choosing Helen over Penelope. The prince was prepared to let his friend die for his homeland, but would not give up the woman he loved in exchange for all the power he needed to put Laertes back on the throne. Or maybe he was preserving himself for Penelope, after all, and the return to Ithaca had been relegated to a secondary cause.

'I have no home, my lord,' Eperitus answered, 'so I don't blame you for wanting to regain yours. Even if you are sometimes rash in your actions.'

Odysseus laughed. 'I don't know what came over me. I know I love her and can barely pass a moment without thinking of her, but last night it was as if all my feelings for her were tied up in a knot and there was only one way to release them.'

Peisandros joined them.

'We're ready,' Odysseus told him. 'Now, give me back the sword.'

'I can't do that, my lord.'

'Don't be a fool, man, and do as I say.'

Peisandros put the goat down, which immediately began gnawing at the tough grass around the trees, and pulled the sword from his belt.

'You know as well as I that Eperitus didn't commit this crime. I don't mean to disrespect your rank, Odysseus, but I won't allow you to kill an innocent man.'

'And I have no intention of doing any such thing,' Odysseus replied. He pointed at the goat. 'What do you think I brought that thing for? A sacrifice to the gods for letting me murder my friend? Of course not, you buffoon – I'm going to kill the goat and dip Eperitus's cloak in its blood. Hopefully that and your testimony will convince them.'

'What?' Peisandros exclaimed. 'You gave them your word without having any intention of killing Eperitus?'

'Just as you told them you'd be a witness to my death,' Eperitus added, 'with every intention of seeing me escape.'

The realization brought a broad smile to the Myrmidon's lips as he handed the sword to Odysseus. 'Yes, I suppose so. Well, let's get on with it, and may the gods forgive us.'

At that moment they heard the thudding of hoofs and turned to see Icarius arrive, mounted on a white stallion. He stopped and looked about himself until he caught sight of the warriors amongst the apple trees. With a sharp dig of his heels he drove the horse into the orchard, ducking his head to clear the branches. Odysseus gave the goat a quick kick and sent it running off towards the city walls, whilst shooting Peisandros a look of frustration and despair.

'I'm not too late, then,' Icarius sneered, looking down at them and noting with satisfaction that Eperitus was kneeling and Odysseus stood over him, sword in hand. 'I was half expecting you to have let him go, Odysseus.'

'You should have more trust in a man when he gives his word,' the Ithacan retorted.

'Trust you? Why do you think I'm here? Now, let's get on with it.'

Eperitus spat blood into the dirt where his horse stood, but Odysseus laid a calming hand on his shoulder.

'Peace now, my friend; at least try to die with honour,' he said as he stepped in front of Eperitus, turning his back towards Icarius. Then his voice sank to a whisper. 'You always said you were a good horseman — now's your chance to show me. Do you understand?'

Eperitus nodded and lowered his head. He heard the stallion shifting as Icarius tried to get a better view, and his mind raced to plan his next move. He raised one knee, ready to spring. Then Odysseus drew himself up to his full height and lifted the sword over his head.

An instant later, Eperitus thrust himself upwards and barged him aside with his shoulder. The prince tumbled deliberately into

Peisandros and the pair of them fell into a heap. Icarius's eyes widened as Eperitus sprinted towards him, but his reactions were too slow and as he tried to turn the horse around Eperitus caught his heel and pushed upwards with all his strength. The king fell to the damp ground with his arms and legs flailing, and Eperitus leapt skilfully onto the animal's back. It continued to turn, snorting loudly in confusion, but its new rider quickly took the reins and calmed it with a hand on its neck.

For a moment he was tempted to drive the horse over the prostrate form before him, but the temptation quickly faded as he saw the terror in Icarius's eyes. Instead, he turned the stallion towards the bridge and the road that led to the Taygetus Mountains.

'Farewell, Odysseus,' he said. 'I'll look for you again after Helen is married. Until then, make sure you choose the *right* daughter of Lacedaemon to keep the thieves from your house.'

With that he spurred the horse out of the orchard and onto the road, then drove it at a gallop towards the mountains. He knew that his place was at Odysseus's side, and so he would hide out in the foothills until the time came for the Ithacans to return home.

The news of Eperitus's escape was greeted with anger amongst the suitors and their retinues, though the Ithacans and a few others were relieved that the cruel sentence had not been carried out. Several mounted soldiers had been sent to hunt for the fugitive, but none had been able to locate him and – against Icarius's wishes – the search was soon abandoned. The feast that evening was subdued, the atmosphere soured by the events of the day. Eventually, Tyndareus could stand no more of the sombre mood in the great hall, and asked Odysseus to walk with him in the gardens.

'This may not be the ideal time, Odysseus,' he said, placing a broad arm about his shoulder and leading him to the very bench the prince had shared with Penelope weeks before, 'but I need to know your answer to the little matter that remains unresolved between us. My daughter awaits your reply.'

'Tyndareus, for these past months you've been like a father to me,' Odysseus responded. 'Indeed, to all of us suitors. You've given us the best of your food and drink, provided us with beds and kept us safe under your roof. No host could be kinder, and nothing would please me more than to become your son-in-law.'

His words pleased the king, who had been rather bemused by his daughter's interest in the Ithacan. He wanted to make her happy, though, and was prepared to break his agreement with Agamemnon for her sake. The king of Mycenae would be disappointed and perhaps angry that Menelaus would no longer be chosen for Helen, especially as the council of war had been such a disaster; but Tyndareus was tired of his power stratagems and wanted an end to the constant – and expensive – feasting.

'However,' Odysseus added, 'the events of last night and today have changed matters. I can no longer marry Helen.'

'But why?' Tyndareus said, clearly shocked and offended.

'It's my duty to marry Penelope.'

'You'd turn down the greatest prize in all Greece for . . . for my niece?'

Odysseus shrugged, as if the comparison between the women was of no consequence. 'She was dishonoured by an Ithacan and I feel responsible for that. That's why, in fulfilment of your debt to me, I want you to persuade Icarius to let me marry Penelope.'

Tyndareus sighed, resigned to Odysseus's inexplicable sense of honour. 'I may hold sway over my brother in many things, Odysseus, but he's very sensitive about his daughter.'

'I've seen that already, though I'm also told he has little love for her. Perhaps he'll be glad of a chance to see her married off.'

'No king has much use for female offspring; they're more trouble than they're worth, as I will gladly swear by any god you care to name. But he relies on Penelope far more than he knows, and might think twice when someone asks to marry her. Especially if that person is *you*, Odysseus. He never liked you.'

'And today hasn't improved his opinion,' Odysseus said, thinking aloud. 'But nevertheless, you'll persuade him for me?'

'I honour my debts,' the king reassured him. 'I'll do what I can.'

Chapter Twenty-three

THE FOOT RACE

The palace gates yawned wide to allow Icarius's speeding chariot into the courtyard. Its wheels spewed up plumes of dust as they traced great arcs across the enclosure, following the circuit of the walls twice round before the king leaned back on the leather reins and brought the vehicle to a sliding halt. The four horses stood hock-high in a brown mist from the dirt they had ploughed up, stamping and snorting impatiently as their master spoke calming words from the chariot behind them.

Half a dozen attendants rushed out of the stables as Icarius stepped down. Beating the dust from his cloak, he watched three of the men unharness the team of horses and take them away to be fed on corn and white barley. The others dragged the chariot over to the stable and tilted it against the wall with its pole pointing up at the sky, before covering the body of the vehicle with a large tarpaulin.

Grudgingly satisfied with their efforts, Icarius turned on his heel and crossed the courtyard towards the main entrance of the palace. His work had given him an appetite and he was just beginning to look forward to a good meal when Tyndareus appeared, blocking the doorway with his well-fed bulk.

'Welcome back, brother. Did you find anything?'

'No. The overnight rain has washed away all hoof-prints, so I assume he has escaped through the mountain passes by now. Though I get a feeling that's not the last I'll see of him. But right now I have a voracious appetite to satisfy. Do you want to join me?'

Tyndareus stepped aside to let his brother pass. 'I'm ahead of you,' he said. 'There's food waiting for us in the hall. You see, I've a little request to make of you.'

Icarius did not wait to ask, but made his way at once to the great hall where two slaves were waiting to serve him. Tyndareus sat and watched him satisfy his hunger, wondering how his brother would react to the notion of Odysseus as a son-in-law, or how best to cajole him into accepting.

'I've some news for you. Good news, I think you'll agree.'

'Oh yes?' Icarius mumbled through a mouthful of pork. 'The best news would be that you've finally chosen a husband for Helen and the palace will soon be free of suitors. They're starting to show signs of restlessness, you know.'

'Not yet. But it's good news, nonetheless, and involves your daughter.'

Icarius carried on eating as if nothing had been said, but Tyndareus refused to play his brother's games. He knew he had caught his interest, whether Icarius acknowledged it or not, so he determined to keep his silence until he received a reply. Eventually, after another mouthful of food, Icarius spoke.

'Which one?'

'Penelope, of course. Odysseus feels ashamed that one of his men was responsible for the offence against her. He wants to restore her honour by marrying her.'

Suddenly whatever Icarius was swallowing lodged in his throat and brought on a fit of choking. One of the attendant slaves stepped up and irreverently thumped him between the shoulder blades, sending a half-chewed blob of meat flying from the king's mouth into the fire, where it fizzed into destruction. '*That* pauper,' he rasped, still struggling for breath. 'I'd rather see Penelope die than marry a trumped-up commoner.'

Concealing the pleasure he took from his brother's discomfort, Tyndareus offered him a cup of wine. 'You should be more generous in your opinions. Odysseus may not be a powerful man, but he has a fine mind and a strong character. He'd make a good son and, besides, I have an inkling Penelope likes him.'

'Do you indeed? And where does her opinion come into this matter? She'll marry who I tell her to, and I have no intention of giving any daughter of mine to an upstart prince without a kingdom to his name. Why should Helen have the greatest suitors in Greece flocking to her, when Penelope has to make do with beggars and peasants?'

'Because she's *my* daughter, of course!' Tyndareus snapped. 'I'm the eldest of us, Icarius, and whoever marries Helen will inherit the throne of Sparta. They won't get that from taking Penelope to wife, will they? That and the fact that Helen is the most beautiful woman in Greece, if not the world.'

Icarius shrank into his chair, withdrawing under Tyndareus's vocalization of his own superiority. But his proud spitefulness forced him to bite back.

'She certainly has the looks of a god,' he retorted.

Tyndareus stood, his eyes blazing at the accusation. 'Watch your wayward tongue, brother,' he warned. 'Now let's say I'm *telling* you Odysseus would be a good choice for Penelope. Don't you always say the girl gets under your feet? More than once you've said how you'd love to be rid of her. Well, now is your opportunity.'

'Damn you, Tyndareus,' Icarius squirmed. 'Maybe I would allow it, if you insisted, but the truth is I can't.'

'Can't?'

'No. Someone has already asked to marry her. One of your guests.'

'That's ridiculous. They came here for Helen, not Penelope.'

'Not this one, I think. He came here with Ajax.'

'Zeus's beard, Icarius. You don't mean Little Ajax, do you?'

'Yes, I do,' Icarius confirmed with a nervous nod. 'He asked me after the assembly this morning. He's besotted with her, in a way I've never noticed anyone to be interested in Penelope before.'

'Perhaps you should pay more attention to what goes on around your daughter, then. But I wish it had been anyone other than that Locrian hothead. There'll be trouble if he gets refused for Odysseus's sake. They hardly see eye to eye as it is.'

'That's good,' Icarius said. 'For all of Little Ajax's anger, I'd much rather have Penelope married to a real prince than a scheming mendicant like Odysseus.'

Tyndareus was in a dilemma. He wanted to honour his promise to Odysseus, who had helped ensure there would be no disagreement when Helen's husband was chosen. Equally he did not want Little Ajax's temper to threaten the hard-won peace that still existed within the palace walls. Especially not over a minor princess such as Penelope. Then an idea came to him.

'Perhaps you'll let them decide the matter between themselves.'

'There's nothing to decide, is there?' Icarius replied. 'I intend to allow Little Ajax to marry Penelope. Odysseus can go to Hades for all I care.'

'I don't think you should make any rash judgements, brother, especially as I've given Odysseus my word that I'll get a reasonable answer from you. Why don't we let them compete for her? A javelin-throwing contest, perhaps. Better still – a boxing match. A woman loves nothing more than to see two men spill each other's blood for her sake.'

Icarius knew better than to cross his older brother once he had made up his mind about something, but long years of being the inferior sibling had taught him how to manoeuvre around Tyndareus.

'I can see you're determined about this. Well, as Penelope's my daughter, perhaps you'll condescend to allow me to choose the nature of the competition?'

Tyndareus had already decided to offer Little Ajax a substantial bribe to under-perform in whatever sport was chosen, so happily nodded his agreement. As an ally he believed Odysseus would prove to be worth the expense.

'Then I suggest a foot race,' Icarius said, hardly able to suppress a smile. 'Three days from today. I'll agree to give Penelope to whoever wins.'

Odysseus groaned. 'A foot race?'

'Are you concerned?' Tyndareus asked. They walked alone through the corridors of the palace on their way to the night's feast. 'I've watched you during the morning exercises and you look fit and strong. What are you afraid of?'

'Little Ajax is the fastest runner in all of Greece, my lord. He may not look quick, but I've heard he can outrun any man alive and could even match Olympian Hermes in his winged sandals. Icarius has fooled you, I think.'

Tyndareus scoffed at the notion. 'Maybe. But perhaps I'm not as stupid as my brother thinks: I've offered your rival a bribe to run slower than you – without making it look too obvious of course – and he has accepted. So much for love, eh?'

Odysseus was not convinced, though he did not say as much to the king. They reached the tall wooden doors of the great hall and walked up to the dais, where the other kings and princes awaited them. Little Ajax was there and nodded to them both in a surprisingly civil manner, which naturally made Odysseus suspicious. They took their usual seats and began the business of eating the food the servants brought to them and dousing their beards with the wine they poured into their cups. But after a while Odysseus rose from his seat and asked to be excused. To the surprise of the other high nobility he walked over to his own men, who were in their usual corner of the great hall next to the men of Rhodes.

As he looked about at their familiar, comforting faces and shared their jokes and laughter, his thoughts were firmly fixed upon the race. Though Odysseus was also a fast runner, he knew that if he was to rely upon his legs alone he would never win Penelope for his wife. Tyndareus's bribe might prove enough to persuade the Locrian to lose, but Odysseus remained unpersuaded. Little Ajax hated to lose in anything to anybody; he competed not so much for the glory as for the delight of seeing others defeated. Odysseus knew he could not afford to take even the slightest risk.

'Where are Halitherses and Damastor?' he asked, suddenly noticing their absence.

'Damastor has skulked off with that slave girl again,' Antiphus answered.

'And Halitherses?'

'Ill. He ate some bad food and now he's too sick to do anything but lie on his mattress and hold his stomach.'

Odysseus's eyes gleamed and he sat up straight. 'Antiphus, you're an inspiration,' he said. 'Now give me some of that wine and let's drink to the old man's recovery. And our homes.'

They lifted their cups and murmured their approval – especially, Odysseus was pleased to note, at the notion of Ithaca. He drank and the troubles of the day became suddenly more bearable, thanks to the idea that had struck him. Then he saw Penelope enter the great hall, tall and elegant like a flower set amongst dull weeds. The heads of the guests and slaves observed her in silence, broken only by the occasional whisper that followed in her wake. He saw her glance at the royal dais and noticed with pleasure the disappointment on her face: he knew she had come in the hope of seeing him, and that her heart sank to observe him missing from his usual place.

He could not bear to be apart from her now that she was here. Before, when she had visited the nightly feasts, she had forced him to keep his distance. Believing that she hated him, he had reluctantly left her to her arrogant isolation. Now, though, he found the temptation of being with her irresistible. The thought that she would greet him with a similar strength of longing was a pleasure he could not wait to taste. He rose from his seat and she turned instinctively towards him. There was a fire in her eyes that burned only for him, oblivious to the watching crowd who knew of her shame. Her nostrils fanned open briefly as she saw him, and then without even the glimmer of an acknowledgement she turned and left the hall.

Odysseus snatched a glance at the royal dais. Icarius sat next to the empty chair that Little Ajax had occupied only moments before, watching his daughter as she retreated from the great hall. But Odysseus had no concern for the king or any of the other nobles who looked at Penelope with accusing eyes. That they suspected her of inviting men to her room, as palace rumour now suggested, did not concern him; that Little Ajax must be moving through the crowd in pursuit of her did.

He slipped out of the great hall, unnoticed by the throng of people who were already discussing the departed princess. Outside in the moonlit inner courtyard priests were sacrificing oxen to the ever-watchful gods. They burned thighbones wrapped in glistening fat, the twisting smoke from the fires mingling with their verbose and wailing prayers, while their attendants cut up the animals' flesh to supply the feast.

Odysseus saw his rival amongst them and ducked quickly out of sight behind one of the pillars that supported the roof of the gallery that circumvented the inner courtyard. From here he watched the attendants shake their heads and shrug their shoulders in response to Little Ajax's urgent enquiries about Penelope. Then Odysseus heard his name whispered behind him and turned to see the princess, hiding behind another of the pillars. She beckoned to him as she disappeared through a side-door back into the palace.

Odysseus followed her into a corridor that, he guessed by the smell of food, led to the kitchens. She turned and in an instant they were in each other's arms, kissing and abandoning themselves to their need for each other. The brief but intense flirtation of the night before had left them unfulfilled and tense with frustrated desire, and only the appearance of a slave returning to the kitchens tempered their passion. Penelope grabbed Odysseus by the hand and led him by a complex route through the darkened corridors and eventually to a room stacked with dust-covered clay tablets.

Odysseus looked about at the room. It was unlit and without windows, and it took a moment for his eyes to adjust to the darkness. From what he saw he doubted the place had been used for years, except perhaps for secret liaisons between the people who lived and worked in the palace. 'You know I'm to compete for you against Little Ajax?' he said.

'Yes. Tyndareus told me,' she replied, smiling at him. Her teeth were white in the darkness of the room. 'He says he offered Little Ajax a bribe to lose, and that he accepted. I can't wait to be yours. I love you, Odysseus.'

He kissed her lightly and stroked her hair, and in response she put her arms about his neck and pulled his face to hers. Moments later she withdrew and looked into his green eyes.

'You would have been my first, Odysseus, if we hadn't been disturbed. I've preserved myself for so long knowing one day I'd meet the man I love, and now you're here and I'm consumed with the need of you. Don't keep me waiting any longer, I beg you, not even for a day.' Then it occurred to her she might have misjudged his feelings. Perhaps the need was all hers, and Odysseus bore no attraction for her. 'Or maybe the other night had no meaning for you?'

Odysseus dismissed her doubts with a shake of his head. 'I swear by Athena, Penelope, I love you more than anything else. You mean more to me than my home and my family, and I'd gladly die for either of those. If I never restore Ithaca to my father's rule, but have you, then I'll be content and count myself blessed by the gods. You're my new homeland. Wherever you are, that is where my heart lies also. But you aren't mine yet. Little Ajax has no intention of accepting Tyndareus's bribe, I'm certain of it, so unless I can find a way of beating him nothing I can do will stop you from being his.'

'But why shouldn't he accept the bribe?' Penelope protested. 'He told Tyndareus he would.'

'And perhaps he means it. But if he can fool me into believing I'll be given an easy victory then his task will be even easier. He intends to marry you, I'm sure of it, and no amount of Tyndareus's gold will turn his mind from taking you back to Locris with him. No, I have to find another way to defeat him.'

'Everybody says he's too fast for you, though. You'll never beat him.' Her chin sank onto her chest. 'Perhaps it's my fate to marry him and spend the rest of my days on Locris. Though I'd rather kill myself first.'

'Don't talk like that.'

'I can't think of anything worse than not being with you, Odysseus. At least if we were lovers I'd have that memory to take with me to Locris.'

'No,' he insisted. 'Your love will be the inspiration that takes me to victory. Only when I've defeated Little Ajax will I take the prize. And I already have an idea of how to ensure victory.'

'How?'

'I'm not certain yet, but if I can put something in his food the night before the race, something guaranteed to make him ill, then he won't be able to run and Icarius will be forced to concede. It might not be the way others would approve of, but my wits are my gift from the gods, just as Little Ajax's is his great speed. The only problem is that I've no idea of herb lore and don't know what I could use to poison him. Even if I could, I wouldn't know how to administer it without the risk of others being made ill too.'

Penelope took Odysseus's hand and held it. 'You may have the method, my darling, but I have the means. Clytaemnestra knows the properties of every herb in the Eurotas valley, as well as how to use them. She'll give me something to put in Little Ajax's drink at tonight's feast. I know the wine stewards, and they'll do whatever I ask of them.'

Odysseus returned her grin. 'You aren't only beautiful and desirable, Penelope, you're also very cunning. The gods could have made us for each other. And one day you'll make the most wonderful queen Ithaca has ever had.'

It was the morning of the race, a fine spring morning with washed blue skies and a strong breeze blowing in from the Taygetus Mountains. Odysseus stood with Agamemnon, Tyndareus and Icarius under the shade of the apple orchard, waiting for Little Ajax to arrive. It was almost half a year since he had come to Sparta, and with spring approaching the prince felt more keenly than ever the urge to return home. Something in his blood told him matters were getting worse back on Ithaca, and that his people were crying out for him.

'I don't think he's coming,' Tyndareus announced.

'Then the competition is void,' Icarius declared. 'Penelope doesn't go to either suitor.'

'Odysseus wins by default,' Agamemnon corrected.

Icarius noticed a faint smile of triumph pass across Odysseus's face and had to bite his lip. 'He'll come. Perhaps he drank too much last night.'

As they spoke, Little Ajax appeared at the entrance to the city walls. He was accompanied by Teucer, who twitched repeatedly at his friend's shoulder as they approached. Odysseus, though frustrated to see his challenger had mustered enough strength to show up for the race, noted the fragility with which he walked. Little Ajax's face was bloodless beneath his tan and there was not a man amongst them who did not notice the weakened state of the warrior. Suddenly he paused, put a hand on his stomach and ran behind the stone wall that encircled the orchard. Moments later loud noises declared unceremoniously the cause of his distraction.

Despite the chill wind that blew down from the mountains, Odysseus threw off his cloak and stood naked on the dirt road, ready to begin the race back up to the palace. When he finally re-emerged, Little Ajax quickly shed his own clothing and took up his place beside his opponent.

'You bastard,' he growled beneath his breath. 'You did this to me, didn't you?'

'I've evened things up,' Odysseus admitted. 'And now I'm going to beat you.'

Little Ajax's innards groaned in response, sending a spasm of pain through him like a punch to the midriff. He seized his stomach with both hands and bit back a grunt of agony.

'Don't be so confident, you Ithacan swine. I know it was you in Penelope's room, though you're too cowardly to admit it. But even blaming one of your own men won't save her for you. I'm still the fastest man in Greece.'

At that, and without waiting for the signal, he sprang off. Odysseus looked in disbelief as the short, muscular man sprinted away from him. Within moments he was already back up to the city walls.

'Go on then!' Tyndareus bellowed.

An instant later Odysseus was in pursuit, running as fast as his legs would propel him. He was a strong runner, confident of his ability to compete with anyone, and he had the endurance for longer races such as this one through the streets of Sparta. He was also exhilarated by the challenge and felt a new release of energy flooding his arteries; the muscles in his legs bore his awkward, heavy frame with ease, and as he used his arms to balance himself and build up a rhythm he could sense his pace quickening. Despite Little Ajax's head start, the race was on.

The air rushed over Odysseus's face and through his thick red hair, increasing the sensation of speed as new bursts of vigour fed his muscles and drove him on still faster, his lungs pumping the air in and out of his body, his heart pushing the blood through his straining chest and limbs. And yet he saw Little Ajax disappearing through the city gates ahead of him and knew his opponent was intent on losing him. He had felt nothing but confidence since seeing Penelope hand a small vial to a wine steward the night before; his sense of certainty had diminished only slightly when, to his surprise, Little Ajax had defied Clytaemnestra's poison to show up for the race; but now it was draining rapidly away as he realized the truly unbelievable speed and power of his rival. The man's reputation was well deserved.

For an instant Odysseus tasted fear. The bitter gall of imminent defeat now replaced the expectation of victory that had accompanied his dreams the night before. Though visibly weakened, Little Ajax had somehow found the strength not only to run fast, but to outstrip Odysseus and keep stretching the distance between them. Dispirited, Odysseus pressed on in his wake, through the city gates that loomed up large before him and past the lone guard in full armour. As he sprinted fiercely to catch up with the Locrian, his thoughts turned despairingly to Penelope and, with a stab of terror, he realized he was about to lose her for ever.

He gasped a prayer to Athena and focused his thoughts on Penelope, trying to forget the exhaustion in his limbs and remember all the things that he loved about her. All he could think of was the way she had humiliated him when they first met, but it was enough. Suddenly a surge of energy filled his muscles. Like a giant hand at his back, it pushed him on to meet the sharp slope of the main street of Sparta, up which he must pursue Little Ajax if he was to win the woman he loved. It wound its serpentine way up the hill on which the city was built, doubling back on itself several times until it reached the palace gates where Menelaus and Diomedes were waiting to greet the victor. The broad route had been cleared of townsfolk for the purpose of the race, so Odysseus knew that the figure disappearing around the bend ahead of him could be none other than Little Ajax.

Encouraged to see his opponent still within his grasp, Odysseus sensed his limbs held yet more in reserve and threw himself into the pursuit. He took the bend, his bare feet finding footholds in the rutted, sun-baked mud, and saw his quarry ahead of him, struggling now against the steepness of the hill. The sweat poured from Odysseus's naked body as he lengthened his stride to close the gap further, but he doubted he was suffering to the same degree as his rival, whose rasping breath he could now hear just ahead of him.

The road bent back again to the left then suddenly gave way to a gentler angle. Both men found a new surge of speed and ran as fast as their flagging muscles would allow, their arms pumping desperately as they sought advantage over each other. They raced on through the winding streets, their hearts thumping horribly inside the stifling confines of their chests, and slowly Odysseus began to close the distance between them. Soon they were barely a sword's length apart, and in desperation Little Ajax threw a punch with the side of his fist. It caught his pursuer in the ribs, but the blow lacked the strength to throw him off his tail. He repeated the tactic, this time moving nearer to the house-fronts on the right-hand side of the street, trapping his opponent before aiming a higher punch at his face. Odysseus, unable to distance himself without falling back, received the blow in his left eye. He lost his balance and crashed into the wall of a house, before stumbling to his knees in a cloud of dust.

He was up again in an instant, but his rival had already disappeared around the final bend in the road. Odysseus heard the cheering of the warriors who lined the last stretch of the race to the palace gates, and for a dark moment he sensed defeat.

Then, as his heart sank, a new resolve stirred within him. The thought of losing Penelope was something he could not accept, or even contemplate. It clanged against the solid core of his character and insisted the race was not yet over. A shock of anger erupted through him, pouring every last drop of remaining strength into his legs. He began to draw fresh speed from his tired limbs. The muscles tensed agonizingly, but with each thrust of his legs he sensed the burden of his body weight decrease. Suddenly they launched him around the final bend and back into the race.

A new roar greeted his appearance. He saw the Locrian turn in surprise, the panic filling his eyes as he knew Odysseus could still rob him of victory. Further on the gates of the palace were open, guarded on either side by Diomedes and Menelaus, waiting to announce the winner. The volume of spectators' shouts was enormous, driving him on relentlessly until he was at his Little Ajax's shoulder once more.

He threw the final reserves of his strength into a last push to be first to the gates. But whatever force had kept his legs moving at such speed and for so long suddenly drained away beneath him. He willed himself on, desperately, but felt only a faint impulse in response. It was barely enough. He fell sprawling into the mouth of the palace gateway, not knowing whether it had been sufficient for victory. The last thing he saw as his mind collapsed into darkness was Diomedes and Menelaus leaping in the air like madmen, to the sound of endless cheering from the warriors of every state in Greece.

Chapter Twenty-four

EPERITUS AND CLYTAEMNESTRA

Eperitus rode to a village below the foothills of the Taygetus Mountains, where he exchanged Icarius's stallion for a blanket, a dagger, and a few days' supply of bread and meat. It was a sorry trade, but he desperately needed food and a weapon. Besides, he excused himself, the horse would only be a burden if he was to hide out amongst the frowning ridges and inhospitable peaks above. Swinging the bag of food onto his shoulder, he started up the crumbling road that struggled into the coppery-brown mountains.

After a while he found what he was searching for: the lip of a rock shelf overlooking the fertile plains of Sparta and the road through the mountains. He made his way carefully and slowly up the loose, scree-covered slopes until, shortly, he was standing in the centre of a shallow bowl that was an ideal place for a camp. It had an overhanging crest of rock to provide shelter from wind and rain, whilst its natural concavity would keep him out of sight from anyone below. And if he needed to make a defence, the only approaches were up steep gradients from the valley or the mountain road.

The westering sun was on his back as he saw out the last of the daylight, dangling his legs over the rim of his hiding place. Soon the brown light of dusk choked the colour and detail from the valley and his mind turned naturally to thoughts of warmth and food. He decided to risk a fire and wandered the slopes collecting dead bushes and branches from the few stunted trees that grew there, before sitting down to make tinder and kindling with his dagger. He shaped a nest of dried grass and put the tinder inside, then sharpened a stick and began vigorously rubbing a groove into a piece of wood. After a few moments he tipped a small coal into the tinder nest and blew on it until a puff of flame appeared. Carefully shielding it from the night breeze, he transferred it to the pile of kindling and soon a crackling blaze was bathing the rocky shelf in orange light.

The rest of the night was lonely and thought-filled. As Eperitus lay in his thick blanket and listened to the spit and pop of the fire, he looked up at the white moon that flitted between the ragged fronds above and thought of the future. Meeting Odysseus had been a blessing from the gods: at the prince's side he had fought men and monsters and brought glory to his name; he had spent months in the company of Greece's finest men, and had even spoken with one of the immortals. But now the fickle gods had forsaken him again, taking back what little honour he had won for himself and leaving him once more destitute and without hope. Unless he could somehow rejoin Odysseus and help him win back Ithaca, he would never redeem himself from the shame of what his father had done. Tortured by the memory, his descent into sleep was slow and fitful.

The next day was spent watching the gleaming walls of Sparta. The courtship of Helen would soon be over, and once a husband had been named the suitors would quickly begin to leave. Odysseus and his men might return the way they had come, but it was more likely they would head south to the coast and hire a ship to take them home, so he kept a watchful eye on both routes.

By the time dusk had fallen, he had seen nothing more than farmers' carts, a few horsemen and the usual traffic of villagers and merchants entering or leaving the city gates, and was relieved to be able to leave his post and search the hillsides for firewood. He also looked for edible plants, conscious that his food supply would not last for long, but came back empty-handed. That evening his stomach rumbled in protest at the measly crust of bread and the strip of beef he allowed himself. After months of feasting on the best food and wine in all Greece, it was difficult to adjust to a harsher diet of restricted rations.

As he lay down to sleep, the howl of a wolf broke the stillness of the night. It was near at hand and its lonely cry rolled emptily off the slopes and cliff faces around him, leaving behind an ominous silence. He drew the dagger from his belt and placed a fresh log on the fire, to act as a brand should the animal or any of its pack have the courage to investigate his camp. Then the moon broke free of the wall of cloud that had contained it for some time. It shook off the last clinging tatters of vapour and threw its unhindered light down across the valley and the mountains. Only then did he notice the tall black figure standing at the edge of his camp.

He seized the flaming brand from the fire and held it above his head, the dagger gleaming in his other hand. He felt exposed and vulnerable without his weapons, and to his dismay saw that the figure was armed with a tall shield and two spears.

'Who are you?' he demanded.

'A friend,' the figure replied, and Eperitus was shocked to hear a female voice. She moved into the circle of orange light cast by the fire, which threw aside the shadows that had veiled her identity.

'Clytaemnestra!'

'I've brought your weapons,' she announced, throwing his grandfather's shield onto the pile of brushwood he had collected to supply the fire. His spears were dropped on top of it with a clatter, followed shortly after by his bronze sword, gleaming fiercely in the firelight. Last of all was the dagger Odysseus had given him, but this she offered across the flames. 'After all, Eperitus, a warrior is nothing without his arms.'

He dropped the brand back into the fire and eagerly took the dagger from her outstretched hands. For the first time since his weapons had been handed in to the palace armourer at Sparta he felt complete again, conscious once more of his own independence, his power to defend himself and impose his will on others by force of arms. He was a man again, able to do and say whatever he pleased, a freedom that was bounded only by the will of the gods and his own sense of honour. He thanked her and put the dagger into his belt, tossing the other over the lip of the slope.

'I've brought food, too,' she said, handing him a small woollen sack.

She turned to warm herself by the fire and Eperitus joined her.

'Thank you again,' he said.

'It's the least I could do. You've been a good friend to me these past months, letting me burden you with my problems.'

'But how did you know where to find me?'

'I have an insight that few possess,' she answered, staring hard at the flames. 'There are gods older than the Olympians, Eperitus, and they can give their followers powers the rest of the world has forgotten. *They* told me you were hiding here.'

Eperitus wondered whether those same mysterious powers had helped her to slip out of the city unseen, and without a horse or a wagon had enabled her to carry the heavy and awkward bulk of his weaponry up here to this shelf of rock. But something inside him was wary of probing further, perhaps for fear of receiving a straight answer. Looking at Clytaemnestra's drawn and prematurely wise face, there were some things in the world he preferred to remain in ignorance of.

'I also know you were with Peisandros the Myrmidon two nights ago, so could not have been Penelope's guest.'

'If that's the case,' Eperitus asked, 'has this insight revealed to you who *was* with Penelope?'

'No. The gift is a double-edged sword. It reveals many things and gives powerful knowledge, but it omits things, too. However, I don't need second sight to know who *was* with Penelope that night.'

'Perhaps it was Agamemnon?' Eperitus said, clumsily trying to divert Clytaemnestra's suspicions – the fewer people who knew the truth, the safer Odysseus would be. 'You've told me he's often unfaithful.'

Clytaemnestra gave a short laugh. 'Agamemnon is sleeping with my mother. He enters her each evening whilst Tyndareus presides over the banqueting, then returns again before anyone can become suspicious. Besides, I know it was Odysseus – I brewed the love potion that brought him and Penelope together. And why else would you take the blame for a crime you did not commit?' She switched her glance from the flames to Eperitus. 'I must go now, but I'll return soon with more food. And don't worry about watching the road – Odysseus won't be leaving for a few days yet.'

She came back three nights later, startling him as she moved noiselessly into the ring of light from the fire and sat down beside him.

'Here,' she said, handing him a sack of provisions. 'Fresh from the night's banquet.'

She held her hands up to the flames and in that dancing light, as her breath blew feathers of vapour into the cold night air, Eperitus noticed how beautiful she was. There was nothing of Helen's powerful attraction in her features, but she had a mysteriousness about her that he found quietly appealing. Her large, sad eyes seemed almost bottomless as they reflected the flickering light; as if the knowledge of all human experience was imprisoned within them, threatening to burst free and flood the world with its misery.

He opened the bag and took out a haunch of brown meat, still shiny with grease, and bit into it in an effort to turn his thoughts from the woman beside him. His stomach craved the taste of real food again, unaccustomed as it was to the mould-scraped bread and leathery strips of beef he had been living off since his retreat to the mountains. Clytaemnestra watched him with an undecipherable look.

'Help yourself,' he offered.

'I've eaten my fill,' she replied. 'It came from the table of your master's wedding feast.'

Eperitus choked, coughing violently until Clytaemnestra had to thump him hard on his back to dislodge the piece of meat. He spat it into the fire.

'Odysseus and Little Ajax both wanted to marry Penelope,' she continued, 'so Icarius suggested they race for her. Odysseus won and they were married this afternoon. All very straightforward and simple; a quick ceremony with Penelope's close family, Odysseus's men and the suitors as guests. No need to plan a wedding feast, just rearrange the seating for the usual evening banquet. You seem surprised, Eperitus.'

'I am,' he answered. 'I knew of his attraction to her, of course, but he always said she treated him with contempt. That's why I couldn't understand why he would be in her bedchamber.'

'I helped with that,' Clytaemnestra admitted. 'Not that Penelope really needed my help. She just needed to have her eyes opened to what her heart really wanted.'

But Eperitus was not listening. He sat staring into the flames until his eyes watered, thinking about the news Clytaemnestra had brought. His emotions were a confusion of jealousy, frustration and anger that he did not understand. Was he annoyed that Odysseus had abandoned his greatest chance of saving Ithaca for the sake of a woman? Or was he simply jealous that his friend had achieved his heart's desire, whilst he was left forgotten on a mountainside with little hope for the future?

Clytaemnestra sensed Eperitus's sadness and put a hand cautiously upon his shoulder. She began stroking him with awkward movements, her long fingers running towards his neck and rubbing against the knuckles of his upper spine. They lingered there and his thoughts, for a moment, were no longer directed against Odysseus and Penelope but dwelt upon her. He thought of what it would be like to return her touch, to hold her slender body in his arms. Women had rarely featured in his martial lifestyle, but he would have given anything to be with her there and then. But the moment slipped away. She withdrew her hand, tucking it into a fold of her clothing as if burnt. She stood.

'Soon my father will announce Helen's husband. I'll return to you then so you'll know when to expect Odysseus's departure – he won't leave before the marriage ceremony. That's assuming you still wish to serve him.'

The question of not serving Odysseus had never crossed Eperitus's mind. Despite his moment of jealousy, he was bound to the prince by an oath and would not go back on his word. His only hope of finding a home lay in the liberation of Ithaca, and he would do everything in his power to help Odysseus win back his homeland.

'I do,' he said.

Without a word, Clytaemnestra disappeared back into the night, leaving him to wonder once more how she would return to Sparta through the perils of the dark. Shortly afterwards he heard the cry of a lone wolf on the valley plain below, calling out into the emptiness of the night.

Despite the news of Odysseus's marriage to Penelope, Eperitus spent most of the next day thinking of Clytaemnestra. As he watched Sparta for signs of any activity, he found himself looking forward to the evening and the possibility of her return. She had a strength and hardness he both admired and pitied. The cruelties she had suffered over the years had made her as tough as any warrior he knew, but beneath her flint-like exterior was a softness that was deep and consuming. He had seen glimpses of the real Clytaemnestra during the months at Sparta – brief, heartfelt smiles or moments of tenderness when the natural beauty of her face shone through – and it saddened him that she was the prisoner of a forced, loveless marriage.

As the sun threw the shadows of the mountains across the Eurotas valley, turning the landscape from sallow ochre to a dun brown, he felt keenly the lack of human company. He missed the closeness he had felt in belonging to Odysseus's men, and it was hard not knowing what was going on at the palace. He wondered how Ajax had reacted to the choice of Menelaus to marry Helen, as Athena had said would happen. And what of Diomedes, the proud warrior who was deeply in love with the princess? How had Little Ajax fared with the loss of Penelope to Odysseus? And what of Helen? With all her hopes of freedom dashed, how would she cope with marriage to a man she did not love? He felt for her most of all, and pitied the girl whose youthful hopes never had a chance of being realized.

These thoughts buzzed around his head long into the night, until the moon was overhead and he knew Clytaemnestra would not appear. Even then sleep was slow in coming, but finally the pressure on his eyelids became too much and he slept until the light of the sun on his face woke him.

There were no signs that he had been visited in the night and so he went about his usual tasks of gathering wood and looking for food. The rest of the day passed in much the same way as the one before, followed by an equally restless and, ultimately, disappointing evening. The next morning he was woken not by sunlight forcing its way through his eyelids, but by splashes of rain on his face. He looked up, blinking against the heavy droplets, to see a ceiling of grey cloud covering the valley and mountains. Quickly he carried his supplies of food and wood into a niche in the rock face and spent the rest of the day hidden beneath the protection of its broken roof as the rain came down.

Making a fire in those conditions was difficult, but as the rain trickled away slowly to nothing he eventually succeeded in his task. Soon a great blaze was burning in the darkness and he stood naked before it, holding first his tunic and then his cloak up to the heat to dry. Then he heard a sound behind him and turned to see Clytaemnestra standing there, shamelessly eyeing his nakedness.

He hastily threw the cloak about his waist and apologized. Saying nothing she approached the flames and picked up his tunic.

He put a hand out to take it from her but, as he did so, she threw it onto the flames.

'What are you doing?' he objected, trying to get hold of a corner of the garment and pull it free of the flames, though without success. 'That's my only tunic. Do you want me to look a fool when I finally get down from this mountain?'

'Of course not,' she replied, calmly. 'That's why I brought you this.' She held up a new tunic and handed it to him. 'I made it myself, especially for you. That old rag you've been wearing is a disgrace for a nobleman, so travel-worn and threadbare. Don't worry, it'll fit you perfectly.'

Eperitus looked at the garment. He could detect Clytaemnestra's scent on it, and imagined her long-fingered hands working on the soft material, just for him. He met her eyes and saw that the veil of cynicism and anger had lifted to reveal a young woman in the prime of her life.

'I'll put it on now,' he said, and walked behind a corner of rock to change.

As Eperitus slipped the cloak from around his waist and stood naked once more in the cool night air, he suddenly felt himself being watched. He turned and saw that Clytaemnestra had followed him, but instead of covering himself he allowed her to look at him. It was exhilarating, and for a moment he felt godlike, worshipped, desired. Then he pulled the tunic over his head and picked up his cloak. She returned to stand by the fire as he followed.

'So Helen's husband has been chosen,' he said, as if nothing had happened between them. But something had. The usual formality of their relationship had been bridged, and the bridge could not be recrossed.

'Yes. They were married today.'

She stood between himself and the fire, her back turned to him, and he could see the silhouette of her body through the thin material of her dress: her bony shoulders; the narrow hips and waist; the gap between the meeting of her legs. A tingling feeling crept across his skin and spread through his whole body, exciting the flesh and shaking off the cold of the night. He wanted her. He wanted to touch her, to kiss her and then to take her, to journey where he had never ventured before.

'It was Menelaus, wasn't it?'

'How did you know?' she asked, turning towards him.

'A god told me.'

Clytaemnestra gave him an inquisitive look that was halfway between disbelief and curiosity, but she did not question his knowledge.

'Anyway, it's over now and the suitors – all but Menelaus, of course – will be leaving over the next couple of days. I hear Odysseus and his new bride are heading for the sea tomorrow afternoon. They'll follow the course of the Eurotas and hire themselves a ship when they reach the coast.'

'So your husband's plans for a war on Troy have failed?'

'Yes. Utterly,' she said, with a grim smile of quiet triumph. 'There'll be no war unless Priam turns his ambitions towards Greece itself. Agamemnon's dream to unite the Greeks can never be revived now.'

'But when Menelaus inherits Tyndareus's throne, the Atreides will rule the two most powerful states in Greece. With the combined armies of Sparta and Mycenae they could conquer all the other states, effectively giving Agamemnon what he wanted anyway.'

Clytaemnestra shook her head. 'He's ambitious, but he isn't a tyrant. He believes in unifying Greece by mutual agreement, not subjugation. If he were anybody else I could almost admire his vision and his commitment. But he isn't anybody else; he's my husband and he's a bastard. I curse him!'

She spat over her shoulder into the flames.

'I don't blame you for hating him, not after what he did to you,' Eperitus ventured, taking a step closer.

Clytaemnestra hung her head and a shining tear rolled down each of her cheeks. Then Eperitus put a hand under her chin and lifted her face. Her large, bewitching eyes met his and something stirred deep within him. More tears, even though her face was proud and defiant, and then he kissed her. Her lips parted and he followed her lead, each action new to him. His hands found her thin waist and pulled her body against his, the twin bulge of her small breasts pressing upon his ribs. Then as her fingers ran into his hair he felt the tip of her tongue enter his slightly opened mouth, a sensation for which no rumour or description of the act had ever prepared him. He felt his whole body respond.

He squeezed her closer still and dropped a hand to her buttocks, only for her to mirror the action on himself. For a moment both of her hands clawed at his flesh, and then began tugging at the hem of his tunic, sliding it up his back until moments later she pulled it over his head and arms and flung it to one side. Instinctively they stood back from each other as she undid the cord that held her dress together. Then she was naked before him and he found his aroused passion momentarily stilled as he stared at her.

Although he had seen naked women before, never had he beheld a body that he knew within moments would be joined with his own. Clytaemnestra, perhaps enjoying the knowledge she was giving herself to him in a way that Agamemnon would never know, allowed his eyes to roam across her body, over the small white breasts with their disproportionately large, starkly pink nipples, down over the flat stomach to the thick arrowhead of red hair between her legs. Then, before his eyes could have their fill of her, she took him by the hand and led him to a patch of dried grass beyond the ring of firelight, out into the shadows where the moon's silver luminance gave their bodies a ghostly, even corpse-like appearance.

When Eperitus awoke the next morning she was gone. He was disappointed – there was so much he wanted to say and ask and talk about with her – but he knew he was not heart-broken. He glanced about for signs of her, just in case she had only wandered off, but there were none.

He lay back on the bed of grass and looked up at the clouds, his mind sliding lazily between the different pleasures of the night before. But for all the foreign delights of experiencing a woman, every thought ran ultimately up against the same barrier, the single revelation that Clytaemnestra had shared with him between their bouts of love-making. Damastor was a traitor. Damastor had wanted Odysseus to choose Penelope over Helen, and it was Damastor who had given the alarm when Odysseus entered the women's quarters.

It all sounded too incredible, and Eperitus wondered whether Clytaemnestra's second sight had failed her or deceived her. But as he sifted through everything he could remember about Damastor's actions over the past half-year, the distant sound of horns carried to him from across the Eurotas valley. In an instant he was on his feet and standing at the edge of the shelf of rock, shielding his eyes from the sun as he gazed towards Sparta. Away in the distance, the first of the suitors was emerging from the city gates. The courtship of Helen was over. The battle for Ithaca was about to begin.

book

FOUR

Chapter Twenty-five

DEATH IN THE TEMPLE

Even from a distance Eperitus's shield and spears would mark him out as a warrior, so he was especially cautious in his descent from the foothills not to make himself visible to any watching eyes on the city walls. Once he was back on the level plain of the valley, though, there were enough trees, ravines and stone walls to provide cover and he made much better progress on his way to the sun-dappled waters of the Eurotas.

The day was a warm one, in contrast to the clouds and occasional rain of the past week, and by the time Eperitus reached a point on the river far enough down from the city gates he was sweating and thirsty. He laid down his shield and spears behind a stone wall and glanced about the countryside for signs of life. There were shepherds on the foothills to either side of the valley and a handful of peasant children in an olive grove on the other side of the river, but neither posed a threat so he walked to the near bank and knelt down to drink. The cold waters were refreshing on his dusty hands, the strong undercurrents driving his fingers apart and chilling them to the bone. He took a quick draught and splashed some on his face and neck, then on his dark hair, hot with the sun. He scooped up more handfuls of the liquid until his thirst was slaked, then sat back with the water dripping from his unshaven chin onto the tunic Clytaemnestra had given him.

As he slouched back against the rich, damp grass of the river bank the sun quickly dried his hair and skin and took advantage of his wearied condition to woo him with thoughts of sleep. The air was rich with the smell of spring blossom, overpowering his senses, and he felt his lids grow ponderous and the tension in his muscles ease away. His breathing grew slower and heavier as the gentle breeze from the river fanned his skin. His chin lolled onto his chest and within moments he was in the depths of sleep.

A noise snagged him back to wakefulness. He opened his eyes and raised his head to listen. Silence. For a moment he thought the noise had not been from the waking world, but then he heard it again. The slow beat of hoofs and the trundle of wheels, followed by the sharp whinnying of horses. Eperitus pulled the sword from his belt and lay flat on his stomach against the steeply angled bank.

The road bent out of sight behind a cluster of cypress trees, hiding whoever was approaching, but soon a chariot with a team of four horses came slowly into view, followed by a large number of fully armed warriors. Because of the size of the escort, Eperitus thought at first that it was one of the more powerful suitors, on his way to the coast and a ship home, but as they came closer Eperitus could see Mentor at the reins with Odysseus and Penelope standing beside him. The couple looked magnificent together, and Eperitus felt a surge of happiness at the sight of them. Behind them came the small band of Ithacans, with Halitherses and Antiphus at their head, followed by a much larger troop of a further forty warriors.

Unable to contain himself any longer, Eperitus stood up and ran to greet them. At a command from Odysseus, Mentor halted the chariot and the prince jumped down to meet his friend.

'I've been praying you would find us before we sailed for Ithaca,' he said, taking Eperitus's hand and pulling him into an embrace. 'I've a lot to tell you about. Penelope and I were married.'

He nodded towards his wife, who was watching them from the chariot.

'You old fox,' Eperitus replied, feigning surprise. He looked up at Penelope and took pleasure from the sight of her calm, intelligent face. She smiled back at him with a happy gleam in her eye.

Odysseus gave him a roguish grin as the other Ithacans gathered around them, their faces full of surprise and joy at the unexpected reunion. Halitherses put his arms about Eperitus and held him in a bearlike grip, a rare sign of affection from the guard captain. As he stepped away, Antiphus gave the young warrior a hug and roughed up his hair affectionately, welcoming him back into the ranks.

'You did a brave thing,' he said. The others murmured their agreement. 'After you escaped Odysseus told us it was him, not you, who had been in Penelope's room, and that your sacrifice probably saved his life. I wonder how many of us would have done the same.'

'You all would have,' Eperitus said, dismissing the compliment. 'Now, is someone going to tell me who these others are?'

'They're Spartans,' said Damastor, stepping forward and offering his hand. 'Tyndareus lent them to Odysseus as a wedding gift, to help him retake Ithaca.'

This was the moment Eperitus had thought about and dreaded more than any other since waking that morning. Should he refuse Damastor's gesture of friendship and denounce him as a traitor in front of everybody, without the slightest proof to support his accusation? Or should he keep silent and bide his time, waiting for some evidence that Clytaemnestra was right? After a moment of doubt, he decided the latter would be the wisest course of action and took Damastor's hand.

Soon after, the march to the sea resumed. Odysseus did not return to the chariot, but walked beside Eperitus. The matter of his sudden appearance still needed explanation, he said.

'Does it?' Eperitus asked. 'You of all men should know I'm a man of my word. I offered you my loyalty and now it's my duty to help you restore Ithaca to Laertes's rule. Did you really expect me to let you and these clumsy oafs you call warriors fight Eupeithes alone?'

'Of course I didn't,' he laughed. 'But I should really like to know where you hid yourself these past few days, and what you lived on. And just how did you ghost into the palace armoury and retrieve your own weapons?'

'That's a story I'll keep to myself,' Eperitus replied, thinking of Clytaemnestra and knowing that the mere mention of her would reveal everything to Odysseus's clever mind. 'But you must answer a question for me: how do you intend to retake Ithaca with the force you have? These Spartans look like good men, fully armed and battle-hardened, but the Taphians aren't children either. We were lucky to beat the ones that ambushed us, and from Mentor's account their army on Ithaca is at least twice our number.'

'The people of Ithaca will come to our aid,' Odysseus began. 'They may only be fishermen and farmers, but they love their country and they're loyal to their king – that's more powerful than the gold Eupeithes pays to his Taphians. But Athena's the one I'm counting on.' He dug into his pouch and brought out the clay owl the goddess had given him. 'Her spear and aegis are worth a thousand men each, and when I use this to call on her no power on earth will be able to save Eupeithes.'

§

Darkness began to fall before they reached the coast, putting an end to the day's journey. As the others made camp for the night Eperitus and Antiphus gathered wood and built a fire. The archer sniffed the air and announced that the sea was only a quick march away. Although Eperitus did not possess his seafarer's senses, the gulls flocking about their camp in the twilight seemed to confirm his verdict.

'I know the coast around here,' Antiphus added. 'The river empties out beside a large fishing village. I stopped there once when I was a lad on a merchant ship, and I remember we came inland to buy livestock for the voyage home. We might even have come this far, though it was a long time ago and it's difficult to recognize a place in this sort of light.' He looked about at the rocky hills on either side. 'But it feels familiar, you know, and if I'm right there's a temple to Athena nearby.'

'What's that you say, Antiphus?' Odysseus asked, who was standing nearby and watching the last of the sunset over the peaks of the Taygetus Mountains.

'A temple of Athena, my lord, on a hilltop not far downstream from here. It wasn't very big, as I remember, but you'd easily catch its silhouette if there's any light left.'

'Then I'm going to look for it,' Odysseus said. 'I'll be back by the time it gets dark.'

'My lord!' Eperitus said, noticing Damastor amongst a group of Ithacans preparing food nearby. 'Surely you're not going alone? At least let me accompany you.'

'Eperitus, if I'd needed a nursemaid I'd have brought old Eurycleia with me. Now, sit down by the fire and stop worrying about me.'

Eperitus felt uneasy as he watched his friend go. Soon he and Antiphus were joined by the other Ithacans, Damastor amongst them. The blaze was already puffing burning embers into the evening air and a few early moths were attracted into its circle of light. One of the Spartans, a tall, bearded man by the name of Diocles, came over and politely requested a brand from their fire. There were too many of them to share a single fire, so Eperitus helped him carry some burning logs over to the stack of wood his comrades had constructed and soon had it ablaze. The Spartans thanked him and he returned to his own group.

The last embers of the day were burning over the western hills, leaving an insipid pink stain on the sky that gave warning of an even warmer day to come tomorrow. But the faint glow was rapidly succumbing to the deep blue of evening and the stars were already beginning to gleam and twinkle at every point on the horizon. As Eperitus watched them his thoughts turned to Penelope, who was in a makeshift tent with her slave Actoris, over by the tethered horses. He was wondering whether she would join them that evening when he was struck by a sudden sensation that something was wrong. It was a feeling of growing fear, though he could not think what had caused it. He looked about and instinctively put a hand on the hilt of his sword, but there was nothing.

Then he knew. He looked once around the circle of faces, illuminated orange by the fire, and his heart sank into his stomach. Damastor was gone.

Odysseus propped his sword against the outside wall of the temple and walked in. The doorway was so low he had to dip his head to enter, and once inside he saw it was little more than a simple, unadorned country altar. There were no anterooms, no columns supporting the broken, sagging roof, no elaborate murals on the flaking walls and no rich ornaments to lend it the required sense of divine majesty. It was perhaps a quarter the size of the great hall in his father's palace and boasted nothing more than a pitted stone altar at the far end. This was watched over by a badly formed midget effigy, which he could only assume was meant to represent Athena.

The stub of a torch had been lodged in a groove upon the wall to his right. It was sputtering its last as Odysseus entered, but by its wavering light he could tell that the chamber was empty. A bunch of early spring flowers lay to either side of the altar, which along with the torch were the only signs that the temple had been visited in months. Even they were probably the work of a lone peasant or local holy man, whose daily duty it was to light the single room and attend to its altar.

Odysseus knelt before the clay figurine and eyed it, making a mental comparison between its stunted, grimacing features and the matchless glory of the goddess it represented. But for all its rude art and rough edges he sensed something of Athena had been caught in the representation; compared with the voluptuous, richly curving statuettes of Aphrodite and Hera he had seen in other temples, the figurine's long body, straight hips and crude breasts reminded him of her boyish masculinity; the jutting brow and the straight nose that shot down from it were every bit as stern as the face of the goddess herself. And as he looked he sensed a new presence filling the temple. Suddenly fearful that the spirit of Athena might be watching him through the thumbed pits of the figurine's eye sockets, he threw his glance to the base of the altar and closed his eyes.

'Pallas Athena,' he said aloud, his voice filling the dusty confines of the temple. 'The journey you sent me on is over. Now the time has come to prove myself in the final battle, as I know you always intended me to. Tomorrow I embark for Ithaca.'

Damastor stood in the shadows at the back of the temple, the torchlight gleaming dully off the drawn blade of his sword. He had removed his sandals and left them outside so that he could enter the temple without making a noise, and now, as his prince knelt before the effigy of the goddess, he took two steps nearer.

Odysseus continued. 'Mistress, you've always guided my spear in battle, as in the hunt. You've kept me safe from harm. It was you who saved me from the boar that tore open my thigh, and you who sent Eperitus to aid me in my trials. You made him swear service to me in your presence, after you gave me the gift.'

Damastor had crept two paces closer and was bringing his sword up to hack down on Odysseus's neck when he heard the strange words. What gift could he be talking about? Was Odysseus suggesting he had *seen* the goddess? Damastor had heard of such things, though the tales were treated with scepticism and the tellers often mocked. But Odysseus had no one to lie to here.

'And it is your gift I'm concerned about, mistress.' Odysseus pulled the clay owl from his pouch and held it up before the figurine. 'I've carried it with me everywhere, and it's here with me now, but the time is near when I'll use it to summon your help. Tomorrow I take my men to Ithaca, to win back my father's kingdom. But you know how weak we are, mistress, how few compared to Eupeithes's hordes. That's when I intend to break the seal and pray for your help.'

Damastor looked at the clay owl and his quick mind half-guessed what it was. In an instant he had questioned whether it would work for himself; he considered the possibilities it might offer him after he had plucked it from its dead owner's fingers; and in his black, ambitious heart he saw himself as the new king of Ithaca, divinely appointed by no less a god than Athena herself.

'So I ask now that you will be swift to honour your promise to me,' Odysseus continued. 'Come quickly into the battle when I call you, mistress, unless every plan and every hope you ever pinned upon me be cut down by a Taphian spear.'

'Or an Ithacan sword,' Damastor said, and raised the weapon high over his head.

§

Eperitus stood up and left the circle about the fire, and as soon as he was out of earshot of the camp he began to run. Following the sound of the river on his left he stumbled like a blind man over the pitted and rock-strewn road, constantly looking up and to his right for sight of a temple on a hill. The light was failing fast and he was beset by fears that he had already passed it, until, after some time of doubt and increasing panic, he was ready to turn back and retrace his steps. Then he saw it.

The very last of the evening light was spread like a purple mould along the low black humps of the mountains. But there in its watery light, barely distinguishable amidst the rocks and twisted figures of leafless trees, was framed the upright silhouette of a building. Despite the darkness he quickly found a path leading up the hillside and began to pick his way along it. But at that moment he was struck by a sudden sense of dread. Looking up he saw, or thought he saw, a figure standing by the temple. It stood between the building's outline and the stump of a dead tree, the sky burning with purple flames behind it as it looked down the hill. Eperitus froze, not wanting to be seen, but then the figure was gone. He did not see it go and could not say whether it had entered the temple or left it; he was not even certain he had seen it at all. And then panic contracted the muscles of his heart and he knew he must run, run without care for the path or the rocks at his feet, because if he did not Odysseus would be dead.

Even in that blunting darkness, going uphill with his heavy sword in his hand he found a speed he would not have dreamed possible. Instinct took over and it was as if he had been lifted in the hand of a god and carried across the boulders and loose stones. He bounded up the slope to the porch of the temple, where he found Odysseus's sword and a pair of sandals. The temple had no door and through its open portal, as the last of the sunset disappeared from the evening sky, he could see the glow of torchlight. The sound of a hushed voice drifted out into the night air and brought him back to his senses.

Heedless now of any need for caution, Eperitus ran to the doorway and looked inside. The scene before him froze his blood. He was too late.

Against the far wall Odysseus knelt in prayer before an altar and a rough effigy of Athena. Damastor stood just behind him, his sword raised high above his head and ready to fall. An instant sooner and perhaps he could have done something, but instead he had failed Odysseus and the goddess who had entrusted him to protect his master. But as despair forced his spirit down, it found there was a place beyond which he would not retreat. His self-condemnation clanged against the bronze core of his character, where it found a new resolve. All was not lost, he told himself; not while Odysseus lived.

Something held Damastor's arm from delivering the fatal blow. At the same time Odysseus's words were slurred and far away in Eperitus's hearing. Almost to the surprise of his conscious mind he found himself running into the small room and timing the swing of his own sword to strike Damastor. In that same moment the invisible grip on the traitor's arm broke and he threw the blade down into a deadly lunge that would cut through the skin, bone and sinew of Odysseus's neck. Odysseus, finally aware he was not alone, began to turn his head. But Damastor had already failed.

The edge of Eperitus's sword thumped into his arm above the

elbow, the force of the blow biting through flesh and bone to send the lower part of his limb, weapon still gripped in its frozen fingers, spinning through the air into one of the dark corners of the temple. Blood spouted from the maimed stump in sporadic arcs, raining large droplets over Odysseus and the altar at which he prayed. Damastor spun round, partly from the impact of Eperitus's sword, and looked with wide-eyed disbelief at his butchered limb, and finally at his attacker.

And then the torch went out.

Everything was sucked into the sudden blackness. For a moment Eperitus was blind and disorientated. Robbed of his sight, he froze and retreated back upon his hearing. But the shock of the darkness had imposed an equally confusing silence within the temple, and in that sensual void only the faint hiss of the dead torch and the red glow of its stub gave any point of focus.

There was a scuffing sound close by and Eperitus took a step backwards. By now his eyes were adjusting to the faint light from the doorway and he could see the dim blue outlines of shapes in the temple. Damastor had fallen to his knees, hugging the remnant of his arm to his side and beginning to sob. Eperitus saw Odysseus stand and retreat against the altar.

'Is that you, Eperitus?' he whispered.

'Yes.'

The sword felt heavy in Eperitus's hand, pulling at the relay muscles in his arm, and for a time he was unsure whether to finish Damastor off or spare his life. Two steps forward and a sweep of the great blade would end for ever his treachery and send his spirit to ignominy in the Underworld. But there was something about the horrific sight of his shattered limb, spraying gore across the altar in a mockery of human sacrifice, that took away any heart Eperitus had for more bloodshed.

He took a step towards the kneeling figure. 'Stand up, Damastor. Your wound has to be bound before the blood loss kills you.'

'Damn you,' Damastor replied, struggling to his feet. The dull sheen of a dagger gave Eperitus a moment's warning, but it was too late.

Before he could even think to move the point was puncturing his chest. Intense pinpricks of pain spread like fire through his body as the blade sank slowly, smoothly and unstoppably into his flesh, ripping an agonized scream from his throat as every muscle crumpled and he crashed heavily against the dirt floor.

He looked up and saw the dark shape of Damastor towering endlessly above him, seeming to rise higher and higher like a tall tree as Eperitus slipped further and further into the earth below him, thrust relentlessly downward by the gigantic, fiery dagger embedded in his heart. Then he felt the warm, glutinous dampness of his own blood pumping out over his fingers – which were closed motionless about the handle of the weapon – and seeping down across his chest. He felt it infiltrate the material of the tunic Clytaemnestra had given him, making it heavy and pasting it firmly against his skin. And then the downward motion stopped and he lay looking lazily upward through dim, misting eyes, skewered to the floor by the searing blade of Damastor's knife.

Odysseus appeared at the centre of his vision, leaping like a lion upon Damastor and carrying him out from the borders of his sight. There were distant sounds of a struggle, and then Eperitus felt the dagger lifted out from between his ribs. No longer pinned to the ground he stood with an easy movement that seemed unhindered by his wound, or even the usual grating of joints and groaning of muscle and bone. He turned to see Odysseus on top of Damastor, leaning his full weight down upon the fingers he had closed about the traitor's throat. Damastor flailed his bloody stump uselessly against Odysseus's flank as he struggled for air, trying desperately to fight off his attacker and breathe again.

It seemed an eternity before the monstrous arm stopped flapping, and even longer before Odysseus finally extracted his fingers from Damastor's throat and stood up. Only then did he turn around and look into the darkness for his friend. Eperitus wanted to say something to him, to draw his attention, but the words did not come. Then Odysseus dropped his gaze to the ground by Eperitus's feet and an agonized groan escaped his lips.

Quickly he moved towards the centre of the room and fell to his knees. He reached out his arms and clutched at something long and heavy, lifting one end onto his lap and bowing his head over it.

'Eperitus,' he said, and the young warrior suddenly knew that the words were not directed at him but at the shape on the floor.

A cold sense of apprehension filled him. Outside, far away though it seemed, he thought he could hear the sound of something approaching the temple, something terrible coming at great speed. He felt a compulsion to get out and run, but just as he had found himself incapable of speech he was equally unable to move a muscle of his body.

Desperately he looked down at the shape in Odysseus's arms. As he began to recognize what it was, as the truth settled upon him with an icy chill, he saw Damastor rise from the floor behind the prince.

But Eperitus felt no panic, no urgent need to draw Odysseus's attention to him, for like himself the figure of Damastor was but a harmless wraith. They were dead, and the sound of rushing air grew nearer, even to the door of the temple.

Chapter Twenty-six
WRAITHS

Eperitus looked at the entrance. For an instant it was clear, the ghoulish moonlight cracking open the darkness of the temple and teasing him with a final glimpse of freedom. He saw the silvered rocks and the starkly illuminated hillsides outside, the sweet, despairing beauty of a world that was now lost to him. And then the light was extinguished. A tall figure in a black robe, his features as magnificent as they were terrible, filled the doorway, looking first at Damastor and then at himself.

Every soldier understood the fate that awaited him. One day he knew a spear point would pierce his guard, a sword's edge cleave his flesh, or a bronze-tipped arrow skewer his heart. Then, as his armoured body crashed into the dust of the battlefield, he knew his soul would stand dispossessed. And soon Hermes would come to lead him to the Underworld, the House of Hades; there he would drink of the river Lethe and forget his former life, becoming a shade and passing the rest of eternity in loneliness, without satisfaction or joy.

Damastor saw Hermes and cowered before him. Though he could not speak, a low and baleful moan left his ethereal lungs and his wraith's limbs shook in terror. At the same time Eperitus, too, was hamstrung with fear. The brief but honeyed tenderness of life was gone, snatched from him before he had barely been able to taste it. Now his spirit would spend perpetuity in emptiness.

Hermes entered and filled the temple with his presence.

323

Odysseus, who still held Eperitus's body in his arms, did not see him, nor did he hear the frightened muttering of Damastor's ghost as the god beckoned to him. Such things were not for mortal eyes.

To Eperitus, though, they were inescapable. He saw Damastor fall to his knees, silently weeping and begging not to be taken, but nevertheless inexorably drawn towards the dark figure. He watched him shuffle forward, resisting every movement until an instant later he was swallowed up in a great sweep of the god's cloak, disappearing from sight altogether. Hermes then turned his gaze upon Eperitus, and in a commanding gesture threw his hand out towards him.

At that moment Eperitus heard Odysseus say his name. From the corner of his vision he saw him lay his dead body back onto the earth of the temple floor and wipe the tears from his eyes with the back of his hand. Still on his knees, the prince looked up and accused the gods of cruelty to all mankind.

Reluctantly Eperitus took a step towards Hermes. He wanted to remain with his friend, not share Damastor's fate, and as he took two more heavy steps towards the god he looked again at Odysseus. He silently implored him to see what was happening, to save him from his fate, but Odysseus's chin now rested upon his chest and his hands were in his lap.

Eperitus's resistance gave way and he took the last few steps towards Hermes. But as he reached out to take the god's hand, the palm was suddenly turned towards him and Eperitus was fixed to the spot, unable to move. Hermes's attention was now rooted firmly upon Odysseus and, following his gaze, Eperitus saw that in his friend's hands was the clay owl Athena had given him.

The prince turned it about in his fingers, blandly studying each detail of the seal, but as he considered what to do with it Eperitus already knew what was in his mind.

'No,' he said, though no sound came from his mouth. 'The seal is your only hope for winning back Ithaca. Without Athena's help you'll never defeat Eupeithes. *Odysseus!*'

But there was not a breath in his ethereal body to give shape to the words. Instead, the only sound was the snap of the seal as his friend broke it between his fingers. The two halves melted away into fine dust and were gone for ever.

Odysseus wiped his hands on his cloak and looked up. After a few moments he glanced over his shoulder, directly through Eperitus's ghost to the doorway, and then into each corner of the temple. Eperitus followed his gaze, but the goddess did not appear. Nevertheless, Hermes's eyes remained firmly fixed on Odysseus.

The Ithacan dug his fingers into the loose soil of the temple floor where the dust of the tablet had spilled, trying to recover any fragment that might remain from the clay owl. There was nothing.

'Athena! Goddess, come to me.'

'What do you want, Odysseus?' said an invisible voice.

The prince squinted against the darkness of the temple but saw nothing. Then he noticed that a faint light outlined the crudely shaped effigy of the goddess. Its features were no different, but as he looked he could see a glimmer from its black eyes. Immediately he bowed his head and whispered her name.

'Why have you called me?' she said. 'I can't see any enemies – at least not living ones – and you haven't even reached Ithaca yet! Weren't you going to call me when you returned home?'

Odysseus lifted his head and looked directly at the clay figure.

'That *was* my intention, Mistress, but circumstances have changed. I have wits and courage enough to defeat my enemies on Ithaca, and yet there's one thing that's beyond any mortal. Only a god can give a man back his life.'

He gathered up Eperitus's corpse into his muscular arms and held it towards the statuette. Eperitus watched with a deep sense of pity in his heart: even Athena would not restore life to a dead mortal, and so Odysseus had thrown away his last hope of saving Ithaca. He heard Athena's voice admonishing Odysseus, telling him that what he asked was an insult to the gods, a request no man had any right to make of an immortal.

But, she added, she was compelled to honour her word.

Eperitus turned to Hermes, ready to be taken under his black cloak, but the god now stood at the threshold of the temple. His cloak was open and in the dark shadows of its folds was the quaking ghost of Damastor. His mouth was open in a soundless groan and his insubstantial arms were stretched out towards him, imploring his help. But there was nothing Eperitus could do, even if he wanted to, and a moment later Hermes had taken him on his final journey. He heard again the sound of rushing air outside, this time receding and accompanied by a low, despairing wail.

Suddenly he felt heavy. His ethereal limbs were seized by an awful lethargy that pulled upon them with irresistible force, dragging him downwards. The sensation consumed his whole body, constricting and crushing it so that he felt himself slowly being sucked into the ground at his feet. Then Eperitus felt a mighty blow knock him to the ground. It plunged him into a spinning blackness where he fell but did not hit the floor. Instead he tumbled downwards, his disembodied senses reeling about him like tentacles, reaching out to clutch at anything that might offer itself in that sensory void. As a wraith, he had at least been granted a grey sort of vision and a dull consciousness of sound; his other senses had been dimly aware of the living world from which they were departing, as if his body was still tenuously attached to it or had been gifted a final memory of mortal experience before being doomed to the Underworld. But in this non-existence the cord had been cut and he knew the true, hopeless meaning of death. For a fraction of worldly time he was held in an eternity of nothingness. It could not be measured, for he did not even have the comfort of his own thoughts with which to fill the vacuum. The only thing Eperitus knew for sure was that he had been given a glimpse of the pit into which all souls must one day be cast. And it was utterly black.

Something snapped. He felt himself in Odysseus's arms and everything was perfectly still. Then he lurched violently upwards as his lungs screamed for air. Simultaneously his heart quivered in his chest and began to spasm into action. Every organ of his body burst back into the unrelenting fight that gives life. His eyes opened and the brightness in the unlit temple was almost blinding.

Odysseus stared back down at him, his eyes wide with shock. Then he turned his attention to the gash in Eperitus's tunic and began probing it with his fingers.

'It's gone,' he declared, disbelief and joy alternating upon his features. 'The wound's gone. You're healed!'

'He's more than healed,' Athena corrected. 'How do you feel, Eperitus?'

Eperitus placed tentative fingertips upon the place where he had been stabbed. Not even the trace of a scar was left to mark the spot. He attempted to sit up and although his limbs and torso still felt heavy there was absolutely no pain. He raised himself stiffly to his feet, anxiously anticipating a stab of searing pain or a gush of blood from the reopened wound. Yet nothing happened. His wound was healed; he had been restored to life.

Eperitus looked at the goddess, wanting to express his gratitude but stalled by the inhuman form she had assumed. Instead he turned to his friend, whose sacrifice had saved him.

'I feel wonderful. The pain has gone. I mean, it's gone entirely.'

'Anything else?' Athena asked.

'Yes. I feel as if I've been given a new body. There's no pain in my chest, or anywhere else either. The throb in my shin where I was hit by a spear on Mount Parnassus has gone; even the ache in my ribs from the beating at Sparta. I feel wonderful!'

'You'll soon learn that your hearing has improved too,' the goddess added, 'and your eyesight and sense of smell. Your whole body has been rejuvenated.'

Despite the joy of his new body, Eperitus remembered he was in the presence of a goddess and knelt before her. As he did so he placed the soft part of his knee onto a sharp pebble and called out in pain. The statuette laughed with a grating sound that reminded him of stones being rubbed together.

'You may have a renewed body cured of all past wounds, Eperitus, but you aren't immune to future hurt. Even we Olympians feel pain when we assume earthly form. But now you must both return to your comrades, who are already looking for you. Tomorrow you will sail for Ithaca, Odysseus, to find your destiny. There you'll meet the greatest trial of your strength and intelligence so far, especially as you can't now rely on my help.'

With that the glimmer in the effigy's eyes died and the darkness in the temple grew deeper. A lonely wind whistled through the branches of the dead tree outside, and they knew that the goddess was gone.

Chapter Twenty-seven

THE RETURN

Ships were easy to find when they reached the coast at dawn of the next day, and Odysseus had soon hired two merchantmen and their crews for the return to Ithaca. Eperitus was the last to board, and as he walked up the gangplank onto the unsteady craft there was a murmur of excitement amongst the Ithacans. They were going home at last and their conversation was full of the sights and sounds of their island, mixed cautiously with memories of family and friends. But they had also regained the sense of purpose that had been denied them in Sparta. As guests of Tyndareus they had been a burden, vagrant soldiers given temporary lodgings for the sake of their master. There, only Odysseus was of any importance and only he could influence their collective destiny. Now they were returning to fight for everything they held dear, and each man would be vital in the coming battle. On Ithaca, for better or worse, they would come into their own again as their spears and swords challenged the usurpers for the right to rule.

Neither Eperitus nor Odysseus told them about the supernatural events of the previous night. All they revealed on their return was that Damastor had shown himself to be a traitor by attempting to kill Odysseus, for which he had paid with his life. If Odysseus spoke with Penelope about it he did not tell Eperitus, and for his own part Eperitus did not share with Odysseus the fact that Clytaemnestra had warned him about Damastor.

Even between themselves, they had exchanged few words about the incident. Eperitus had thanked Odysseus in the straightforward manner of a soldier, and Odysseus had accepted his words of gratitude with a simple nod. The fact that he had sacrificed his best hope of regaining his homeland was not mentioned by either man, and they now turned their minds to the challenge that lay ahead. But both men knew that the bond between them had deepened. Each had saved the life of the other, and warriors do not forget such matters, even if they do not talk about them.

Rough seas and heavy rain made the passage difficult. They sailed all day and night, battling high winds and squalls with the Ithacans busy helping the ships' crews in their struggle against the elements. Eperitus sat in a corner and was ill throughout the whole of the journey, an experience made much worse by the sensibility of his restored body. The only consolation was that the Spartan soldiers shared his agony, gazing emptily out from their own wretched corners of the deck, their faces pale and their half-lidded eyes filled with despair. Not one of them managed any sleep, and when the next morning there were shouts from the Ithacans that their destination was in sight, they were incapable of sharing in their jubilation. Only Penelope seemed unconcerned by the constant buffeting of the waves, and joined her husband at the prow to stare at the low silhouette of her new home.

Thick grey clouds meant they did not see the face of the sun that morning, although they sensed the sunrise in the east. The sea had calmed sufficiently for the merchant ships to anchor by a rocky cove off the south-eastern tip of the island – the only place on that rugged coast where they could disembark their human cargo with any degree of safety. Odysseus knew the spot well and had directed the ships' captains here deliberately. To have landed anywhere else would have risked their being spotted, and the prince was keen to retain the element of surprise.

As soon as the last group of passengers had been rowed to the small pebble beach, Odysseus paid the remainder of the agreed fare and the ships hauled up their anchor stones once more. The crews waved to them and wished them well before setting sail again and drifting back out to sea.

The Ithacans spent a few silent moments looking about themselves and listening to the sounds of the breakers hitting the rocks and the wind whistling across the rugged cliff-face before them. Odysseus stamped his feet on the shingle, as if to convince himself it was real, then put his fists on his hips and took a deep breath, filling his lungs with the air of his home. The men felt no need for ceremony or pompous words to mark their return, and when Odysseus started up the narrow, ill-defined track that climbed awkwardly to the top of the cliff, they followed.

After considerable difficulty they assembled again on its rocky summit, where great black birds circled and cried into the wind. Penelope stood to one side and looked out at the sombre, white-tipped waves below. Eperitus watched her and wondered in that lonely moment whether she was thinking of the home she had left behind. Perhaps she was already missing Sparta's sun-baked plains, the security and comforts of its palace, and even the familiar faces of her family. She turned and looked at him, the breeze tearing at her clothes and hair. For a moment he saw doubt in her eyes. Then she smiled and the strength of her character returned. For better or worse, she had committed herself to her husband and his beloved island, and now she was determined to make Ithaca her home too.

'Thank the gods we're back,' Antiphus said, standing at Eperitus's side. 'We've only been away for half a year, and yet it feels like twenty.'

'And the hardest part is still to come,' Eperitus said.

'Still, it's better to die here than on foreign soil.'

Halitherses cuffed the archer round the ear. 'Don't plan on getting killed just yet, Antiphus. We have a battle to fight before I accept your resignation from the guard, and there'll be no dying without my say-so. Now stop your daydreaming and come with me. Odysseus wants some of us to do a bit of nosing about before we start chasing Taphians all over the island. You too, Eperitus.'

Intrigued by the prospect of a scouting mission, Eperitus followed the old warrior to where Odysseus was waiting for them with Mentor and Diocles the Spartan.

'Take off your armour and leave it here with your spears and shields,' Odysseus ordered. 'My father has a pig farm just over the crest of that ridge and the herdsmen there are loyal to him. Before we make any plans for recapturing the palace I want to ask them a few questions, but I don't want to panic them by arriving in full war gear. Keep your swords handy – and you can bring your bow, Antiphus – but nothing more. Mentor, I want you to take charge whilst we're gone. Set a guard and make sure everybody gets a rest and something to eat. Don't be afraid to use up the provisions we have, as there'll be ample food at the farm. And there's plenty of water at Arethusa's spring, just north of here.'

'I know it,' Mentor said, before running to give orders to the others.

Back out amongst the choppy seas, far away from the eyes of any who might have been watching, one of the merchant ships turned its sail to catch the southerly wind. The canvas flapped noisily as it bellied out and drew the vessel slowly away from its companion, slicing through the waves to claw its way steadily north and into the channel between Ithaca and Samos.

❧

Before they even reached the crest of the ridge Eperitus could hear the grunting and snuffling of pigs, mixed with the occasional shouts of men. He felt a moment of nervous anticipation in the pit of his stomach and then they were on the hill and looking down over fields of mud. Fat hogs and sows wallowed in the filth, honking with satisfaction as their little pink offspring tottered around them in play-filled happiness. Two young men were ankle-deep in the sludge, carrying sacks over their shoulders filled with acorns and cornel berries, with which they were feeding their charges.

They saw the newcomers, but instead of shouting a greeting dropped their sacks and ran back to a large walled enclosure in the middle of the muddy pastures. Moments later they emerged from a stone hut with two companions, all four of them armed with staves and in no mood to welcome strangers. They had a number of dogs with them that began a vicious barking the moment they set eyes upon the party of warriors. One of the youths walked to the wall and shut the gate, as much to keep the dogs in as the unwelcome visitors out.

'Who are you and what do you want?' he called.

'Isn't that Eumaeus?' said Halitherses, squinting. 'He always used to be friendly to strangers.'

'Things have changed on Ithaca since we left,' Odysseus reminded him. 'And he won't be expecting our return.'

He stepped forward and held out the palm of his hand in a sign of peace.

'Put down your weapons. We come as friends, loyal to the king.'

The men made no sign of lowering their staves, whilst their black dogs barked even more furiously.

'Which king?' Eumaeus called back. 'Polytherses or Laertes?'

The returning soldiers looked at each other in quiet astonishment. The implication that Eupeithes had been overthrown by the infinitely more brutal and ruthless Polytherses did not come as good news.

'We honour the lord Laertes, true master of these islands. And our swords will speak against any who deny him.'

Eumaeus opened the gate and ordered the dogs back into the farm. 'Then you're welcome here, friends,' he said, as his comrades lowered their weapons. 'Come and eat with us, so we can learn your names and your purpose here.'

'You know both already,' Odysseus replied as he walked down

the hill and along the low causeway that led to the farm. Eumaeus gasped and fell to his knees with tears of happiness in his eyes. The others followed his example, murmuring Odysseus's name to each other in disbelief.

'You've returned, my lord!' Eumaeus said. 'May the gods bless this day, and may you forgive us our lack of welcome, but terrible things have happened since you left. Eupeithes took advantage of your absence to overthrow Laertes and put himself on the throne, then Polytherses replaced him and now rules with a fist of bronze. Any show of open disloyalty is punished with death. And we've had no news of you, my lord, though we've prayed every day for your return.'

Odysseus took his slave by the hand and lifted him to his feet, signalling for the others to rise also. 'I've heard about Eupeithes – Mentor escaped and found us in the Peloponnese. But I didn't know about Polytherses. It's a traitor's reward to be betrayed, and Eupeithes knows all about that now, but I fear Polytherses will prove a more difficult opponent if I'm to win back Ithaca.'

Eumaeus nodded. 'It's true. Mentor will have told you about the Taphians, no doubt, but he couldn't have known there are a full hundred garrisoned here now. It'll be a difficult task, unless you've brought an army with you.'

As he said the words he looked up with a sudden glimmer of hope in his eye, but Odysseus shook his head.

'We have forty Spartans on loan from King Tyndareus – they're resting on the other side of the ridge – but there are fewer than sixty of us all told. What about Taphians on the other islands?'

'Zacynthos, Samos and Dulichium are ruled by those who supported the rebellion. If there are ever any signs of trouble Polytherses sends a shipload of Taphians over for a day or two until things are quiet again, but mostly they remain here. Polytherses is no fool; he has always feared you'd one day come to claim your inheritance, so concentrates his forces here for your return.'

'And my family?' Odysseus finally asked, though this was the question that had been burning at the forefront of his mind all the time.

'Your mother and sister are kept at the palace, whilst Laertes is a prisoner in the former home of Eupeithes, under the guard of Koronos. Eupeithes was much too afraid to have him killed, but the rumour from the palace is that the new king intends to execute him.'

'Then we've arrived just in time,' Odysseus declared with a determined look. 'Tell me, are you or your men taking any of these pigs up to the city today?'

'Yes, two of us were planning to go at noon.'

'Good. Now listen to me, I want you to question the most loyal men in the city. Tell them I've returned and find out who's prepared to fight with me against Polytherses. Those who are must be ready to join us at any time. Find one who'll let you stay with him overnight, so when I call on you you can gather a force as quickly as possible. And be prepared – I may need you sooner than you expect.'

'I'll see to it, my lord,' Eumaeus said.

Half a dozen swine were killed and the carcasses dressed for roasting, whilst Antiphus was sent to bring the rest of their party to the farm. By the time they had arrived and had eaten it was mid-morning, so Eumaeus and the other swineherds hurriedly gathered together a dozen pigs to drive down to the city. They whistled for their dogs and with their long staves began to shepherd the pigs into a group, ready to move. As they were taking their leave, Odysseus put his hands on Eumaeus's shoulders and looked him in the eyes.

'Penelope and her slave will stay here,' he said. 'I'm leaving a couple of her uncle's men to protect her, but if we don't return you *must* see they get a ship back to the mainland. Do you understand?'

Eumaeus was about to answer when he caught a quelling glance from his master's new bride. She had been talking with Actoris,

GLYN ILIFFE

but on overhearing the words of her husband she walked over and stood before him.

'You've misjudged me, Odysseus, if you think I'll allow myself to be left in the care of others. If you go then I will follow.'

'A battle is no place for a woman,' her husband replied, his voice even but commanding. 'If we're defeated the Taphians will show no mercy to their prisoners. For a woman, death would be a blessing compared to what they'll do to you. No, I must believe you're safe, Penelope, and know that if I die you'll be taken back to your home.'

She met his stern look with defiance, her royal breeding there for all to see. '*Ithaca* is my home now,' she said. 'I live here or I die here. I'll not go back to Sparta to spend the rest of my days in widow's rags. My place is to be at your side and share your fate, whatever that may be.'

They stood facing each other. The shadows of their inevitable parting settled around them, bringing sudden uncertainty and fear as they realized they might not meet again. She looked at the rough features of the man she had once convinced herself she hated, and found the thought of being apart from him unbearable. He met her gaze and realized she was the foundation of the rest of his life. In her he would find the wholeness he had lacked as a young prince.

Tentatively, tenderly, he reached out and stroked her arm with his knuckles. As he felt her soft flesh he remembered the words of the Pythoness and took heart. Here, already, was the Spartan princess of whom the priestess had spoken. And had she not also said it was his fate to reign as king? He smiled encouragingly at his wife.

'You'll not become a widow yet, Penelope,' he told her. 'Unless the gods have deceived me, I can't die until I've first become king of these islands. So have courage and do as I ask. If you've learned anything about me, you'll already know I won't permit you to refuse me.'

She stared at him for a moment, then nodded and lowered her eyes. Odysseus immediately turned to Diocles, who was close by. 'Assign two of your best men to remain here with my wife and her slave. The rest of you make ready. We'll march to Mount Neriton now and see what preparations Polytherses has made for our arrival.'

With a nod the prince signalled for Eumaeus to be on his way, while the rest of them began pulling on their armour and preparing for the battle that they sensed would soon be upon them. Without a final word or glance at her husband, Penelope turned and went into the stone hut.

From the slopes of the hill to the south of the city they saw all that they needed to know of Polytherses's defences. His full strength was based inside the palace walls, with only an occasional patrol leaving the gates to roam the streets of Ithaca. Even with a hundred armed soldiers, though, the high palace walls, the thick wooden gates and the open killing ground before them presented enough of an obstacle to deter even the most numerous and well-armed enemy.

During the long march from Eumaeus's farm speculation was rife amongst the men, most believing they would attack upon arrival. But even with the element of surprise and support from the men of the city, the sight of the heavily defended palace made them realize that an assault by daylight was impossible. This did not deter Odysseus, however, who remained full of confidence, energy and purpose. He ordered the remaining Spartans to make camp whilst the Ithacans, who knew the island intimately, were split into two groups to scout each flank of the town. Their primary task was to ensure there were no Taphian outposts to warn of their attack, but Odysseus also told them to watch for weaknesses and gather intelligence about the defences.

'Our best hope is to kill Polytherses,' Eperitus suggested. 'I can climb over the wall after dark, while they're eating, and find my way to his room. When he goes to his bed he'll be unprotected, and that's when I'll kill him.'

Mentor disagreed. 'Even if you knew which room is his, you'd never get into the palace without detection. There isn't a ruler in Greece who doesn't fear assassination, and I guarantee that some-one as hated as Polytherses will have a personal guard of his best men close to hand. Our best hope is an attack just before dawn – ladders against the walls and into the palace whilst most of them are still sleeping.'

'I don't plan to do either,' Odysseus countered. 'I've been discussing the matter with Halitherses and we're agreed the best way is to draw the Taphians out.'

He briefly explained his plan to have the townsfolk murder one of the Taphian patrols, then flee to prepared positions on Mount Neriton. Polytherses would not fear a group of peasants without armour or proper weapons, of course, but neither could he allow their dissent to go unpunished. So he would send out a significant part of his force to overthrow the rebellion – and straight into an ambush of nearly sixty fully armed soldiers. The storming of the undermanned palace would then be a bloody but brief formality.

He smiled confidently, then led Mentor and the rest of his party away through the trees to skirt the harbour and the western edge of the town. Eperitus set off with Halitherses in the opposite direction, accompanied by Antiphus and five others. They moved in a cautious file, using the rocks, bushes and trees to keep them hidden from the city below as they descended slowly towards it. All around them birds sang freely and the wind sighed in the leaves, whilst the warm air was thick with the strong smell of the sea. Since his life had been restored by the goddess, Eperitus's senses had improved greatly, to give him a richer awareness of his surroundings: not only could he see better by day or in darkness, but his hearing and sense of smell were also much sharper and more far-ranging. But the new life he had been given had not only improved his physical senses. Now he was aware of things beyond the world of sight, sound and smell. Suddenly he would know if someone was about to speak to him, and would turn to them before they had opened their mouth. Similarly, he would instinctively anticipate movement an instant before it happened, enabling him to react faster and move with a speed that unnerved others. Initially his new abilities were disorientating, but he was fast growing used to them.

Another benefit was a sense of the presence of others. After they had been creeping through the thinly wooded slopes for some time, getting ever closer to the outermost settlements of Ithaca, Eperitus realized that they were being followed.

The trees began to thin out, offering less cover, so they climbed a wall into a vineyard to screen their progress from unwelcome eyes. Here, as the others moved forward, Eperitus ducked down and doubled back to wait behind the chest-high wall. Moments later he heard the sounds of someone approaching with great stealth – a small, light person who made little noise as he reached the wall. Had it not been for his improved hearing Eperitus doubted he would have detected him; but, after a brief pause to listen, their pursuer put an arm on the wall above Eperitus's head and began to clamber over.

In an instant the warrior was upon him, grabbing him by the tunic and hauling him with a thud onto the ground. He drew his sword and placed the point against his captive's exposed throat.

And saw that, with his newfound stealth, he had captured a boy of no more than ten years.

'Don't worry,' Eperitus reassured him, withdrawing his sword. 'I'll not kill a child. Now get up and tell me who you are.'

'Arceisius, my lord. My family are loyal to the king. I know you must be a friend of Laertes, too – I saw you with Halitherses.'

'Is that young Arceisius?' said Halitherses, returning with the rest of the party. 'Where are your flocks, boy?'

'Mostly eaten up by the Taphians, sir. The scrawny animals they've left us are back up there on the hillside. Is Odysseus with you?'

'He is, lad, and if you want to help us stop the Taphians stealing your sheep you'd better answer us a few questions.' The captain of the guard knelt down so that he was eye to eye with the boy. 'Don't exaggerate now, Arceisius, but tell us how many of these folk there are.'

'Five score and three, not including Polytherses, or Eupeithes, who is his prisoner now.'

'That's a very clear answer,' Halitherses replied, looking up at him and raising an eyebrow. 'Now, lord Odysseus will want to speak to your father. Where is he?'

'The Taphians killed him when he tried to stop them stealing his sheep.'

Halitherses tousled the boy's long hair and stood up. 'Then we'll make them pay, Arceisius, don't you worry. You head back up to your sheep and let us get about our business.'

He turned to go, but the boy tugged at his cloak.

'The Taphians are paid with wine, partly, but the shipment is a week late. It's due this evening in a ship from the mainland, and they're sending some men to escort the wagon back from the harbour. I thought I should tell you because the Taphians are getting angry and Polytherses is scared they'll take it out on him if the wine doesn't arrive safely.'

'Good lad,' Eperitus told him, understanding the suggestion. If they could somehow stop the wine reaching the palace, perhaps the Taphians would revolt and do their job for them.

'There's something else, my lord,' the shepherd boy said. 'It's the reason I was following you. There are Taphians in the woods. They left the city a while ago and headed for the top of the hill. I thought maybe Odysseus was up there.'

'Zeus's beard!' Halitherses exclaimed. 'They'll find the camp. Come on. We haven't a moment to waste.'

Chapter Twenty-eight
TAPHIAN WINE

They ran headlong through the trees without caring whether they could be seen from the city below. Everything now depended upon them reaching the camp before the Taphians: if Polytherses's men took the Spartans by surprise, they would be massacred. At a stroke Odysseus would have lost over half his warriors, as well as the element of surprise that was so essential to the success of his plans.

Halitherses's training regime at Sparta had made the Ithacans fit enough to run all day, but their armour and weapons weighed them down. The heavy accoutrements sapped the strength from their limbs as they struggled to climb the steep slopes, frustrating their progress and making them curse beneath their breath, but as they neared the area of their camp they slowed to a cautious walk. Set in a hollow in the ground and surrounded by a screen of trees and bushes, it was visible only to those on the topmost point of the hill. However, the approaches to the hollow were also obscured to within a short distance, enabling them to come quite close before Halitherses signalled for the group to halt. Eperitus was with him at the head of their file and, leaving the others crouching amongst some rocks, the two men crawled up to a knot of bushes for a better view.

'I can hear voices,' Halitherses whispered.

'Yes, and there's an armed man over in those bushes. You see him?'

'My old eyes aren't as good as they used to be. He must be a sentinel, but is he a Spartan or a Taphian?'

'He's neither,' Eperitus answered. 'He's an Ithacan.'

'Then Odysseus has beaten us back,' Halitherses said, getting to his feet. He raised his spear to catch the lookout's attention, then stepped out into the open. Eperitus waved for the others to follow.

The soldier came out to meet them, his face gloomy. 'You'd better go and see for yourselves,' he said, pointing back towards the camp.

Eperitus felt a cold weight sink through him as if he had swallowed a stone. Halitherses gave him a look that revealed his own misgivings, and then with reluctant curiosity they pushed through the trees and walked down into the hollow. The others came after, bringing Arceisius with them.

Before them was a scene of devastation. Spartan bodies lay strewn everywhere, intermingled with bits of armour and broken weapons. The dust was stained with blood in many places, not just where the Spartans had fallen, and from that alone Eperitus knew they had killed some of their Taphian assailants before being overwhelmed. Odysseus and the others stood looking at the litter of corpses. At the sight of Halitherses and his men their spirits rose visibly, glad to see they were still alive, though they offered no words of greeting.

'The shepherd boy told us there were Taphians on the hill,' Eperitus said, pointing at Arceisius. 'But how did you know to return so soon?'

Odysseus shook his head in dismay. 'We slipped over the road between Ithaca and the harbour, hoping to climb the hill to the north-west of the town. From there we saw a ship drifting out of the bay and into the straits; it was one of the Spartan ships that brought us here.'

Halitherses spat in the dust. 'Treachery then.'

'They sold us and their own countrymen for a few pieces of silver. It's my guess Polytherses sent a large force of men to hold the isthmus between the two halves of Ithaca, and some malevolent god led them straight to our camp.'

'So what do we do now?' Halitherses asked. 'We can't stay here: Polytherses is certain to send up another force at any time. The ship's captain will have told him how many men were landed, so he'll know there's only a handful of us left. At the very least he'll want to check the bodies to see if you're amongst them, Odysseus.'

'We'll have to find a boat to take us back to the mainland,' Mentor said, despondently. 'I can't see any other choice: if the Spartans killed as many as they lost, Eumaeus will still need to recruit seventy loyal Ithacans before we can match the Taphians man for man. Even then, Polytherses has the advantage of defended walls and a better-equipped force, and we've lost the advantage of surprise. Winning back our homeland was always going to be hard, but now it's become impossible.'

'None of that matters any more,' Odysseus said. 'Look.'

He pointed at one of the Spartan bodies. He had short black hair and a beard and his eyes were closed as if in sleep. The shaft of an arrow stood up from his stomach, where a crimson circle of blood had spread out from the point of entry. Eperitus did not recognize him or know his name.

'What of him?' he asked.

'He was one of the men Diocles assigned to guard Penelope; the other's over there. They should be back at the pig farm with her. The fact they aren't means Penelope persuaded them to follow us. You heard her say she would follow me, and that's exactly what she's done.'

'Then she's been taken by the Taphians?' Halitherses asked.

'I've no doubt about it, which leaves me no choice in the matter. If there are any that will follow me, I intend to attack tonight.'

Halitherses looked grim. His reply was stiff and tight-lipped.

'And every man here will attack with you. This island's their home and there's not a man amongst them who doesn't have wives and children to fight for. The only man I can't speak for is Eperitus. I've come to respect you in the time we've been together,' he said, turning to Eperitus, 'and I would trust you with my life. But you've only spent a handful of nights on Ithaca and I'd think no less of you if you returned to the mainland to seek your fortune there.'

'Yes,' Odysseus agreed. 'I owe you my life, Eperitus, and you owe me yours, but I can't ask you to give it up for the sake of an island you know nothing about.'

'Know nothing about?' Eperitus scoffed. 'Haven't I heard you and your men talk about every rocky crag, every wooded hill, every olive grove and every young maiden on Ithaca? I know the names of each different place on this island from its homesick warriors, and its sights are so familiar to me I feel like I was born here. Ithaca's my home now and my allegiance is to its prince. I'll kill Taphians with you, even if it means certain death, but if you'll listen to me I have a better suggestion.'

The others looked at him quizzically.

'The shepherd boy told us something we can use to our advantage. He says the Taphians are getting restless because their wine shipment is late. The only thing stopping them from rebelling against Polytherses is the promise it will arrive today.'

'That must have been the merchantman I saw coming in as the Spartan ship left,' Odysseus said.

'Then we don't have any time to spare. Polytherses has sent some men to escort the wagon back up to the palace, but if we can kill them and smash the shipment then the Taphians will rebel. We might not even have to fight them.'

'The boy has brains, as well as brawn,' Halitherses said, slapping Eperitus on the shoulder. 'I say the idea's a good one. How about you, Odysseus?'

'I say you two should stick to fighting and let me do the thinking. The wine shipment is the key, but we shouldn't destroy it. On the contrary,' he said, snapping his fingers and grinning at them, 'I want to make sure it arrives at the palace safe and sound.'

❧

Odysseus and his men watched the sail of the merchant ship drift out of the harbour. The sun was sinking behind the hills of Samos on the other side of the channel that divided the two islands. Its departing beams set fire to the surface of the water, making it boil red about the charred hull of the vessel as it slipped away northwards, dragging the long, oblong shadow of its sail beside it. After a while the ship disappeared from their view and, released from its spell, they settled themselves for the ambush.

Before long they heard the squeal of an overladen wagon making its way up the road from the harbour. It was the same road they had marched down to the cheers of the townsfolk half a year before, though now the only voices they heard were those of the approaching Taphians, the only sound the occasional crack of a stick on some poor beast's hindquarters.

Eperitus waited with Odysseus, hiding amongst the poplar trees where he had fought Polybus and knocked him into the town spring. Antiphus and five others were with them, waiting anxiously for the Taphians to appear. The remaining warriors, led by Halitherses and Mentor, were concealed behind a stone wall on the other side of the road, readying their weapons for the fight.

Eperitus's sword was in his hand and Odysseus had an arrow fitted in the great bow of horn that Iphitus had given him in Messene. Beside them Antiphus slid an arrow from the quiver at his hip and readied the notch in his own bow, to wait with stilled breath for the first soldier to come into view. No sooner had he half-tensed the ox-gut string than a man appeared where the road bent down towards the bay. He was followed in quick succession by two others – all of them were tall and heavily armed – and a pair of oxen drawing a large, high-sided cart. A further two warriors, older and fatter than the others, sat behind the labouring animals. They were backed by stacks of earthenware vessels, placed in baskets to prevent them smashing against each other during the journey and spilling the precious wine.

Nobody moved. The Ithacans had been in enough fights together now to know that the time to strike was still moments away. Before the Taphians had come into sight Eperitus had felt a knot of anxiety in his stomach, but now battle was at hand the tension eased out of him and an intense sensitivity to his surroundings took over. He was aware of every slight movement, every sound and, despite the twilight, every detail of each of his enemies. He could see the redness in their cheeks from sampling the wine, and the light of life in their eyes, shining with cheer because tonight they hoped to drink themselves into a stupor. But for them the night would never come, and their eyes would soon be dark for ever.

Odysseus signalled quietly to Antiphus, pointing at himself and then the driver to indicate his chosen target. Antiphus nodded in reply and indicated the lead Taphian. In the half-light of early evening neither shot would be easy, but Eperitus trusted both men to find their marks. Then Odysseus raised himself on one knee, waited for Antiphus to do the same, and in the same instant their bows twanged.

Both of the chosen men fell. The driver pitched sideways out of the cart, whilst the lead soldier half-raised a hand to his throat – where Antiphus's arrow had struck – before dropping to the ground. The squealing cart halted and for a brief instant everything was silent as the surviving Taphians looked about themselves in consternation. Then Eperitus leapt to his feet and ran at them screaming, his sword raised above his head. The others followed, yelling insanely as they dashed across the short distance separating the trees from the road.

One man made a clumsy effort to loosen the shield from his back and turn it towards them, but failed to hold its weight in his hurry and dropped it. An instant later Eperitus's sword had swept his head from his shoulders and sent it bouncing back down the road to the harbour. The remaining man on the wagon burst into tears and threw his arms out in supplication, pleading for his life in a garbled and hideous-sounding dialect. Realizing he had no heart for a fight Eperitus ignored him and looked for the other man, who he saw duck beneath a swathing cut from Halitherses's sword and sprint up the road to the town.

Antiphus fell in beside his captain and raised his bow to shoot the man down, but before he could release the arrow from between his thumb and forefinger, Mentor and another soldier hurdled the stone wall and dived upon the fleeing Taphian, smashing him to the ground beneath their combined weight. He struggled ferociously, and not until more help arrived did they manage to control him.

Strangely, when the two men were hauled before Odysseus for judgement their attitudes reversed. When Odysseus revealed his identity, the old man who had gibbered insanely for mercy became silent and stared at the prince with defiance; the younger man, however, crumbled with fear and began begging for his life. He fell to his knees before the prince and wrapped his arms about his legs.

'Don't kill me, lord,' he cried, his accent thick and barely intelligible. 'Spare me and I'll fight for you against Polytherses. We came here to support Eupeithes, but since he was deposed many of us have lost our reason to be here.'

'Shut up, you grovelling piece of snot,' growled his comrade.

Mentor cuffed him about the back of the head, persuading him to silence.

'I'll spare you,' Odysseus said. The kneeling man looked up in surprise. 'If you help us get into the palace.'

'Say nothing, Mentes,' ordered the other Taphian, earning himself another blow. This time blood trickled from one of his nostrils, proof that Mentor's patience was thinning.

'What do you say?' Odysseus persisted. 'I give you your life, and in exchange you get me into the palace.'

The man seemed suddenly uncertain, but as Odysseus raised the point of his sword and placed it against the soft flesh of his throat he swallowed quickly and nodded.

'I'll do it. I can tell you all you need to know about Polytherses's defences. If you let me return now, I can open the gate for you in the middle of the night.'

'Don't mock me, Mentes,' Odysseus replied with a frown. 'I intend to drive this wagon up to the palace gates with you at my side. And in return for your life you'll not only tell the guard I'm one of the wine merchants, you'll also see I'm made welcome for the night. Then, when the palace is sleeping, you can help me open the gates so that the rest of my men can enter. I want you close to me the whole time, close enough for me to slit your throat if you show any sign of revealing my name. And only when Ithaca is rid of Polytherses and your countrymen will I spare your life. Do you understand?'

'Yes, lord,' Mentes nodded fervently. 'I've told you I have no love for Polytherses – I'll do all these things you ask, and more if required.'

'I don't believe him,' Mentor said. 'He'll say anything right now, when your sword is pricking at his soft neck. But what about when he's surrounded by his friends, safely tucked away inside the palace with nothing but your dagger to threaten him? The coward'll find his courage and sense of duty quick enough then – duty to Polytherses! Some god has robbed you of your wits, Odysseus, if you let yourself be led into the palace by this serpent.'

'I give you my word of honour as a warrior, as all the gods are my witness,' said Mentes, standing and facing his accuser.

'I don't trust the word of a Taphian,' Mentor replied, sliding his sword out of his belt. He presented the hilt to the Taphian. 'But if you kill your comrade . . .'

'No!' Eperitus protested. 'That's barbaric.'

'It's the only way to be sure,' said Odysseus, looking expectantly at Mentes.

The older Taphian shifted uneasily. Then Mentes took the

sword and stuck it deep into his guts. He twisted the blade once and pulled it back out, unplugging a stream of dark, glistening blood that sluiced down the man's groin and legs and onto the road.

He turned from the body and handed Mentor his sword. 'Is that proof enough for you?'

'It will do,' Odysseus answered coldly. 'Now hide these corpses and listen to what I have in mind.'

*

The gate guards heard the squealing of the wagon long before it came into sight. The sound carried easily through the silent streets of Ithaca, which had already settled down for the night after an unusually busy day, and brought great joy to the wine-starved hearts of the soldiers gathered in the compound. Although the noise of the burdened vehicle was painful to hear, the Taphian warriors had been eagerly anticipating the shipment for several days and listened to its strained music with suppressed excitement.

The rumour that Odysseus had returned to the island meant nothing to them in comparison with the prospect of getting drunk. There had almost been a riot when Polytherses announced the wine would be kept in storage until further notice. Although the king wanted his warriors to remain sober to meet any attack that might come in the night, faced with the mutiny of his army he was forced to relent. Instead he took a core of volunteers who agreed not to drink in exchange for gold, and kept them garrisoned within the royal quarters.

'Who's that with you, Mentes?' called one of the guards as the wagon screeched to a halt before the gates.

'Merchants,' he answered. 'They want to stay in Ithaca for a while, so I said they could sleep in the palace until they find a house in the town tomorrow.'

'After our money, I suppose.'

'Why else would anyone want to come to this rock?' Odysseus answered.

He smiled at the three guards, who looked back with stony faces. They were tall men wrapped in thick cloaks, each one armed with two long spears and a shield and wearing leather caps on their heads. They looked more than ready for a fight.

'There speaks a wise man,' one of them replied. 'Where are the others?'

Odysseus squeezed closer to Mentes and pressed the point of his dagger against his ribs, the blade concealed beneath the cast of his cloak. On either side of the wagon Mentor and Antiphus prepared to pull their swords from between the jars of wine, where they had been concealed in rolls of matting.

'Drunk in one of the huts by the harbour,' Mentes shrugged. 'They couldn't wait.'

The guard shook his head resignedly and waved them through the tall wooden portals. Odysseus and Mentes had to duck their heads slightly, and then they were inside the familiar courtyard of the palace.

'Do you trust me now?' Mentes whispered as he applied a stick to the backside of one of the oxen.

'We'll see,' Odysseus replied, nudging the point of his dagger against his ribs.

He looked about himself at the two or three score of warriors who were approaching the wagon from every corner of the courtyard. Although it lifted his heart to see again the familiar surroundings of his home, it dismayed him to see this place – his childhood playground – filled with foreign soldiers. He halted the wagon and ordered Mentor and Antiphus to pass down the wine.

The Taphians cheered with delight and eager groups of men gathered at the back of the cart, ready to receive the heavy clay jars and pass them back to their waiting comrades. Others called on servants from the palace to bring food and, more importantly, water to mix with the wine. That was when Odysseus saw his father's ageing housekeeper come out of the palace at the head of a column of slaves bearing food and water.

As she began directing them in their duties, Odysseus called quietly on Athena to keep the old woman from looking up at the wagon and seeing him. The least sign of recognition from her or any of the slaves would bring a swift doom upon the disguised Ithacans. But Eurynome did not look up from her work, and as soon as enough water had been fetched and the food brought from the kitchens, she and the other servants retreated as far from the unruly Taphians as possible. Not one slave remained in the court-yard as Mentes drove the now empty wagon over to the stables against the eastern wall of the compound.

He prepared to jump down and unyoke the oxen, but was quickly deterred by the press of Odysseus's dagger against his side. Instead of sitting back down, though, Mentes slowly closed his hand over the blade and, looking the Ithacan in the eye, moved the weapon aside.

'You cannot stay beside me all night long, Odysseus. I have friends here who will want me to join them, and then what will you say? You have no choice but to trust me.'

Odysseus knew the Taphian was right. The fact they had not been detected thus far showed that the gods were with them, and if they were to succeed he would have to trust much more in them and in Mentes. So he tucked the knife into his belt and nodded.

'You're right. But I want you to stay with us, no matter who wants you to join them. And you aren't to drink anything. Is that understood?'

Mentes smiled, then jumped down and went to unharness the team, leading the beasts individually into the stables. As he did so a handful of Taphians approached, shouting friendly greetings in their rough dialect. Odysseus looked behind himself to make sure their weapons remained well covered, then waited for their enemies to reach them.

'Welcome to Ithaca, friends,' one of the men began. He was tall and had a scarred face. 'Why don't you join us for a drop of your own merchandise? We'll be happy to hear news from the mainland.'

Mentes reappeared and met each of the group with a quick embrace, speaking their names in turn.

'These men have travelled far and are tired,' he said. 'Let them keep their own company this evening. I will stay with them and act as host, so that they do not think we Taphians are inhospitable. There'll be plenty of time in the morning to hear stories from far-off lands.'

'No,' Odysseus said, to the surprise of his companions, 'we aren't so tired that we can't share a bit of news with men who want to hear it – and some of what I have to say might be of great worth. If you have a few portions of meat and a cup of wine to spare, we'll be glad to share with you.'

'Then come and join us by the main fire over there,' the scarred man said, pleased at the prospect of a tale or two to go with the new abundance of wine. 'We will go and see that spaces are made for you, and food and wine set aside.'

'Are you insane?' Mentor hissed as the Taphians returned to the fire. 'You'll get us all killed, and for what?'

'Have some faith in your old friend. All you need to do is remember you're a wine merchant. And don't reveal your true name, of course – there'll be a time for that tomorrow.'

Soon they were seated in the midst of their enemies, the very men who had stolen their homes from them and imposed a brutal regime upon their families and countrymen. Unless their identities were revealed, by dawn of the next day they would be fighting to kill each other with all semblance of friendship forgotten; but for now they could do little else but eat the food placed before them and sip at their wine.

Then the scar-faced man asked Odysseus his name and lineage, and on being told he was called Castor, son of Hylax (this time of Athens), demanded to hear what was happening on the mainland of Greece. Others echoed the call – all Greeks love a story – and Odysseus began without delay. He told them of the affairs of state back in Athens, which were true events told to Odysseus by Menestheus when they had courted Helen together. Though they were mundane issues, he was able to embroider them to make each event lively and interesting. Eventually he mentioned the departure of their king to Sparta, which, as Odysseus had intended, brought immediate demands for news of the now famous gathering. What did he know? they asked him, and when he admitted to knowing very little they begged him to tell them whatever information he could spare.

At the time of their leaving Athens, he said, King Menestheus had not returned from Sparta, though there was rumour that a suitor had been chosen. This caused a stir amongst the Taphians, who had been made excitable by the amount of wine already consumed, and inevitably one amongst them asked the question they had all wanted to ask – what had he heard about Odysseus of Ithaca?

Odysseus wetted his lips with the wine in his cup and looked about at the wall of faces, bathed orange by the firelight. From what he knew, he said, the Ithacan prince was highly regarded amongst his fellow suitors. He was supposedly a great warrior – the equal of Ajax or Diomedes – who carried a horn bow given to him by the god Apollo. He had already defeated a much larger force of bandits on his way to Sparta (at this, the Taphians muttered energetically with each other), and shortly afterwards had single-handedly saved the goddess Athena from a gigantic, man-eating serpent (at this, Mentor coughed loudly and shot Odysseus a stern glance).

The prince continued undeterred. What was more, Odysseus was reputed to be a man of irresistible charm. Not only had the great Helen of Sparta chosen him for her husband, he had also gained the sympathy and support of the other suitors. It was even rumoured that a combined force of Spartans, Mycenaeans, Argives, Myrmidons and others were gathering from all over Greece, preparing to liberate Ithaca. On hearing this there was a great uproar amongst the Taphians, at which Odysseus stood and held up his hands for silence. He stressed it was nothing more than a bit of hearsay he had picked up from another merchant, which he himself did not believe. However, the truth of the rumour would be easy to prove: if such a gathering really was taking place, then it was also said that a small vanguard of Spartans were to be sent to Ithaca to prepare a camp and scout out the rebels' defences.

Again the crowd of Taphians erupted. Fear and panic seemed to seize the courtyard as scores of voices were lifted in debate about Odysseus's return, and whether he was really bringing an army with him. The Ithacans took the opportunity to slip away unnoticed.

'You've got guts,' Mentor told his friend as they settled down on the soft ground beneath their wagon. His voice was even, but seethed with disciplined anger. 'And yet I can't understand why you took such a risk, just to give them a fright. It'll only put them more on their guard.'

'Or make them throw down their arms in surrender as soon as our attack begins,' Antiphus added.

'They are uneasy,' said Mentes, who had returned with them. 'That is understandable, when you live each day wondering whether the true heir to the kingdom will return to take his revenge. But I could have told you that without the need to risk your lives and mine.'

Odysseus covered himself with his cloak and lay down, looking up at the stars and listening to the riotous noise of the Taphians. He caught snatches of arguments, voices raised in drunken dispute. Then he heard female voices, servant girls who had been forced – or came willingly – to entertain the warriors. He instantly thought of his sister, Ctymene, but did not stir as the cold stars sparkled overhead.

'I didn't go just to see their fear at the sound of my name. No. I wanted to see the faces of the men who have invaded our homeland. I wanted to know what sort of people they are, how different they are to us, or how similar. I wanted to know who I'll be killing in the morning. Now get some rest and I'll wake you before first light.'

It was still dark when he shook them from their sleep. The fire in the middle of the enclosure had died to leave a pile of glowing embers, and the revelry of the Taphians was long since over, leaving only the faint harmony of their snores. Mentor and Antiphus were quickly awake and drawing out their weapons from beneath the matting in the back of the wagon. Last of all, Odysseus woke Mentes.

'I'll not ask you to accompany us in what we must do now,' he said. 'But you haven't betrayed us, despite being given every chance, and so I'll entrust you with one more task. You told us last night there were a number of Spartan prisoners held in one of the storerooms. Release them and wait until the fighting is over. If I'm still alive I will free you from your oath.'

Mentes nodded and, pulling his cloak about his shoulders to keep off the early morning cold, crept off towards the palace. Odysseus turned to Mentor and Antiphus. They stood close by, two black figures with only the dull gleam of their naked swords to distinguish them in the darkness.

'It's time,' he announced. 'We've thought about this moment for over half a year, but now it's here. It'll be bloody work, but this is no time for mercy. As you hold your daggers to their swinish throats, think of what they've done to your homeland and how long your families have had to endure their yoke. And remember that Ithaca's freedom depends on us opening those gates.'

He drew his dagger and led them by the faint starlight to where the gates sat slightly ajar. The guards were on the outside, watching the terrace between the walls and the city, unaware of the peril their sleeping comrades were in. The humped shapes of the unprotected men lay all about the Ithacans, motionless as if dead already, each one ignorant of the inglorious fate that awaited him.

Quickly, as if afraid that he might lose his determination for the grim task, the prince knelt down beside one of the soldiers and placed the palm of his hand firmly over the man's mouth. His eyes flickered open and looked up, but before he could react Odysseus had cut open his throat. The first victim died at once, his ruptured arteries jetting thick gouts of blood up Odysseus's bare arms.

Without pausing he moved to his next victim, this time sitting astride the torso and leaning his weight onto the hand with which he covered the man's mouth. In an instant he sawed through the soft flesh of his windpipe and stood again to move to the next Taphian.

Mentor and Antiphus waited no longer and joined in the butchery with silent determination. They gave little thought to the work, beyond the occasional grimace of disgust at the amount of blood that covered them, and very soon two dozen men lay murdered in their sleep. Not one had made a noise and few had even woken to set eyes upon the avengers who killed them.

Then the air changed and Odysseus looked up from his tenth victim. There was a faintness now in the sky above the stables, and he knew that if the attack were to come it would be soon.

He stood. The others finished the work at hand and stood with him. Odysseus tucked his gore-drenched dagger into his belt and drew the long sword that hung there. He gestured his men towards the gates: to surprise the sleepy guards and kill them would be the work of moments. Mentor and Antiphus drew their swords beside him and together they looked through the open portal at the shadowy city beyond. And then they heard a noise behind them.

'Stay where you are,' said a familiar voice. They turned to see the scar-faced Taphian, standing with a bow in his hand and an arrow fitted. It was aimed directly at Odysseus. 'I knew there was something not quite right about you,' he continued. 'You've got too much of the warrior about you to be a mere merchant, and now I find you slitting the throats of my countrymen. But before you die I will find out whether you are more Spartan scum, or one of Odysseus's men.'

Odysseus drew himself up and looked scornfully at the Taphian. 'Don't trouble yourself – I've concealed my name for too long as it is. I am Odysseus, son of Laertes, and you are trespassing on my father's property.'

For a moment the concern on the Taphian's face was visible, even in the darkness. After months of living uninvited under this man's roof, helping himself to his food and wine, he felt now like the trespasser he was and longed to be anywhere other than in his presence. But he soon quashed his own dismay and, realizing that the key to Polytherses's ultimate victory was at his mercy, smiled with satisfaction.

'Guards!' he called to the men outside. 'Guards! Get in here and shut the gates. Bolt them. I think we can expect visitors soon.'

His loud voice woke the surviving men in the courtyard, who propped themselves up on their elbows to see what was happening. Somewhere in the town outside a cockerel cried out to herald the first light of dawn. And at that moment a horn sounded a single note, rising clear and strong through the morning air.

Chapter Twenty-nine

THE BATTLE FOR ITHACA

'Come on then, lads,' Halitherses said. 'These Taphians have already overstayed their welcome; let's send them to a new home in Hades's halls. Eumaeus! I want you at my side with that hunting horn.'

He stood before a mixed force of guards and men from the town. There were over fifty of them, waiting for the first grey light of dawn to edge the darkness. Those who had escorted Odysseus to Mount Parnassus and Sparta had seen battle already and were calmly preparing their weapons and armour for the coming fight. The younger townsfolk, though lacking training or the proper arms and protection, were buoyed by thoughts of glory and making a name for themselves on their tiny island. The older men were stern-faced, thinking of the consequences of failure and determined to accept nothing less than victory. They knew that if Odysseus had been successful they would be inside the palace before the Taphians could wake, with every possibility of catching them entirely by surprise. But if he failed and the gates remained shut, then their attack would be short, bloody and fruitless.

As Eperitus loosened his sword in his belt and hefted the weight of his spear in his hand, he thought not of Ithaca but of Alybas. His father's treachery had brought disgrace on his family, and he could almost hear his dead grandfather calling out for revenge. But Eperitus knew he could never go back to the valleys in which he had grown up, once again to be walled in by its dead mountainsides or to sink into the mire of its humdrum troubles. Who had he met in the great palace of Sparta that had heard of Alybas, an obscure little place where the sum of its entire wealth was worth less than Agamemnon's golden breastplate? And which of the girls in Alybas was even fit to serve wine to Helen, whose beauty was perilous to look upon? No, he would remove the shame of his father's sedition by fighting the traitors who had overthrown Laertes. Ithaca was his home now, and Alybas but a memory.

A low mist had crept up from the sea and shrouded the legs of the small army, making them appear to float as they followed Halitherses through the town towards the palace. Eperitus and the other guardsmen were close behind him. As the only trained soldiers, they were to secure the gates whilst the others entered the courtyard and led the assault on the palace.

There were no fires or torches, but by the first light of dawn that pervaded the already failing night they could see the white-washed palace walls through the murk. There was a dark hole where the gate stood and they could not tell whether the portals were open or shut, but they were encouraged by the silence that met them as they formed a line along the edge of the terrace.

A cockerel crowed. Halitherses pointed at Eumaeus, who raised the horn to his lips and blew a long, clear note. For a moment they waited, listening to the lonely sound shiver the darkness, and then they were running steadily towards the gates.

Their weapons weighed them down, making it difficult to run. Eperitus's sword banged against his thigh and he was conscious of the bronze greaves upon his shins, stiffening his movements and checking his speed. His feet became quickly sodden from the wet grass, and yet the palace walls seemed hardly any closer. Suddenly someone called out.

'The gates are closed!'

Some of the men slowed down to look at the tall wooden doors. Though they were still some way off, they could see the gates remained shut against them.

'Come on, you dogs!' Halitherses shouted grimly. 'Get moving! We'll scale the walls while they're still waking up.'

But it was too late even for that. Taphian bowmen were already climbing onto the walls from the other side, unslinging their bows and taking aim. Halitherses was leading the Ithacans headlong into a trap, yet even so Eperitus ran on after him, hoping to close the remaining distance before the archers' deadly arrows stopped them. After waiting so long to return, it angered him that they should fail so early in their mission. Now only death and honour awaited them, and he was determined to fight his way into the compound and die with Taphian blood on his sword.

The attack had almost stalled behind them, but encouraged by the example of their captain the guardsmen ran screaming at the high walls, followed by most of the townsfolk. Eumaeus, unencumbered by shield or armour, outstripped them all. He passed Eperitus at a sprint and caught up with Halitherses, seeming as if he would run straight up the walls and over into the compound beyond.

Then the archers fired.

Their bows sang in the cold morning air. Eumaeus fell into the layer of mist and was gone. Halitherses turned towards him and was brought down under a second volley, disappearing into the vapours like the squire before him. Eperitus thrust his shield out before him and ran towards where his captain had fallen, shouting with rage and heedless of the flying darts from the walls. They split the air about his ears and thumped into the layered ox-hide of the shield, and in the growing light he could see yet more Taphian archers clambering up to shoot at the easy target he presented for them.

But Athena had heard his prayers. As he searched amid the swirling vapours only a spear's throw from the walls, he was not brought down by an arrow but by an obstacle on the ground. He stumbled forward into the welcoming mist and his shield fell on top of him, just as two more arrows thumped into its thick hide. There was a tense pause as the archers looked for him through the concealing vapours, then, thinking him dead, they turned their attentions to the mass of retreating Ithacans.

Eperitus lay still as the noise of battle receded from him. The grass was damp under his stomach and its fresh smell filled his nostrils. Close by someone was crying. Looking to his right he saw Eumaeus, whose legs he must have tripped over. The mist was beginning to evaporate as the sunlight grew and he could see the swineherd lying slumped and motionless on his front, a pair of arrows protruding from his left thigh. It also exposed him once more to the archers on the wall, and another arrow buried itself into the ground perilously close to his side. Eperitus sprang to his feet and, with his shield and spear in one hand, lifted the wounded boy with his free arm and ran as fast as his burdens would allow, back across the terraced plain towards the town. The bows twanged behind him again and he watched the arrows pluck at the last swirls of mist. There were dark humps on either side as he ran, barely distinguishable as bodies in the weak light of dawn, but ahead of him he was encouraged to see the remainder of his comrades, crouched beyond the reach of the Taphian arrows.

They stood to welcome him as he joined them, elated that two of their number had returned from the dead. He threw down his spear and shield and passed Eumaeus into the hands of one of the townsfolk, a giant bronze-smith who lifted the lad easily in his giant arms and set off with him back through the streets.

The rapid defeat had strained every man's nerves, and Eperitus wondered whether the Ithacans had the courage for another attack. Too few of them were seasoned warriors; the majority were ordinary men who had decided to join the fight for their country with whatever weapons were to hand. Now, with the loss of their captain, possibly of their prince, and with the palace gates barred against them, they were faced with the reality of a bloody fight and little hope of survival.

Eperitus brushed the dirt from his tunic and looked about at their anxious faces. 'Anybody who wants to abandon the fight now is welcome to do so; if you can face the shame of it, then your homes and families are waiting for you. Besides, I'd rather fight with brave men at my side than cowards. The rest of us have a duty to fight Polytherses and free our homeland. Halitherses has fallen and we must avenge him. Odysseus may also be dead, but as long as there's a chance he's still alive then we must go back and take the palace. If we don't fight for him now, all hope is lost and the Taphians will *always* rule Ithaca.'

'I'm with you!' said a grey-bearded old fisherman, his face stern and uncompromising. He was joined by a chorus of agreement from the rest of the men. 'I'd rather die fighting than live under Polytherses.'

'Good. Then let's go to glory, or an honourable death.'

Eperitus lifted his shield before him and signalled for the other guards to do the same. Together they made a wall of shields and marched once more towards the palace, the arrows parting the air above their heads again. Those without armour fell in behind them for protection from the deadly hail, and for a while, at range, they remained safe. But as they approached the walls two or three arrows found their mark, spinning men backward into the grass to kick out the last moments of their life. Eperitus peered around the edge of his shield and an instant later an arrow thumped into the top of the hide. But ahead of them their objective was getting progressively closer.

'We'll use our shields to make a platform when we reach the wall,' he shouted. 'It won't be easy: we'll be under fire from their archers as we climb, and they'll be waiting for anyone who gets over alive. But when Ithaca is free again, the bards will make songs about us that will be told long after we're all dead.'

They cheered at the prospect of glory, and at the same time shrank behind the cover of the shields as the palace defences grew tall before them. A man fell heavily, making no sound as an arrow pierced his heart and took his life. His comrades shrank down even further as more arrows rattled against the line of shields.

Suddenly Eperitus noticed a slight figure break away from the huddle of attackers and stand exposed before the walls. It was

Arceisius, the shepherd boy, who must have slipped unnoticed into the Ithacan ranks. Without a care for his own safety, he fitted a pebble into the woollen pouch of a sling and spun it rapidly about his head. Another cheer erupted from the Ithacan line as the stone found a target and one of the Taphian archers tumbled from the walls. A second pebble followed, hitting one of the defenders in the face before a flurry of hastily aimed arrows forced the shepherd boy back behind the press of his comrades. As he watched Arceisius send a further missile flying at the walls, Eperitus regretted not having any more slingers or archers; although he carried Odysseus's horn bow on his back and his quiver of arrows at his waist, his own place was at the forefront of their attack. Arceisius would have to work alone.

Having seen the first Taphians fall, Eperitus was also keen to press the attack on the wall and take his spear to the elusive enemy. They were almost up to the gates now and he was ready to break into a run, when suddenly he saw the body of Halitherses lying in the grass. At the sight of his grey hair and the distinctive, old-fashioned armour Eperitus felt the hot tears pricking at the corners of his eyes, provoked to sadness by the loss of his good friend. And then Halitherses moved.

It was only the slightest twitch of an outstretched arm, but overwhelmed to discover the guard captain was alive Eperitus ran from the Ithacan front rank towards where he lay, determined to bring him safely away from the foot of the walls. But before the Taphian archers could shoot him down, their rain of arrows suddenly stopped and they slipped back into the courtyard. Eperitus looked back at Arceisius, who shook his head in reply.

Then the answer came. They heard the rasping sound of the bar being lifted from the back of the great gates and saw the doors fold outward, ready to unleash the Taphian counter-attack.

༄

As the gates were slammed shut, Odysseus and his companions were hurriedly escorted into the palace by the scar-faced Taphian and four others. There was no time to bind their wrists, but with two guards in front of them and the sword points of the others pressed painfully into their backs, the Ithacans knew any attempt to escape would be futile and swiftly dealt with. The commotion of battle was already starting behind them as they entered the torch-lit passageway that skirted the great hall.

They marched rapidly towards the steps leading up to the royal quarters, but were stopped by the sudden appearance of Mentes from a side passage, his sword held menacingly at his side. When Diocles the Spartan joined him, the guards knew something was wrong.

'What do you think you're doing, Mentes?' asked the leading Taphian. 'And why isn't this prisoner with the others?'

Without a word, Mentes plunged his sword into the man's gut, killing him instantly. Diocles, though unarmed, crumpled the other man with a single blow from his large fist. Five more Spartans joined them from the side passage; two of them picked up the weapons of the fallen men and, with Mentes at their head, rushed at the remaining Taphians. Odysseus, Mentor and Antiphus twisted away from their captors as their rescuers drove them back down the corridor, their swords clashing angrily against each other.

'Mentes, you traitor,' hissed the scar-faced warrior.

Mentes replied with a thrust of his sword. His opponent parried the hasty lunge and laid the younger man's guard open, but in the narrow passage was unable to bring his own weapon up to find the exposed torso. In desperation he resorted to punching Mentes in the stomach, winding him. Mentes slumped against the wall, but before his former comrade could finish him one of the armed Spartans stepped in and skewered the Taphian through the groin. He fell to the ground, screaming with the agony of the mortal wound.

Though the two remaining guards had been pushed back, they showed no signs of wanting to run to the safety of the courtyard. Instead, they stood shoulder to shoulder and raised the points of their swords, smiling grimly at the thought of a fight to the death. Odysseus picked up their dying comrade's weapon, ready to answer their challenge, but before he could advance on the waiting Taphians Mentes stepped between them and faced his countrymen.

'Join us,' he said. 'We came here to serve Eupeithes, not Polytherses. There will be no dishonour in laying down your arms and refusing to fight, and tomorrow we can return to our beloved homeland.'

The men looked at him with scorn in their eyes. They were warriors, proud men who were ready to die in battle; they had also come to prefer Polytherses's brutal style of leadership to the soft indecision of Eupeithes, and had every intention of fighting for the new king of Ithaca. One of them spat into the dirt at Mentes's feet.

Odysseus wasted no time in rushing at them and severing the sword arm of one with a single blow. Shocked, he fell backwards clutching at the gushing wound, and Odysseus finished him with a stab through the throat. The other man was engaged by a Spartan and quickly slain, the victor savouring revenge for the massacre of his comrades the day before. The scar-faced warrior, still groaning, was quickly dispatched, but Mentes insisted they spare the life of the man Diocles had knocked unconscious.

As they tied his hands and feet with belts taken from his dead comrades, Odysseus explained the desperate situation at the gates to the others.

'It troubles me to fight against my own countrymen,' Mentes said, gagging the prisoner with a strip of cloth torn from a bloody cloak. 'But, equally, I hate Polytherses and the way he is putting good soldiers to ill use. If I help you open the gates, maybe the gods will bring some of them to their senses and they will join with us against our true enemy.'

Odysseus thought of the two guards they had just slain and doubted whether many, if any, of the Taphians would switch allegiance. They were too proud, even for Greeks. But he was nevertheless glad of Mentes's continuing loyalty, and knew if he could help them open the gates there would still be a slim chance of victory. Something else concerned him, though, and he could no longer restrain himself.

'Diocles, where is Penelope? I know she was with you when the camp was ambushed.'

'She was captured with us, but we were separated the moment they brought us inside the palace walls.'

'Then I have no choice,' Odysseus announced. 'Diocles, I want you and your men to open the gate. Antiphus and Mentes will go with you. They won't be expecting an attack from within the palace so you'll have the advantage of surprise, but you still have to open the gates and hold them until Halitherses can reach you. When he does, then you must do what you can to defeat the Taphians inside the courtyard.

'As for Mentor and I, we will search the palace for Penelope. Any victory will be a hollow one for me if my wife is harmed, so I must be sure of her safety. Then, if the new king is anywhere to be found, I'll make sure of him too. But first I must find where Eupeithes is being kept.'

'He was imprisoned with us in a storeroom, down there,' said Diocles, pointing to the passageway from which they had emerged earlier. 'Have pity on him, Odysseus.'

'May the gods be with you,' was Odysseus's only response, then with Mentor he went to find the man who had brought so much trouble to Ithaca.

The corridor was lit by a single torch, which Odysseus freed from its holder and took with him into the storeroom. For a moment they could see nothing but large clay jars amidst the flickering shadows cast by the flame. Then, as their eyes adjusted to the darkness, they distinguished a man in the far corner, his legs sprawled out before him. They stepped closer and held the torch up, causing the man to squirm away from the light, cowering and whimpering as he covered his eyes with his forearm.

It was Eupeithes, though only just. His once proudly fattened physique was diminished through starvation, and his previously clean-shaven, fleshy cheeks were drawn and covered in a scrawny beard. So this was the man who had deposed Laertes, and for fear of whom Odysseus had taken the palace guard across the Peloponnese to Sparta. He lowered the torch.

'Let's go.'

'And leave him?' asked Mentor, shocked. 'You've wanted to kill this rat for the past half-year; surely you aren't going to turn your back on him now? He deserves death, Odysseus!'

'Maybe,' Odysseus answered, 'but I haven't the heart to murder such a pathetic creature.'

He turned and, without a further glance at the former king, walked back out of the room to the main corridor. The others had gone already and, with no time to waste, Odysseus flung the torch into the dirt at his feet and pulled the sword from his belt.

'Come on, old friend,' he said, looking at the steps to the royal quarters. 'Let's see this thing to its finish.'

They mounted the steps two at a time to the floor above, where they turned to scan the dimly lit corridors for guards. Seeing none, they moved cautiously to the point where an intersecting corridor ran to the right. Both men knew the palace intimately; the turn led straight to the royal quarters.

Odysseus had been born and brought up here. This was his territory, the very heart of his home, where he, his parents and his sister had lived in happiness for as long as he could remember. The sight of the familiar walls and doors, the faded murals and the worn mats on the stone floor made Odysseus suddenly realize the depth of the offence that had been caused to his family. That he had been forced into exile, his father taken to the northern tip of the island and his mother and sister imprisoned in their own home; that their enemies were now enjoying the food from their own kitchens, cooked and served by Laertes's slaves; that foreigners bathed, dressed and slept in their own rooms, filled him with a murderous anger. Gripping the hilt of his sword until his knuckles were white, he turned the corner.

Two guards lay propped sleepily against the door jambs of his parents' room. The first barely saw Odysseus as he clove his head open to the base of his neck. Though the second threw the shaft of his spear up as a defence against Mentor's sword, he was killed by the follow-up thrust that split open his stomach.

They jumped over the corpses and into the large room where his mother sat gripping the edge of the bed. Beside her stood Koronos, the traitor who had deceived the Kerosia into sending the palace guard to Sparta. He held a sword in his hand, but appeared calm and collected before the unexpected appearance of Odysseus and Mentor.

'So, the fledgling has returned to the nest,' he scoffed. 'But a little too late to save your darling wife, I fear.'

Suddenly another guard leapt at them from the near corner of the room. Mentor, whose sword was in his other hand, instinctively held up his forearm to ward off the blow. The force of the Taphian's blade cut through the flesh and bone of his wrist, severing his hand and spraying blood across the smooth floor. He fell against the bed, shouting with pain and clutching the stump of his hand beneath his other arm.

Simultaneously, Koronos launched a ferocious attack on Odysseus. Their swords clashed noisily as the prince checked the traitor's well-aimed swing. For a moment they stood face to face as their momentum pressed them together, their blades crossed between them. Then they withdrew again, their weapons rasping as they slid apart. Koronos renewed his attack, lunging skilfully at the bulk of his opponent, but Odysseus was quicker than he seemed, easily twisting away from the deadly thrust and in the same movement swinging his blade around to slash at Koronos's exposed flank.

The older man's reactions were equally good. He straightened up from the lunge that had so nearly skewered his opponent, and then lithely stepped away from the arcing point of the counter-stroke. In the same instant, the Taphian guard jumped over his wounded opponent and joined Koronos in pinning Odysseus back against the corner of the room. The prince retreated under their alternating cuts and thrusts, twice being wounded on the sword arm as he narrowly beat aside blows that would have split open his belly. Then, with all the strength his great arms would lend him, he not only stopped their advance but began to beat the two men back.

A single opponent could barely have withstood the ringing blows. Odysseus slashed from side to side, forcing the two men onto the defensive. They gave ground before him and became quickly exhausted by the effort of parrying his blows. Then the Taphian slipped in Mentor's blood and fell at the foot of the bed. Though wounded, Mentor used the last of his strength to pluck a dagger from the unconscious guard's belt and slashed open the man's throat. He died with a final blood-choked sigh, just as Mentor collapsed with exhaustion.

'What did you mean by "wife", Koronos?' Odysseus grunted as he renewed his attack on the old man.

'Don't try to fool me,' Koronos laughed. 'Penelope told us she was your wife as soon as she was captured. She seemed proud of the fact, though I wonder whether she will show such arrogance when she's a widow.' He beat aside a sudden probing jab from Odysseus. 'When you're dead, Polytherses intends to make her his plaything.'

Odysseus lunged angrily, but was checked and had to defend against a rapid return thrust from Koronos.

'Penelope would die before she gave him the pleasure,' he snarled.

'Really?' Koronos retorted. 'The king enjoys a good hunt. Says it makes the meat taste better. She's with him now, you know, down in the great hall with four Taphians. Do you think that if they want to satisfy themselves with her, she'll be able to stop them?' He parried another angry thrust. 'Perhaps if I kill you now, my reward will be a turn with your wife, too.'

Odysseus resisted the impulse to throw himself into another furious attack. Koronos was easily his match in swordsmanship, if not in physical strength; he was also a cunning man, and Odysseus sensed that he was deliberately trying to provoke his anger. Already his lapses of concentration had nearly allowed the older man inside his guard. He stepped back and eyed him with caution.

'You know I have Laertes held prisoner in my home?' Koronos continued. 'Before you arrived I was telling your mother how he begs to see her again. I find his pleas very moving. If I die, though, my slaves have orders to kill him. Is that what you want?'

Odysseus sensed an undercurrent of desperation in Koronos's calm voice, the voice that had once persuaded him to leave his family undefended. Now it was trying to convince him that his wife would be raped and his father murdered. And yet for all his skill and power, the old man could not conceal his fear from the prince.

'Don't be a fool, Koronos,' he responded in an even tone. 'Your slaves hate you. Once you're dead and I'm standing at their door, they will never dare kill the rightful king of Ithaca. For all your delusions that Laertes was an unfit ruler, the people of this island know different. And before this day is out my father will be back on the throne. Only, you won't be alive to witness it.'

Odysseus had bided his time carefully. He had watched the beads of sweat on his opponent's forehead, heard his struggling breath and noticed the wavering grip on his sword. In the meantime he had allowed Koronos to take the offensive with his voice, encouraging the traitor to switch his thoughts to goading and dissuasion. Then he struck.

He scythed down with all his strength. Koronos attempted to divert the blow and had his weapon swept from his hand, to clatter noisily across the stone floor and leave him defenceless. The traitor stared in disbelief at his empty hand, then fell slowly to his knees. But Odysseus was in no mood for mercy. The sight of Koronos pleading for his life only made him think of his father, imploring his former friend and adviser to let him see Anticleia. Without a second thought on the matter, he plunged his sword through the man's black heart.

Turning at once to his mother, he gathered her into his arms and pressed his cheek to hers. They held each other for a few moments, then Anticleia sobbed and pushed him away.

'Find your wife, Odysseus. Let me tend Mentor; you just go — and hurry.'

Odysseus was loath to leave his mother unguarded, but was racked by the sense that Penelope was in urgent danger. He kissed her on the cheek, then ran from the room and down the steps to the lower floor. Beyond the passageway where the bodies of the Taphians lay he could hear the clash of bronze upon bronze in the courtyard. Men were shouting, though the words would not carry to him, and the cacophony of battle was punctuated by the screams of dying men.

Without pause, he turned right and followed the passageway until he reached the entrance to the great hall. There was no guard, so he raised his sword point and walked boldly in to meet whatever perils lay in wait.

The hearth burned low in the middle of the room, just as it had on the day that he and his men had left for Sparta. The previously smoke-stained walls were now bright with a fresh coating of limewash. Upon this were sketched the ghostlike outlines of murals yet to be painted, giving the familiar hall a curiously alien feeling. The great doors that gave access to the courtyard beyond were barred shut, ensuring nothing would disturb Odysseus and the men who had taken his father's throne.

They stood on the other side of the hearth, their shapes distorted by the heat from the flames. The Taphian warriors were armed with bows, each aiming an arrow at the lone intruder. Between them stood Polytherses, his arm wrapped about Penelope's waist and holding her to him. His free hand held a dagger to her throat.

Chapter Thirty

KING OF ITHACA

A Taphian warrior stepped out from the gates. His face was covered in blood and rivulets of gore stained the sword he carried, which Eperitus could only think was the blood of Odysseus, Mentor or Antiphus. He beckoned the Ithacans to come to him.

Eperitus drew the sword from his belt and moved towards the Taphian, determined to cut him down, but at the same moment Antiphus appeared next to the mercenary and shouted for them to come. Suddenly they could hear the sounds of battle from the courtyard and realized that the man at the gate was Mentes, his features hidden by the mask of blood. Eperitus ordered Arceisius to help Halitherses then, half-turning to the remainder of the Ithacans, pointed his sword at the gates. No words were needed. As a single body they ran towards the palace, cheering in their hunger to meet the Taphians in battle. Most of the men had lived under their cruel regime for too long and wanted revenge; the guards who had accompanied Odysseus to Sparta had dreamed of this moment for months and were no less fervent in their bloodlust. Within moments they were cramming through the gates and into the courtyard.

Diocles and his Spartans were desperately holding off a great press of Taphians, but as the Ithacans joined them the enemy's advantage was lost and they backed away. Dismayed by the loss of the gates and the number of men pouring in through them, they retreated across the compound and re-formed before the pillared threshold of the great hall, ready to confront the assault. Meanwhile, the last man through the gates was the bronze-smith, who had left Eumaeus with the waiting townsfolk and returned to the fight. He was accompanied by a dozen new recruits from the city, who had found their courage in the dawn light and decided to risk everything for their true king.

They formed up to face the enemy horde, absorbing Mentes, Antiphus and the Spartans into their ranks. Eperitus looked about in surprise at the carnage within the courtyard, where the corpses of several Taphians lay as if sleeping. Then he saw their opened throats and realized that Odysseus and the others must have been busy with their daggers whilst their hosts slept. It explained the smaller force of Taphians who faced them – their numbers were now evenly matched – but raised his concerns about the whereabouts of his friend, whose bloody corpse could be amongst the trampled bodies.

'I hear Halitherses is injured, and that you're leading us now.'

Eperitus turned to see Antiphus. He was barely recognizable, bathed in gore and armed with the strange weaponry of a Taphian warrior.

'Yes, unless Odysseus is with you,' he answered, hoping the prince would suddenly appear from amongst the throng of men.

'He and Mentor are inside the palace, searching for Penelope,' Antiphus explained. He briefly summarized all that had passed since they parted company the night before. It seemed Odysseus's plans had been more successful than expected, despite his being captured as they were about to open the gates. Athena had been faithful to her beloved Odysseus.

As they spoke a flock of arrows fell amongst them. Most of the townsfolk had no shields and quickly took shelter behind the guards, who instinctively moved forward to form a wall against the enemy archers. Antiphus took a few of the men to retrieve the bows and arrows of the dead Taphians by the gates, then, taking shelter behind the ranks of their colleagues, began to return the fire of their opponents. The exchange of arrows inflicted casualties on both sides, but the Taphian archers outnumbered the Ithacans and most of the fallen were amongst the unshielded islanders. Seeing this, the mercenaries were happy to remain safely ensconced before the doors of the great hall, waiting for the time when the advantage of numbers would weigh in their favour. Then they would engage them in face-to-face combat, when the recruits from the town would prove easy prey for the long spears of the fully armoured enemy warriors. Realizing this, Eperitus picked up a discarded spear and stepped out between the two opposing armies.

The Taphian arrows stopped and were replaced by jeers and insults from their ranks. It reminded him of the day he had first met Odysseus on the foothills of Mount Parnassus, when he had killed the Theban deserter. Kissing the shaft of his spear as he had done then, he launched it at the massed ranks before him. A man toppled backward with a scream, the spear held fast in his groin, and suddenly the Taphian jeers were replaced by a triumphant shout from the Ithacans. Drawing his sword, Eperitus led them into the attack.

The enemy archers only had time to fire a half-volley of arrows before the Ithacans were amongst them. Eperitus clashed shields with a spearman in their front rank, knocking him sideways with the momentum of his attack and slashing at his exposed back with his sword. He gave a scream and toppled into the dirt, where Eperitus left him to be finished off by the men behind. Two more Taphians now faced him, jabbing at him with their long spears whilst keeping out of reach of his sword. He tried desperately to knock the weapons aside and slip inside their reach, but whenever he succeeded with one spear the other would press him back.

Then, in the few moments before the weight of numbers behind him would push them inevitably together, he was joined by an Ithacan armed with a spear. He was young, frightened and knew little of warfare, and quickly fell victim to a skilful jab from one of the Taphians. But in that moment Eperitus was able to force himself inside the long reach of their weapons, where only a sword would be effective. He hacked at a face above one of the tall shields and split the man's features across the bridge of his nose. He dropped his weapons and turned away, clutching at his eyes and screaming with pain. Eperitus finished him with a thrust of his sword.

He turned to engage the other man, who had discarded his spear and drawn the long blade from his belt. With the press of struggling men all around, it was hard to remain out of striking distance as they eyed each other closely, trying to guess when and how the first attack would come. The Taphian, like all his countrymen, was tall and had the longer reach, but in the crush of battle Eperitus knew that could be just as much of a disadvantage. He edged closer and his opponent lunged at his face with the point of his weapon. Eperitus deflected the thrust with his shield, then swept his sword across the outstretched arm and severed it at the elbow. The man reeled away in pain and Eperitus left him to retreat into the mass of his comrades, clutching at the stump of his arm.

Suddenly, Eperitus felt a sharp blow to his shoulder and staggered backwards, pursued by a wave of pain that crashed over his senses and plunged him into the blackest night. For a moment he seemed to float, his head swirling like skeins of mist before the hard ground rose up to meet him, jarring him back to consciousness. He lay there amidst the sandalled, dancing feet of friend and foe alike, a curious peacefulness pressing him to the ground like a heavy weight. The sounds of battle receded, though he still sensed the sluggish thumping of feet all around him. Or was it the beating of his own heart?

Trying to draw breath, he felt something buried inside the flesh of his left shoulder. From somewhere deep within came the pounding approach of a fresh surge of pain, and instinctively he closed his eyes against it. Then it bit, hot and sharp, jerking him back to his senses.

He reached up and seized the shaft of the arrow. He tugged at it, feeling the barbs tear new furrows into the flesh that had closed about them. Fortunately it had missed the bone, but his muscles screamed with agony as the arrow slid free and dropped into the dust at his side.

He collapsed again, exhausted from the effort. Moments later he felt hands under his arms, causing yet more pain as he was hauled up and dragged away from the fighting. He looked up to see the faces of Mentes and Antiphus staring down at him. The archer looked into his eyes for a moment before lifting Odysseus's bow over his head and pulling aside his cloak to look at the wound. Mentes joined him, probing the skin with his fingers until he was satisfied there was no danger. Then he tore strips of cloth from his cloak and bound them about Eperitus's shoulder.

'The gods are with you,' the Taphian said in his thickly accented voice. 'A flesh wound only. It will heal, but you can take no further part in this battle.'

He turned and rejoined the fight that still raged about the portals of the great hall. Antiphus looked at Eperitus, the relief visible in his eyes, and told him he would take command. Then he drew his sword and followed the Taphian into the thick of the fighting, leaving Eperitus amongst the dead and dying at the edge of the battle.

Eperitus looked down at Odysseus's horn bow beside him and suddenly recalled that the prince was somewhere inside the palace. A sense of urgency gripped him and, picking the weapon up out of the dust, he struggled to his feet. His countrymen, as he now thought of them, were still at close quarters with the Taphians, and though his left arm could not support the weight of a shield he knew that he could still use a sword to help them. But despite their need his mind was now bent upon his friend. He looked about the large courtyard and saw the door that led to the pantry and kitchens. Retrieving his sword, he stumbled towards the door and found it unlocked.

He stepped into a narrow passageway. No torches burned there and the only light came from the doorway behind him, but his keen eyes penetrated the shadows with ease, picking out doorways on both sides of the corridor and a flight of stairs to the right. Suddenly he heard the sound of voices from somewhere within the palace and paused to pick up their direction. Straining his heightened hearing against the din of battle – filled with the screams of the wounded and dying – he listened for a particular voice, the voice of Odysseus. Moving slowly, he passed the stairs to the upper level of the palace and followed the passage around to the right. As he moved cautiously through the shadows, his sword gripped tightly in his hand, the voices became clearer. Then he recognized the unmistakable tones of Odysseus.

Within moments the short corridor had led him to the great hall, where he found the prince faced by four Taphian archers and Polytherses. The latter held Penelope to his side, with a gleaming dagger poised at her throat. Eperitus saw her and his heart sank, knowing he had arrived too late. Without any force of men behind him, there was little help he could offer Odysseus now other than to die at his side.

'So, your *army* has arrived,' Polytherses mocked.

Odysseus turned and for a moment the look of concern left his face, to be replaced by relief and even joy.

'I knew I could rely on you, Eperitus,' he said. Then his looks grew dark again, though determined, and he turned to Polytherses. 'Release my wife and I'll spare your worthless life. But if you harm her I will make your death so terrible you'll beg me to kill you.'

'You oaf,' Polytherses retorted. 'Don't you see that your life is in *my* hands? One word from me and you'd be dead in an instant.'

'Then why do you wait?' Odysseus demanded. 'Kill me now. Unless you *fear* to kill me.'

'I fear nothing and no man, least of all you. No – I want you to kneel before your king, and then I will kill you. And if you want Penelope to live, you'll do as I command.'

'No, Odysseus,' Penelope shouted fiercely, struggling against the strong grip that held her. 'I'd rather die than be this man's whore.'

Polytherses placed his hand over her mouth and pressed the

tip of the dagger into her neck, pricking the soft skin so that a bead of blood rolled down over her chest. Odysseus took a step forward and the archers drew back their bows; the slightest twitch of their fingers would release the arrows.

Eperitus put a hand on his shoulder and pulled him back. The ungainly prince, with whom he had shared so many hardships, looked at him and there was anger in his eyes. But in that same moment Eperitus handed him Iphitus's bow and a single arrow he had taken from the quiver. Odysseus snatched them from him and in an instant had fitted the arrow and was aiming it at Polytherses.

Silence fell in the hall. Polytherses's eyes were wide with terror as he dragged Penelope in front of him to act as a shield against Odysseus's arrow. The four Taphians strained their bowstrings even further and waited only for a word from their leader. Meanwhile, Odysseus focused his concentration on Penelope and Polytherses. Penelope met his eyes and nodded imperceptibly. Odysseus whispered a prayer to Apollo for the sureness of his aim, then released the arrow from his fingertips.

The darkness in the hall and the shimmering heat from the flames obscured the usurper of his father's throne and made his aim almost impossible. Indeed, very few could have hit such a mark: Teucer, possibly; Philoctetes also, but only with the magical arrows that Heracles had given him; Apollo, certainly. But with Iphitus's great horn bow Odysseus was as deadly as any archer in Greece, and the arrow flew from his fingers straight into Polytherses's left eye. It passed through his brain and killed him before he could even think to cut his captive's throat. The Spartan princess stepped free of the dead man's hold and the corpse collapsed in the dirt behind her.

In the same instant, the Taphian bowstrings shivered the air in the great hall. One of their arrows nicked Odysseus's forehead, and another his upper arm. The third missed completely, but the fourth thumped into his thigh, making him shout in pain. Eperitus drew his sword and charged towards the enemy archers, but at that moment Mentes burst in through the twin doors, followed by Antiphus and a group of Ithacans. The Taphian held up his hand and ran to the centre of the hall.

'You are victorious, Odysseus,' he announced, and then to his countrymen: 'Lower your weapons, my friends. The battle is over.'

With their leader slain, the archers realized they had nothing more to fight for and threw down their bows. Polytherses's brief reign as king of Ithaca was over, and fittingly he was the last to die on that fateful day.

Odysseus plucked the arrow from his leg and tossed it into the shadows, then limped across the hall to embrace his wife.

The courtyard was filled with the nobility of Ithaca, Samos, Dulichium and Zacynthos. An honour guard, commanded by Antiphus, lined the newly whitewashed walls; it was drawn from the survivors of the battle for the palace six days before, many of whom still wore their bandages like badges of pride Beyond the gates, hundreds more people filled the broad terrace hoping for a sight of their king and queen.

A large space had been left clear before the threshold of the great hall, and Eperitus stood between Mentor and Halitherses in the first rank of onlookers. Both men had been severely wounded in the battle and would not fight again: with his hand severed, Mentor would no longer be able to hold a shield, whilst it was a miracle that Halitherses had survived at all. The old warrior had been hit in the foot and the arm and had lost a lot of blood as he lay beneath the palace walls, and it took all the skill of Eurycleia, Odysseus's childhood nurse, to revive him. When Odysseus and Eperitus visited him two days later he swore never to lift a weapon in anger again, and with tears in his eyes resigned his position as captain of the guard there and then.

Odysseus was saddened, but recognized the will of the gods. That same evening he conferred the captaincy on Eperitus, as a reward for his services and a recognition of their friendship. To the young exile from Alybas it meant the security he longed for – a permanent home among friends, as well as a true sense of purpose and fulfilment. And at last, Eperitus felt he had absolved himself of the disgrace that had been brought upon him by his father. Though he remained the son of a treacherous usurper, by fighting to put a rightful king on his throne he had lessened the shadow on his family's honour. His grandfather's ghost would take satisfaction from that.

Eperitus looked about at the throng that filled the courtyard, but recognized only a few of the faces he saw. Mentes was on the opposite side of the cleared space, standing a full head above those around him and attracting much curiosity. Diocles and the surviving Spartans were on either side of him. Like many of the Ithacan guards, their necks were draped with garlands of flowers given to them by appreciative islanders. Eumaeus was there too, leaning on a crutch with his leg bandaged; he had been so badly hurt from the arrow wound that Eurycleia predicted he would carry a limp for as long as he lived.

Standing next to the swineherd, with her arm linked through his elbow, was Ctymene. The young girl's attractiveness had grown in the time Eperitus had been away, and it was obvious she was fast becoming a woman. But Eperitus, too, had matured: he had seen Helen, the most beautiful woman in Greece, and he had slept with Clytaemnestra, queen of Mycenae. The princess, though disappointed at the indifference that her brother's handsome friend had shown since his return to Ithaca, quickly tired of flirting with him and diverted her attentions to the many more responsive young men at the celebrations.

In the centre of the clearing, two high-backed chairs faced the entrance to the great hall. These were occupied by Laertes and Anticleia, who held hands and chatted quietly to each other, their words lost in the noise of the crowd. Then the doors of the great hall swung open and the courtyard fell into silence. A moment later, the king and queen stood as Odysseus and Penelope appeared beneath the pillared threshold and walked out into the bright sunshine.

Despite the solemnity of the occasion, Eperitus's heart swelled with happiness as he watched his friends cross the courtyard to stand before Laertes and Anticleia. The prince was dressed in a fine purple tunic with a white robe about his shoulders, clasped together by a golden brooch. His wife wore a light green chiton with a white sash about the waist, reminding Eperitus of the new growth of spring that was already filling the island. She looked relaxed and confident as she held her husband's hand, and Eperitus knew she had quickly become enamoured of her new home. When Odysseus was not dealing with the aftermath of the rebellion, he had spent time showing her his beloved Ithaca. Often Eperitus would be invited to join them as they walked its woods, climbed its mountains and explored its coastline. On these occasions he had seen how Penelope had taken to the island, and heard her talking of starting a family that would be safe from the wars and political rivalries of the mainland. She reminded him of Helen then, and made him pity Tyndareus's daughter, whose looks had condemned her to a life as the trophy of powerful men.

That the people loved Penelope was clear, and the huge crowds outside the palace walls had gathered as much to see the new queen as the long-awaited succession of Odysseus. But it remained Odysseus's moment of triumph. It was his leadership, intelligence and courage that had led them to Sparta and back, and had brought about the downfall of the rebellion. Because of him, their great task had been a success and Ithaca was free again. The long journeys, the battles, the treachery and the mesh of love and politics were behind them. And now Odysseus was to replace his father, just as the oracle had predicted.

Laertes looked his son firmly in the eye, but did not move. As a captive of Koronos, the old man had long before decided that his son should take his place as king if he overthrew the rebels; but as the two men stared at each other, Eperitus feared that Laertes might revoke his decision. Then the moment passed. The old man kissed Odysseus on both cheeks and placed a short staff in his hand – the symbol of rule on Ithaca. Then he and Anticleia bowed low and moved aside.

Odysseus and Penelope now stepped up to the vacant seats and turned. They held hands and stared about at the silent faces for a long moment. Then they sat down and the simple ceremony was complete: Odysseus had become king of Ithaca, and Penelope was his queen. The courtyard erupted with cheering that was echoed in the streets beyond, marking the start of many days of celebration.

As the cheers continued, Odysseus found Eperitus amongst the crowd and gave him an irreverent grin. Eperitus returned the smile, happy to share in his friend's moment of triumph. Yet circling vulture-like over his joy was a nagging doubt: Odysseus had found a Spartan wife and was the ruler of his people, but the second part of his oracle remained, distant but threatening. And if Odysseus's doom took him to Troy, as the Pythoness had warned, then Eperitus would go also. For that was the will of Zeus, which he had naively sought a lifetime ago at Mount Parnassus.

AUTHOR'S NOTE

The Greek myths are rich with characters and adventures that span time from the creation of the universe to the end of the heroic age, when gods and men mingled freely and the lines between them were often blurred. At the centre of this menagerie of tales is the Trojan War, a great hub of legends from the Bronze Age that dominated classical Greece and Rome and have continued in Western culture right up to modern times.

Whether these myths had any basis in real events is a question that has rattled on for centuries. Archaeology has uncovered some of the cities that stand so large in the prose of Homer, while recent studies of Bronze Age texts suggest a historical basis for several of the central characters. Nevertheless, combining Greek myths with historical facts and portraying them in the format of a novel presents an interesting challenge. Sometimes the pieces simply don't fit: different myths contradict each other about the same events, whilst the events themselves are often incompatible with historical reality. Also, although the war took place around 1250 BC, the myths were compiled or written down several centuries later and therefore include elements of different historical periods.

Facing this challenge, I have tried to tell the original stories in the correct historical context, while allowing for the essential ingredients that give the Greek myths their enduring popularity. Unfortunately, for all his heroism and boyish naivety, Eperitus comes from my imagination and is not taken from myth. The same applies to the invasion of Ithaca. However, Helen and her many suitors, her marriage to Menelaus and the oath between the kings – thought up by Odysseus to keep the suitors from quarrelling – are all taken from well-known tales. Indeed, in these seemingly minor events lay the seeds of the Trojan War, which started around a decade later when a Trojan named Paris dared to come between Menelaus and his wife.

But that's a different story.

THE GATES OF TROY

Read on for an exclusive extract from
Glyn Iliffe's second book featuring Odysseus,
which is available now.

Chapter One

UNWELCOME VISITORS

Odysseus, king of Ithaca, lay on his stomach amongst a clump of fern. Leaves and twigs were tangled in his thick, red-brown beard, and his face and hands were smeared with earth so that only the whites of his eyes were visible in the undergrowth. He remained perfectly still and silent as he looked down the slope towards a clearing in the dense woodland, where two dozen men sat around a large fire and ate stew from wooden bowls. Their features were grey and blurred in the twilight, but it was clear from their armaments and the sound of their heavily accented voices that they were not Ithacans.

'That's them, Eperitus,' Odysseus whispered, nodding decisively. 'They're not a hunting party or a group of woodsmen – they're the bandits we're looking for. Can you hear what they're saying?'

Eperitus, captain of Odysseus's guard, lay shoulder to shoulder with the king. 'Most of it,' he replied, turning an ear towards the circle of men. Despite the distance, his acute hearing – which, like the rest of his god-gifted senses, was unnaturally sharp – could easily pick out the words of their conversation. 'Something about a troupe of dancing girls and . . . well, you can probably guess the rest.' A roar of harsh laughter broke out below them. 'They met the girls in Pylos, but from their accents it sounds like they're Thessalians.'

'Then they've a long journey back home,' Odysseus said,

watching the men thoughtfully and tapping at his teeth with a nail-bitten forefinger.

Eperitus scratched at his closely cropped black beard. 'The problem is that we were told there were six of them, not four times that amount. And we've only brought twenty men with us.'

Odysseus leaned his large, muscular torso to one side and looked at his old friend, a glimmer of playful mockery in his green eyes. 'When we landed on Samos yesterday morning you told me you were itching for a fight. In fact, hardly a month's gone by in the past ten years when you haven't reminisced about the old days or longed for a proper battle to come along. Now the opportunity's arrived, all you can do is complain.'

Eperitus screwed his lips to one side and fixed his eyes on the camp below. Even though he knew Odysseus was poking fun at him, the king's words still stung. No other man on Ithaca – not even Odysseus himself – desired glory in battle as much as he did. The islanders were simple folk whose happiness was found in their homes and families, but Eperitus was an exile from a distant city who had never lost the unsettling need to prove himself. It drove everything he did, and though he had long since earned his place amongst the Ithacans he struggled to share their contentment. The handful of skirmishes he had fought in the past few years had left him hungry for a real chance of glory, and it was not until the news that a large group of bandits were terrorizing Samos that he had realized how deep that hunger had eaten into him.

'I'm not complaining,' he replied. 'I'm a warrior, and a warrior wants nothing more than to kill his enemies. It's just that you're the king, Odysseus, and I'm sworn to protect you. Zeus's beard, if we take these lads on as we are there's a good chance they'll win and you'll be killed. And just look at them: I thought brigands were supposed to be armed with daggers and rusty swords, not breastplates, shields and spears!'

He pointed to the weapons piled against the mouth of a cave

at the back of the clearing, and then at the armour worn by each man and the long swords hanging from their belts. Both he and Odysseus knew that the men who had been robbing the people of Samos were not a band of disorganized thugs, stealing at need and fleeing back into the woods; they were soldiers, turned to common robbery for survival in a country where peace had reigned for a decade. They had arrived from the Peloponnese by ship several days before, and if they were allowed to establish themselves on Samos they would not only continue to threaten the welfare of the islanders, they would soon pose a challenge to Odysseus's own power and authority.

'Well, we need to deal with them,' the king said, resolutely. 'And I can't wait for more of the guard to be fetched from Ithaca – we have to defeat them here and now, with the men we've got.'

'What about Penelope?' Eperitus responded, noticing the look in Odysseus's eye at the mention of his beloved wife. 'She's three weeks away from giving birth to your first child, the child you've been trying for ever since you were married. This isn't the time to go risking your life.'

'I love my wife,' Odysseus said, simply but seriously. 'And no pack of outlaws is going to prevent me from returning home to her. But a king who isn't prepared to risk his life for his people isn't worthy of the title, and for the sake of my unborn son I have to live up to who I am.'

Eperitus looked at his friend and knew he had spoken truly. 'Well, evening's not far away,' he sighed, glancing up at the azure sky through the canopy of budding branches overhead. 'And there'll only be a faint moon tonight. We could bring the rest of the guard up here after dark and . . .'

'And kill them in cold blood? We won't need to resort to that.'

'Why not? You slit the throats of a dozen sleeping Taphians once, so what's the difference?'

'I had to do that,' Odysseus answered. 'They were invaders, whereas these poor swine,' he pointed a thumb towards the men below, 'are just soldiers fallen on hard times – warriors, like you and me. I won't kill them without giving them the chance to leave peacefully first.'

Eperitus shook his head resignedly. It was not that Odysseus was too proud to accept advice, it was just that he always thought he knew better. And he invariably did: if anyone could think of a way to defeat the bandits, it was Odysseus, the most clever, devious and resourceful man Eperitus knew.

'I assume you've got a plan,' he said.

'Of course I have,' the king replied with a grin. 'Now, let's get back to the others and tell them what we've seen.'

He raised himself on all fours and backed away from the screen of ferns, followed by Eperitus. Once they were sure they would not be spotted by any of the men around the campfire, they stood and quietly made their way back through the wood, picking a route between the silvery-grey trunks in the darkness. Soon they found the path they were looking for – a rutted cart track that crossed from one side of the forest to the other – and began the trek east toward their own camp.

'I dreamed about her again last night,' Odysseus said after a while. He was looking up at the early evening stars, which could be seen pricking the sky through the fissure in the canopy overhead.

'Athena?' Eperitus asked, pausing to look at the king, who avoided his eye and carried on walking. Eperitus ran to catch up with him. 'What did she say? Was it about Penelope again?'

He knew Odysseus had long enjoyed the blessing of the goddess. As a child he had often seen her in his waking dreams, sitting on his bed at night and comforting him when he was lonely. She had once saved him from a wild boar, and when he became a man he had repaid her by making her his patron goddess. Ten years ago she appeared before him and Eperitus on Mount Parnassus – where they had gone to seek the advice of the oracle – and then at Messene. A few months later she brought Eperitus back to life after he had died saving Odysseus from the knife of an assassin.

But since then the king had seen or heard nothing of her – until she came to him in a dream two nights ago, telling him Penelope would shortly give him a son.

'She didn't speak this time,' Odysseus said. 'We were standing on a plain under the moonlight, with the sound of the sea behind me and the smell of brine in my nostrils. Before me was a great city built on a hill. Its walls and towers were gleaming like silver, and it was both beautiful and terrible at the same time. Even though Athena was beside me the sight of that city struck me with fear and sadness, as if it were a symbol of the end of my happiness. Of all happiness.'

'What does it mean?'

'I don't know. Perhaps nothing, but I don't think so – it left me with a feeling that an evil doom is approaching. You remember the words of the oracle, of course: I will be king over my people for ten years, and then I will have to choose between my home and Troy. This is the tenth year of my reign, Eperitus.'

Eperitus recalled the meeting in the caverns beneath Mount Parnassus, where the priestess had spoken the prophecy that had haunted the king for so long. It was there, also, that she had told Eperitus his fate was bound up with Odysseus's, for good or bad.

'I hadn't forgotten the words of the Pythoness,' Eperitus replied. 'Yet I can't see what will happen to force such a choice on you, or, if it comes, why you can't just remain on Ithaca.'

But Odysseus did not reply. Before long they saw the orange light of a fire through the trees. As they approached, a man stepped out from the shadows and levelled his spear at them.

'Not a step closer,' he ordered, brandishing the weapon threateningly in an attempt to disguise his own nervousness. 'Who are you and what do you want here?'

'Apollo and Ares, come to bring death and destruction to all who stand in our way,' Eperitus replied, pushing the point of the spear away from his chest.

The man was similar in height to Eperitus, but had short, hairy legs and a large stomach that hung down over his belt. He squinted at Eperitus through his small, pig-like eyes, then with a half-sneer of recognition raised his weapon and stepped back.

'Oh, it's you,' he said with badly disguised contempt. Then, turning to Odysseus, he gave a quick bow before offering his hand. 'Welcome back, cousin. I'm sorry I didn't recognize you in this darkness.'

Odysseus gripped the other man's wrist and smiled. 'Who let you stand guard, Eurylochus? Everyone knows you've got the eyesight of a mole.'

Without waiting for an answer, the king clapped his cousin on the shoulder and strode off toward the welcoming light of the campfire with Eperitus at his side. They could see the figures of several men eating and drinking around the vivid orange flames, and the rich aroma of roasted meat made their mouths water in anticipation.

'I don't know what you've got in mind for dealing with those bandits,' Eperitus said, 'but I pray to the gods you'll leave Eurylochus here. He should never have been allowed to come with us, Odysseus – he's a clumsy, self-important idiot with no idea about fighting. If we're not careful he'll put us all in danger.'

'Laertes insisted he come,' Odysseus replied with an indifferent shrug, 'and I wasn't going to argue with my own father about the matter. Besides, if you're lucky Eurylochus'll get his head chopped off and you'll never have to put up with him again.'

Eperitus ignored the comment. Eurylochus had shown him nothing less than disdain since he had been made captain of the royal guard ten years ago, a position that Eurylochus, as Odysseus's cousin and a lesser member of the royal family, felt should have been given to him by right. The fact he had skulked out of the greatest battle in Ithaca's history – against a rebellion supported by a Taphian invasion force – did not stop him from despising Eperitus's good fortune. Nevertheless, Eperitus did not want to see the fat fool slain needlessly.

'And how do you intend to defeat two-dozen heavily armed warriors, assuming they refuse your invitation to return peacefully to the mainland?' he asked as they paused at the edge of the broad clearing.

'That's easy,' Odysseus answered blithely. 'You've been itching for a chance of glory, Eperitus, so I'm going to send *you* to fight them.'

extracts reading groups
competitions books new
discounts extracts
competitions
books new
events
extracts books
new reading groups
interviews
events extracts
discounts
new books events
events new
discounts extracts discounts

www.panmacmillan.com

extracts events reading groups
competitions books extracts new